Empress of Dust

Other works by Alex Kingsley

Short Stories:
The Strange Garden and Other Weird Tales
The Things I Made
The Small God of West 54th St
Shroomscape
Three-Inch Grave
The Fog Man and the Fox
Would You Still Love Me if I Was a Wyrm

Plays:
Unplanned Obsolescence
The Dreamless Patron
The Bearer of Bad News

Empress of Dust

BOOK 1 OF THE BASTION CYCLE

Alex Kingsley

Space Wizard Science Fantasy
Raleigh, NC
www.spacewizardsciencefantasy.com

Cover art by MoorBooks
Editing by Courtney Brooks
Illustrations by Ines Maria Eckermann
Book Layout © 2015 BookDesignTemplates.com

Empress of Dust/Alex Kingsley.— 1st ed.
ISBN 978-1-960247-26-1

Author's website: Alexkingsley.org

Noa believed in my work, even when there wasn't yet much work to believe in. It's not easy to come across devotion like that. Thank you, angel.

CONTENTS

Part One: The Ivies

I pray that the Earth remain still where I stand
I pray to remain above ground
I pray that the dust stay away from my lungs
I pray I be left safe and sound

I know Earth is hungry
I know Earth is thirsty
I know it will not try to hide it

I pray to remain one more day on this Earth
And not yet be taken inside it

- The Earth's Mercy Prayer, transcribed in *Legends of Bastion*

CHAPTER ONE

A Refined Child

Harvard had a tremor for all nineteen (twenty?) years of his life. He'd grown accustomed to always shaking a little—or a lot—when his mother was angry at him, or when he didn't know the answers to a quiz, or when there was a monster trying to eat him.

He'd hoped after two years of facing desertwalkers of all shapes and sizes, he'd learn to face the crabs without fear, but still he turned into a quivering mess before the serpentine creature skittering toward him on spindly legs.

"Now, Harvard! Spray it!"

But Harvard's body was useless. He fumbled for the canister of vapor he carried in his pack and aimed it at the charging beast, but his trembling hand hardly put any pressure on it. The nozzle only coughed up a pathetic cloud of gas into the dry desert air.

"Spray it!" Princeton commanded again.

"I can't!" he cried as the creature closed in. A hand gripped him by the collar and yanked him backward, his feet kicking up dust. Someone wrenched the metal cylinder from his hands, scraping his fingers.

With a flick of his wrist, Princeton effortlessly turned the canister toward the encroaching beast and gave it a long, hard spray. The white mist shot forward into the gaping mouth of the reptilian monster. The beast recoiled, whining, scampering back on its insectoid legs. Its top half writhed in fluid spasms while its angular legs jerked around haphazardly. One more pathetic wheeze, and its legs collapsed under it. It twitched in agony, stirring up dust, and finally lay still.

Harvard looked on in horror. He'd seen the same sight many times, and it never became any less off-putting.

"I let you hold the canisters for *two quaking seconds,* and you let this happen!" Princeton snapped him back into reality.

"I— I tried!" Harvard said. "It came up behind me, and— and I didn't see it—"

"Useless piece of garbage," Princeton grumbled, shoving the near-empty canister into Harvard's chest. He didn't protest. He could delude himself, imagining Princeton had been talking about the faulty canister, but he had very little hope that was the case. It was not the first time one of his crew members had easily snatched him from the jaws of death, and if he were being honest with himself, it wouldn't be the last.

"Leave him, Princeton," Yale said. The two turned to see the captain of the Ivies approaching with Columbia trailing close behind, faces obscured with dustscarves and goggles. Columbia, as always, remained silent, keeping whatever judgements she was making to herself. And Harvard knew she *was* making judgments. He wasn't sure which embarrassed him more—that Yale had to come to his aid, or that he didn't have an inkling of what Columbia thought about him. At least Princeton made his opinion on the matter clear.

"If that thing tore through him, we'd be fending for ourselves without a vapor canister!" Princeton said, a little too comfortable with the prospect of Harvard's death.

"Well, it didn't," Yale said matter-of-factly. "And be careful with those. We're running low."

"Oh, I'm sorry, should I have let it eat him?" Princeton retorted.

"Just don't use so much."

Yale turned their gaze to Harvard.

"You okay?" they asked. Harvard nodded, still clutching the canister to his chest like a talisman.

Satisfied, Yale turned away.

"We've got a long way to go before sunset. Get moving."

Harvard looked back again at the corpse of the crabsnake. He couldn't help but feel sorry for the thing. Had it been inches away from devouring him? Yes. But still...it didn't deserve such an excruciating death. He didn't know what it felt like to inhale scuttler vapor, but he couldn't imagine it was pleasant. But if the creature wasn't dead, then he would have been. *A refined child does not draw attention,* his mother had told him. *A refined child knows how to handle himself.*

Harvard had known how to handle himself, once. Not anymore.

* * *

The Ivies made camp while Harvard, told to "make himself useful," idly drew with one finger in the sand, lying on his stomach with his head perched on his palm. He scratched out the patterns the crabsnake had on its scales, to the best of his memory. Before he'd been to the dusts, he had no clue monsters could be so beautiful. From afar. Harvard had once offered to keep a record book of the creatures they came across in the dusts, but everyone at the Commission had mocked him for the idea.

As he dragged his finger along the sand in curves and jagged lines, he could hear the hushed tones of Yale and Columbia's conversation. He hazarded a glance in their direction, brushing ginger curls out of his eyes. Columbia ran a hand along her box braids, looking worried. Yale was explaining something to her with quiet intensity. They had sleek dark hair Harvard had only seen down a few times because they kept in a tight bun and kept the sides of their head shaved. Harvard thought that was a shame, but then again, luxurious long hair could be a hazard in the dusts. Still, Harvard liked to watch them, just like sunsets or birds or anything else graceful and beautiful. From afar, of course. Their rectangular glasses gave them a kind of serious look that intimidated Harvard. Perhaps that was why his stomach gave a nervous flutter every time the captain gave him an order. Yes, that was probably the reason.

He ached to return to Bastion. They were already due back at the Commission and hadn't yet reached quota. This dig had lasted a few days, and they hadn't found a single silicon chip, or car motor, or anything else the Commission would pay them for. Harvard was beginning to worry that after years of scavengers like the Ivies, the dusts had finally been picked clean. If there was nothing left in the desert for them to sell, then what would they do? Last dig had only turned up old rations, which would extend the new dig a little, but wouldn't sell for much.

As he fell asleep shivering under a too-thin blanket on the desert floor, Harvard wished he could have been with Yale and Columbia on their previous scavenging crew. Maybe they would have been friends with him. They were roughly his age, after all, even though his crew sometimes treated him like a child. Maybe he would have learned a thing or two. Learning to be a scavenger was a slow and painful process, but he wished he'd been able to learn when he was younger, not when he was already out here with a real scavenging team, staring scuttlers in the face.

Harvard could have sworn as he drifted off to sleep, he heard Yale murmuring the Earth's Mercy prayer. Probably not. Probably just the wind.

* * *

"Right here, guys!" Princeton called, working to uncover the structure from underneath the layers of thin rust-colored dust.

The angular form looked out of place jutting from the smooth curves of the sand. The Ivies helped Princeton unearth the find until they discovered a window, its ancient glass still preserved. Yale jerked their shoulder back, and their sledgehammer unlatched itself from its holster and slid into their hand.

Yale swung the hammer into the window, shattering it easily. The glass was brittle with age, and the screen beyond ripped instantly. None of the protections from newer buildings. This must be a very, very old dig.

Princeton slipped the rubber grips onto the soles of his boots. A baby scuttler sidled up next to him, no larger than the palm of Harvard's hand, headed for the open window. Though he knew the creature would grow up to be a towering beast, now it was hardly larger than a beetle. Harvard found the babies a bit endearing. They had no idea what behemoths they would grow up to be! They were just little baby crabs with little baby claws.

"Nasty!" Princeton spat and stomped the creature with his rubber-coated boots. Harvard heard the sickening crack of chitin. He flinched with a quiet shriek, as though he were the one who'd been crushed. Princeton ground his boot in the dust, complaining about getting scuttler guts on his shoes, before kicking the crushed crab away and ducking into the window, careful to avoid the shattered glass.

Harvard looked to Yale for some kind of support, but they were more interested in the sunken building than Princeton's wanton cruelty.

"How's it look?" they asked.

"Looks like an office building, at least two hundred years," Princeton said from inside. "We might find some good tech down here. Don't know about vapor canisters, though. This one might be too old." Yale and Columbia both donned their boot grips and followed Princeton into the darkness.

Harvard did not follow his crewmates. Harvard was always the one on watch, since his tremor made it difficult for him to safely descend into the sunken buildings.

"He's perceptive," Yale had said by way of justification when they first decided on this. "He has a good eye."

"You can't be serious," Princeton had complained when he thought Harvard couldn't hear their conversation.

"What, would you rather he go down with us?" Yale had responded.

Harvard remembered feeling his stomach sink when he overheard this. Every time he began to convince himself Yale was starting to like him, comments like this proved him wrong. It was only Yale's leadership instincts, Harvard guessed, that kept them repeatedly taking pains to make Harvard feel welcome. In truth, they probably felt just as stuck with Harvard as the other two.

I don't want to be here either, Harvard wished he could tell them. *I wish I wasn't like this. I wish I wasn't holding you back. I wish I hadn't gotten placed with you. I wish that too.* He couldn't say that, of course. What good would it do?

Harvard rolled his head from side to side idly, hoping this dig would be more fruitful than the last. He scanned the desert for the first sign of an approaching desertwalker. Nothing but dust and the sound of the wind stirring it up. He sighed and began drawing swirls in the sand with the toe of his boot.

At the edge of his vision, something moved.

Harvard jumped. He laughed at himself when he saw it was only a baby scuttler meandering toward him. The same one Princeton had stomped, still doggedly making its way for the window with two crooked legs pointing awkwardly in the wrong direction.

"You lived!" Harvard cried. The crab ignored him, climbing the cracked concrete toward the broken window, but each time it neared the edge, its little legs lost their grip and it slid down, flopping onto the dusty ground.

"Whatcha tryna do, little guy?" Harvard cooed, leaning down to the little creature. It continued its pathetic attempts to climb. Once again it fell, this time landing awkwardly on its back.

Harvard scooped the creature up in his hands. "I'm sorry about Princeton. He's like that. I think he'd do the same thing to me if he could." *But I have Yale to protect me,* he thought, *and you're completely on your own.* Well, maybe the crab wasn't *completely* on its own. Maybe it was part of a whole army of huge, mean desertwalkers that would one day slaughter them all. This crab was not his friend. Harvard had to remember that.

He wanted to help it anyway.

He examined its shell, gently petting the crab's back. Its carapace was covered in intricate gray fractals tinged with burgundy, like a knot weaving in and out of itself. Harvard wondered if it would maintain those markings as it grew into adulthood. He never got the chance to look at the big ones up close as they tried to kill him.

"You're so beautiful," he told the creature. "Do you know that? You're the prettiest little crab I've ever seen."

Gingerly, he set the crab down on the windowsill. It leapt into the building and scuttled forward with a lopsided, lurching gait. Despite its injury, the little creature moved with remarkable speed.

"Be careful in there," Harvard called after it as he watched it go, wondering what kind of mission the determined crab could possibly be fulfilling.

He glanced around. No desertwalkers in sight. Surely it couldn't hurt if he took a peek inside the building to figure out what the little crab was after?

He should do what he was told. He knew that.

But what if that little crab got hurt again? He couldn't just stand here doing nothing—and he was doing nothing—when there was a little creature that might need him. The idea of being needed, even if by an animal that would one day grow into a hulking beast hungering for his flesh, made an aching kind of sensation in his chest.

Or maybe the crab was going to call upon its desertwalker compatriots to corner the Ivies. Harvard hadn't thought of that. Had he just put everyone in danger? Then maybe his *crew* would need him.

Harvard scanned the dusts one more time, just to be sure. Nothing but barren, empty sands.

"I'm coming, little guy," he said, and gripped the edge of the wind to lower himself into the building.

CHAPTER TWO

Unnecessary Danger

Careful to avoid the broken glass, Harvard clambered into the dark portal. It took him a moment to get his footing. He slid into a desk, which gave a metallic clang. The floor was slanted enough that he struggled to stay upright. Only three scavengers were supposed to descend during a dig, so they only had three pairs of grips.

Harvard had never been in one of these sunken buildings before. He'd always imagined what they must look like, but never witnessed it for himself. The room was covered in chairs and desks in various stages of decay. And of course, everything was coated in a thin layer of orange dust.

Undisturbed dust. That was good. Other scavengers hadn't hit this one yet. Maybe actually find something the Commission could sell.

Harvard spotted the crab crawling down the incline toward a hallway across the room. *Funny*, he thought. *This little guy seems to really know where he's going.* Without the grips on his boots, Harvard struggled to follow the crab without falling forward. He had to repeatedly grab onto desks and drawers to keep himself from sliding down the hall and colliding with the back wall.

Harvard followed the crab all the way down the hall, by an old elevator shaft, until it disappeared into a vent.

"Aw," Harvard said aloud. He'd really wanted to know what that little thing was up to. Maybe—

The elevator, which must have been in disrepair for over three hundred years, screeched open. Harvard yelped.

"Harvard?"

Harvard turned to see Yale, who had shoved the lopsided metal door aside, hanging from a thick metal cable that now slanted diagonally like the building floor. They leapt from the shaft to the floor easily, as though they'd done it a hundred times. In fact, they probably had.

"What the hell are you doing here?" For Yale, who was always so cool and calm in the face of everything, and the anger creeping into their voice was like storm clouds gathering on the horizon.

"I...um—" Harvard sputtered, stepping away from them and realizing for the first time just how much *bigger* Yale was as they towered over him.

"You're supposed to be watching the window!" Yale scolded.

"I just... I..." Harvard was at a loss for words since, "I followed a tiny crab," seemed like a pretty stupid reason to abandon his post, all things considered.

"We don't know what's out there right now! There could be all kinds of desertwalkers waiting for us! We're making our exit totally blind!"

Harvard heard the pounding of footsteps behind him and whirled to see Columbia and Princeton emerge from a stairwell opposite the elevator, summoned by the sound of Yale's reprimands.

"Harvard?" Columbia asked sweetly. She looked confused, not angry.

"Get back to the quaking window!" Princeton commanded, less sweetly.

Before Harvard could say anything to defend himself, Yale grabbed him by the bicep and led him back up the hallway toward the room he'd originally entered, like a teacher leading a misbehaving child to the principal's office. The other two followed, but when they got to the mouth of the hallway Princeton pulled them back.

"Look!" he hissed, pointing to the upper right corner of the room, near the open window. Rooting around the rusting metal desks was a massive megacrab, easily twice Harvard's height and as wide as a car, pincers that could easily cleave a person in two with one snap, and behind them eight thick spidery legs. The window Harvard had entered through was now a crooked hole lined with jagged concrete and steel where the creature had forced its way in. Was it just bad luck, or was it drawn by their scent? The creature overturned drawers with its thick claws, its speckled carapace scraping against the walls. Its legs extended so far, the creature filled half the room. It made a sort of clicking sound as it tore apart a filing cabinet with its claws and teeth. Yale's grip tensed on Harvard's arm, and his heart pounded violently as he watched the thing searching for something to sate its hunger. Three thoughts crowded Harvard's mind at once. *I'm trapped in here with a scuttler and it's going to kill me. I'm trapped in here with a scuttler and it's going to kill my crew.* And, most importantly: *I'm trapped in here with a scuttler and this is all my fault.*

Princeton raised the vapor canister, but Yale placed their free hand on the nozzle and lowered it.

"It's distracted," they whispered. "If we can get out fast enough, it won't give us any trouble."

"Do you see the size of that thing?" Princeton shot back, gesturing with the hose. "It's quaking huge!"

"I know," Yale said levelly, "which is why I don't want to engage it in a fight. Besides, we can't waste a canister on it."

"It's not a waste if it saves our lives," Princeton hissed.

"We've only got two more of those, and we're a long way from Bastion. Besides, if we spray it and we miss, we're dead. It's better to try to avoid catching its attention altogether. This is what we do: when I say so, we're all going to run for the window. First you and I will help Columbia up. Then Harvard. Then you. Then me. And with any luck, we can do it all before that thing has had a chance to figure out what's going on."

"And if we're not fast enough?"

"Then it eats us, obviously."

"Okay, so maybe you can see why I'm not on board with your plan?"

"If we wait long enough," Columbia cut in, "it will eat us regardless."

"Exactly. Which is why we're not waiting to do a vote, Princeton."

Yale waited for a fraction of a moment until the scuttler was angled away from the window, distracted by the contents of a desk drawer.

"Now!"

The four bounded up the incline toward the open window. But Harvard wasn't wearing the same rubber grips as the rest, and now that Yale was too focused on helping Columbia out the window, they weren't dragging him up with them. After a few attempted footsteps up the incline, Harvard slid back down the hallway and slammed into the back wall. The scuttler poked its head up and looked in his direction, ignoring the other three as they clambered out the window.

Princeton and Yale easily hoisted Columbia out, but the moment she landed she shouted back down, "We've got some desertwalkers up here too. Princeton!"

"On it!" he shouted in response, pulling himself up after her.

Harvard's view was suddenly obscured when the hulking body of the crab appeared at the door of the hallway, blocking the entire room behind. Harvard screamed in horror as he saw the thing angle itself awkwardly to squeeze through the narrow walls, inching toward him. It used its thick legs to pull its body closer, the rim of its shell tearing the plaster, pincers snapping wildly in Harvard's direction. He reached for the door to the stairwell, but the creature's long legs were already holding it closed. Instead, he dove to the left, toward the elevator, though its metal door had once again fallen shut. He desperately attempted to pry it open, but his feeble arms didn't have the same strength as Yale's. A pincer grabbed him by his shirt and threw him backward, before ripping the fabric and losing its grip. He slammed against the floor with a painful thud. Once he managed to gain his footing, he found himself staring into the crab's gaping mouth.

As he was certain he was about to be torn apart and ravaged, the whole creature jerked backward, letting out a pained screech as its legs bent awkwardly. Its mouth snapped again at Harvard, this time too far to catch him in its jaws. It jolted away from him.

"Harvard!" he heard a voice cry from behind the megacrab. "Can you get under it?"

Yale. They had come back for him. They had come back, and they were *pulling* the monster back by its legs to give him enough room to escape. He stood there in shock, watching the scuttler once again lurch backward.

"Harvard!" Yale called again, this time more strained. Snapping back into reality, Harvard dove under the scuttler's torso. It tried to skewer him on one of its many legs, but Harvard slipped underneath before it had time. He emerged next to Yale, who immediately released the leg and shoved the scuttler further down the hallway, wedging it between the walls so it had no way to turn itself around. They scooped Harvard up and threw him over their shoulder like a rag doll, bounding up the incline toward the window. They practically threw him out of the building and into the harsh desert daylight.

As his eyes adjusted to the light, he saw a crabsnake skittering toward him. He gave a panicked yelp and knelt in the sand, feeling for where he'd left his pack. Columbia and Princeton were shouting not too far off. So they were still alive, which was good. But definitely in trouble, which was not as good.

Harvard felt his fingers close around the familiar shape of his pack just as Yale emerged from the sunken building. Harvard gave a little shriek as the crabsnake darted toward Yale, who was still too focused on pulling themself up to notice the new creature about to sink its teeth into them. Harvard screwed his eyes shut, swinging the bag blindly and hoping to connect with something. He felt it make contact with a thud, and a hideous screeching followed. He opened his eyes to see he'd managed to knock the thing off balance, and it was scampering backward on its spindly legs.

He let out a sigh of relief. Not too much relief, since he could now see Princeton and Columbia were fighting another one, an empty canister of vapor discarded on the ground. He extended a hand to help Yale out of the building.

They took a moment to assess the situation before shouting, "Ivies! Retreat!"

"But—" Princeton protested, his hunting knife held aloft and dripping with scuttler blood. Columbia did not hesitate to follow the command. She ducked past the creature and ran.

"Princeton! Now!"

Reluctantly, Princeton followed the other three as they fled on foot.

"That thing is gonna catch up to us!" Princeton cried.

"It was gonna kill us if we stayed. We had no more vapor!" Yale responded.

"So now it'll kill us when it catches up to us!"

Harvard looked over his shoulder. Sure enough, the crabsnake was pursuing them hungrily. And it was faster. Much faster.

"Um...guys?" he asked shakily.

"Don't look back, Harvard," Yale commanded.

Harvard, however, simply couldn't stop himself from looking back at the towering creature pursuing them, tripping over his own feet in the process.

Interlude One: Ronan

There was a ghost living in Bell Manor. At least, that's how Ronan Bell liked to think of himself. Before he was Harvard, he was a shadow creeping soundlessly through the corridors, unnoticed, unseen. On the occasion one of the staff did notice him, they acted as though he were a spirit.

"Oh!" they'd shriek, nearly dropping the linens they carried. "Master Bell! I didn't see you there!"

It was a talent, in a way, making himself so small. Something he practiced through years of scoldings and slaps on the wrist. He could not avoid his mother's gaze, but for the most part he was as insubstantial as a phantom haunting his own home.

It meant he could slip out to the courtyard unnoticed during his "study" hours and feed the crows. He soundlessly crept through the garden gate and watched as the birds congregated to meet him.

Ronan wished he could be a crow. Not just any bird. A crow specifically. Crows were smart—they had relationships and rituals and hoards full of shiny things. Ronan wanted to be smart, to have little corvid friends who would never leave him, and to have his own wealth to do with as he pleased. And of course, to have wings. And fly far, far away from Bell Manor and never have to see his mother or Kathy or any of these people ever again.

He sat on his usual stone bench in the garden, the one where he always sat to sketch pictures of the birds. He looked up from his unfinished drawing, pencil tapping the page idly, leaning against an oak tree trunk, and stared out at the vast ocean. He knew he was lucky to have this view. Bastion was placed right on the edge of the Infinite Ocean, and those fortunate enough to have their property overlooking the Upper Bastion cliffs could afford such a vista. Most of the city dwellers, Ronan knew, would never see the ocean in their lives. He couldn't imagine that. He spent most of his days sitting on this bench, staring out at the expansive emptiness, tossing food to the crows.

He put the sketchbook aside gingerly and reached into his pocket, pulling out a golden earring he'd swiped from his mother and tossing it to the birds. This was even better than feeding them. With something shiny, a crowd of crows would stare curiously, mesmerized by the sparkling oddity. Then one of them would claim it in its beak, eliciting squawks of dismay from the others, and promptly fly away with it before any could purloin its bounty. *So human*, Ronan thought. *See something shiny. Take it for themselves.*

"Everything has a pecking order," his mother would always say in regard to running the family business, "Someone has to be on top."

That was why, she claimed, she had to be so hard on her children. To prepare them for the real world. To inherit and run Bell Enterprises to reach its full potential. To be on top.

This was why Ronan was terrified of his mother. She never hit him. She never even touched him, as far as Ronan could remember. Part of him almost wished she would hit him, just so he'd have a reason for feeling the way he did. The way he withered when she looked at him. If she'd actually struck him, then he wouldn't be stuck feeling like it was his fault, that she had every right to be disappointed in him the way she was.

Ronan didn't truly think crows were the way his mother described people to be. They weren't sitting atop piles of gold like miserly dragons. They were just animals with instincts, not selfish aristocrats. They had no "pecking order." They had no history exams or piano recitals. They did not tell their hatchlings to be "refined." They simply survived.

Ronan tossed them a handful of peanuts.

When he went back inside, he found Kathy in their shared study, hunched over a stack of papers.

Kathy spared one moment to glare at him, then looked back down at her work. "Mom gave me some accounts to deal with."

Ronan groaned. He hated numbers.

"Why is she making us deal with company stuff?"

"Not us, Ronan. Me."

Ronan cocked his head. "But...she always makes us do the same stuff?"

"You really *are* stupid, aren't you, Ronan?" Kathy slammed her pen down on the desk.

"Um...yeah, I guess?"

"What Mom needs is someone to help her run the business. One person to help her run the business. And if you look at the marks Mr. Jenks gives us, it's pretty obvious who that should be."

"Oh. So, if you're gonna help with the company, what am I going to do?"

"I don't know. Probably they'll send you away."

Ronan tried not to notice the hint of a smile that appeared on Kathy's face at the thought of being rid of her brother.

"Send me away?"

"To one of those boarding schools on the edge of the city. Ya know, where they send kids no one wants to deal with?"

He'd heard of those schools. Though Ronan's mother had never struck him, he knew the instructors at those schools would not have the same type of restraint.

"You're just trying to scare me," he guessed, hoping she couldn't see that she had succeeded.

"Am not! I heard Dad talking about it."

Ronan frowned. He knew his mother didn't like him, but his father too? Did everyone in this household want him gone? He felt a lurch in his stomach, and—not for the first time—he wondered why he'd been born at all. What was the point of twins if one of them was useless? Wouldn't the Bell family, maybe the world as a whole, be better if Kathy was the only one?

"Leave me alone," Kathy commanded. "You're distracting me."

Ronan retreated to his room, numb.

CHAPTER THREE

Conditional Immortality

Yale had made a promise to themself: never to lead their crew into unnecessary danger. This is what they were hoping to avoid when they made the split decision to flee, though perhaps it was accidentally exactly what they achieved. *Maybe*, they wondered, *I should have promised myself to stop making split decisions.*

They heard an *oof* behind them, followed by the impact of a body hitting sand, and knew Harvard must have fallen.

"Pick him up, Princeton!" they demanded. They weren't going to lose Harvard. They weren't going to lose anyone. They didn't know *how* they were going to save everyone, but they would. The how part would come later.

"Dusts," they said under their breath when they surveyed the land ahead.

They froze, skidding on the sand, kicking up a cloud of sand.

"Wait!" they shouted, pointing forward. "We got another one!"

The rest of the Ivies stumbled to a halt to see the lumbering crab in the distance making its way toward them from the other direction.

Well, this is it, Yale thought, surprised at their sudden serenity. *I have led my crew to their death, just like I was always going to.* Still, they owed it to their team not to give up yet.

"This way!" Yale shouted, leading the team to the right, off in the direction where there weren't monsters running after them. Columbia grabbed their arm.

"That's not a crab," she said. Yale glanced back at the hulking creature, then processed the metal creaks of its joints. A machine?

"We gotta go!" Princeton said, shoving them toward the mechanical beast.

"We don't even know what that—" Yale began to protest, but at that moment the crab-that-was-not-a-crab angled its shell down and a door swung open, revealing a human figure leaning out, urging them forward.

Yale made another split decision, this time based on a key piece of information: human better than crab.

"We're going for the machine!" they decided, and the Ivies followed without protest.

As they neared, they could see the figure was an old man, smiling congenially as though he wasn't watching four scavengers about to be consumed by desertwalkers. When the mechanical crab met up with them, it turned on its legs with a screech, keeping pace with them away from the pursuing crabsnakes.

"Wanna lift?" the old man said.

In answer, Yale scooped up Harvard and half-lifted, half-threw him toward the metal hatch. With surprising strength, the old man pulled him in through the door into the relative safety of the pod.

At least one of us won't die, Yale thought, then hazarded a look over their shoulder. The crabsnake was closing in.

"Columbia!" they called, and she allowed herself to be lifted into the pod, a little more gracefully than the unsuspecting Harvard had.

"Princeton!" Yale commanded next. He looked as though he might protest, but a crabsnake just a few paces behind him shot out its tongue and licked him on the ear, which seemed to make up his mind. He needed no help in jumping up toward the hatch and grabbing the swinging door, expertly launching himself inside.

Harvard reappeared at the door, though they could see from the brown arms wrapped around his waist that Columbia was attempting to hold him back.

"Yale!" he cried, arm outstretched. The old man just laughed and shook his head before leaning down himself and offering a hand. They took the hand and allowed themself to be pulled into the metal pod.

The hatch slammed closed behind them, and everything was silent except the muffled sound of metal stilts navigating the sand.

* * *

Harvard sank to the ground, trembling violently. He wrapped his arms around himself and looked at his crewmates. Yale leaned against one of the metal walls, head tilted back, eyes closed. Columbia checked her pack. He met Princeton's eyes and his breath caught.

"You little *idiot!*" Princeton shouted, shattering the silence four had been settling into. He took two big strides over to Harvard, balled both fists into Harvard's shirt, and hoisted him up against the wall with a loud thud. Harvard gasped. He struggled to get free, but his shaking made him feel weak.

Columbia's head snapped up.

"Whoa!" She held up a hand to signal Princeton to stand down, but he wasn't paying any attention to her.

"You had one job!" he said. "All you were supposed to do was keep watch! That was it!"

"I...I'm sorry!" Harvard stammered, holding back tears. "I didn't mean for...I didn't know...I made a mistake."

"No shit, you little turd!" Princeton shook him.

"Princeton!" Yale shouted. "Let go of him!"

Princeton didn't seem to hear. "You could have gotten us all killed, shit-for-brains!" he pressed on. "You ruined the dig, and then you almost got us all quaking eaten!"

Columbia tried to pull him back by the shoulder, but Princeton shook her off easily. Harvard could no longer keep his sobs at bay, and now tears were streaming down his freckled cheeks.

"I'm sorry!" he cried. "I'm sorry!"

"You're *gonna* be sorry, you stupid—"

"Princeton! Put him down!" Yale commanded with ferocity that Princeton was pulled out of his frenzy. His head swiveled to face his captain, who was standing upright in the center of the pod, facing the other three, and the old man watched the whole scene unfold from by the door. The two scavengers stared each other down, a silent challenge passed between them, and Harvard couldn't help but feel painfully small.

Eyes still fixed on Yale, Princeton lowered Harvard to ground in defeat, releasing his grip on him. Harvard sank to his knees, burying his face in his hands.

"We survived," Yale said. "And the only reason we survived is because we worked as a team. The moment we stop working as a team, we die. Understand?"

Harvard glanced up to see how Princeton would take this. He looked as though he would protest, but then thought better of it. In the end, he only nodded meekly.

The old man coughed, and Harvard remembered they were not alone.

They turned to the man watching patiently from his spot by the hatch, only a few wispy gray hairs on his head and a thin gray beard on his chin.

He wore a tattered plaid shirt with tattered brown pants, complete with tattered work boots.

He gave a sheepish smile.

"I don't mean to interrupt," he hobbled forward, "but I figured I oughta introduce myself."

Princeton reached for his knife. Columbia shook her head, and he loosened his grip.

"I take it you're scavengers?" the man asked, his eyes flicking around to each of them. Scavengers were easy to recognize since the Commission outfitted them with the same dustscarves and goggles. Besides, Harvard didn't think there were many other people willing to brave the dusts. If you bumped into anyone out in the desert, which was already an unlikely event, they were almost certainly there under the Commission's auspices.

Yale only nodded in response. The old man smiled fondly.

"I've had more than a few groups of scavengers come through here," he said, almost conspiratorially, "and they've told me all about your whole organization. You're like a big family, you Commission kids, aren't ya?"

Whatever scavengers the man had been talking to, Harvard had never met them. Nothing about the Commission had ever felt "familial" to him, save for perhaps his own crew. Even then, after two years with them, he worried the other Ivies only liked him begrudgingly, out of obligation. "Tell me, what's your, um...your..." he continued.

"Brand name?" Yale guessed.

"That's the one!" the man clapped his hands.

"We're called the Ivies. I'm Yale, and I'm the captain." They flashed their captain's band instinctively, even though it probably had little meaning to the old man. It was a simple leather band with a metallic plate screwed into it, bearing only the text: "Ivies. Captain." It was intended to be used as proof of authority when coming across other groups of scavengers. They gestured to the other members of the crew. "This is Princeton, Columbia, and Harvard."

The old man chuckled fondly. "And what are your real names?"

"We don't give out that kind of information," Yale shook their head.

"Pssh," the old man laughed. "I've heard about you scavengers and your customs. Silly, if ya ask me. Here, I'll give you mine. Name's O'Neill! Now how about you all?"

Yale glanced toward Columbia, and the two had one of their patent silent exchanges. Harvard wished he could understand all the wordless conversations that passed between the two of them.

"We don't share our real names," Yale said levelly. "Not even with each other. It's a custom that—"

O'Neill waved a dismissive hand. "I know, I know, you scavengers and your traditions. You're a superstitious bunch, aren't you?"

"It's not about superstition," Yale protested so weakly that Harvard wasn't sure if he believed them. Admittedly, he never asked about the reason why they were required to abandon their previous names at the Commission's doorstep. In fact, Harvard had welcomed it as an opportunity to start his life anew, maybe become someone different. Yale had been very strict about the rule as long as Harvard had known them, but he'd never guessed there was some kind of mystical reason behind it. He remembered how he thought he'd heard them praying the other night.

"So, this is your place?" Yale changed the subject abruptly.

"It sure is," O'Neill grinned proudly.

Harvard glanced around the capsule. The pod was cramped, giving the five of them barely enough room to move around comfortably. There was a window with a table below it and a kitchenette, but every surface was covered with equipment. Most were items that would be familiar to any scavenger, basic equipment for the dusts: canisters of scuttler vapor, a few sets of sheathed knives, traction pads for boots, the usual stuff. The rest, however, was alien to Harvard: tubes and glasses, vials holding colorful fluids. Suspended from the ceiling were bundles of different dried plants, all swaying with the movement of the pod.

"You're a scientific researcher?" Columbia guessed, and Harvard marveled at her. She recognized all this?

"Sure am!" the old man banged on the metal wall, beaming. "This is my research pod!"

"What are you researching?" Columbia lit up. Harvard hadn't thought anyone could be so excited about the idea of research.

The man smiled, then gestured to a glass case on the counter holding—

"Whoa!" Yale threw their arms out in front of the other Ivies protectively, holding them back from getting close to the glass, "You have a baby scuttler on board!"

"Oh, that's no baby," O'Neill tapped the glass of the terrarium affectionately. "That's just Little Liza. Her breed don't get no bigger than that. Nothing to fear."

"You have a scuttler as a *pet*?" Princeton gaped.

"Not a pet, exactly. More of a...test subject?"

"Test subject? What kind of tests?" Colombia asked, watching the creature with wide-eyed curiosity.

O'Neill rubbed his leathery hands together. "Have you ever heard of a thing called 'conditional immortality'?"

All four shook their heads as Yale slowly lowered their arms. O'Neill smiled that same gleeful smile once again, the smile of any person experiencing the joy of sharing something they're particularly passionate about.

"Did you know," he asked, "that if a scuttler is not killed, it will just get bigger?"

"Well, duh," Princeton said, "that's how growing works."

O'Neill laughed fondly. "You misunderstand. I mean that if nothing kills it, *it won't die*. Why do you think all the desertwalkers around here are so big? Because they've been around for centuries."

"That doesn't make sense," Yale said. "If that were the case, then we'd have even larger desertwalkers than the ones we have. They'd get to be the size of—"

"Well, that's the thing about conditional immortality," O'Neill winked, "it's *conditional*. No one can live out in the dusts without getting killed eventually. No one. Not even the kings of the dusts themselves. Ain't that right, Little Liza?"

He gingerly placed a hand in the terrarium and the tiny crab crawled onto his outstretched palm. He held her up for his guests to see. Yale flinched, pushing their crewmates away from the miniscule creature as if by instinct, but Harvard wanted to see it. He placed a hand on Yale's arm and lowered it, stepping forward to take a look at the little creature in the old man's hand.

"She's beautiful," he whispered, examining the complex patterns on her back. It looked to him as though the intricate swirls of purple and gold on her shell had been painted by hand.

"Harvard," Yale warned, "that thing—"

"Oh, she don't bite!" O'Neill interrupted. "I told ya, her breed doesn't get any bigger than this! Otherwise, I wouldn't keep 'er around. C'mon boy, gimme your hand."

Obediently, Harvard opened his palms and O'Neill dropped Little Liza inside them. Harvard giggled at the tickle of her little legs on his skin. She tilted her little crab body toward him, and Harvard could have sworn she was looking at him.

"Hello Liza," he smiled, "my name is Harvard."

She poked around Harvard's hands tentatively before deciding he was a safe place to be, then started a slow crawl up his arm. Again, he laughed at the sensation.

"O'Neill," Yale said, "If that thing hurts any of the members of my crew—"

"She's completely harmless!" O'Neill insisted. "I just use her for some genetics samples. Let him have his fun!"

"Why don't the scuttlers give you any trouble?" Columbia cut in. "You're out there collecting..." she waved her hand at the vials and dried herbs surrounding them, "materials. And you live in this, well, for lack of a better word, easy target. A scuttler could get through this thing easily. And they can always smell a human inside. No offense, but...how are you still alive?"

"You see, little lady," he explained, turning to a control panel in an alcove at the back of the room so he could maneuver the pod, "the scuttlers don't give me any trouble because they think I'm one of their own. This pod is a beauty. Twelve meters across, three meters deep, about as large as the biggest megacrab. And when I burrow the thing in the sand, the telescoping entry hatch has five meters of runway." He jerked a lever to the left, and Harvard felt the pod's trajectory shift beneath him, the mechanical legs hard at work beneath the metal floor. "Ah! That looks like a good spot, don't you think?" He gestured out the front window to a spot in the dusts, still navigating the controls.

Harvard didn't know what a "good spot" meant by O'Neill's standards, and evidently neither did the rest of the Ivies, so they watched wordlessly as the pod ambled to a location that O'Neill found acceptable. Another press of a button and the whole mechanical creature folded its legs and nestled itself into the dusts, nearly covered by sand. O'Neill slammed his fist on a button and the pod jolted. O'Neill opened the hatch to reveal the telescoping entry hatch that he had mentioned, an accordion of corrugated metal, inclined toward the surface.

"This," he said, "is the secret to modern research. Can't study the desertwalkers any other way."

Harvard turned his attention to the back window, watching two megacrabs fight over some long-dead meat of a now unidentifiable creature. He'd never seen the creatures from safety before, so he'd never had a chance to marvel at their beauty. Harvard felt a hand on his shoulder and whipped around to find Yale kneeling next to him. Beyond them, Harvard saw the other two disappearing through the hatch.

"Harvard," Yale murmured, "are you alright?"

Harvard's mouth hung open in surprise, overwhelmed by Yale's sudden closeness and warmth. There were many things about Yale that he could never seem to get used to, but one of them was how quickly they could shift from attack mode to caretaker. Even though Yale had been defending Harvard a moment ago, he still found himself terrified of their anger. How could this be the same person—at one moment the commanding captain, and the next suddenly tender?

"I...I'm fine," Harvard stammered. He laid Little Liza on the table. Yale gave a little smile, and Harvard found himself unable to meet their gaze, looking down at his boots and wringing his hands.

"I really am...*so, so sorry*," he said, his voice barely above a whisper. He was afraid if he tried to raise his voice any higher, he would only start crying again. Even though he knew all the Ivies were around the same age, he couldn't help feeling that everyone saw him as the baby of the group. Harvard worried another breakdown would only give Princeton more ammo.

"It's alright," Yale said, tightening their grip on Harvard's shoulder. "You're still shaking," they observed.

"Yeah, it, um...it takes a while to go away," Harvard said.

"You were scared?"

Harvard nodded meekly.

"Of the desertwalkers or of Princeton?"

Harvard could feel his face flush.

"Is it bad if I say both?"

They glanced over their shoulder to ensure Princeton was behind the pod door in the entrance corridor.

"I'm sorry about that," they said. Harvard could hear genuine regret tinge their voice.

"It's not your fault," he said. "Princeton is just like that."

"Well, he shouldn't be. I'll make sure of that. And, um, Harvard?" They used their free hand to gingerly turn Harvard's chin toward them. "You're not gonna leave your post again, right?"

Harvard could feel himself shrinking like a chastised dog. Of course that was what this was about. Yale just had to do damage control after a crisis. Harvard desperately wanted to see Yale's kindness as a display of genuine affection, but he constantly had to remind himself that they had a job to do: to keep the scavenging crew intact. And Yale had been a scavenger twice as long as Harvard, which meant they had twice as much training and hard-won wisdom. Of course they were looking after Harvard's feelings. It's not that they cared about Harvard's feelings, no. They can't have Harvard getting overly emotional and ruining a dig, now could they? If Harvard didn't feel at home with the Ivies, would he snap under the pressure? Run away, and become a liability? That must be what Yale was really thinking. *Poor Harvard*, they must be thinking, *that little idiot boy that I'm stuck with is having another breakdown and I gotta clean up the damage before he gets my crew into trouble. Poor little Harvard. Poor little, stupid Harvard.* That must be what Yale was really thinking. Of course it was.

"No," Harvard whispered, fighting the instinct to break Yale's gaze. "I won't."

Yale gave an encouraging grin, and patted Harvard on the back.

"Good. I'm glad to hear it."

Princeton peaked his head out of the pod door, gesturing for Yale to come join him.

"Wait here, okay?" they said as they stood. Harvard nodded, and Yale walked out of the pod door to the entrance corridor.

Harvard crossed his arms and sunk deeper into the chair, turning his head toward the window to watch the scuttlers again. He felt a scratching sensation at his leg and yelped, pulling his legs up onto the chair.

O'Neill laughed.

"It's only Little Liza!" he said, scooping up the little crab and putting her on the table in front of Harvard. "I think she likes you."

Harvard gave a sad laugh and held out a hand for the creature to crawl on to. She settled into his palm immediately. Harvard imagined that if crabs could purr, Little Liza would do just that. He stroked the back of her shell with two still-trembling fingers.

"That captain of yours is really looking out for you, huh?" O'Neill asked. Harvard frowned. He knew the old man was only trying to make conversation, but he didn't want to be reminded of the way his superior condescended to him.

"They're just trying to smooth things over so I don't get upset and run away or something," Harvard sighed, looking into Liza's diminutive eyes. "They think I can't handle myself. None of them do."

"Well, can you?" O'Neill challenged, leaning against his research counter with a knowing grin.

Harvard's head snapped up to face the old man. He hadn't expected this question.

"I...I mean, yeah, of course I can!" Harvard asserted.

O'Neill shrugged, unconvinced.

"I can!" Harvard repeated, but he realized the more he insisted upon it, the more unlikely it seemed. He turned his attention back to Liza, who had begun crawling up his arm and onto his shoulder. He raised the opposite hand to pet her. He worried his trembling would upset her, but she hardly seemed to notice. In fact, when he touched her shell and she rubbed up against his fingertip, he felt his body relax.

"You're shaking quite a bit, son," O'Neill observed.

"I *know*," Harvard said with barely concealed exasperation in his voice, "I have a...I have this condition, it...I get shaky really easy."

The old man eyed him up and down.

"Looks more than a little shake to me."

He hobbled over to his little kitchenette and put a kettle on the stove. He pulled out a mortar and pestle and began crushing something with them, though Harvard couldn't quite make out what.

"What are you doing?" he asked, lifting Little Liza from his shoulder and placing her gently on the table.

"As you may recall," O'Neill said as he ground the pestle, "I happen to specialize in the medical sciences."

Harvard, unsure of how to respond, simply nodded. Did O'Neill think he could cure Harvard's condition? Some of the best doctors in Bastion had tried and failed.

"I expect," the man said between pumps of his arm, "that you might be needing some medicinal herbs."

"Medicinal herbs for...shaking? There's not a cure. That's what all the doctors said when I was little, anyway."

The man poured his crushed concoction into a tea strainer, dropped it into a mug, then showered it with the now-boiling water.

"No no no. Dustsickness."

Harvard cocked his head to the side. "I've never heard of dustsickness."

The old man gave a hollow laugh. "Well, you haven't been a scavenger very long, now have you?"

Harvard shook his head, embarrassed.

"When you're a scavenger, you breathe in all sorts of particles," O'Neill explained as he brought the steaming cup of tea to Harvard. "Now, normally these particles ain't an issue because the human body is used to filtering out a certain amount of debris, but far out here there are all sorts of substances that can make a person sick. Plants, animal parts, that kind of thing. Sometimes a little bit of one of those substances gets carried in the dust, and a scavenger breathes it in."

Harvard went pale, cupping his hands around the mug. It was scalding.

"I think I would know if I breathed something in that made me sick," Harvard said, though he didn't entirely believe it.

The old man lowered himself in the chair across from Harvard, chortling. "Would you? If you caught it right when you first joined up, maybe you wouldn't! I mean, look at you now. You're not just shaking; you're pale, sweating, and I bet you've got a headache. I wouldn't be surprised if your body's feeling pretty weak, too."

"Is that not...normal?" he asked. He assumed he felt weak because, by comparison, he *was*.

"It is. For someone with dustsickness. Oh, don't worry. Most dustsicknesses are easy to cure. But if it goes untreated..." he trailed off meaningfully.

"Then what?" Harvard asked.

"Well, that doesn't matter, 'cause we're gonna treat it!" He gestured to his collection of herbs, fluids, and other substances. "I do happen to study remedies, after all."

Harvard gestured to the tea. "This is supposed to make me better?"

O'Neill nodded. "There's a fine mix of herbs in there. Whatever kind of sick you got, it should be gone soon. You may experience more symptoms than what you're already experiencing, though."

Harvard felt his trembling become more violent.

"This can't be right," he said, more trying to convince himself than he was O'Neill. "I've been trembling ever since I was little." He held out his hand to demonstrate. "I don't know what it is. I'm just...I mean, I just shake, I guess. But it's not...I mean, it can't be a disease, right?"

"It gotten worse since you've been out here?" O'Neill asked.

Harvard frowned. Had it?

O'Neill placed the back of his hand on Harvard's forehead. "You've got a bit of a fever."

"Oh...I didn't...I didn't notice," Harvard could feel the panic setting in, feeling his own face to see if he, too, could pick up on his symptoms.

O'Neill laughed again, scooping up Little Liza and putting her back in her terrarium.

"It ain't nothing to worry about, little guy," he said, covering Liza's enclosure with a mesh screen. "Just drink your tea."

* * *

The moment the hatch closed behind Yale, Princeton and Columbia both converged on them.

"We gotta do something about the kid," Princeton said.

"Harvard is not a kid. He's just as old as us."

"I think he is a *little* younger," Columbia pointed out quietly. "I can't imagine he's more than nineteen."

"It doesn't matter how old he is!" Yale snapped. "Harvard is a member of our team, okay? We don't have control over who the Commission assigns to us."

"Sure," Princeton conceded, "but if you were to file an incident report claiming that Harvard was a hazard to our safety..."

"He's not!"

"He kind of is, though," Columbia admitted. Yale shot her a look, not one of malice but one of surprise.

"He almost got us killed!" Princeton said.

"He didn't almost get us killed. A band of desertwalkers almost got us killed."

"Yeah, that he was supposed to be on the lookout for!"

"If anything, it's a good thing Harvard wasn't at his post. They would have skewered him, and we'd still have been caught off guard, but be down a team member."

"Yeah, and we'd probably have been better off that way."

Yale said nothing. They only stared at Princeton long enough to make him start to squirm.

"Princeton," they said in a voice like a cold blade being drawn across skin, "you do *not* talk about your crew member that way."

Princeton rolled his eyes.

"You don't have to treat me like a little kid. You keep trying to give me these lessons on 'teamwork' and 'responsibility' like we're in quaking kindergarten."

"Maybe I'll stop giving you lessons once you start acting like you've learned them," Yale retorted. "Listen to me: I'm not trying to make you a better person. I don't care if you come off this scavenging team a bigger asshole than you were when you came on. This is not about your character development. This is about me trying to make sure that you don't fuck up and get us all killed, understand? I just don't want your inability to cooperate to end up with all our bodies out in the dust. You understand?"

Princeton stared at them wordlessly before murmuring, "Yes, Yale."

"Yes, *Captain*."

"Yes, Captain."

"Good. You are dismissed."

Princeton pushed past Yale and entered back through the hatch. *He'll get over it*, Yale thought. *That guy lightens up in no time.*

"You are dismissed," Colombia mocked quietly. Yale gave a half-smile, pushing her playfully.

"Shut up," they mumbled.

"No, no it's good," she said. "Someone's gotta keep him in line."

"You could do it better."

"I don't think that's true."

"He respects you."

"He respects you, too."

"I don't know," they looked after him, fiddling with their captain's band. "Whatever little respect he has for me, I have to work hard for it. What is it that you have that I don't?"

Colombia shrugged.

"I think it's all in your head," she admitted.

"It's not, though."

The two stood there in tense silence for a moment. Yale wrung their hands, feeling Columbia's eyes on them, deciding whether or not to put words to their question.

"Columbia, you can't possibly agree with this," they finally said.

She shrugged as if to say she *could* possibly agree with it.

"Okay, what is this really about? You've never agreed with Princeton before, and I'm guessing you didn't just start now."

"I don't think you have to get rid of Harvard, no," she admitted.

Yale nodded. "Good."

"I just think you should make sure you're keeping Harvard on for the right reasons."

"What do you mean?"

"You know what I mean."

"I—" Yale fell silent.

"I know you think you're doing a good thing here. But don't disobey your own rule: you have to do what's best for the crew. And I think you just need to entertain the possibility that the best thing for the crew might be letting Harvard go."

"It's not," Yale responded reflexively.

"I'm just saying," Colombia held up a gentle hand, "to consider it. I know you feel bad about Minty, and you want to make up for it. That's a good reason to try and do the right thing. But is it a good *enough* reason?"

Yale took a deep breath.

"It's not about that," they said. Maybe it was, once, but their attachment to Harvard stopped being about Minty a long time ago. They didn't know how to tell her that. "But...I'll think about it, okay?"

Columbia nodded, then gestured for them to go back into the main section of the pod. When they entered, they found Harvard nursing a cup of tea, standing outside the cockpit as O'Neill showed Princeton how the controls to the mechanical legs work. When faced with such novel machinery, Princeton's anger seemed to have evaporated.

"Guys, look at this thing!" he exclaimed. "We gotta get ourselves one of these."

Yale smiled fondly and glanced at Harvard. He was shaking still. More than normal, in fact. He seemed to even be struggling to get the teacup up to his mouth.

"Are you alright, Harvard?" He asked.

Harvard nodded vigorously.

"O'Neill thinks I might be a little sick," he explained, "but he said he knows all kinds of cures." He took another shaky sip from the mug. "I'm totally fine!" he insisted, though he sounded more like he was trying to convince himself than Yale. Yale glanced over to O'Neill, who sidled past Princeton to come address the situation.

"I noticed your friend had a few symptoms I was familiar with, so I took the liberty of taking some preventative measures."

"I'm feeling much better I think," Harvard agreed. His eyes fluttered, and Yale caught him just before he collapsed onto the ground, spilling sweet-smelling tea all over the metal floor.

Interlude Two: Ronan

At the age of fourteen, Ronan Bell was an excellent pianist. Just not when anyone was watching. When he was on his own, without the weight of others' stares, he didn't shake like he did when he was forced to perform in a stuffy concert hall. His fingers effortlessly glided over the keys, fitting the melodies together like pieces of a jigsaw puzzle sliding neatly into place. Ronan loved counterpoint. He loved that he could see how the notes fit together on the page, and how they corresponded to the way his fingers danced. He liked the way that piano didn't require him to *think*—it had never been his strong suit. Whenever he was required to *think* under pressure, Ronan had a tendency to panic. But when he was sitting on the bench letting his fingers take over, he achieved a state of mind he could only reach through playing music. A kind of...emptiness. But a pleasant emptiness. Like he was holding nothing and everything in his mind all at once and making music while doing it. Very little could calm the constant churning in his stomach, the constant shaking of his limbs, the constant fears chasing each other around in his mind—but playing the piano did that.

Ronan Bell was playing a melody alone in the parlor, staring absently at the notes, his fingers easily sliding over each other, each note fitting neatly in place like pegs sliding into wooden holes.

"Ronan."

It was not a shriek. It wasn't even a scream. That was the funny thing about his mother—she never raised her voice at him. Sometimes he wished she would—the cold intensity of her voice scared him so much more. The way she whispered his name, like she was breathing out a knife made of ice, filled him with a desire to flee and hide. That's exactly what he'd done, when he was little. He'd hear his mother call—no, not call. *Speak* his name. And he'd hide under tables, or under his bed, or out in the gardens, or in the servants' quarters, or in the kitchen. Each time his father, at his mother's request, would wordlessly drag him out by his shirt collar and drop him at his mother's feet. So he stopped hiding. The instinct, however, was still there.

At the sound of his name, Ronan jerked in alarm, his fingers hitting the piano at awkward angles and striking an ugly, off-key chord, leaving the piece unfinished, the notes unplaced. He turned to see her standing in the doorway, hands clasped behind her back, elegant scarlet gown reaching down to her feet. She looked like a statue, one that was supposed to display ancient pre-Quake virtues— Moderation. Balance. Discipline.

"Mr. Jenks is expecting you," she said.

Ronan stood abruptly, the piano bench scraping against the tiles.

"Oh! I...um..." he glanced at the clock on the wall. *Dusts.* He'd lost track of time. Again.

"I wasn't...I didn't..."

"I don't very much care for your excuses," Madame Bell held up a hand, and Ronan's mouth snapped shut. "Just go downstairs before you waste any more of your tutor's valuable time."

Ronan hung his head. "Yes, ma'am," he responded, and brushed past her to the marble staircase that led to the classroom.

"Thank you, Ronan," he heard her say as he left. The way she hissed his name, like she couldn't wait to get it out of her mouth, always made him wonder if she hated it. She wasn't pleased when he'd asked to change his name, certainly, but he'd at least picked a good Bell family name, hadn't he? And she'd approved it? Yet somehow, he still felt as though she weren't entirely pleased with the decision, like he'd shunned a precious gift that she'd given him, and she couldn't let the rejection go. It wasn't even that he particularly liked the name Ronan. It was just better than the alternative. But the way his mother said it...he wasn't sure if she hated the name, or she just hated *him*.

When he reached the door, he could already hear the scratching of a pencil inside.

She's already here, he thought. Of course she is. *And she's already started, too.*

He swallowed and pushed open the door, steeling himself for the inevitable rebukes. The scratching stopped as the sole pupil in the room turned to look at him. He was met with his own face, his own eyes staring him down disapprovingly.

Katherine Bell sniffed disparagingly, then whipped her head around to look back at her paper, two perfect ginger braids swaying against her back.

"Master Bell," said the tutor, leaning against his desk nonchalantly. "So kind of you to join us for your exam."

"Sorry, I...Sorry I'm late," he sputtered, and he could feel his face reddening under the man's stare. Or maybe it was the awareness that despite Kathy's show of concentration, she was certainly thinking nasty thoughts about him that very moment.

Mr. Jenks stalked over to Ronan's desk and slapped a thick stack of papers down on the surface.

"Sit," he commanded. Ronan did as he was told.

"I...Um..." he patted his pockets.

Mr. Jenks rolled his eyes and slapped a pencil onto the desk.

"Come prepared, next time. And while you're at it, come on time next time. Hm?"

"Yes. Yes sir. Yes."

"Excellent. Now get to work. You've already wasted"—he checked his watch—"twenty-six minutes."

Mr. Jenks rapped his knuckles on the desk twice and walked back over to the desk.

Ronan flipped through the pages and felt the fluttering in his stomach grow more violent. A history test. He'd never been much good at history. He'd never been very good at most subjects, to be honest, but especially not history. It was all names and dates and events and documents—and Ronan wasn't one for memorization. He could understand things that he could see—like notes on sheet music, or keys on the piano. If he could see it, he could understand it. That meant he did alright when it came to geometry or even geography, but most subjects were entirely lost on him.

He didn't even remember *learning* most of these things. Who *was* the representative of the Satsuki Group at the Bastion Summit? How *had* the first code of law been written? How was the new Head Enforcer of the Delian Group chosen? What did the Rubira Association specialize in?

The moment Mr. Jenks left to get another cup of tea, Ronan turned to his sister.

"Kathy," he hissed, "help me."

She didn't look up from her page.

"That would be cheating," she said.

"So cheat! No one cares."

"Mom cares."

Of course. Mom would care. And Saoirse Bell would never have her perfect daughter, heir to the family enterprise, sully herself by helping her idiot twin brother.

"You're still gonna get a perfect score anyway," Ronan groaned. She always did, and she lorded it over him every time.

"You should have studied," she said, pencil still scratching.

"I did study!" Ronan complained. "I didn't remember any of it, though."

This was partially true. He *had* looked over his notes yesterday, but he very quickly concluded that it was a hopeless endeavor and spent the rest of his evening sitting in the garden throwing peanuts to crows.

"How it is my fault," Kathy turned her head toward him, her blue eyes flashing with annoyance, "that you're an idiot, Roe?"

He slumped down in his chair, defeated.

"I'm not an idiot," he murmured, though he wasn't sure if it was to his twin or to himself. She laughed a sharp, derisive laugh and went back to her scribbling.

"I'll do something for you," he pleaded. "I'll...I'll give you my dessert for a week."

"I don't like dessert."

"I'll help you fake a cold so you don't have to do your singing lessons on Saturday."

"I like my singing lessons."

"I'll clean your room."

"My room is clean."

"I'll—"

"You can't *bargain* with me, Roe," she snapped her pencil against the desk. "You don't have anything I want."

He crossed his arms, thinking—and he resented her for making him think under pressure because she *knew* he hated that.

"I'll steal something for you," he suggested.

Kathy froze.

"What?"

Ronan shrugged. "I don't mind. I get in enough trouble as is, what's one more thing? But I wouldn't get caught. I'm good at stealing. I do it all the time."

"Ronan, I'm not going to steal—"

"No, *you're* not," he clarified. "I will."

Kathy stared at him blankly. He wasn't sure if she was shocked, disgusted, or actually considering it. Before she could respond, Mr. Jenks walked back into the room.

"Is Master Bell pestering you, Mistress Bell?" he asked.

"Yes, Mr. Jenks," she said coldly.

The tutor gave Ronan a quick bat upside the head.

"Get back to work."

The two worked in silence—well, Kathy worked in silence. Ronan sulked in silence, unable to think of a single thing to write on the pages. He drew pictures, just to have something on the page that wasn't boring, stupid words.

Only when Mr. Jenks left the room again did Kathy sigh and whisper, "Mother has this...brooch. Amethyst, I think. She never wears it, but she refuses to part with it."

Ronan stared at her in amazement.

"You want a *brooch*?"

"*I* don't want a brooch. But...I know someone who would like it." She blushed deeper than Ronan had ever seen. She'd never had occasion to be embarrassed in front of him before.

"Done. It's yours," he said. "Now *help me*."

"Fine," she grumbled. "Start with the first page. Bastion as we know it was found three months after the First Crisis Summit, which was held during the third and final wave of Quakes. That's when the big six corps were established. First Delian, then Satsuki, then Taheri..."

CHAPTER FOUR

Better Off

O'Neill flipped a metal twisting lock and a shelf fell into place, containing a sleeping palette. Yale effortlessly lifted Harvard's inert body onto it.

"Your gang is certainly not my first group of scavengers," O'Neill said as they situated Harvard on the makeshift bed, "so I've seen this plenty of times before."

"You said it's some kind of...infection?" Columbia asked. She was standing far off, arms crossed, leaning on the kitchenette counter.

"Yes, from particles carried on the dust," O'Neill explained. "The fatigue phase usually only lasts a day or two. Your friend should be just fine in the morning."

"Right. Good," Princeton said, a little too "right" and "good" for Yale's liking. "Could I, uh, could I talk with you all again?"

"Princeton—" Yale began.

"Oh don't worry about me!" O'Neill interrupted. "I'll be doing doctorin' and the like. I won't be paying attention so you can discuss whatever you want."

Yale shook their head. "We have nothing to discu—"

"We should go on a dig without Harvard," Princeton cut in. Yale opened their mouth to protest, but Princeton continued too quickly.

"It's the perfect opportunity to actually get some good work done. We leave him here while he recovers, and we get some good cargo for once."

Again Yale moved to speak, but Princeton held up a hand.

"I'm not *saying* we kick him off the team," he made meaningful eye contact with Yale. "I'm just *saying* this would be a good time to give the kid a break while we, ya know, get out there."

"We can't just leave him with O'Neill. That's not fair," Yale countered.

"Oh, it's fine by me!" O'Neill responded from where he was puttering around by Harvard.

"I thought you weren't listening," Colombia said.

"Well, I mean, you said my name so..." he shrugged.

"Would you really be alright taking care of Harvard for the day?" Yale asked. "I guess we could...we could bring you something in return. A share of the haul, perhaps."

"Oh, it would be my pleasure to care for your friend!" O'Neill said. "It's been so long since I've had any company. No payment required." He went back to his work, paused, then turned back around to face Yale. "Though, come to think of it, it *is* a bit difficult for me to collect herb samples what with my bad leg and all. Perhaps if you see any interesting looking plants out there..."

"Yeah, totally cool plants, got it," Princeton interrupted. "So, we're doing it? We're going out tomorrow?"

Yale sighed, then nodded reluctantly. "Yeah. I guess we are."

Princeton bounced around from foot to foot eagerly.

"This is gonna be so great! You'll see, Yale! It's gonna be awesome!"

The implicit meaning was clear: *you'll see that we're better off without him.*

Yale looked away in hope that Princeton couldn't see the truth on their face: he was probably right.

* * *

Harvard didn't have many reasons to be thankful that he was bound to the Commission, but he did have one: he found the desertwalkers fascinating. There weren't many animals in Bastion, only those who had managed to survive the Great Quakes—dogs, cats, and birds. Without being shoved out into the dusts, he would never have had the chance to see the megacrabs for himself.

O'Neill had provided him with pencils and paper, and he was thankful for that as well. He hadn't had it this nice since he was a child. He watched Little Liza from the fold-out bed, watching her scuttle around her terrarium and capturing images of her from every angle. *She's so majestic,* he thought. *She's a beautiful creature. Perfect, almost. If we weren't so scared of the desertwalkers, I wonder if we would worship them.*

"Your hand doesn't shake when you draw!"

"Ah!" Harvard yelped.

"Sorry," Yale said, pulling out a stool. "I didn't mean to scare you. I can leave you alone if you—"

"No, no, it's fine!" Harvard sputtered. "I just...I didn't know you were there."

"It's just, um, interesting," Yale nodded to Harvard's pad. "That it only happens sometimes."

"Yeah, I know. When I was little, none of the doctors knew what it was. It happens almost all the time, like when I'm nervous or scared or someone is watching me. But every once in a while when I'm alone, I realize that I'm just sort of...still? Never lasts very long though. The stillness."

"Huh. It must be difficult."

Harvard shrugged. "You get used to it. Kind of. It's just..." Before he could finish, he worried he was telling them too much. No one wanted to hear him complain. "Never mind."

"What?" Yale asked. Harvard studied them, trying to gauge whether they really wanted to know. He decided he'd risk it.

"It's funny," he said. "Every time I feel like I've finally gotten used to it, I hear someone swear by the Quakes, and I think...that's me, isn't it? It's hard to hear someone say, 'quaking piece of shit' and not feel like they're talking about me. The Great Quakes were Earth's biggest disaster, and sometimes I feel like..." he struggled to find the words. "Like I'm Earth's next biggest quaking disaster."

Yale laughed, and Harvard flushed unexpectedly. He hadn't meant it to be funny, but it felt like a triumph to make them smile.

"You're no disaster," they grinned, and though it was not exactly a compliment, it still made Harvard's heart flutter. "I never really thought of that, honestly. The connection between the Quakes and your...um, condition. I'll try not to use that word much anymore, if it makes you feel better."

Suddenly Harvard worried he was being too needy, or oversharing, or asking too much, or all of those things at once. He waved a hand hurriedly. "It doesn't really matter," he assured them.

"It does matter," they insisted. "To me. I'm your Captain. I'm not going to go around using words that make you uncomfortable."

"Oh. Um. Thanks."

Harvard's eyes darted between Yale and his unfinished drawing, not sure what to say next, or if he was even supposed to say something next. He thought maybe Yale had been waiting for an exit to the conversation, but now they sat in silence together and they didn't leave.

"Can I...watch you draw?" they asked. "Or will that make you nervous?"

"No, no it's fine if you watch! You don't make me nervous." This was only a partial lie. Yale did make Harvard nervous, and he probably wasn't hiding it very well since his pencil was already starting to shake when he pressed it against the page, his previously confident strokes now wobbly and unclear. But he didn't want Yale to *think* they made him nervous, and he didn't want them to leave. Yale was the only person he'd ever known who showed him kindness even when he wasn't useful to them. He'd grown up without much kindness at all, and the first person he called a friend only tolerated him because she'd discovered a way to profit off him. Yale wasn't like that. Harvard knew he wasn't an effective crew member; everyone knew that, and Yale still seemed to care about him regardless. Harvard was aware that this was probably only because they were Captain and the Captain was supposed to care for the whole team, but still, it wasn't something he was going to take for granted.

"It looks...really nice," they said. "I mean, I don't really know anything about art, like I don't know how to tell good art from bad art, but I think yours is good."

"Thanks," Harvard said, though he was fully aware it wasn't true. He was too aware of Yale's eyes on him, and he couldn't manage any precision with his shaking hand. He couldn't tell if Yale really didn't notice, or if they were politely avoiding commenting on it.

They folded their arms on the edge of Harvard's bed and laid their chin down on them. Harvard could see their eyes darting across the page, watching the movements of his pencil with rapt attention. He felt a flicker of warmth in his stomach. No one had ever taken an interest in his drawing before. Maybe it was a good thing he'd ruined everything, landing them in O'Neill's pod. Maybe this was a well-needed respite.

Probably not, though. Probably this was a huge waste of time, and he was wasting even more time by being sick.

"I'm sorry," he murmured. "I'm slowing you guys down. I know we're due back at the Commission already, and we haven't reached our quota, so we're probably not even going to make any points of this trip—"

"—that doesn't matter," Yale's brow knit, as though they couldn't even understand why he'd be worried. "We'll have plenty more chances to dig around in the sand for garbage. You're sick. We'll wait."

"Thanks," Harvard said, and he wished he could shrink away and fade into nothingness, just so that he wouldn't be a burden anymore.

"Just keep drawing," Yale suggested. Harvard did.

* * *

"Are you sure I can't help with anything?" Harvard asked as he watched O'Neill puttering around. The pod was barely large enough for him to maneuver in, yet he seemed to be constantly moving. "I feel like I'm wasting space sitting here while everyone else is out digging."

O'Neill shook his head. "I wouldn't hear of it," he said. "You just rest. I've been doing this work on my own for years."

"Er." Harvard pet Little Liza, who had taken a liking to resting on his shoulder and nuzzling into the crook of his neck. "I don't actually understand what your work is, to be honest."

"All the better! I get to teach you!" O'Neill limped over toward Harvard and reached up to the bookshelf over his head. He displayed its contents like a kindergarten teacher showing a picture book to the class.

"Ya see, back in Bastion they think they know all the answers. But out here! Plants have been evolving. Animals have been evolving! There are all sorts of new critters and no one bothers to look for them cuz they're too afraid of the giant crabs."

"Um, okay," Harvard said tentatively. "I still don't see how that's important though."

"Something has gotta be keepin' these creatures alive! Is it what they eat? Is it something about their bodies? Their cell structures? Their organs? We gotta study these creatures, boy! Find out all their secrets. That's what I'm out here researchin'! It's the only way to unlock mankind's dream: immortality!"

Harvard gave a polite smile and nodded, hoping to hide his skepticism. O'Neill handed him the notebook, signaling for him to peruse the notes and sketches.

"What's this?" he pointed to the illegible scribbles on the page. He'd heard that before the quakes there were many ways to write, but now everyone wrote in Bastion Common. How did O'Neill write in a different language?

O'Neill only laughed.

"Just have a look at the pictures," he said.

He did so, if only for etiquette's sake. He flipped through a few pages of plants and flowers before he came across the creatures.

"Whoa!" he exclaimed, pointing to an illustration of a thick lizard with pincers extending from the top of its front legs. It wouldn't have been so notable if there weren't a human drawn for scale only reaching about half of the thing's height. "What's that thing?"

"Ah," O'Neill leaned over Harvard's shoulder to see where he was pointing. "You've never seen a pinchdragon?"

Harvard shook his head.

"One of the most dangerous creatures in the dusts."

"Why's that?" Harvard had a hard time imagining anything more dangerous than the crabs and snakes that he and the Ivies dealt with daily. "Is it a carnivore?"

"Nope. Filters out edible particles from the air when it breathes. Doesn't hunt."

"So...what makes it dangerous?"

"It's blind. And it doesn't give a shit."

"What?"

"You see one of those things barreling toward you, you best run. Those things are heavy, fast, and ruthless. They don't know what they're doing, and they don't care."

Harvard silently hoped that he would never encounter one of those terrifying creatures and turned the page, only to find another terrifying creature. This one looked like a turtle with a birdlike beak and crablike legs.

"Tortoisecrab," O'Neill dismissed it. "Very common around these parts. This one *will* eat you, though. That sharp beak sure is a bitch."

"*Common?*" Harvard repeated.

O'Neill shrugged. "You probably spend more of your time 'round the East, yeah? Near Bastion?"

"I guess."

"Mark my words, boy: the further west you get, the weirder the creature. That's a saying among us scientists: more west, more weird."

"I can't even believe that there are even other researchers *out* here!" Harvard marveled. He'd been loath to come out in the dusts himself, even when he'd known he had no choice. He couldn't imagine doing it of his own free will. *Still better than the alternative*, he reminded himself.

"Oh yes, there's a whole slew of us. We're the only ones crazy enough to live out here full-time. Us and the sandheads, that is."

Harvard nodded gravely. He'd heard all about the sandheads, though he'd never seen one in real life. Their formal title was the Congregation of the Earth's Mercy, but most scavengers just dismissed them as lunatics. Harvard didn't know how he felt about that. It seemed too simple, to explain away a whole belief system just by calling them "crazy."

Their religion was as old as Bastion itself, which is to say, very young. The Congregationalists refused to take part in the founding of Bastion, claiming that it was human ambition that caused the Earth to swallow humanity in the first place. They believed forming a city upon the remains of the sunken human society was the deadliest of sins. They vowed to make their lives out in the deserts, shunning the comforts Bastion could provide. They claimed the sun was an unholy beast, and refused to let the light touch their skin, so even in the heat of the desert they wore staunch black-hooded robes. The original city-dwellers figured they'd soon die out, and perhaps most of them did. No one had since bothered to check.

But Harvard had heard the tales. Some scavengers back at the Commission had claimed to have once run into a sandhead. One scavenger who claimed to have seen a sandhead monk said he thought it was death itself come to claim him, what with the black robes and face so ghastly white that it looked like a skull. Instead, it was a Congregationalist admonishing him for his sinful ways, and praying his death was swift and painful. Sandheads, it was said, believed scavenging was an insult to the Earth, and a robbery of her bounty. And on the rare occasion they came across scavengers, they were said to do terrible things. Someone on another scavenging crew said they saw a sandhead cut off someone's hands and feet and watched them bleed into the dust. Harvard thought they just said it to scare him, but still, he would avoid anyone he found wearing black robes in the desert, just in case.

O'Neill, however, did not seem to treat them with the same dread seriousness that Harvard did.

"Well, keep reading!" he goaded, clearly bursting with pride over the compendium of his work. O'Neill taught him about the venomous Gila crabs, the aquatic crabsquid, the dual-brained netherworm, and many others Harvard lost the names for.

"Do you happen to have a pen and paper I could use?" Harvard asked, hating how his voice pitched up whenever he made a request of anyone.

"Sure," O'Neill shrugged. "You're taking notes?"

"No, I...I want to practice drawing some of these. If it's okay with you. I haven't, um, been able to draw with a real pen and paper in a while. It would be nice, I think."

O'Neill obliged, and Harvard spent the rest of the evening sketching his own renditions of scuttlers, or carcines, as O'Neill called them— lizards, plants, and more. While it didn't do much to lessen his dread about what lurked in the desert, capturing the creatures in ink at least gave him the illusion he had some power over them. Or an understanding, at least.

Eventually, however, the exertion was too much for Harvard's sick body. He fell asleep with Little Liza perched on his shoulder, still holding the thick tome of research.

* * *

The first dig without Harvard was the first uneventful one the Ivies experienced in a while. Columbia kept watch. When she saw a crabsnake getting dangerously close, she called them back. The other two down below hurried up and vacated the area before the creature even noticed they were there. They returned to the research pod with two more vapor canisters, a whole sack full of dried food rations, a computer chip, some plastics, and plenty of herb samples to take back to O'Neill.

Yale sat by Harvard's side and told him every detail of the dig, boring as it was. Harvard did his best to listen, though it was hard to keep from dozing off and jerking back awake. Yale would occasionally use a tissue to mop the sweat from Harvard's forehead, where it beaded and dripped down his face.

"I wish I could have gone with you," Harvard murmured weakly.

"Next time," Yale said, brushing some red curls away from Harvard's eyes.

Harvard coughed, the spasms wracking his whole body.

"I don't know," he wheezed.

"You'll be better tomorrow," Yale said.

Harvard looked up at them with big, hopeful eyes. "Promise?"

"I promise."

CHAPTER FIVE

A Dig Up North

Harvard was not better tomorrow.

In fact, he was considerably worse. O'Neill informed the rest of the group about this during a huddle in the entry hallway.

"Believe me, I'm doing all I can," he wrung his hands, "but I don't think he'll be, um, in the best shape for going on your next dig."

"We can wait," Yale said firmly. Columbia only eyed them, but Princeton let out a groan.

"We can't, though!" he whined. "We're supposed to be back to the Commission today. And we haven't filled our quota. Our debt is gonna be through the roof. If we get back—"

"If we get back a little late, it's fine," Yale snapped. "We're not leaving Harvard."

"I'm not *saying* we need to leave Harvard," Princeton held up his hands in defense. "I just—"

"Look," O'Neill cut Princeton off. "I want to be perfectly honest with you folks. You seem like good people and I...I just don't wanna lead you astray. I'm gonna do everything I can to get that boy on his feet again. I just don't know how soon that's gonna be. And to be quite frank with you..." his eyes flicked between Princeton and Yale, "I don't know if it's gonna happen at all."

A tense silence passed.

"What do you mean, O'Neill?" Yale finally asked, and each word was spoken with the weight and precision of a stone dropped in a pond. The old man glanced at Columbia for guidance. Everyone knew what he meant, of course. But he didn't seem to have the courage to look Yale in the eyes and say it.

"You think Harvard might die," Colombia translated. Yale did not turn their gaze from the trembling old man.

"I think...it is a possibility," he nodded his thanks to Colombia. Yale breathed in sharply, then clasped their hands together.

"Well, thank you for being upfront with us," they said coolly. "I'm sure we've kept you from your work too long. Please, don't let us take any more of your time."

The old man made a sort of appreciative grumble and hobbled back to the pod door, glancing back at Columbia for approval before stepping through and shutting it hurriedly behind him.

"You don't have to scare him like that," Colombia chided as soon as they were alone.

"I wasn't trying to scare him," Yale snapped. "I was just trying to get him to speak plainly. I wish people would just say what they mean."

"I think he was afraid that if he said what he meant, you were going to beat him up."

"I wouldn't—" Yale cut themself off. They turned around to see that she was raising an eyebrow at them.

"I know he's doing what he can," Yale adjusted their glasses, looking down, "and I...appreciate that."

They glanced at Princeton, who had been oddly quiet. He was staring blankly at the door O'Neill had just left through.

"Guys," he said distantly without breaking his stare, "do you really think Harvard is gonna die?"

Yale and Columbia exchanged glances.

"I don't know, Princeton," Yale said. "I have no idea how any of this works. Harvard is completely in O'Neill's hands here."

"I just...I didn't..." he swallowed, then took a deep breath. "I've never been on a team where someone died before. And like, Harvard...I don't know, I mean, I always thought he was annoying, but he's just a little guy, ya know? I don't...I don't want him to die."

Princeton's face had started to turn bright red, and Yale could see tears just beginning to sparkle in his eyes. He turned abruptly to head out through the pod door.

* * *

"You don't seem too concerned," Columbia observed as the two surveyed. Surveying was not as involved as a full dig and certainly not as dangerous. Just a simple search for anything that might be useful, like canisters from a dead scavenger. The corpse of a scavenger was considered to be a great find, since it was often dripping with useful equipment.

Yale did not look up as they stirred the dust with a paddle.

"Harvard's not going to die," they asserted.

"You sound confident."

"I am."

For a moment, there was no sound but the wind whipping the sand around them. Columbia extended a tentative hand toward their shoulder.

"Yale—" she began.

"What?" they snapped, turning to face her. She recoiled in surprise.

"Talk to me," she pleaded.

They turned away from her.

"I have nothing to say." They started trudging back toward the pod, so they could speak to Harvard before they left. O'Neill protested, claiming that they should just let Harvard rest, but Yale insisted that Harvard knew maps better than anyone else on the team, and it was worth waking him for a bit of guidance. It also didn't hurt that getting Harvard's input would at least allow him to feel like he was a part of the dig, even if he was now too weak to even stand, let alone go out scavenging.

"Your path veers a little too far west here," Harvard pointed a shaky finger at the map Yale had drawn. "There's still a big concentration of unexplored buildings here, and if you miss it, you'll have to turn back around."

Yale handed him a pen and he made some notes on the crumpled pages, then handed it back to Yale.

"This will help you," he said. Yale nodded and pocketed the map. They moved to stand, but Harvard placed a hand on their arm.

"Yale," Harvard murmured, his voice weak and raspy. "Yale, I don't think I'm going to make it."

"Of course you are," Yale reassured him, patting his red hair. "We'll make it back to the city before you know it."

"No," Harvard shook his head almost imperceptibly, "I don't think I will. I don't think I'll even make it until you all get back from the dig."

"Harvard!" Yale toed the line between comforting and scolding him. "Don't talk like that. We'll do this dig as soon as we can, and by the time we're back you'll be all better and you can go home."

Harvard's body was too feeble to sob, but still tears formed in his eyes and fell down his face and he shook his head again.

"Yale, listen to me. I can tell. I'm not getting better. I need," he pulled Yale close. "I need to tell someone. Please. I can't die without telling anyone my real name."

"No," Yale pulled away, gripping Harvard's hand. "No, that's not going to happen. You're not going to die and you're not going to tell me your name. Understood? Once we're all super rich from all the stuff we find out here, then you can tell me your name. But not today. I will see you when I get back. You got that, Harvard? When I get back from this dig, you're going to be right here, and you're going to think of how silly you were for ever thinking you were going to die. Because you are going to make it. Understand me?"

Harvard no longer had the strength to continue the conversation. He simply shook his head, closed his eyes, and allowed one final tear to slide down his face.

Once they were satisfied that Harvard was asleep, Yale extricated their hand from Harvard's and stood.

Their stomach roiled with guilt, leaving Harvard like that. They tried to convince themself it was better this way. He'd be safer. He already had his tremor to deal with, and now he was sick. It was best to keep him out of harm's way, for the time being, even if the nasty side effect was that it might further his sense of alienation.

They watched the gentle rise and fall of his chest. Yale knew it wasn't their job to protect him, but they couldn't fight down the urge. *He's so kind, in a world that's so unfair to him.*

"Are you ready to go?" Columbia's voice sounded from the pod entry. Yale remained staring down at Harvard.

"He tries so hard not to hurt anyone. Or even crabs, for that matter. He doesn't even like to use the vapor."

"He's a good person," Columbia agreed.

"Better than me," Yale whispered. They didn't need to turn to her to know she was wearing that familiar disappointed frown.

"You try your best," she said.

"But I *do* hurt people. I can't be like him."

Columbia didn't deny it. Why would she? She knew it was true.

"Let's go," she finally said. "We have work to do."

Yale took a breath and nodded. "We'll be right back," they whispered to Harvard, even though they knew he couldn't hear them.

* * *

"You're sure you think this is wise?" Columbia asked as she carefully lowered herself into the sunken building, gripping Yale's hand for support. They nodded solemnly.

"Given the fact that we didn't encounter any kind of desertwalker on the way here, I'm pretty confident that we're not gonna have any trouble."

"Still, the last time we didn't have someone keep watch..." Columbia started.

"Three of us doing this dig is better than two. This time it's more important that we be fast, not careful."

Princeton peeked his head out of a doorway, holding a scavenged pre-tremor device, something flat with a shattered screen in the front. He had pried off its metal case and was picking through the innards for anything useful.

"Not a lot of scuttlers up here, but I hear they're *fast*. There's, like, pinchdragons and shit. Lenovo told me she and the Computers saw one it almost crushed their whole crew."

Columbia removed her hand from Yale's as she gained her footing on the grimy carpet of the ancient apartment complex.

"We better not run into one of those," she glanced cautiously back out the window, as though she expected one to appear at its mention, like summoning a demon.

Yale shrugged. "They're not dangerous, just stupid."

Columbia watched Princeton cheerfully dive back into his scavenging.

"Same thing," she murmured, before carefully making her way down the incline toward another apartment, the rubber grip on her shoes clinging to the inclined carpet.

Yale kicked open the door next to them, and it was so rusted one of the hinges came loose with a *crack*. They whipped out their flashlight and shone it over the room. A hoard of small scuttlers were poking around the kitchen, looking for leftover scraps. A few seemed to have made a den in the armchair in the corner. A doorway next to it looked as though it led to a bedroom, and with a wave of dread Yale saw a motionless lump under those covers. It would not be the first body they'd found in the sunken buildings; usually someone who thought they'd found a refuge and soon discovered that the predatory crabs had the same notion.

They walked toward a sloping bookshelf pressed against the back wall, hoping the cabinets might hold something useful. Where they expected to find the floor flush with the wall, instead was a gap, exposed steel rod jutting out of concrete. At a glance it looked rusted, but Yale knew better than that. They froze.

"Nobody move!" Yale shouted, but the other two Ivies were too far away to hear them clearly.

"What?" came Princeton's echoing reply from another room.

"I said, don't—"

They heard the sound of Princeton's lumbering footsteps coming toward them.

"No! Stop! Don't—" they stammered. "This building has steelmites."

Princeton let out a yelp of surprise and his footsteps stopped abruptly.

"Founders! Don't scare me like—"

"Stop. Moving," Yale could hear Columbia command coolly. They took a cautious step toward the door. Only now that they were aware of the danger could they hear the subtle creaking of the reinforcement beams with every step.

"What...what's going on?" Princeton asked, nervous laughter creeping into his voice.

"Steelmites," Columbia explained. "Scuttlers that eat steel. They weaken a building from the inside out."

"So..." Princeton processed the information like a lagging computer, "the building is unstable?"

"Yes. And we have to get out *very carefully.*"

At this point, Yale had crept to the doorway. Princeton and Columbia stood at the other end of the inclined hallway. Yale could easily reach the window and climb to safety, but the other two would have to climb up the entire hallway without upsetting the fragile supports keeping the floor in place.

"How do you guys know about these?" Princeton asked. Columbia and Yale shared a glance but said nothing.

"Just don't," Yale instructed levelly, "make any sudden movements."

Princeton and Columbia both nodded slowly.

"Walk toward me. Carefully."

Columbia took the lead, taking one heel-toe step up the incline. Princeton mimicked her, but his footfall was heavier. The floor creaked under his weight.

"Sorry!" he hissed.

"It's fine, just...go slow, okay?"

Princeton nodded, and he lifted his foot to take another step, but his toe caught on a wrinkle in the decaying carpet.

"Wait—" Columbia started, but he tripped over his feet. He slammed against the ground with a reverberating *smack*.

First, the left side of the floor came loose, sending the Ivies slamming against the left wall. Then the right side snapped as well, and the whole floor began to tremble and sink. The floors shuddered down the shaft of the building like a violent elevator, plummeting down into the depths.

* * *

Columbia dragged herself to her feet, examining herself for injuries in the darkness. The shock of hitting the ground had rattled her body. She could have sworn she could feel her bones shake, but it didn't seem she was injured. Had they suffered a free fall from that height, they'd all be dead for sure, but standing on the sinking floor was more like being rapidly and aggressively lowered to the ground.

She probed her legs, her arms. Nothing broken. A few bruises here and there, but that was nothing new. It was rare that a dig didn't result in a few minor injuries.

"Is everyone okay?" she called out into the darkness. A moment of silence shot a knife of panic through her stomach.

"Yup!" she finally heard Princeton's voice somewhere ahead of her. "All good here."

She waited for another response but was met with silence.

"Yale?" she asked shakily.

"Yes," came a whispered reply behind her.

"Dark as shit down here," Princeton grumbled. "Lemme find my—"

"No," Yale hissed behind her. "No light. No sound. Be quiet."

Columbia felt her body tense.

"What...what's going on?" Princeton asked.

"Nobody panic," Yale said in a strained voice, "but there is some kind of creature in here with us."

"What," Colombia matched her captain's tone, "kind of creature?"

"I can't quite tell," Yale responded, "but it's big. It's wet. And it has some kind of tentacles."

"How do you know that?" Princeton asked. "It's fucking dark."

"Again, nobody panic," Yale reiterated, "but I know because one of the tentacles is wrapped around my leg."

Columbia fought down the urge to dive toward the sound of their voice, knife drawn, and blindly stab at whatever was preying on them. She knew better than that, knew that the creature would probably panic and strike, killing both of them. Besides, she had never made a habit of jumping into danger without careful calculation. She'd seen the results of an uncalculated risk, and she wasn't going to let those consequences befall anyone on her team.

"How does it feel?" Princeton asked.

"Unpleasant," came Yale's cool reply.

"Don't be a smartass. I mean what does it feel like?"

"It feels like a tentacle wrapped around my leg."

"He's trying to ask, how big do you think it is?" Columbia clarified. "And what kind of scuttler—"

"It's not a scuttler. I mean, it's not...it's not crab shaped."

"How do you know?"

"It's *wet*. I think this is a crabsquid."

"That's not possible. Crabsquids only live in water," Columbia said.

"Which brings me to my next unsettling conclusion. I think somewhere around here this is a large pool of water."

"Why hasn't it pulled you into the water then?" Princeton asked.

"It's *trying*."

"Okay," Columbia said slowly. "So, everyone, watch where you step."

"I can't, Columbia, because, let me reiterate, *it's fucking dark*," Princeton snapped.

"Better yet," Yale hissed. "Don't move at all. I am going to *slowly* draw my knife and try to cut myself free. You two, just—be quiet, okay? And *don't move*."

Columbia found herself nodding, despite the darkness. She waited for the sound of metal cutting into slippery flesh, perhaps for the squeal of an unseen creature taken by surprise. The sound didn't come. She waited in silence, biting down on her questions. She willed something, anything, to make a sound, just so she could know what was going on, so she wasn't suspended in this stasis wondering if her captain was free.

She heard a sound. In fact, she heard five in quick succession.

A body hitting the ground. A yelp of surprise. A knife clattering to the ground. Something being dragged through the dust. And a splash.

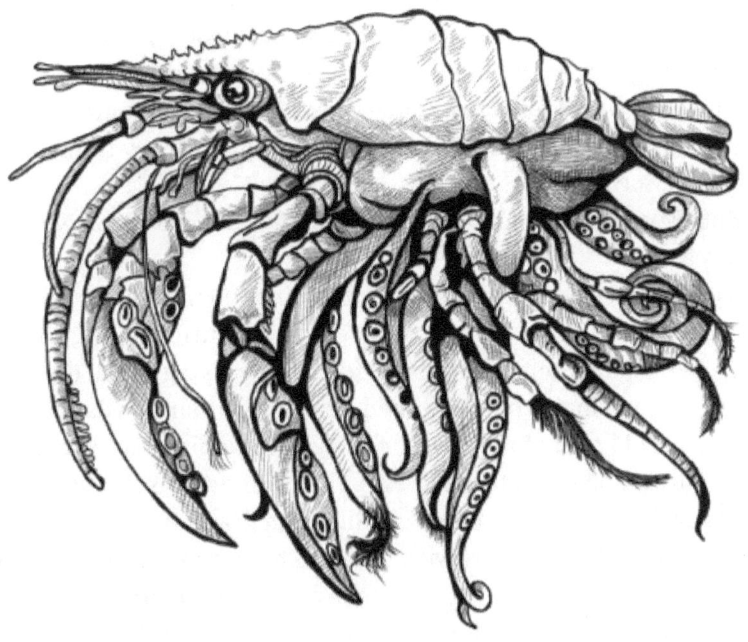

Interlude Three: Chavi

"I don't understand the problem," Avi said as Chavi kicked up dust underneath the swing. The chains creaked under the weight of the three children, idly swaying back and forth.

"It's not that hard to follow the rules," she declared haughtily.

"It is, a little," Chavi protested. "I mean, sometimes rules are stupid. So why should I have to follow them?"

"Because if no one followed the rules, then the world would descend into chaos," Avi explained, wearing her usual I-know-better-than-you expression. She loved talking about chaos. She constantly reminded Chavi and Jasmine about how the world was going to end in entropy. Jasmine asked her to stop saying that because it made her nervous. Chavi said they hoped it would happen soon, so they could see what it looked like when the world fell apart. They were always disappointed that they hadn't been alive to see the Great Quakes, so this entropy thing better be pretty cool, too.

"But everyone else follows the rules. Just not me. See? No chaos," Chavi reasoned.

Avi rolled her eyes and leapt off the swing, then began brushing dirt from her overalls. She'd been looking for worms during recess, which had earned her a gentle but firm talking-to about "playing in the dirt."

"I'm *not* playing!" she'd stomped her foot petulantly when a teacher cheerfully told her that recess was for *clean* fun only. "I'm *researching!*"

She barely got any of the grime off, then shrugged as if to say, "Eh. My parents will buy me new ones." Unlike Chavi and Jasmine, who were both attending the Academy with financial help from elsewhere, Avi was a Taheri, an heiress to the largest real estate conglomerate in Bastion. A Taheri could pay their way into the Bastion Academy of Arts and Sciences ten times over.

"You know they're supposed to treat you differently in secondary school," Avi crossed her arms.

"Yeah, they keep telling me that," Chavi shrugged.

"It's true," Jasmine agreed.

The other two turned to look at her. Jasmine did not speak often, so when she did, it had to be something important.

"I've heard that they can do bad things to you when you're in secondary school," she murmured.

"Like what?" Chavi pressed.

"I don't know," Jasmine admitted, looking down at her diminutive pink sneakers. "Lots of things."

"Well, I haven't heard that," Chavi turned away. Jasmine leapt off the swing, standing next to Avi.

"Just stop making the teachers mad, okay?" Jasmine asked, still looking at her shoes. Then she ran off abruptly, leaving the other two alone.

"What's her problem?" Chavi asked.

"She's right," Avi chided. "If you don't—"

She was cut off by the sound of giggling from somewhere nearby. She turned to see a few other schoolchildren had gathered to watch them talk, snickering.

"Chavi and Avi, gonna fall in love-y!" one of them taunted. This always made Avi flustered.

"Stop it!" she cried. "Stop! We are not!"

Fed up, she stomped off, throwing a backward glance at Chavi over her shoulder.

Chavi never really minded the mockery of the other children. They were pretty certain they *weren't* going to fall in love with Avi, and they were *definitely* certain Avi would never fall in love with them. But apparently this was a thing that was supposed to embarrass them? Admittedly, the joke was completely lost on them. Still, they knew how much the chanting bothered Avi, so when they heard a classmate mocking her with the stupid little rhyme, a swift threat of violence would shut them up.

The moment they stood up off the swing, the offending students' eyes widened, and they dispersed like frightened mice. Another thing Chavi didn't really understand—were the other kids afraid of them? It's not like they'd *actually* beaten anybody up. Yet.

It was only a few weeks into the fall semester. Chavi, Avi, and Jasmine were in their first year at secondary school, and already suffering the consequences, which at this point simply meant an onslaught of homework. Jasmine did it quickly and studiously. Avi could get away with doing a poor job on everything but her biology work, which was her focus that semester. Chavi did poorly on everything and couldn't get away with it. The whole situation left them feeling irritable and jealous. That's how they ended up getting into a fight with another student and punching them in the nose, which was what landed them in the principal's office once again.

"I'm...disappointed to see you here again, Mx. Chakrabarti," Principal Santo sighed.

"Well, I'm disappointed you made me *come* here again, for what it's worth," Chavi retorted.

Principal Santo put his face in his hands. "I don't like to do this to students, you understand. It's not pleasant for any of us. But it's necessary for your *own* wellbeing."

Chavi stared blankly and said nothing. The principal sighed again, growing weary of having to explain everything piece by piece to the same child over and over again.

"If you keep up this kind of behavior, you will not learn," he explained. "If you do not learn, you will do poorly on your Aptitude Exam. If you do poorly on your Aptitude Exam, you will not be admitted to a university. Do you know what happens then, Chaverim?"

Chavi shrugged. "I get a job."

Principal Santo smiled sadly and shook his head. "No, no, I don't think you *do* get a job. Jobs are scarce, what with all the jobless good-for-nothings clogging the city these days scrounging for anything they can get," he waved a hand as if to indicate the riffraff *out there*. "Surely, you've seen what an absolute *mess* Founder's Square has become? No, a job doesn't seem like an option without that degree. So, what do you do?"

"I don't know!" Chavi complained. "That's in seven years!"

"Oh, but *I* know," the principal closed his eyes and drew a deep breath. "Because I've seen it, time and time again. You graduate. You don't get into school. You can't find a job. You become a scavenger."

Chavi rolled their eyes. "I don't think I'm going to do that."

The principal ignored them. His face had gone hard. "Do you have any idea what it's like, being a scavenger?" he asked darkly.

Chavi had heard tales—all the students had. Rumors of monsters lurking outside the Bastion walls, creatures hungering for human flesh that could crush your whole skeleton with one stroke of a massive claw. But Chavi wasn't about to let the principal know that. They shrugged again.

"You dig, right? Doesn't seem too bad. Avi digs all the time." It was a bluff, and the principal knew.

"Avi Taheri is a natural born researcher," he raised a knowing eyebrow. "You will not be doing research. You will be out in the dusts, diving into cold, dark, crevices, all with a team of strangers who could care less whether you live or die. Is that what you want, Chavi?"

"It doesn't sound—"

"And of course you have to leave everyone else behind," the principal cut them off.

"What?" Chavi asked.

"Well, scavenging is a dangerous profession, Mx. Chakrabarti, as you know. The Commission has certain customs to keep its people from getting distracted. After all, Bastion couldn't function without them."

"I don't get it," Chavi said.

"You'll understand when you're older. The important part is this: When you become a scavenger, you'll have to take on a new name, a new identity. You won't be able to see your mother while you're a scavenger. And those two little girls you spend so much of your time with? They'll certainly be admitted to universities. You'll likely never see them again."

"That's not fair!" Chavi protested.

"No. No, it's not. So my advice to you," the principal gave them a stern look, "is to behave, so you can stay in school while you still have the chance."

With that, one of the women from the front office laid a hand on Chavi's shoulder. They thought she was going to guide them out of the office, but instead gently pushed him toward a different door, one Chavi had never paid much mind to.

"Where are we going?" they asked.

"Let me be clear: I don't like to do this," the principal sighed. "But with kids like you, there's really no other way to get the lesson through your head. You do *not* want to become a scavenger, and we'll have to show you why. Believe me," he took off his glasses and rubbed his face. "This is for your own good."

Before Chavi had a chance to respond, the secretary opened the door and shoved them in. They stumbled, falling down the stairs in complete darkness. They hit the floor bruised and scratched, but once they managed to get back to their feet, the door had already closed. They heard the click of a lock.

"Hey!" they shouted. "You can't do this!"

They scrambled back up the stairs to bang on the door. "Hey! Let me out! Hey!"

But no response came. Defeated, they went back to the base of the stairs to explore the room they'd been trapped in. Is this really what it was like to be a scavenger? Alone in the dark? Perhaps it wasn't so bad. Perhaps they could get by like this.

No one came to check on them for twenty-four hours.

The following night, Chavi dreamt they were a scavenger, digging around in the dusts looking for something, anything, to keep them alive. They heard a rumbling as the tunnel began to collapse around them, trapping them in the dirt. The dream felt so real, the dirt walls closed in around them, the dust filled their lungs and choked.

They awoke gasping for air, flailing in their bed. Their mother rushed into their room, sitting by their side and running her hand across her child's back in gentle circles.

"Breathe," she murmured. "You're okay. Just breathe."

Before trying to go back to sleep, Chavi said the Earth's Mercy prayer. It became a personal ritual, and while it didn't prevent the nightmares from coming, Chavi liked to imagine it lessened them.

So, they prayed every night.

Just in case.

CHAPTER SIX

Exploration

"They should have been back by now," Harvard said. A day had passed. Still no sign of the Ivies' return. A dig should never take more than a few hours.

"Probably hit some difficult terrain," O'Neill shrugged, engrossed in his work. Harvard was never quite sure of the specifics of O'Neill's work, though he often talked at length about the different species he was studying. Harvard wasn't particularly interested in any of these things, but he was both too weak and too polite to protest. Perhaps O'Neill thought his rambling was a welcome distraction, from the pain and the absence of Harvard's crew.

Harvard petted Little Liza, who was sitting on his chest, a habit she had made during his illness. If she were much larger, she would resemble a cat perching on top of its human for warmth. She gave him little comfort as he imagined the gruesome fates that could have befallen his crewmates. It was not as though he was all that useful in protecting his team, but he still wondered if he could have prevented whatever happened had he been there. Now they were in danger, or maybe dead, and it was all his fault for getting sick and not coming along. He groaned, at the thought and at the growing pain in his muscles. He'd had the flu once, as a child. He remembered it being like this, only this pain was unyielding, gripping every inch of his body, making his limbs so heavy that he could hardly move.

"About time for your tea, isn't it?" O'Neill observed, putting up the kettle. "It'll put ya right to sleep."

Harvard struggled to sit up and crossed his arms. Little Liza slipped down, so he placed her in the front pocket of his shirt, where she could still peek out without falling off him.

"Maybe we should go looking for them," he suggested. "It's not normal for them to stay out this long. We know exactly where they went; I could lead the way—"

O'Neill laughed, not a mean-spirited laugh, but one with a touch of condescension.

"And let's say they were in some kind of trouble, what would we do? An old man with a bad leg, and a boy who can barely walk?"

"I'm an adult," Harvard grumbled, but O'Neill was already busying himself with his mortar and pestle. As he watched the man at work, Harvard made a promise never to be useless again. If his crew needed him, then he would be there.

When O'Neill served him the tea that was supposed to help him sleep, he thanked him heartily before feigning drinking it and dumping it out the window when the old man couldn't see. The relief from the pain would have been welcome, but he couldn't allow himself to sleep tonight.

Only once O'Neill was snoring quietly, curled up by his research station, did Harvard pull himself off the sleeping palette. Careful not to make any noise, he slid a few items into his pack; some food, a flashlight, and a small vapor canister. He donned his goggles and dustscarf, then carefully pulled the hatch door open. It protested creakily, and Harvard cringed, turning to see if it had woken the old man. He stirred but didn't rise. Harvard let out a sigh of relief and slipped through the cracked hatch into the entry hallway.

Though there was now a thick metal door between him and O'Neill, he still tread carefully. One of the benefits of being relatively small was that he could easily move around without being detected. This was something he had discovered when he was very young. He'd made good use of it before becoming a scavenger.

Harvard unlatched the locking mechanism on the front door of the pod and stepped out into the cool night air. It felt nice, being out in the world again. Even his body aches seemed to recede as he started his trek to the north.

* * *

Being slow and sickly, Harvard knew the course would take him much longer than it would have normally taken the crew. Traveling slowly was dangerous in the dusts, as it made you vulnerable.

Harvard's ears pricked up at the first hint of pursuit. He'd become well-versed with the signs of a desertwalker in the area. A regular scuttler often made a thunderous rumble with its legs when approaching. The sound Harvard heard did not sound like the sustained murmur of an approaching crab. It was large, heavy footfalls. He pulled out his flashlight and flipped it on to see the creature lumbering out from behind a rocky outcropping.

He looked up at the thing, feeling dwarfed by its size. He'd never seen one in real life, but he recognized it from the illustration in O'Neill's creature books: A tortoisecrab.

The thing's crab legs were as thick as tree trunks, and its shell was thick and rounded, with a sinuous neck extending forward. Its huge black eyes, reflecting the glow of Harvard's flashlight, watched him curiously, hungrily. Its beak gave an expectant twitch. Harvard began to slowly back away, fearing any sudden movement would cause the creature to snap at him. It could easily crush his whole body with its powerful mouth. He felt his knees get weak, and he began shaking so violently that he worried his legs would collapse under him.

It set its jaw on the ground, and its mouth gaped so widely Harvard could have walked right into it. In fact, that's probably exactly what the tortoisecrab expected Harvard to do. He'd read in O'Neill's book that smaller scuttlers couldn't tell the difference between the beast's maw and a nice moist cave, so they would crawl in thinking they found a pleasant new burrow only to be digested seconds later.

The beast snapped at him, and he leapt backward, yelping in surprise and horror, narrowly avoiding being sliced down the middle. The tortoisecrab took another step, its tall legs stretching a seemingly impossible distance. Harvard scrambled to his feet, eyes fixed on the gargantuan creature.

What could he do? The thing was slow, but its legs were long enough to keep pace with him if he were to run away. It could extend its neck and clamp its beak closed on him. And of course, fighting it was out of the question.

Hands shaking, Harvard removed his pack and fished around for the canister of vapor he'd brought with him. It wasn't much, but if he managed to aim it correctly, he could get away while the tortoisecrab wheezed.

Just as his hand closed around the canister, something hit Harvard in the stomach, forcing the breath out of him and knocking him to the ground. The vapor canister and flashlight flew out of his hands. Gasping for air, he tried to stand but found that something heavy was pinning him to the dust. When he struggled to rise, it only pressed on him harder. As the wind died down and the dust settled for a moment, he could clearly see a megacrab leg, thicker than both of his own legs combined, held him against the earth. The creature could easily have shoved that leg right through his torso, but instead the megacrab planted its leg firmly on his stomach. Each time Harvard wriggled to get away it only pressed harder.

Harvard lifted his head awkwardly at a noise from the tortoisecrab. It was still approaching, jaw snapping. And here was this giant crab holding him down, making him easy prey. He was not nearly strong enough to break away from the leg that held him down, despite his wriggling.

Be still, child.

Harvard froze. Had someone spoken? Or was he hearing voices? Was the dustsickness loosening his grasp on reality? Perhaps this new voice was something inside of him, something that his panic had unleashed.

Do not move, idiot boy. Stay very still. Then maybe you will live.

It certainly didn't *sound* like a voice in his head, but perhaps the mind does strange things when you're about to be eaten by a giant monster. Were the two going to fight over who got the privilege to eat him? Would their battle be enough of a distraction to let him slip away? But no, instead the two creatures made a series of clicking noises, gesticulating with their legs. Harvard wondered if they were communicating, or simply threatening each other. It reminded him of the way he'd seen cats hiss before one would bat at the other with a paw as a warning. The tortoisecrab snapped its head forward and Harvard flinched, but the megacrab smashed a thick pincer down on it. The tortoisecrab wailed, taking a heavy step backward and retracting its head. The megacrab made some more clicks and gave a demonstrative snap with its pincer. The tortoisecrab gave a pitiful little whine, then began to walk away.

The tortoisecrab's retreat would have done a lot to quell Harvard's terror if it weren't for the colossal crab hovering over him. He was going to be eaten by a desertwalker, whether or not it was a giant turtle or a giant crab didn't matter much to him. He braced himself for mandibles digging into his flesh. It didn't come.

Instead, the pressure on his stomach lifted. The megacrab moved its leg off Harvard and back onto the dust. He was so shocked that for a moment he lay on his back, dumbfounded.

Stand.

Harvard did as commanded, though he still didn't fully understand where the command was coming from. He brushed the dust from his clothing, which didn't do much as he was covered in the rusty residue.

He was still trembling violently. The crab watched him with beady marble eyes, disproportionately small for its hulking body.

You should not be here, child. This is no place——

The megacrab staggered, wailing. Harvard gasped, stumbling backward. A flashlight beam landed on the creature, and Harvard could see the beast in all of its insectoid glory. As much as Harvard had an affection for little crabs, seeing the huge creature's mouth in such detail made him feel sick. Its maw was stretched wide, letting out an unholy screech. It took Harvard a moment to see the harpoon extending from the side of the crab's shell.

The creature snapped its mouth shut, and Harvard feared it would seek reprisal. Instead, it whined softly, and retreated into the night.

For one sacred moment, Harvard felt safe. He let out a sigh of relief.

"Damn it, boy!" said a familiar voice behind him. "I told you you'd get yourself killed out here! What were you thinking?"

Harvard turned around, suddenly blinded by the glare of the flashlight. He held up a hand to shield his eyes. He couldn't see anything until a hand closed around his arm dragging him back the way he came. Only then did he get a glimpse of O'Neill's face as it made its way toward him. The old man hauled him toward the pod, which Harvard realized had moved. No wonder O'Neill had found him so quickly. He had a mechanical desertwalker to ride in.

"What kind of idiot are you?" he shouted as he half-pushed, half-threw Harvard through the entry hatch. "You think you can face those things on your own? You can't! If I hadn't been there, that thing would have—"

"It wasn't going to hurt me!" Harvard protested as he opened the interior door to the pod. He wanted to say more, but if he spoke his thought aloud, O'Neill would surely think he'd lost his mind, or completely given in to the hallucination of dustsickness. Still, he could not dismiss the suspicion that had wedged itself in his mind like a splinter turning into a festering wound: *That crab just spoke to me.*

"Like hell it wasn't! I *saw* it!" O'Neill shuffled into the pod behind Harvard, waggling his harpoon gun. "If it weren't for me, that thing would have torn you apart!"

Harvard leaned against the table in the back of the room, eyeing O'Neill up and down. His mind raced, his heart hammered, his whole body trembled, and slowly pieces began to fall into place like two hands weaving their fingers together.

"What is it, boy?" O'Neill shouted. "Spit it out!"

"Your limp is gone," Harvard murmured.

He expected O'Neill to protest, perhaps to give some explanation. But he didn't. He only grinned.

Interlude Four: Ronan

Ronan Bell had been preparing for years to make a hasty exit from Bell Manor. He had his pack ready to go, complete with food, some changes of clothes, even a small pocketknife. Every once in a while, he would go over its contents, scrutinizing whether he needed to add something, fantasizing about the day he would finally make his daring escape. But each time he would set the pack aside for another day. He simply didn't have the courage. He wondered what would eventually push him over the edge; maybe his mother would finally snap and lay hands on him. There had certainly been moments when she looked tempted to hit him. Perhaps one day she would lose her restraint, and that would be the point little Ronan finally decided he'd had enough.

In the end, there was no violence. There was no dramatic reckoning, no screaming match, no tearful parting in which the Bell family begged for their only son not to go. It was, like everything else in Ronan's life, painfully mundane.

It started when Ronan prepared to make good on his promise to Kathy. Swiping things from the Bell household was nothing new to him. He'd discovered one of the benefits of being small, meek, and overall easy to ignore was as long as his parents and tutor weren't watching, he could generally get away with things. Nothing big, of course. But the occasional extra tart from the kitchen, or the occasional ring from his mother's overflowing armoire? He had to find *somewhere* to get shiny things for the crows, after all. He'd never snuck into his parent's bedroom while they were *in it* before, but if he'd been able to creep away from three different caretakers at his parent's yearly Winter Ball to go hide in the topiaries in the west garden, he was pretty certain this would be comparatively easy.

His parents kept to a strict schedule, so he knew they'd be in their room by nine and asleep by ten. He put on the softest socks he owned and gently pushed open his bedroom door. Of course it didn't creak. Madame Bell would never tolerate a creaky door in her manor. His parents lived on the floor above their children, so he padded toward the mahogany stairs.

On his way up, he wondered who Kathy wanted to give the brooch to. Who wears a *brooch* these days anyway? Or was it more of a gesture?

Kathy didn't have any friends, as far as Ronan knew. Perhaps she'd developed a crush on the girl who worked in the kitchen. Ronan thought he'd seen Kathy staring at her when she served dinner. Or maybe Kathy was having a *secret* affair with someone from the city proper. No, that certainly wasn't it. Kathy, sneaking out? The idea was laughable.

Ronan reached the top of the steps without making a noise other than the gentle hiss of his breaths. Rolling from heel to toe with each step, he gradually inched toward his parents' door.

Or maybe she had a "suitor." Ronan's mother had often told the twins that as heirs to one of the most lucrative corps in Bastion, both of them would soon have all manner of interested parties pursuing them for their hand in marriage. Wasn't fourteen a bit young for that, though? Or were his parents already trying to marry Kathy off? If that were the case, though, Kathy probably wouldn't need to give that person a *gift*. So there must be another reason—

Ronan stared into his parents' room, frozen. Instead of finding them nestled in their bed, asleep at their firm bedtime of nine-fifteen, he saw them standing, arms crossed, in the center of the room. By their side was Kathy.

"I bet he steals things all the time, the little scuttler. I bet once he got away with this, he was going to start siphoning off all your jewelry and start selling them," his sister narrowed her eyes.

"Quiet, Katherine," Madame Bell put a hand on her daughter's head. Her husband stood silently behind her, wordlessly, more gargoyle than patriarch. Still, he watched his son with the same cold eye that his wife did.

"Is it true, Ronan?" she asked, speaking his name with the same quiet acid that she always did. "Katherine tells us that you bragged to her of your many little 'heists' and that stealing some of my belongings would be 'easy' for you. Is that so? Have we really raised you so poorly?"

What could he possibly say? *No, Kathy told me to do it in exchange for cheating on the test?* First of all, that would be admitting to another scandal, which would not help his case. Second of all, they would never believe him. *Kathy* complicit in a crime? Unheard of.

"Is this why my earrings keep disappearing? I assumed it was the staff. I've had three different servants sacked for that, you know."

Ronan stared at the three of them, dumbfounded.

"Well?" his mother prodded. "Do you have anything to say for yourself?"

No. He didn't.

His mother gripped his arm and dragged him downstairs to the parlor. "Wait here," she hissed, "while we discuss what to *do* with you."

Kathy didn't have to wait there, of course. She just wanted to watch the show. She sat primly in her pink nightgown, watching him, as their parents stormed into the adjoining room and slammed the door behind them.

Ronan stared down at his interwoven fingers, his stomach twisting at the thought of his parents having to "do something" with him.

"You just wanted me to get caught," he murmured without looking up.

Kathy crossed her arms and rolled her eyes. "'I'm so good at stealing.' You can be so cocky, Ronan!"

Her twin looked up. "That's what this is all about? Because you think I'm cocky?" He wasn't even sure if that was true. When had he ever bragged about something to her? When had he ever been good enough at something to brag about it?

"No, it's—"

"You just like when I get hurt, don't you?" Ronan whispered. It was the most direct he'd ever been with his sister, the first time he'd addressed the tacit understanding between them: you really hate me, don't you?

"What did you get out of this, anyway? They gave you some reward, didn't they? For telling on me?"

Kathy said nothing. She just stared at him. Then she grinned almost imperceptibly.

"Everything has a pecking order," she said. "Someone has to be on top."

"What did they promise you?"

She didn't answer. She stood up wordlessly and walked back up the stairs to her room.

Ronan sat alone for a moment before creeping over to the closed door that his parents had disappeared into, deciding his fate on the other side.

"How did we let this happen?" he could hear his mother asking. "They were born the same day at the same time. They were given the same nurses, the same teacher. We gave them the same toys, the same lessons. How did we get one natural lady and one miscreant?"

"We've done everything we can," his father replied. "He's a lost cause."

"And you still believe reform school is the only option?"

"I don't see anything else we can do with him, Saoirse."

Ronan felt his stomach plunge. They wouldn't really send him away, would they? It wasn't as though he relished life at Bell Manor, but at least they didn't hurt him. He'd heard the "students" never saw sunlight. He'd never see the ocean, or draw the birds, again.

"What would they say about us, then? When the news spreads that we had to send our son to...to one of those institutions."

He breathed a little easier hearing his mother's rebuttal, but still gripped the bottom of his shirt so tightly that his knuckles were white.

"What will they say if our son grows up to be a common thief?" his father retorted.

"Perhaps you're right. There's no point in keeping him around here any longer. He either can't learn, or he refuses to. That boy will never be a worthy heir to us. Could you imagine *him* running the company? *Him* dealing with accounts? *Him* hosting social events? He can hardly keep track of what day of the week it is, let alone keep track of a schedule! And that damn *tremor*. How can he be expected to be taken seriously in high society when he's shaking all the time? The boy is useless."

Useless. The word echoed in Ronan's head as he numbly plodded back to his room, numbly scooped up the bag he'd prepared all those years ago, and numbly made his way toward the front door as his parents continued to squabble about his fate.

That was the first time that Ronan Bell ran away from something, and he had a sense that it would not be the last.

CHAPTER SEVEN

Exodus

Harvard backed away from the scientist, bumping into the table by the window of the pod.

O'Neill laughed. It was not that maniacal laugh of villains in stories Harvard had read when he was little, just the amused chuckle of an old man who continues to find himself surprised by the world.

"And here I was thinking all scavengers were dumb as rocks," O'Neill shook his head, closing the pod's hatch. "Guess you do have a few brain cells after all."

"But what...why...*why* would you fake something like that?" Harvard stammered.

"I'll let you puzzle that out," O'Neill said, making his way to his research station, pointedly *not* hobbling this time.

"I don't understand," Harvard shook his head, his mind racing. If O'Neill had lied about his injury, what else was he lying about? "I'm not really sick, am I?" Harvard wondered aloud. For the first time since he'd slipped out of the pod, Harvard took stock of his body. He no longer felt those muscle aches, or the weakness that had kept him in bed for days. In fact, other than his usual shakiness, he felt pretty much normal. But what had changed? How had he—

Oh, of course. Obviously. He didn't drink the tea.

"I'm so stupid," Harvard reprimanded himself.

O'Neill nodded, his back still turned. "Yes, you are."

"So...what was this all for?" Harvard demanded, though it came out as more of a nervous request than a demand. "What was the point?"

"Let me tell you how it usually goes," O'Neill said, still working away at whatever was keeping him busy at the counter.

"A group of scavengers in danger stumbles upon my pod. They're so thankful to me for taking them in, for saving them from the big bad desert. Then one of their number falls ill. Scavengers have a tendency to be a loyal bunch, so they don't wanna leave anybody behind. So they go out and run some errands for me, bring me food and samples, while I take care of their poor, sickly comrade."

"You poison them...to make them help you with your research?"

"There are a lot of important people back in the city waiting on this research, son," O'Neill said. "And I have deadlines to meet. Besides, those scavengers *want* to help me. They're so grateful for my hospitality! But, of course, their patience runs thin. They figure, 'we gotta get to Bastion to get some real medical help,' and they start to get antsy. That's when their buddy up and dies. Very tragic. I'm very distraught, as you can imagine, but since I was so obliging they agree to do one last job for me. I gotta maximize my returns, ya see. And on the off chance any of them to figure me out...well, the dusts are dangerous. They never do make it back to Bastion."

Harvard swallowed. It was no strange thing for scavengers to go missing. The dusts were full of dangers and everyone knew this. Returning to Bastion was never a guarantee. Even in his short time with the Commission, he'd known other scavengers to go missing, even whole teams. How many of them had met this same fate? Had Harvard once known someone O'Neill had already killed?

"How...how many times have you done this?" he asked, and he could feel that uncontrollable quivering beginning to set in. *Not now,* he willed himself, *please not now.*

"Oh, enough to get by, kiddo. Enough to get by. Usually, I can get them to stay for a month at least, and then I'm stocked up for ages. I was certainly hoping our game would last a little longer than this. I guess all good things have to come to an end."

He turned around, and Harvard saw he held a syringe between his fingers.

"This one'll be a faster death than the tea, but it'll really sell it. By the time they get back, you'll be right on the brink of death," he explained gleefully. "Oh, they will just be *crushed*! And you will be so weak and tired you won't even be able to speak. Then you'll die and they'll cry and cry and do all sorts of nice things for me because I cared for you so well."

Harvard felt his face grow pale.

"You're going to kill me?"

O'Neill shrugged. "Well, I was always going to eventually."

Harvard dove for the door, but O'Neill easily caught him in the stomach and slung him back. He was deceptively strong for an old man. Harvard crashed against the table and dropped to the ground.

"Wait! Stop!" he pleaded from the floor of the pod, holding up his trembling hands as a feeble attempt at defense. "We'll do whatever you want! We'll bring you food and supplies and equipment and...just, please don't hurt me!"

O'Neill knelt next to Harvard and placed a firm hand on his shoulder, pinning him to the ground.

"It's a shame, kid, I know," he said almost apologetically, "but if any of you all get back to the city and spread word of my little operation, well, that would be a whole lotta trouble for me, now wouldn't it?"

"What are you going to do to them when they get back?" Harvard asked, momentarily more worried about his friends' safety than his own.

"Depends on how smart they are. Oh, don't give me that face. I'm doing you all a favor, you realize," O'Neill chuckled. "Better to meet a calm and quiet death in here than a violent one out it in the dusts. It's a dangerous place, out there in the desert. A kid like you could get hurt."

As if illustrating his point, he jabbed the syringe down toward Harvard's neck. He just barely managed to wiggle out of the way.

"Stop squirming," O'Neill grumbled, as if berating a particularly wayward dog.

Harvard, however, was a master squirmer. For once in his life, his violent trembling served him well, since it made it all the more difficult for O'Neill to get a firm grasp on him. He reached for the leg of the table behind him and jerked down, slamming the corner into O'Neill's back. The man grunted in surprise and momentarily released Harvard, giving him enough time to get to his feet and make another dive for the door.

But O'Neill shot a hand out and caught Harvard by the ankle. Harvard's momentum slammed him onto his back, head crashing against the metal floor with a painful clang. The man pulled him away from the hatch, dragging him along the ground, and planted a knee on his stomach, forcing air out of Harvard's lungs. He was a small man, but Harvard was even smaller, so this time he had no hope of breaking free.

Once again, he brought the syringe toward the exposed flesh of Harvard's neck and, unable to dodge, he caught the man's wrist with both hands, pushing up with the little strength he had.

For a brief moment, the two were caught in a violent tableau, an arm-wrestling match Harvard was destined to lose.

"Say, Harvard," O'Neill grinned as he pushed down, "Don't you feel yourself getting shaky?"

"Stop it!" Harvard cried, but the harm was already done. The more aware he was of his tremor, the more aggressive it became, making him weaker. O'Neill brought the needle even closer to his neck.

Harvard used all the strength he had to push back on the man's wrist, but it wasn't good enough. He felt the cool metal brush against the base of his neck, and he cried out in terror.

At that moment, Little Liza, who had been tucked safely in his shirt pocket, appeared on O'Neill's shoulder. The old man, focused on jabbing Harvard, didn't seem to take any notice of the little crab perched by his head. She reached a little claw up to the side of O'Neill's head and snapped it twice, two elegant pinches.

And his ear fell off.

O'Neill's hands immediately flew to his ear, screeching in shock and pain. Little Liza fell to the ground as he rose, and Harvard reflexively scooped her up and put her back in his pocket, for fear she would be stepped on.

"You little bitch!" the scientist screamed, and Harvard wasn't sure if he was talking to him or to the crab.

Seeing his opportunity, Harvard leapt for the door. O'Neill reached to stop him, but his hand was now too slick with blood to get a good grip. Harvard slipped away, first out of the pod, then out of the metal entry hallway, leaving a wailing O'Neill behind.

"If you walk out that door, your friends are dead!" the old man shouted through the metal door. "You hear me? They're *dead*!"

But Harvard was already running into the dusts, diving into the vast nothingness before him. The wind tore at him, sand scraping his skin with such force that little specks of blood began to appear on his arms and legs. With a sinking sensation, Harvard realized he hadn't brought his dustscarf or his goggles. His eyes began to water as they were barraged with dust particles, soon too irritated to stay open. He pushed himself forward blindly, hoping he would stumble upon some kind of shelter. He couldn't go back now.

The dust he inhaled began to tickle his throat. He pulled his shirt over his mouth, but the damage was already done. He fought the urge to cough, but his throat spasmed, causing him to gasp. The breath only made him inhale more of the airborne dust, and his gasp became a full-blown hacking fit. Harvard stumbled, falling to his knees. He flopped forward, body wracked in throes of agony. He dug his fingers into the dust, feeling as though he were drowning upon land.

He started to feel lightheaded. He knew if he passed out, there would be no hope for him. A desertwalker would find him and feast on his body in no time. Fighting to maintain his grip on consciousness, Harvard lowered himself to the ground, wheezing.

But no relief came. As his lungs continued to fill with dust, Harvard sank into darkness, his body spasming until suddenly it lay still.

Part Two: The Empress

The story of the Earth's hunger is not the only cautionary tale circulated in Bastion. Far from it. As a culture that prides itself on rational thought and progress, every story told in Bastion must have a clear and instructive moral. If practical information is not conveyed, why tell a story at all?

By far the most famous of these tales is that of the Crab Prince. Every child likely grew up with one of the many iterations of the fable told to them at their bedside, but if for whatever reason you're unfamiliar with it, these are the details that most versions seem to agree on:

There was once a little boy.

This boy was kind of heart, and showed that kindness to all creatures, from the people around him to the flies in the desert air.

One day, the boy found a tiny scuttler that had wandered in through the city gates, as the little ones are wont to do. The oblivious little thing had no clue it had ambled into the middle of the main street, and that a car was barreling toward it. Seeing the plight of the crab, the boy threw himself in front of the vehicle and scooped the scuttler up just in time.

"Poor thing," he said, "you must be lost! I'll take you back home."

So the boy walked directly down the main thoroughfare, right through the city gates, into the desert.

"Hello?" he asked. "Are there any crabs here? I have one of your children!"

And the creatures arrived—all manner of desertwalker, all ugly and evil, and for the first time in his short life the little boy felt repulsed by another creature. He tried to run from them, but it was no use. He was too far from the aegis of the city walls, the protection of humanity.

He cried out and there was no one to hear him.

This is the point where some stories differ. Some say they devoured him on the spot. Most, however, claim they took him captive, and he lived among them against his will until the end of his days. The more grotesque versions claim that when he grew older, he even bred with the crabs, siring half-human, half-crab abominations that to this day roam the desert in disguise, searching for unsuspecting wanderers to feast upon.

Moral: Have no compassion for the creature of the desert. They exist only to hurt you.

Footnote: It seems the only aspect all versions can agree on is that he is dubbed The Crab Prince. Scholars have been perplexed for years by the origins of this title. If he was taken captive, how could he be a prince? Is it not too reverent a title for a character that was crafted specifically as a bad example? Perhaps the honorific makes him more threatening a figure in Bastion mythology, though this would come in stark contrast to his naivete. Though the legends claim he still lives in the desert, no one truly fears The Crab Prince. There are much more real dangers in the dusts to be afraid of, after all.

CHAPTER EIGHT

Arrival

Yale flailed in the water as they were pulled deeper, fingers clawing for anything to pull themself back to the surface. Their fingertips brushed the stone at the edge of the pool and their hand closed around the rusty nub of a crab-eaten steel rod. They gripped it with both hands, fighting back against the pull of the beast.

They had never experienced darkness like this. Even their days in detention didn't compare to the oppressive, all-encompassing darkness that came with drowning.

Stay calm, they told themself, hoping it would slow their hammering heart. *Get the knife. Cut yourself loose. And do it before you drown. Just—*

The knife. They'd dropped it on the surface.

Dusts.

The tentacle yanked at their leg, and they nearly lost their grip on the rod they clung to.

I really am going to die here, aren't I? they thought. *I'm sorry, Mom. And Harvard. And even Minty.*

* * *

The moment she heard the splash, Columbia leapt toward the source of the noise, hoping she could find where Yale had been standing.

"I'm going in!" she shouted to Princeton.

"Wha—" Princeton began to respond. She dove forward and found herself encased in icy blackness.

Columbia propelled herself into the water, reaching for something to grasp onto. She could hear thrashing somewhere to her right. She clawed at the water blindly, hoping to close her fingers around anything. Something whooshed past her head, nearly knocking her in the head. She reached out to grab it.

An ankle.

Clutching Yale's ankle with one hand, Columbia sawed haphazardly at the tentacle pulling them down. Even dulled by the water she could hear the creature's scream of agony, and she hoped it didn't have any spare tentacles or claws to try and pull her down too. Without the use of her eyes, she couldn't tell if she was making any progress and cutting Yale loose. All she had to go on was the cries of the hungry beast somewhere in the darkness down below her.

Columbia felt her grip slip temporarily as the creature jerked Yale deeper, but the pull stopped abruptly. She gave one more powerful thrust of the knife, and she could feel the sinews of the tentacle cut loose, the creature wailing in protest below her.

She felt a hand grasping at her clothes, and realized Princeton was at the edge of the water, trying to pull the both of them back up. She let him haul her out of the water, and she saw he'd grabbed Yale first, who now lay on their side, hacking up water. The ankle where the tentacle had grabbed them was bruised and dotted with pinpricks of blood.

Once it was clear everyone was alive and going to stay that way for the time being, Princeton gave a breathless laugh.

"Well, that was a fun team bonding exercise. Right guys?"

* * *

When Princeton was little, his father used to take him and his siblings to a community center in Lower Bastion. His father always grieved the fact that he wasn't able to take them someplace nicer, but children don't generally know how to tell the difference between something that's a "nice" place and something that isn't. To him and his siblings, it was a veritable paradise. There was a pool, a track, and far more toys than the children could ever hope to have at home. And there had been a rock-climbing wall.

In retrospect, it was a major safety hazard. It had clearly been constructed by a well-meaning parent, and there were no safety harnesses attached. A child could easily get hurt. And Princeton did, many times. In fact, once he fell from the top of the rocking climbing wall and broke his arm. As soon as it healed, he was begging his father to go back so he could climb again. As a child, Princeton was very stubborn and very stupid. Neither of those things had really changed in his adulthood, and he knew this.

Princeton thought of that rock climbing wall and the thrill it brought him as a kid, a minor danger compared to scaling the skeleton of a rotting building. But when he decided he was going to do something dangerous, no one could deter him. Especially when he wanted to help. If Princeton was going to help you, then by the name of the Founders, he was going to do it whether you liked it or not.

Yale definitely didn't like it, but Princeton, respectfully, couldn't give a shit. It was better he took a little risk than the three of them just sitting around waiting for any other creatures. So he leapt expertly from crumbling ledge to crumbling ledge, imagining they were the stones of the makeshift climbing wall that he'd spent hours scaling in his youth. It was easy when he thought of it like that. Just a game, a game his father hated, but still a game—

The rusted metal girder below his foot snapped.

He felt his stomach lurch before his body started to fall, and he caught himself with both elbows against a concrete ledge, his legs dangling below him. He heard Columbia yelp, and Yale asked, "What? What's going on?"

He hazarded a glance down—Founders, he was high up—to see that while Columbia was watching him, her hands pressed against her mouth in alarm, while Yale was covering their eyes. He laughed, just before remembering he could fall to his death.

"What?" Yale asked again.

"Nothing!" Princeton called down as he heaved himself onto the ledge. "I'm just doing sick backflips and stuff and Columbia is amazed."

"Shut up."

"No, really!" he insisted as he searched for something else to grab onto. "I just did a cartwheel." He pulled himself up, and heard Columbia breathe a sigh of relief.

After that, he tested every foothold before putting his full weight on it. He had a few more wobbles, which elicited gasps from Columbia, but each time he made a point of giving her a big smile and thumbs up to prove he was so totally *not* going to die.

"I maaaaade it!" he sang as he pulled himself out of the window they'd come in through.

"Was that so bad?" he heard Columbia ask Yale.

"Yes," they grumbled.

Princeton staked a shovel in the ground, tied the rope around it, then threw the other end into the dark void of the building. He heard the other end hit the ground with a *thud*.

"Honk honk! All aboard the Princeton-mobile!" he called down to them.

* * *

"Ha!" Princeton shouted when he'd finally pulled his friends to the safety of the sandy surface. Columbia's relief was overtaken by irritation in an instant.

"See! I told you I could do it! It told you! I told you—"

Yale laid a hand on Princeton's shoulder. "Good job, Princeton. I'm glad you're okay." This seemed to deflate his gloating.

"Yeah, sure. I mean, no problem. Anything for the team, right?"

"Yeah. Anything for the team."

That night, the Ivies camped out beside the apartment complex that had almost claimed their lives, too exhausted to start the long trek to the pod that night. Neither Columbia nor Princeton wanted to ask Yale to walk on their bad leg, though Columbia knew they would insist they could do it. Even the next day, they refused the support of Columbia or Princeton, despite the fact that they were very obviously limping.

"It's a long way back," Columbia coaxed.

"Yes, I remember from the first time," Yale spat, unyielding. She sighed but did not try again. She knew once they had made their decision about something, they would not go back on it.

Luckily, they found the pod even closer than where they had left it. Columbia guessed O'Neill had taken it upon himself to come closer to them, which certainly made their trek easier.

"Welcome, welcome," he ushered them in as he hobbled up to the front entry hatch. He clocked Yale's injury immediately.

"Run into some trouble, didja?" he ventured.

"It's nothing," Yale muttered as they made their way into the pod.

"Happens to the best of us," O'Neill grinned, giving Yale a pat on the shoulder as he indicated his own bad leg.

"What happened to your ear?" Columbia asked, nodding to the bandage on the side of his head. It looked as though he'd tried unsuccessfully to cover it up with his hair, but his sparse gray locks were thinning too much.

"Liza got a little feisty," he said with an embarrassed grin, putting a self-conscious hand on the injured ear. "Don't poke the old girl too hard!"

Once they got into the main pod, the three began unloading their packs of the few items that had managed to scrounge. Columbia glanced toward the terrarium, only to find Little Liza strangely absent. She frowned but stayed silent.

"We figured we'd split everything five ways," Yale explained, "with the exception of things you specifically requested. If it interests you, we have a bit of crabsquid tentacle—"

"Oh, that will be fascinating to dissect! Give it here!" O'Neill outstretched his hand, and Yale gave him the slimy cloth package where they had stored the remains of the monster.

"We're not great at, er, the whole plant thing, but we tried to pick up any of those herbs you wanted if we saw them. Sorry if they're not the right ones though. We just wanted to make sure you had enough for—"

They glanced over at the sleeping palette to see it unoccupied, and neatly made, then turned to O'Neill.

"Where is Harvard?" they asked. Behind them, Columbia shot Princeton a worried glance. O'Neill wrung his hands, looking down.

"I'm...I'm sorry, Yale," he said. "He was...he was very sick, you know."

Yale's face froze. For one moment, Columbia thought they might strike O'Neill. But they stayed completely still.

"You said he was getting better," they whispered, their voice tight. Columbia never remembered O'Neill saying this, but sometimes Yale heard only what they wanted to hear.

"He...was really fighting, you know," the scientist wrung his hands. "He wanted to hold off until you got back. He wanted that so badly. He told me all the time how badly he wanted to see you again. But this morning, I was getting up to go fix breakfast and..." he looked anxiously at the empty bed, "it was too late. He was gone."

Yale took a deep breath, then walked placidly up to the window.

"I'm so sorry—" O'Neill began.

"It's not your fault," Yale said.

"I did my best to—"

"I said," Yale snapped, "it's not your fault."

All four stood in that silence, thick and heavy like a stew. Then finally Yale said, "What did you do with him?"

"Hm?"

"The body. What did you do with his body?"

"Oh, I, um, I buried it a little that a-ways," O'Neill gestured out the back window. "I can show you to the place, if you want. Tried to find a nice spot for 'im."

Yale nodded.

"Yes. Show us the place."

The old man began to move to the door, but Yale held up a hand.

"Not now."

They turned abruptly, pushing past Columbia and Princeton to get to the inner hatch. Princeton made a move to go to them, but Columbia pulled him back, shaking her head.

In a sudden burst of violent rage, Yale slammed a fist into the metal wall. The whole room shook. Then they lifted the lever and walked into the entry hall, out toward the night. The hatch slammed shut behind them.

Princeton looked to Columbia for guidance.

"Leave them," she murmured numbly, staring off into nothingness. "They need some time."

* * *

Night had fallen, and Yale hadn't returned. Princeton could tell it was eating at Columbia, who bit the inside of her cheek so aggressively he feared she would chew a hole in it.

"I'll go check on them," he announced, standing.

"No, you—" Columbia started to protest. He guessed what she was going to say: *You don't know them as well as I do.*

"Yeah, yeah, I know," Princeton waved a hand to silence her. "But...I just feel like it shouldn't always have to be your job, right? And besides, I..." he trailed off, not entirely sure where the sentence had been going. *I feel like this is my fault? I don't want them to blame me? I'm sick of you two always having your secret little discussions and leaving me out?*

So he just shook his head and walked toward the hatch. Surprisingly, Columbia did not object.

Princeton found Yale sitting in the dust only a short walk out from the pod, cross-legged, gazing absently out at the horizon.

"You...you doin' okay, buddy?" It was weak, and he knew it. *No, obviously they're not doing okay, dipshit,* he reprimanded himself. *Harvard is dead.* The thought still shocked him, even though he knew it to be true, like he was still trying to convince himself of it. *Harvard is dead.*

Yale didn't respond. They didn't even look up as Princeton trudged up next to them and sat in the sand.

"Do you wanna...talk about it?" he tried again.

"No."

Their voice was empty, lifeless almost. At a loss, Princeton scratched the back of his head.

"Um. I mean. It might help, though. If you do."

Again, Yale didn't respond. They just stared out into the vast emptiness of the desert. Finally, they spoke.

"He was going to tell me his name, Princeton," Yale said dreamily. "He was so scared he was going to die and he just...he wanted someone to know. He wanted me to know who he really was and I...I didn't give him that chance. I don't know why. Out of stubbornness, maybe? Maybe some part of me thought that if I just *willed* it enough, it would make him live. Columbia always said I'm too headstrong about things. That I always say, 'don't worry, things will be fine,' and...well, they're not, obviously."

Princeton nodded, wondering what "always" meant. When had Columbia said that? How many times had this happened before? How often was Yale caught in the trap of strong-willed optimism, only to be violently let down?

"It's not your fault," he said lamely. "You...you were just following the rules."

"What's the point of the rule?" Yale asked. "I mean, seriously, what harm is a first name?"

"We could die," Princeton shrugged. "And if that happens—when that happens— it's easier—"

Yale turned to face him. "And does not knowing Harvard's 'real name' make this easier?"

Princeton was silent.

Yale turned away again. "It's ridiculous. I've always thought it was ridiculous. It's like...it's like a stupid little bow that we tie onto the world's ugliest gift. Like, surprise, you have to go risk your life out in the desert, but at least you get a cutesy codename out of it. It's...it's dehumanizing, is what it is."

"It's for our own safety," Princeton said lamely.

Yale shook their head. "It's a scam. I sort just thought...I don't know, it feels stupid when I say it. I have always been really bad at following rules, and it's never turned out well for me. I thought maybe if this time I could just *follow the rules for once*, then everything would be okay." They placed a hand on the ground and curled their fingers, clawing into the sand. "Princeton, I don't want to be like Harvard. I almost died out there and it could happen again. Easily. Like you said, I got lucky. I might not always be lucky. And I don't wanna...without the knowledge that my team really knows who I am. Before I was a scavenger—"

"Whoa, c'mon," Princeton cut them off. "Don't tell me your name. It hasn't come to that."

"I just—"

"Listen. I know I give you shit, but, like, you're a good captain, Yale. Don't lose your cool over this."

Yale laughed sadly, drawing spirals in the sand idly with a finger. It reminded Princeton of the way Harvard used to draw in the sand, and he felt a pang of remorse remembering how he'd mocked Harvard for wanting to draw the desertwalkers. It wasn't a bad idea, really. He should have told Harvard that, huh?

"If you can believe it, Princeton," Yale said. "I've lost my cool over far less than this."

"No, actually I can't believe it," Princeton laughed. "Because you stayed calm even when you were about to get eaten alive by a squid monster. I would have absolutely gone to pieces, dude! And you were all like, 'whatever, it's nothing.' Look, I know this is a hard loss for you. But you're gonna bounce back. And you're gonna lead us just like you always do. You're gonna lead us back home."

Yale's finger froze mid-spiral. "I guess we do have to get back home eventually, don't we?"

"Yeah, and we're like, mega late," Princeton reminded them gently. "They're gonna have our asses for this one."

"It won't be so bad. We'll get a stern talking to about not meeting quota, then our next quota will be a little higher to make up for it. We'll live."

"The debt's gonna get deeper."

"Next time we'll undeepen it. None of us are in that deep. Not anymore, anyway." They winced, as though this were something they weren't supposed to say.

"I'm just saying...I know it sucks, but we're still counting on you."

Yale laughed, a cold chuckle that made Princeton shiver.

"I get it now," they said.

"Get what?"

"When they first made me a captain, I couldn't believe it. I said, 'there's no way I'm qualified for this.' And they said..." Yale trailed off, looking up at the stars. They sighed, and though they still wore a smile, Princeton could tell there was no good humor behind that mask. Just a well of pain he could see through the cracks.

"Never mind," they said. "You wouldn't understand." There was no condescension, no derision in their voice. Just an honesty that... sounded almost like envy.

"No," Princeton said slowly, "I guess I wouldn't."

The two sat in silence, staring out into the night; the only light was the sliver of moon, and the only sound was the whipping of the wind.

* * *

As promised, O'Neill took the three of them to Harvard's grave. He had found a small cluster of desert foliage to mark the spot, looking dry and brittle swaying in the wind. He indicated a patch of freshly dug sand at the base of the plants.

"You dug this yourself?" Columbia asked, impressed. Maybe the old man was stronger than she'd given him credit for.

O'Neill nodded. "I tell ya, it wasn't easy," he gave an awkward chuckle, "but I felt the little guy deserved...a proper resting place."

"Thank you, O'Neill," Columbia gave a polite smile, but it faded quickly when she turned her eyes toward the nondescript burial site.

The four stood without speaking for a painfully long moment, standing around the little patch of dirt in solemn contemplation.

"Would you like to say anything, Yale?" Columbia offered.

"No," they said, eyes locked on the barren grave. All was silent but the sound of the wind pelting them with dust.

Interlude Five: Chavi

Anyone who didn't know that Chavi and Avi were childhood best friends would assume that they hated each other, based on their constant bickering. The pair sitting behind them in their home economics was treated to a constant chorus of, "Don't put that there!"

"Well, where am I supposed to put it?"

"In the third dish!"

"Well, you could have *told* me that!"

"I did tell you that! *You* could have listened."

"I was listening!"

"I said the third dish! Can't you count?"

"Literally, no! I failed math like five times, Avi!"

But no one *did* assume they hated each other, because the strength of their friendship was common knowledge. Chavi and Avi, the dynamic duo, sun and moon, of Bastion Academy. There was Avi: sharp, cold, devilishly intelligent, and fiendishly rich. Then there was Chavi: boisterous, flirty, willfully ignorant, and—this was their most controversial characteristic at the academy—an unrefined commoner.

Then there was Jasmine. Jasmine had no reputation that she knew of but this: she was quiet. Very quiet.

Every student and Bastion Academy knew that the three of them were inseparable, though no student and Bastion Academy could understand precisely why. They were three planets drifting around each other in their own private little galaxy—an outsider could peer in with a telescope, but never feel the force of the gravity that held them all together. And that's exactly what it was—a force. Some kind of natural pull that kept them all in the same orbit.

Each, famously, had their own specialty. Avi studied medicine. Jasmine studied pre-Quake history. Chavi's specialty was being the bane of Bastion Academy's renowned faculty.

"A child so stupid has no right to be so arrogant," one of their professors had berated them in front of their entire remedial math class.

"Aw, you flatter me," they'd responded, eliciting a hearty laugh from the class and leaving the professor furious.

"You have allowed the fact that you are friends with two brilliant girls to convince you that you, too, are brilliant," she crossed her arms. "You are not."

"Professor," Chavi laughed, "I'm okay being stupid! I think it suits me."

Chavi was one of the three children of staff at Academy, and the other two hung together in the entourage of the weaselly dazzle dealer named Callum. Ariel, the custodian's child, had a wispy sort of quality about them, gliding across campus more like a puff of smoke than a person, and a subtle grin that made Jasmine nervous. Then there was Mellie, daughter of the bookkeeper, who Jasmine recognized by her hot pink braids and jeering laugh. It wasn't that Jasmine distrusted the people in Callum's circle; she hardly knew any of them. But she didn't like the way they nearly worshipped the wealthy boy and the narcotics he provided.

"It's like a cult," Avi once complained when she saw Chavi ingratiating themself with the Callum parade. Not that Avi had much experience with cults, other than her limited knowledge of sandheads.

There was one table in the Bastion Academy Library the students tended to avoid. That was because there was a tacit understanding that it was reserved for the three who could be found sitting there nearly every day, studying—or at least, something like it. Often their time in the library consisted more of Avi and Jasmine studying while Chavi distracted them, Avi attempting to get Chavi to study, failing, giving up, and leaving Chavi to their own devices. On the few occasions Jasmine actually joined in, the two together were often successful. It was a rare sight, but some students rumored that they had seen the trio sitting in silence, all three engrossed in their work. The sight of Chaverim Chakrabarti studying was more elusive than a scuttler in the city, but apparently it had happened before. In fact, now that mock Aptitude Exams were just around the corner, Avi had doubled down on her effort to shove her friend down the throat of any university that would take them.

"Read," she said, slamming a book down on the desk. Chavi looked at the cover—*Introduction to Organic Chemistry*.

"I'm not even in this class," they complained.

"Yeah, I know, you're like three levels of science behind, which is why I am trying to catch you up here."

"How am I going to understand it if I'm three levels of science behind?"

"It says 'Introduction' on it, doesn't it? You just have to get introduced."

"Why organic chemistry? Like, what's inorganic chemistry?"

"Why don't you read the book and find out?" Avi suggested sweetly, before sitting down across from them with her own book—*Behavioral Neuroscience: Vol. Three: Pathologies.*

"Oh, I almost forgot," she slapped a pencil down on the table. "Take notes."

Chavi was already looking away from her, eyeing the boy in a blue sweater and glasses perusing the library shelves near the next table over. When the boy looked over, Chavi gave a subtle nod and a grin. The boy blushed, clutching his book to his chest, and laughed sheepishly before scurrying away.

Avi picked up the pencil and poked Chavi in the arm.

"Ow!"

"Notes!"

Chavi snatched the pencil.

"Fine," they grumbled, leaning over the text.

Jasmine watched the exchange silently from her corner of the table, flipping through the pages of her literature textbook. The next page had been completely crossed out with a marker. She frowned and turned to the next page. It, too, was completely obscured with black squiggles. She sighed and closed the book, hoping they could find another copy that hadn't been so badly vandalized. Strange, though, that this library would have lent this book to someone else first, since it was reserved for her as soon as it arrived. She wondered who would even waste their time scribbling on the pages of their—

Chavi was scribbling on the pages of their textbook.

"Chavi," Jasmine chided gently, "you're supposed to be reading it."

They looked up in alarm, as though they hadn't actually realized that they had *stopped* reading.

"Right. Yeah. Sorry," they got back to work, and Jasmine gave a little satisfied smile as she stood up to exchange the book. *Maybe we don't have to be so worried,* she thought to herself. *With a little gentle encouragement, they seem to do just fine. Avi is too hard on them. It's not that difficult to get them to sit down and work, all things considered.*

When Jasmine returned to the table, Chavi was gone.

"Avi," Jasmine said quietly.

Avi looked up from her book and saw the empty seat across from her.

"Dusts!"

CHAPTER NINE

Skrack

Harvard awoke with a gasp, lying in darkness. His memories came flooding back—the confrontation with O'Neill, his flight into the desert, the dust particles catching in his throat. He thought for a moment he must be dead, but the sensation of cold stone against his back reassured him he was still in the material plane. That and the slight glow at the edges of his vision. He lifted his head—a difficult task—and found some kind of bioluminescent fungus growing in the cracks of the rocks, giving him just enough light to see by.

Perhaps it would have been better if he couldn't see, because then he wouldn't have discovered what was causing the tickling sensation on his skin. Baby scuttlers covered every inch of his body, a thick, pulsating mass of torsos and legs holding him to the ground. They poked at him gently, not nibbling yet. Perhaps they were searching for what part they would most like to eat.

He yelped in horror, not daring to make any sudden moves for fear they'd realize he'd awoken and begin feasting lest their prey made an attempt to escape. Now the course of events crystallized in Harvard's mind: a colony of scuttlers had found his near-dead corpse out in the dusts, figured it would make an excellent shared delicacy, and carried it into their subterranean den to feast upon.

Was it too late for him to fight them off? Even if he were to free himself of the hundreds—no, thousands—of writhing creatures holding him down, would he even be able to navigate his way out of the labyrinthine tunnels? How far down was he? The earth was packed tight as opposed to the thin sand on the surface, so he must be deep. Too deep for him to climb back up on his own. Still, the prospect of being eaten alive was not a welcome one. Why couldn't they have just been merciful and eaten him while he was unconscious?

Harvard gave a sharp gasp as a figure appeared at the mouth of the den, a hulking megacrab that could crush him easily with one blow of its leg. He was not a meal for the hatchlings. They were only exploring him until their parent crab came back to feast.

The wide mouth of a crab was an all-too familiar sight for Harvard. He waited for the creature to begin picking him apart with its pincer, sliding bits of him into its mouth.

It didn't.

Instead, it made a clicking noise deep within its shell, then pivoted to the right so Harvard could see its side. Penetrating its left flank was a harpoon, glimmering in the light of the glowing mushrooms.

"It's you," Harvard said aloud without meaning to, attempting to rise. The babies leapt off his body obediently as he stood, moving toward their gargantuan parent.

Harvard extended a shaking hand to the harpoon shaft. He could hardly blame his tremor this time. Wouldn't anyone be shaking in a situation like this? But he was comforted that he knew how this story went. Human saves deadly creature from harm, deadly creature rewards human with its loyalty. Or, at the very least, not killing the human. That's what happened in the Crab Prince, wasn't it? He'd heard the story so long ago that he couldn't remember all the details, but the boy did become a prince, after all, so he was pretty sure it had a happy ending. And this creature was smart enough to understand Harvard was a good guy, right? Harvard still wasn't sure if he'd heard the crab speak, but if it was smart enough to ask Harvard to remove the harpoon, then surely it was smart enough to understand the basic concept of *quid pro quo* and not to eat him immediately after.

Harvard gripped the shaft tightly and pulled. There was more resistance than he expected, and the crab gave a pained squeal as the thing slid through its innards. Harvard made a few inches of headway but had to take a break before he could go any further.

"Just a second!" he panted.

This was one of those times when Harvard envied the strength of people like Princeton and Yale. If Yale were here, they could have freed the harpoon as easily as one removes a toothpick from a sandwich. Harvard wished he could be more like that. He missed Yale already.

With renewed fervor, Harvard pulled at the harpoon again, eliciting more wails of agony from the injured creature.

"I'm sorry!" he exclaimed breathlessly as he pulled. A few more inches of metal rose out of the crab's body, dripping with bright blue blood. He placed one of his hands at the site of the wound, pressing the crab's shell down, and with his other arm gave a firm yank. To his great relief, the harpoon came free. He dropped it immediately, and it clattered dully on the dirt floor.

Harvard looked the crab in the eyes, and perhaps it was only his imagination, but he could have sworn that he saw some gratitude in that face.

"You're okay now, bu—"

A thick leg slammed into his stomach and pinned him to the back wall, knocking the breath out of him. He gasped for air as the creature inched toward him, still holding him in place with its spiny limb.

Do not become arrogant, human boy, just because you have done me a service.

Harvard gaped—partially because he struggled to breathe with the crab leg pressing down on his lungs, but mostly because this time, there was no doubt: the crab was *talking to him.*

But how was that even possible? Crabs did not have vocal chords, or lips, and, in fact, the crab's mouth hadn't even moved. How was this happening?

"I...I'm sorry," Harvard wheezed pathetically, something he found himself saying a lot lately. "I was just trying to help."

Your help means little to me. I am an ancient creature, eternal and strong. You are flesh, and in your little life you will never know Serenity. I do not require your assistance, and your presumptuousness offends me.

"But...weren't you asking me to help you?"

Your excuses fall on deaf ears, boy child.

"I'm really confused."

The leg pressed further into his stomach, and Harvard gave a pained groan.

"Are...are you going to eat me?" he asked. A painful silence passed between human and crab, as though the creature were giving this consideration.

No, the crab finally responded, sounding almost disappointed. *It is not permitted.*

Harvard feared any more questions might cause the scuttler to change its mind, so he said nothing, just breathed slowly in hopes to quell his trembling. The crab said nothing more, just stared at him with those black marble eyes, and the only sound in the den was Harvard's shaky breathing. Harvard finally found it in himself to ask the question that was hanging between them.

"Why?"

Because you bear the Empress.

Harvard said the only thing he seemed to say more often than he apologized, "What?"

As if in answer to his question, he felt scratching on his chest. He looked down to see if one of the baby scuttlers had made its way back onto his body, but no, they all lined the edges of the den, watching him reverently. Instead, it was Little Liza who peeked out of his chest pocket.

"Liza!" Harvard exclaimed, having forgotten that he'd tucked the small creature in there for protection. He scooped her up in his hands.

"I'm so sorry I forgot you were in there! It's been kinda a crazy day and I—"

Release him, Skrack, came a new voice. This one was lighter, gentler, and though the voice simply *appeared* in his mind the same way the first had, he could tell the source was different. The hulking crab lowered its leg obediently, freeing Harvard from the wall.

His mind reeling with the impossibility of it all, Harvard looked down at Liza, then up at the towering crab, then down at Liza, then up at the massive crab. Then finally, stupidly, he wagered a guess, "Liza...is your Empress?"

There is no word in your inadequate human language for what Kryaka is to us. But for your simple mind, "Empress" will suffice.

"Kryaka?" Harvard repeated. The crab in his hands tilted her shell up to look at him.

You hold the Empress Kryaka in your hands, boy child. Though I cannot fathom the reason, she has taken a liking to you.

Interlude Six: Ronan

Midtown Bastion was *loud*. That was the first thing that struck Ronan as he wandered down the sidewalk, taking in the bright lights, the bike bells, the shouts of vendors, the smoke coming from...well, coming from everywhere, it seemed. Even the parks were filled with shouts, the cries of children playing, and the ding of bicycle bells. And there were *cars*. Not many, of course, since they could only be manufactured out of pre-tremor parts. But ugly as those patchwork contraptions were, owning one was expensive, so when Ronan saw a car sputter by, he knew the driver was almost as rich as his parents. Almost.

He wandered the Midtown streets with his mouth agape, watching street performers wink at the crowd, watching people *dine* at tables on the *streets*—who does that?—but mostly watching everyone bustle about their business. So much purpose and energy and...and life! Compared to this, Bell Manor was a marble corpse, an old stony husk. *This* was real life, and he'd been kept away from it for so long.

More jarring than the sound and colors and energy was *his own name*. Every construction site—and there were a lot of construction sites, since Bastion was always growing and changing—bore a sign on the fence that read "This progress was brought to you by BELL ENTERPRISES." As much as he hated his name, it was hard not to swell with pride a bit at the thought that *his* family was the one behind the city's progress. It was one thing to know that his family was the leader of Bastion infrastructure, but another thing entirely to see it with his own eyes. He watched construction on what looked like a new shopping mall, an ugly vehicle wheeling synthetic lumber over to the workers. Two signs hung from the fence: the one reminding onlookers that the Bells were responsible for the progress, and another that read "Land licensed by TAHERI ADMINISTRATION." Ronan was vaguely aware of the existence of Taheri Administration. His mother seemed to have a bit of a personal rivalry with them, which confused him, because they operated in totally different fields. Why would his family's infrastructure company care about an admin company? He was certain the corps were supposed to have some kind of agreement to work with each other, so he didn't—

"I hear there's gonna be an ice cream shop in there. I'd like to try ice cream one day."

"Ah!" Ronan yelped, startled at the sound of a voice so close to him. In all the time he'd spent walking through the city today he'd heard a lot of people talking, but no one had actually spoken *to* him. In fact, come to think of it, no one had even acknowledged his presence since his parents the previous day. The ghost of Bell Manor had become the ghost of Midtown Bastion.

Except, apparently, to the girl who now stood next to him, looking down at him with shining brown eyes, her hair pulled into two tight braids went down to her waist.

"Um," Ronan wasn't sure how a normal, non-Bell person would respond. Did normal people not usually have ice cream? What about other deserts? Did people in the rest of Bastion not have sugar? What did they eat, then? Potatoes? Everyone had potatoes, right?

"M...me too," he stuttered finally. Luckily, the girl seemed to find his hesitation amusing, not incriminating. She laughed.

"Have you ever had a croissant before?" she asked.

Yes. Often. But that wasn't normal, was it?

"What's a croissant?" he asked. The girl laughed again.

"You're stupid," she smiled. She didn't say it like an insult, more like a statement of fact—one that endeared her. Ronan wondered what had drawn her attention in the first place, but a quick glance at her appearance gave him enough clues. Her worn, broken shoes, and a satchel that matched his backpack. She recognized him as a fellow childhood drifter.

"I was headed over to Founders' Square. Do you want to come with me?" the girl offered.

"What's that?"

The girl stared at him. "How have you never heard of Founders' Square?" she asked. "It's right in the center of the city."

Ronan felt himself flush, wondering what kind of lie could account for his glaring gaps of knowledge about Bastion proper. He couldn't very well say, "Oh, I ran away from an incredibly rich family. One of the six richest in Bastion, actually. I'm here by choice." She'd dismiss him as a privileged brat. No, he'd have to come up with something else.

"My parents didn't let me out of the house," he improvised. Well, it was kind of true. He was rarely ever allowed off Bell property. The key missing detail was that the Bell Estate was enormous, not to mention dripping with luxury.

The girl's eyes widened.

"Are you for real?" she gaped. "Never?"

Ronan shook his head with all the sincerity he could muster.

"No wonder you dipped. I would have done the same, probably. What was their problem? I mean, like, why would they do that?"

"They..." Were overprotective? Were criminals? Thought I was an abomination no one else should be allowed to see?

"...were convinced I was sick. They said I had this, um...this blood disease."

"You have a blood disease?" the girl cringed, stepping back a little, as though she assumed blood diseases were contagious.

"No, they just, uh, they thought I did. Because I shake so much!" He held up a slightly trembling hand to demonstrate, internally congratulating himself for incorporating so much truth into his rapidly woven lies.

"But I thought they were wrong, so I left."

Convinced that Ronan's condition wasn't going to be leaping out of his blood and into hers, she leaned forward again.

"But what if you *do* have it?" she pressed with morbid curiosity.

"I...I don't know," Ronan admitted. "Maybe it was stupid. But I just couldn't live at home anymore."

That was the truest sentence he'd spoken so far.

"Then you've definitely gotta come with me to the Square!" the girl grabbed him by the wrist and yanked his arm.

"But I still don't...ouch!"

"Sorry!"

"It's okay, it's just...your grip is really strong."

"Or maybe you're just weak from all your stupid blood, blood boy."

"Don't call me that."

"What should I call you?" She didn't look back as she dragged him through the bustling street.

"Ronan. My name." He wondered an instant too late if he should have lied about that, too, but what harm could it do? As long as she didn't know his last name, he was in no danger.

"Hm. Alright. Fine," she approved. He had a feeling that if she didn't like his name enough, he would be "blood boy" forever.

"And what do I call you?" he asked.

She slowed her pace a bit as she considered this, and Ronan wondered if she was doing the exact calculation he had failed to do just moments ago.

"Shila," she decided.

"Is that your real name?" Ronan asked. She shrugged.

"What's a real name, anyway? You asked me what you can call me, and that's your answer."

There was a kind of wisdom in this, Ronan decided. As long as you got to tell people what to call you, it didn't matter if it was "real" or not. He supposed some might not even consider "Ronan" to be *his* real name. He vaguely remembered studying something about this in one of his literature classes—only remnants survived, so Bastion had access to a patchwork smattering of pre-Quake literature. Someone had once asked what was in a name and concluded not much, except a few letters. A lot of people had remembered that for some reason. Ronan couldn't remember it, though. He'd never been very good with that kind of thing.

Shila, as she had decided she would be called, came to a halt. Ronan gasped when he saw the sprawling square, brimming with activity. The plaza was lined with patios for various restaurants, each with its own corralled section of umbrellas and seats. Hawkers sold their wares, everything from jewelry to dried fish to wind up toys. At the center of the square was a stone pedestal, and atop it was a brass sculpture depicting a scene: five figures, all crowded around one man at a writing desk.

"Who are they?" Ronan asked. Again, Shila stared at him in amazement.

"Did your parents really not teach you anything?" she gaped.

He shook his head. Well, they had tried to. It just didn't stick. Then again, it's much harder to understand the world around you when you can't see it for yourself. In the one day he'd been away from the manor, he already learned more than he had in his whole fourteen years.

"It's supposed to be the First Bastion Summit. It probably didn't look like that—actually—but ya know, statues like to make everything look prettier than it really was."

"So that's—"

"That's why it's called Founders' Square, duh." She pointed up at the statue. "That man on the right, holding the pen? That's Yagi Satsuki. And then next to him, with the papers? Nisa Taheri. In the middle with the book is Rubira. Um...I can't remember their first name. Dari, I think?

Yeah, Dari sounds right. The one with the hammer on the left is Arlo Bell."

"Bell?" Ronan cut in, again feeling his face betray him with its telltale blush. Shila didn't take any notice.

"Yeah. Then on the far left that's Arun Zuri, with—honestly, I can never tell what he's holding. I think it's supposed to be, like, wires maybe? Some people say they think it's flowers, or a snake, but that's like—why would he be holding a snake? At a summit? It's stupid."

"Who's the guy in the middle? At the desk?"

"Oh, we don't know. He's the anonymous dude."

"Right. Yes," Ronan nodded at the history he definitely did not remember. He'd heard all the names before, though. Zuri, Rubira, Satsuki...and his own, of course. Hadn't there been one missing?

"Delian," he said. To his great relief, Shila nodded.

"Yeah, he's the guy who founded the Delian Group. Didn't want anyone to know his name, though. Don't get it, to be honest. If I invented, like, the biggest company *ever,* I'd want people to know who I was." She shrugged.

"Maybe," Ronan ventured gently, "it's nice when people don't know who you are."

Shila considered this.

"Maybe," she concluded, then promptly started pulling Ronan forward again, evidently not one for extended philosophical contemplation.

"But where are we going?" Ronan whined.

"To make money!"

At the base of the statue was a crowd of children—no, crowd was the wrong word. They stood in a line, like they were guarding the pedestal. They didn't look much like guards, though. Most wore tattered clothes, dirt smudged on their faces. Many of them were Ronan's age, though a few looked as young as six or even as old as twenty-five. Perhaps "children" was not the right word, but they were all certainly young.

"Here, take some of this," Shila produced dirt from her pocket.

"Wha...why? And why do you just carry dirt in your pocket?"

In answer, Shila started smearing the dirt on Ronan's face.

"What are you doing?" he asked in horror.

"I'm making us look more *pathetic*," she explained. "People come here just to pick the saddest looking kid they can and give 'em some extra points."

"But—"

Shila clamped a hand over his mouth. "Shut up! Someone's coming!"

A man in brown work pants and vest strode up to the crowd. He looked dignified, but by no means wealthy. He scanned the group of assembled kids until his eyes landed on a particularly muscular looking teenager in the back. He strode up to them, withdrawing a slip of paper from his pocket.

"Can you lift some boxes for me? Twenty points in it for you if you can."

The burly teenager nodded curtly. "Yes sir," they said.

"Excellent. Follow me," the man jerked his head, and the two disappeared down a side street.

"I didn't want that one anyway," Shila crossed her arms. "Lifting ones suck."

"So you just wait here all day...trying to get jobs?"

"Well, how else are you going to get points?"

Ronan had never considered this. He didn't even know much *about* points, to be honest. He'd never made a purchase in his life. He wondered how that slip of paper the man provided could be a useful currency.

"It's a slow day today," Shila observed, looking at the hopeful children waiting for employment. "Most of these kids are probably gonna end up in the dusts by the end of the year, I bet. The older ones, at least. They tend to get tired of waiting around, and then one day they disappear and...well, you kinda know what happened to them. Either the Commission got 'em, or they started selling dazzle. Or they got arrested and they're rotting in some Delian Detention Center somewhere."

Ronan looked at the older kids, most of them hanging back in a group at the edge of the statue. Unlike the younger kids, who were most attractive to potential employers because of their adorable pitifulness, the teenagers tried to give the appearance of cleanliness and dignity. Some even wore ill-fitting formal clothes, perhaps as a display of professionalism. Ronan didn't know why, but he found it sad.

Shila tugged at his sleeve.

"This one's for us," she said. "I can feel it." Before he could respond, she was dragging him in front of an elderly woman who'd waddled her way up to the statue.

"Can we be of assistance, ma'am?" Shila smiled sweetly. "I'm watching my little brother, see, and we could really do with some points to get him dinner."

Ronan frowned. First of all, he could hardly pass as her little brother. His unruly ginger hair and against her smooth black was a dead giveaway, in his mind. Not to mention his freckles. The woman, however, didn't seem to take any notice.

"Of course, love," she crooned, handing Shila a crumpled slip of paper. "Be a dear and pick up some packages for me. I can't walk all the way down to the post office on this knee."

Shila closed her fingers around the paper hungrily.

"We'll be right back, ma'am!" she gave a little salute before she started dragging Ronan downtown.

"We could be a good team," she considered aloud. "You just look so...frail and sad. It helps, I think."

"But what did she give you?" Ronan asked. Shila unfurled the papers to reveal a series of digits scrawled in pen.

"Account code," she explained. "We take this to a Points System Kiosk and we can transfer whatever's in it."

"We can transfer whatever's in the kiosk?"

"In the *account*, dummy!"

"Oh."

"Now hurry up! The faster we go, the more points she'll drop in the account!"

Shila shoved him forward, and he found suddenly they were sprinting. Ronan felt elation bubbling up inside him. He'd never had a reason to *run* before, not like this. He'd never been allowed to run in the manor, and while the estate itself was sprawling, it was mostly gardens and ponds. He'd never had the opportunity to move with this much freedom...and purposefulness! He had a job, a task! And even though it was a little errand for a small reward that he didn't fully understand, it was something to do, something he could work for, and that made him happy. And maybe he even had a friend, which was not bad either.

Shila had taken a liking to Ronan—or, at the very least, she had found a use for him. As far as he was concerned, he'd rather be used than ignored, so it didn't matter which it was. They spent the whole day racking up points together, and at the end of the day Shila showed Ronan how to use one of the Kiosks to put the points into an account.

"You have to remember this number," she said, pointing to a list of digits on the screen. "That's how you buy food and stuff."

"Um...can you write it down for me?" he asked tentatively. Shila rolled her eyes and produced a piece of paper and pencil stub, something she evidently carried around for the express purpose of writing down account numbers.

"Whatever, Blood Boy," she grumbled, but he could tell that she took a bit of pleasure in mentoring him. She ripped the sheet of paper and thrust it in his hands, glancing up at the position of the sun.

"C'mon," she gestured for him to follow, "we gotta get back to the Shack before we run outta light. It's kinda scary in Lower Bastion at night. There's like murders and stuff."

"Murders?" Ronan gaped.

"Probably not really," Shila shrugged. "That's just what the older kids say to get us home on time."

"To the Shack?"

"Yeah. You never been?"

Ronan shook his head. Wordlessly, Shila grabbed his wrist again and led him west, into the bowels of Lower Bastion.

The Shack was not a shack. It was a disused building on a backstreet of Lower Bastion, repurposed by a group of children as a makeshift haven.

The older "kids" bustled around making sure each child had a plate with something on it, even if that something was little more than a few morsels of dried fruit. Shila, for all her brazenness, nodded to the older kids deferentially. There was a hierarchy here, a pecking order, as Ronan's mother would undoubtedly have said. This hierarchy was not based on power and control, but instead responsibility.

Ronan recognized a few of the kids in the Shack from Founders' Square. Shila greeted some of them.

"Where does the food come from?" Ronan asked as he watched the older kids placing rations on every plate.

"We get a lot of food cheap from the Commission."

Ronan gasped. "You buy food from them?"

"Well yeah, sure," Shila shrugged.

"But they get stuff from the dusts!"

"Yeah, like…food. That you can buy cheaper than you can in the city cuz it's old. And people are scared of stuff from the desert."

"But…but it could be dangerous!"

"It's not dangerous. It's how, like half of Lower Bastion gets fed."

"This food is from scavengers? All of it?"

Shila shrugged again. "Some of it. I don't know. It's not that big a deal. There's nothing wrong with desert food. Most of us will probably have to become scavengers anyway. It's just how it goes."

"But, my mother says scavengers hardly ever survive." Admittedly she'd also had some other commentary about it being "their own fault" and searching the desert for resources was "a waste of time and money that just feeds a grimy slum" when those workers could "easily get a real job." Ronan decided against sharing that last bit.

"Some do," Shila said hopefully. "I know a few scavengers who made enough to get out. Or, I mean, I know about them. They're older than me."

"Do you really think you're gonna end up doing that?"

"Me? No. But a lot of them will."

"That's terrible."

"I don't know. It's just how it is."

Ronan imagined the kids in the room before him, fighting for their lives in the desert against monsters he'd only heard of in tales. Surely, he could find some way to save them from this fate. He was a Bell, after all! And Bells were leaders. Well, his parents didn't seem to think that *he* was much of a leader, but perhaps he had it in his blood. His not-actually-diseased, secretly aristocratic blood. Ronan made a secret vow to help Shila, to help all the kids in the Shack, in hope they would never be tossed out to the dusts.

CHAPTER TEN

Confrontation

"I need some space, I think," Yale told Columbia and Princeton. "I'm going for a walk. Don't wait up, alright? O'Neill says we're moving the pod tomorrow, and that means we'll have a new area to survey. You both should rest."

They saw Columbia bite the inside of her cheek. They'd expected she'd be resistant. She'd always hated them wandering at night.

"I don't like the idea of you going out in the dusts on your own at night," she admitted.

"I do it all the time," they reminded her.

"Yes, but—" she cut herself off. It didn't matter. Yale knew what she meant. *That was before one of us was dead.*

"Yeah, I'm, uh, I'm with Columbia on this one," Princeton chimed in. "You should just stay in here with us."

Yale frowned, eyeing him meaningfully. "The two of you have been agreeing a lot lately," they observed. The other two Ivies shared an uneasy glance.

"I mean, it's just—" Princeton stammered, looking to Columbia for guidance. "You might not be...as alert, as, um, before...and, I mean your ankle—"

"My ankle is healed."

"It's just—" Princeton began.

"It's fine," Columbia cut him off. "I've never liked it when you go out in the dusts alone at night, for what it's worth, but..." she exhaled, defeated, "if it's what you need, then that's fine. Just...stay close to the pod, okay? And if you see anything—"

"Yes, obviously if I see anything I'll come back," they grumbled, making for the pod entrance. "I'm not an idiot. Don't wait for me, alright? It's already late."

Yale did not go for a walk. They stood in the darkness just beyond the reach of the illumination streaming out of the pod's back window and waited for the light to be put out. The pod cast a dark shadow in the pale moonlight, and Yale stood, watching, as that shadow stretched to encase them.

After they were convinced everyone was peacefully slumbering, they crept back into the pod and silently sifted through O'Neill's supply cabinet until they found what they were looking for. Soundlessly, they exited the pod again and stalked into the cool desert night.

It wasn't a long walk to Harvard's grave. Yale had not bothered to check their maps. They knew where they were going.

When they arrived at the barren patch of land, marked only by some dying desert flora, they jerked their shoulder back to unlatch the holster across their back and unslung a shovel.

* * *

Columbia stood by O'Neill as he maneuvered the pod southwest, right at the edge of the Crags. No one, scavengers and scientists alike, ever crossed the Crags. There wasn't much point in risking your life trying to cross the impossibly wide canyon, full of jagged peaks and sharp edges, just to get to—what? More desert? Perhaps once all the sunken buildings on the east shore of the Crags had been mined, sure, but for now there was still a lot to be found underneath the earth Bastions-side.

"No one even likes to get close," O'Neill explained, as he maneuvered the levers expertly, making the pod jolt and shake as the mechanical legs carried it toward its destination, "which is why I imagine it's rich with species that have yet to be explored. And, for you all, some buildings that have yet to be mined."

"We appreciate it," Columbia nodded, gripping the edge of the pod as it shook. This kind of movement was not something she used to. She had never even been in a car before, though she'd seen the wealthy pilot their refurbished ancient automobiles down the streets of Bastion. They all breathed a collective sigh of relief when O'Neill settled the contraption into the sand, and they could once again stand on solid ground.

"Between you and me," O'Neill leaned into Columbia conspiratorially, eyeing Yale, "it's probably best we get away from that whole area anyway."

Columbia nodded her assent.

"I want you two to survey the new area, alright?" Yale gestured to the pod hatch.

"Are you coming with us?" Princeton asked.

Yale shook their head. "I'm working on something else."

The other two watched their captain expectantly, but Yale only stared back.

"Yale—" Columbia started.

"I'll be with you soon," they cut her off, and she recoiled. Something was certainly wrong, but Columbia wasn't about to point that out. If Yale wasn't going to open up about it now, they would probably retreat further if pressed. She held their gaze for a moment, hoping to pull the truth out of them with her stare, but they were silent.

"C'mon, Princeton," she said, defeated. "Let's go."

* * *

"Hanging back?" O'Neill asked as he busied himself with whatever science-y bullshit he was so fond of doing. Yale didn't much care.

"Yeah," they said, kicking the table in the corner of the pod to the center of the cramped room. "I was wondering if I could talk with you."

O'Neill laughed good-naturedly. "I'm not sure I'd have anything to say that would be of much interest to you, but sure, we can chat."

The old man took a seldom-used folding chair from where he had it tucked away behind his research station and sat down across the table from Yale, folding his hands together. Yale turned to a cabinet behind them, pulled out the contents, and dropped it on the table with bang so abrupt that the old man nearly leapt out of his seat. On the table were three empty vapor canisters, dented and covered in dust.

"I found these canisters," Yale announced matter-of-factly.

O'Neill gave a patronizing chuckle. "We don't have much need for *empty* canisters, now do we? Why—"

"I found them where you said you buried Harvard."

O'Neill froze. "Is that so?"

"What happened to Harvard?" Yale asked levelly.

"It don't matter," O'Neill simpered. "Yeah, I might have told a fib, but your friend is still dead."

Without breaking eye contact, Yale reached for their hunting knife and drew it from its sheath. They lifted it with the point toward O'Neill.

"What," they repeated, "happened to Harvard?"

O'Neill didn't so much as glance at the knife. He kept his gaze fixed on Yale.

"He ran away," he said matter-of-factly.

Yale shook their head. "He wouldn't do that. You...you did something to him. What did you do?"

O'Neill's smile widened. Yale slammed their palm on the table, making the cannisters jump with metallic clang.

Yale heard Columbia and Princeton came in through the inner hatch.

"Alright chief, we did a whole perimeter and—whoa! What is happening here?" Princeton jumped back.

"Harvard isn't dead," Yale told them, their eyes locked on the grinning old man. "He did something to him."

"Yale," Columbia put a gentle hand on Yale's shoulder. "I know how badly you want Harvard to be alive, but—"

"He admitted it, Columbia!" they jabbed the knife in O'Neill's direction. The old man didn't even flinch. "He did something!"

Columbia bit the inside of her cheek, considering this, her eyes sliding over to O'Neill.

"The little dude was super sick," Princeton crept up behind them. "And I know you're real upset about it, which probably got your brain all kinds of messed up."

Columbia's hand fell away from Yale's shoulder, and her eyes went distant. Yale had seen this look on her many times, when she was trying to puzzle something out.

"No. He wasn't," she finally concluded.

"What?" Princeton asked. But Columbia couldn't hear him. Her gaze was trained on O'Neill.

"You were poisoning him, weren't you?" she asked dreamily. "To keep us around?"

O'Neill gave a self-satisfied nod, and it made Yale feel sick.

"See, I told you!" they exclaimed.

O'Neill maintained his infuriating calm. He sat at the table, hands clasped, placid grin on his face, watching the scavengers piece everything together.

"So what happened to him?" Yale demanded again.

"Listen," the old man sighed. "It don't really matter what happened, now does it? He ran off on his own, and that was already a day ago. You know what it's like out there. You think he could make it on his own? That boy is dead."

Yale was about to protest when the whole pod shook. O'Neill's smug demeanor melted away in an instant. He shot up moved for the front window by the control panel.

"What the hell—" he mumbled. The metal beast jolted again.

"Is that a creature out there?" Columbia asked.

"I thought you said this thing fooled the scuttlers!" Princeton said.

"It does! I don't know why they've decided to pick a fight now." O'Neill hobbled over to his cockpit, where he could see out the front window. Sure enough, a crabsnake was extending its spindly legs, trying to pry the pod out of the sand.

"Hey!" Yale shouted. "We're not finished."

"Um, Yale buddy? I think the scuttler trying to kill us is probably priority number one," Princeton said absently, watching from the main room of the pod as the creature prodded at the glass. It stood at the same height as the pod on its stilts, and though the pod was much wider, it certainly didn't outweigh seven meter's worth of serpentine muscle and bone. "I know you're angry. But maybe you could stop antagonizing the guy who controls the giant robot crab?"

"I don't *care* if he controls the giant robot crab."

"We're inside it, Yale. You have to care."

O'Neill fiddled with controls and the whole contraption rose onto its metal legs.

"See, ya little carcine idiot? I'm a crab, alright, just like—"

The crabsnake gave the pod a push, and the mechanical crab stumbled backward.

"Has this ever happened before?" Columbia asked, gripping the handle of one of the cabinets to keep from falling over as the floor shook underneath her.

"They always thought it was a *crab* before!" O'Neill exclaimed.

"Move us away!" Yale demanded.

"It's not that easy, ya know!"

With one whip of its tail the creature sent the thing hurtling backward, tripping over its metal stilts.

"So just so we're all on the same page, the Crags are right behind us," Princeton said.

"Yes, we are all aware," Columbia said as she watched O'Neill struggling to push forward with the pod controls. "And if we—"

The creature placed one of its spindly legs against the pod's windshield, then shoved, sending the entire vessel off the edge of the cliff and down onto the jagged rocks below.

Interlude Seven: Chavi

Simon Foster was trembling. He took a shaky breath and willed himself to resume searching for the books he needed. He felt silly, honestly. He just wasn't used to getting any kind of attention. From anyone. At all. And someone had just noticed him. No, not *someone*. Chaverim Chakrabarti. Of course he'd fled immediately. He was too nervous to actually have a conversation with them. But just their acknowledgement was thrilling.

Simon was familiar with Chavi through reputation only. After all, he hadn't been attending the Academy for very long. His test scores had been high enough to be admitted for a year now, but the Foster family was tight on funds, and scholarships were a limited commodity. This was the first year he was lucky enough to be awarded merit aid, a rarity for the Academy. To him, the Bastion Academy of Arts and Science was the academic wonderland he'd always dreamed of. He hadn't made any friends yet, but he'd thrown himself into his studies. Why socialize when he finally had a chance to become an engineer? He'd never have been able to achieve that level of expertise at the Institute.

Once the shaking had subsided, he searched the shelves for a volume he could use for his research project. There was one that looked promising on the top shelf, but he couldn't quite reach. He stood on his toes, his fingers just brushing up against the sign. A dark-skinned hand closed around the book and lowered it, handing it to him.

"You wanted this?" Chaverim Chakrabarti asked, leaning against the bookshelf casually. Simon nearly jumped at the sight of them, suddenly so close. He gripped that book to his chest.

"Th—thank you," he stammered.

"What are you studying right now?" Chavi asked, nodding to the book. Simon's eyes flicked down at it.

"Oh. Um. Physics. I...wanna be an engineer. I think."

"Cool," Chavi nodded.

"Um. What are you studying right now?" Simon asked. Chavi grinned.

"You."

"Oh," Simon's eyes widened.

"I'm not really into studying, to be honest," Chavi admitted, shoving their hands in their pockets. "I'm only here because my friends dragged me. Maybe I should come here more often though, if I get to see you."

Simon felt his face burn. "Hah," he squeaked. This seemed to give Chavi pause.

"You don't say much. Are you usually this quiet, or am I just making you uncomfortable?"

"No, um...I mean, I'm just, uh, not used to conversations like this." *I'm not used to talking to attractive people*, Simon really meant. *I'm not used to talking to people much at all.*

"Do you...like conversations like this?"

"Well I like this one. I just..." Simon's stomach churned as he searched for words. His broad vocabulary was suddenly barren.

"I don't know what to say."

"That's okay," Chavi smiled warmly, leaning in. "I like quiet boys."

A book came down on the back of Chavi's head with a thunk, jostling their glasses.

"You little shit!" complained a voice behind them. "I can't leave you alone for five seconds!"

Avi Taheri appeared, fuming. Chavi's hand flew to their head.

"Ow! Fuck!" they complained. "You didn't have to—"

"Yes, I did," Avi shot back, before noticing Simon. "Were you harassing this poor boy?" she demanded.

"I was not—"

"You've got work to do. C'mon," she pulled them by the arm. To his surprise, Simon noticed a familiar face hovering behind the two of them. Jasmine Reyez watched the exchange with a worried expression, arms crossed, eyes sparkling behind her glasses. Simon didn't know many people at the Academy yet, but he did remember her as the brilliant girl who sat next to him in Physics.

"Oh. Um. Hi, Jasmine," Simon waved meekly.

"Hi, Simon," Jasmine waved back. "Are you studying for the test this week?"

"Yeah," he pushed his glasses up self-consciously. "I'm kinda nervous about it, to be honest."

Chavi looked back and forth between the two of them.

"Oh, so like...like you two know each other?" they asked.

"Yeah," Jasmine said, and Simon let out a little sigh of relief. He was afraid she would say, *This guy? Nope. He's no one*, which would have been super embarrassing.

"Well, Simon," Avi interrupted. "We are sorry about the annoyance. *We* are going to get back to work now."

She glared meaningfully at Chavi, who groaned but allowed themself to be dragged away.

"My dorm is 23A in the West Hall!" they shouted over their shoulder as Avi guided them, turning some heads in the otherwise quiet library. "Come by! My door is always open!"

Simon was left alone, somehow feeling out of place.

* * *

The mock Aptitude Exams were in five days. Avi and Jasmine had taken it upon themselves to sit Chavi down for at least a good few hours every day and make them study *something*.

They sat staring absently ahead of them as Avi placed another book in front of them.

"Read," she commanded. Chavi didn't respond. They just continued staring forward blankly. For a fleeting moment Jasmine worried something was wrong. Was this some kind of depressive episode? A break from reality? Or were they made at Avi? Were they mad at *her*? Or...Oh. The realization hit her a moment before it hit Avi.

"Are you dazzed right now?" Avi asked.

Chavi blinked.

"No," they answered a second too late.

Jasmine only stared at them skeptically, but Avi was more brazen. She grabbed the lapel of Chavi's school uniform and sniffed it.

"I *knew* it!" she hissed. "What kind of idiot are you? Smoking before studying for *the most important test of your life*?"

Chavi stared up at her with unnatural passiveness.

"It's not a big deal," they said slowly. "Just something to calm me down."

"You don't need to 'calm down.' You need to focus!"

"I am focused!" they insisted as their eyes darted around the library.

"You're *high*."

"I—" Chavi stared at her, their eyes suddenly vacant. Maybe they were about to apologize. Maybe they were about to cry.

"What were we talking about?"

Avi made a desperate grasping gesture before burying her face in the heels of hands.

"I am so *sick* of this! I am so sick of *you*! There are other things I could be doing with my life, you know. Big things. But instead, I'm here helping your sorry self get into a university, which is probably a hopeless case anyway—"

"I know," Chavi cut her off, their voice distant and numb. "I know it's a hopeless case. And every time I study with you two I remember that, and it hurts, right? Because I know I'm doing this big thing that I'm destined to fail at."

Avi's face softened. She retracted her hands and sat back down.

"You're not destined to fail," she said.

"I am, though," Chavi said matter-of-factly, and though their tone of voice was callous and removed, tears started to glimmer in their eyes.

"I'm not like the two of you. It doesn't matter how you do on your exams, Avi, because you're going to get into the best research institute in Bastion, and Jasmine doesn't even have to study because she can ace the exam with her natural genius—you two don't know what it's like to actually have to work for it. And I'm working and working and—and nothing is helping. So yeah, of course I wanna smoke before studying. I'd do anything to distract myself."

They stared absently forward. Jasmine gingerly reached for their hand and squeezed it.

"Please," she murmured. "Please keep trying. I want you to pass this test. I don't want to lose you."

Chavi looked up at her, and she felt a pang of pity mixed with—somehow—guilt. They sighed.

"Okay. For you, Jasmine. For both of you."

So, the three went back to studying.

Chavi never showed up to those study sessions high again. In fact, they gave up dazzle altogether in preparation for the test. Avi and Jasmine stayed up late with them every night, going over notes, taking practice tests, doing quizzes. Perhaps had they taken the exam, they would have even passed.

But Chaverim Chakrabarti never *did* take the Bastion Aptitude Exam.

CHAPTER ELEVEN

The Crevice

The research pod bounced against the jagged edges of the Crags like a child's rubber ball dropped into a particularly spiky gutter. It halted its downward descent with a jerk, wedged awkwardly on its side between two steep boulders.

Yale put a hand to their temple and found hot blood seeping from where their head had slammed against the pod floor.

"Who is not dead?" Princeton asked from where he lay on the ground.

"I'm not," Columbia said.

"I'm not," O'Neill said.

"That's a damn shame," Yale said.

"You guys, we have got to stop falling down holes," Princeton observed astutely, rubbing his head from where he'd banged it against the counter during the descent. It hadn't been a pleasant ride, but thanks to the Crags' rockiness, it wasn't a straight drop down.

"It's not exactly like we've been searching for holes to fall down," Yale growled, picking themself up from where they'd fallen by the window, which was now facing the rocks below them. The whole pod was turned on its side. Yale extended a hand to Columbia, who was carefully avoiding placing her palm in the broken glass now littering the floor.

Yale stepped over O'Neill, who was still on the ground, groaning, and wordlessly opened his research cabinets. Petri dishes and vials clattered to the ground, some shattering. Yale found the vial where O'Neill was storing the crabsquid tentacle. They examined it, then tucked it into their boot for safekeeping. They could have it delivered to someone who would make good use of it when they got back to Bastion.

"So, not to make things worse," Princeton started as he watched Yale sifting through the remains of O'Neill's samples, "but I do have to pee."

"Princeton!" Yale scolded.

"What? You expect me to hold it?"

"We're trapped at the bottom of a canyon—"

"Yeah, and I wanna know where I can piss!"

Yale huffed and kicked one of the empty canisters aside. They stepped in the gap that was once the window, broken glass crunching underfoot, and examined the rocks below them.

"So like, are there any bottles around, or—"

"Shut up!"

O'Neill was not the fragile old man he pretended to be, but he was still much frailer than the far younger Ivies. He gave an agonized whine as he righted. No one moved to help him. When he saw his spilled samples, years of research dashes to pieces, he let out a visceral sound of dismay.

"You'll get over it," Yale said without turning to face him.

"Yeah, you don't get to complain," Princeton agreed. "I mean, dude, in terms of worst people to get stuck in a crevice with, you're, like, easily really high on the list."

"So what was the plan?" Columbia asked. Yale could hear some rare acid in her voice. "Get us to work for you while you cared for Harvard, then what? We wouldn't have stayed forever."

"No, you wouldn't have," he admitted. "I would have let you go once your friend died."

"Okay, dude," Princeton said, "don't take this the wrong way, but like, why can't you just get your own shit? Go pick your own plants, find your own crabs? It's not like, that hard."

O'Neill sneered. "I may not be injured, but I'm still old. I couldn't possibly collect everything I need fast enough. Not on my own."

"Fast enough?" Columbia asked. "Fast enough for—"

Yale banged on the metal wall.

Columbia jumped.

"What are you doing?" Princeton asked.

"I'm trying to find a way out," Yale explained.

"Dude. That's like, metal."

"Yes, I know that, Princeton. It's metal against rock. But if we can find a place that isn't against rock, maybe we can start taking apart the pod and make a hole for ourselves to get out."

"Uh-uh," O'Neill shook his head. "There is no way you're making a hole in my quaking research pod."

"Oh, I'm sorry. Would you rather die?" Yale snapped.

"This is my vessel—"

"Shut it! You lost your say when you tried to kill Harvard!" they hissed. At the mention of his name, they felt their stomach twist with guilt and...something else. Worry. Harvard was stranded in the desert, and it was all their fault. Well, not *all* their fault. They glared at the old researcher.

"You're lucky I haven't decided to end you yet," they said.

"Yale!" Columbia rebuked them.

"What?" they whirled on Columbia with such ferocity she jumped back. And that was when Princeton said the worst possible thing, "Dude, just...calm down."

"No! I am sick of being calm! I am over it! I am done! 'Calm' got us *here!*"

"Actually, no. A crabsnake pushing us off a cliff got us here," Princeton countered. "So if you find some chill—"

Yale laughed in the kind of humorless way a person laughs when there is nothing else to do. "Find some chill? Harvard is out there, right now, alone, and it's our fault for leaving him—something you were all too *happy* to do—and it's all because this *sick fuck* tried to con us, and we're such idiots that we fell for it!"

They scooped up one of the few vials that wasn't broken and lobbed it against the wall, spraying glass and sticky blue liquid everywhere.

"If I weren't too busy trying to *find a way out of here,* I would be busy *killing him.* Which, by the way, I might still do once we get out of here, so don't feel too safe," they shot a glance at O'Neill, who was watching the episode impassively from the corner of the pod.

"Listen. We're going to get out of this pod. We're going to find Harvard. And we're going back to Bastion. And you," Yale pointed at O'Neill, "aren't coming with us."

"I told you, he's already dead," O'Neill shrugged. "The four of us aren't doing much better. But even without the pod up and running, we've still got supplies. And the girl and I, we've at least got enough brains to not get killed. But Harvard? That kid is dumb as rocks. *Was* dumb as rocks. I guarantee you, the scuttlers are picking at his bones right n—"

"Alright, that's it!" Yale shouted, and they launched themself at O'Neill, arm swinging. Just before their fist connected with the old man's grinning face, Princeton wrapped his arms around them and lugged them back.

"No no no no no, we're not doing that. Not here, not now. Fuck, I can't believe *I'm* the one that has to tell *you* that."

"Let me go!" Yale protested, struggling against Princeton's grip.

"No! You're losing your shit right now, and I'm actually being the bigger person which is really cool and dope of me and I'm not letting you ruin it."

Columbia gracefully stepped between Yale and O'Neill.

"Stop it," she commanded. Yale froze.

After a moment of tense silence, Princeton whistled under his breath. "Founders. Wish I could do that." Yale jammed their elbow into his ribs. He grunted and released them.

Columbia turned to face O'Neill, who looked on, almost amused.

"I'm not doing that again," Columbia warned. "Next time, I'll let them kill you if they want to. So, I'd be careful if I were you."

"I won't say another word," he promised cheerfully. "I didn't realize your captain was so sensitive. Not a great quality in a leader if I—"

"What did I *just* say?" Columbia snapped. This time, O'Neill fell silent.

"Good," Columbia murmured, turning back to her friends. She laid a hand on Yale's arm.

"This is a bad situation. To say the least. And I know you want to help. And I know you want to save everyone. But you can't right now."

Yale understood her unspoken words: *the last time you got like this, it didn't go so well. And the time before that...*

"Yeah, yeah, I know you're right," they sighed. "Let's get out of here."

Both jumped at a bang behind them. Princeton had taken up Yale's practice of methodically banging on the metal panels of the pod.

"This one sounds hollow!" he announced. "I think we can get out this way!"

Columbia dove for O'Neill's tool cabinet, which was now slanted at a dangerous angle, and sidestepped as she pulled the door. A toolbox, along with various pliers and wires, came tumbling out. She fished around for a screwdriver, then hopped over the mess to join Princeton.

"You can't do this," O'Neill said forlornly.

"Uh, yeah we can, and we kinda have to," Princeton said as Columbia methodically began removing screws from the metal panel.

"You have no idea how this thing was constructed. You don't know how many—"

"I think we're about to find out," Columbia cut him off, and working with incredible precision and accuracy, she removed the first metal plate from the wall of the pod. She brushed a stray braid out of her face.

"Gimme a few minutes. Then we'll be out of here."

* * *

Columbia found the walls of the pod were so armored and insulated it took her a few hours to finally break a small hole into the outside world.

"I want you all to know that I have been holding my pee this whole time, just for you," Princeton declared. Yale, now mollified, patted him on the shoulder.

"We're very grateful, Princeton. Thank you."

Columbia sat back, surveying her work. The wall of the pod was about ten centimeters thick, comprised of multiple layers of metal, insulation, and wiring. Through a process of unscrewing, hacking, and calling upon Yale to hit things with a hammer, she'd managed to make a hole almost large enough for a person to fit through, out into the rocky cavern outside.

O'Neill had not protested all the while, just watched her dejectedly as she hacked away at his life's work.

"Looks good," Yale nodded approvingly. "I think we could—"

A thud above them shook the whole pod.

Princeton groaned, "What is it this time?"

Another thud, so forceful that it dented the upward-facing side of the pod.

"Doesn't matter. We're leaving," Yale said, nodding to Columbia. She picked up the pliers and reached her hand through her newly made escape hatch, frantically pulling at the outer metal shell to widen the hole enough for a body to slip through. She took a deep breath before thrusting herself through the narrow opening. Surprisingly, she made it through with only a few strands of her clothing catching on the jagged metal edges. Once on the outside, she peeled the metal away, widening the hole even further so her compatriots could make it through.

"What is it?" Princeton asked from inside the pod. Columbia looked up. From her vantage point, she couldn't quite see past the curve of the pod, so she couldn't get a good view of what was on top without climbing up on some rocks. *The good news*, she thought, *is that it can't get a good view of me either.* However, she did see a claw about the size of a human head digging into the metal, though the rest of the creature was obscured.

"Can't tell," she said. "Some kind of reptile, I think."

"What color?" O'Neill asked from inside the pod.

"Does it really matter?" Yale asked.

"Depends on how much you care about living. Some reptiles will kill you. Other reptiles will kill you slowly and painfully. Best to know what you're dealing with."

"Um," Columbia pulled herself away from her work long enough to glance up. "It's black, mostly. But with splotches of—"

"Yellow?" O'Neill ventured a guess.

"Yeah."

"Is that bad?" Princeton asked.

"Could be good or bad."

"Elaborate," Yale demanded.

"If you're a fan of venomous lizards, then no, this isn't bad at all."

Interlude Eight: Ronan

Saoirse Bell had often made her opinion on the residents of Lower Bastion very clear. She was convinced anyone stupid enough to wander that far west would be stabbed, and rightly so. What Ronan found at the Shack was something his mother could never have dreamed of.

The walls were plastered with art, notes, and letters the children had made for each other. The older kids welcomed him with open arms. At the end of each night, one kid told a story. It didn't have to be true—in fact, some kids clearly made up their story on the spot, which usually got a lot of laughs from the listeners. Some were true, though, and Ronan could tell by the way the storyteller would get a sort of dreamy look about them as they got lost in their memories. There was a warmth about the Shack that Ronan had never felt in Bell Manor. The Shack was a home. Not Ronan's home, but still a home.

At first, Ronan was resistant to go back out with Shila. Wouldn't there be people looking for him? He'd been gone a few days now. Surely his parents had discovered that he was missing and would hire people to search for him. The Delian Group was the corp in charge of Bastion safety—surely the Delian Guards were patrolling for him. But when he was out with Shila looking for tasks and Delian Guard caught his eye, causing a stab of panic to run through him, she only smiled and nodded politely, continuing in her patrol. His parents hadn't even tried to find him. He'd always suspected, of course, that his parents hadn't liked him very much, or didn't think much of his potential. Only then did he have confirmation of what he'd always suspected: they did not love him. And if his parents did not love him, that meant no one did.

Perhaps Shila loved him, in her own way. But it was not the kind of love siblings might share, or even best friends. It was a sort of business partnership. They were helping each other survive, but at the end of the day, she didn't much care about him. She still insisted on calling him "blood boy" even though he'd repeatedly told her he hated it. He wanted to care about her, wanted to love her the way that he hadn't loved his sister, but it was hard when she seemed so determined to keep him at arm's length. The other kids were friendly enough, but they all saw him as Shila's boy because she was the one who brought him in, so no one was particularly interested in his friendship, despite his desperate attempts at companionship.

Still, he sat with them every night to hear a story, and even told a few stories of his own. As it turned out, he was a pretty compelling storyteller. He told stories from the books he'd read as a child—apparently most of the kids at the Shack had never had access to these, so they'd hadn't heard any of them before. He told them all the classic Bastion tales, from the Crab Prince to Creatures of Ruin. The younger kids liked it when he did voices. Ronan never thought he was good at performing. He'd botched enough piano recitals to know that. But something about telling a story to an eager audience of his peers was different. They didn't expect perfection—all they expected was a story. And that was something he could provide. Growing up in Bell Manor, stories were all he had. That and the birds and a view of the ocean. Maybe in another life, he could have been a performer. Maybe that would have been nice. Not in this life, though.

After some months of running errands in Founders Square, Ronan was struck with an idea. He wasn't quite sure how it had come to him— probably in a moment of elation as he ran down the street on his task, weaving easily through crowds, taking shortcuts that it seemed only he knew, weaving through the city as though it were a labyrinth and only he held the thread that would guide him home. As he darted between walls and under arms and through legs, it occurred to him: *I'm difficult to catch.*

So he told Shila.

"At this rate, we'll be running errands in Founders' Square forever. If we want to actually make money, don't you think we need to set our sights a little bigger?"

"What did you have in mind?"

"Well," Ronan flushed, "I've been thinking a lot about the vendors around the Square—and everywhere in town, really. If we could start swiping from them, then resell at a reduced rate to the kids around the statue, they could trade us for their account codes—I mean, the number of points we get for delivering a message must be about half what you need to buy a bag of dried fish, right? So I bet a lot of the kids would take us up on it—"

"You know if we get caught, we'll get arrested, right?"

"I mean, yeah, but...I won't get caught."

"What makes you so sure of that?"

"Never been caught before." Except once. But she didn't need to know about that.

And thus, Shila and Ronan created their own little crime ring. Shila did most of the people work, while Ronan made the map. Having run through the city on odd jobs, he practically had the layout memorized. For once in his life, he felt like he had a skill worth contributing. He coached his fellow thieves on the best escape routes to avoid getting caught—alleys and passages that most people wouldn't remember were there.

It wasn't as simple as telling the rest of the kids to knock themselves out. No, there had to be some sort of organization, and Ronan knew this. He drew maps of every quadrant of the city with scavenged pens borrowed from the other Shack kids, tracing out the best routes back to the Shack that were sure to lose any pursuers.

"We've got to have a rotation," he figured, "otherwise people will recognize you." He didn't follow this rule himself, as he had a knack for going unseen, but he enforced it for all the others. He'd propose his plans, standing on an overturned fruit crate and pointing at his maps on the Shack wall, and the kids would look up at him, nodding eagerly, those who could write even taking notes. For the first time, he was in charge of something. And oddly enough, he was good at it. Kids reported back to him—what shop had a new security guard, which booths were too crowded to be unobserved, even stores that had such sub-par offerings they weren't worth hitting. He'd nod, taking notes and thanking the scouts heartily for their work. They'd always beam, blushing—Ronan, *the* Ronan, had thanked them!

Ronan's parents always said he wasn't suited to run a business. It turned out this wasn't entirely true. He wasn't suited to run *their* business. His own, however, flourished. Ronan and Shila ran their enterprise for something like three years, though Ronan couldn't be certain. He had lost track of time. He no longer had any need for a calendar, no lessons to make, no appointments to keep. He wasn't sure if he was seventeen or eighteen when everything fell apart.

CHAPTER TWELVE

Harvard's Mission

I am Kryaka, Empress of the Southwest Planes. This is Skrack, my Guardian. And these are his hatchlings, my Guardians To Be.

Harvard wasn't sure how to greet a royal crab, especially one that he didn't know if he'd imagined or not.

"What...what do you want from me, Empress?"

Your assistance, sweet Harvard. And your compassion.

Harvard felt himself blush at being called sweet, even if it was by a crab that might be a hallucination.

"I...I'd love to help you," he said, meaning, *I'd love to get out of this crab den uneaten,* but he hoped neither scuttler picked up on that.

If you refuse, Skrack interjected, *my hatchlings will feast upon your flesh.*

Harvard waited for the Empress to deny this threat, but she did not. Harvard took a shaky breath and decided just in case this *wasn't* a fever dream, he should go along with it, so as not to get eaten by crabs. He looked nervously at the thousands of little eyes from thousands of little crabs, staring at him from the edges of the den. The Empress noted his glances.

My Guardians To Be serve as my eyes in the lands I rule, and even those I do not. They report back to me what they find, so I know all that occurs on my end of the desert.

Harvard surveyed the tiny crabs lining the walls of the den, thousands of miniscule creatures. He was reminded of the injured crab he followed into the sunken building during that dig. A creature with a mission. Had he followed that scuttler, where would it have led him? To Liza—Kryaka—in O'Neill's pod? Or to Skrack in his den?

"But...you were trapped in the pod!" Harvard said.

I was not imprisoned. I was there by choice.

"But...why?"

I have a certain fascination with humans, I must admit.

"So while he thought he was studying you..."

I was studying him, yes.

A futile endeavor, Skrack added. *Humans are not worthy of our study.*

And yet I learned many things, Kryaka said, and though the sensation of her voice was strange in his head, Harvard could still somehow make out the defensive edge.

I now know enough to send Harvard on his mission.

"So what, uh, what is my mission?" he asked tentatively. "I've never been very good at, um, missions." Even his brief period of success at the Shack had ended in failure and landed him in the hands of the Commission.

It is nearly time that I pass on my title, Kryaka spoke into his mind, *I have ruled these plains for many centuries. It is time I begin to seek the Serenity. I must pass my title to an heir.*

Harvard was no stranger to the idea of needing an heir. It was, after all, what he would have been, had his sister not claimed the entire family business for herself.

"But, I mean, I thought crabs were immortal. Why would you need an heir if you live forever?"

I do not expect your mortal mind to be able to grasp our ways. Nothing is forever. One day, we must all seek Serenity.

Harvard nodded, not to indicate he understood, but to indicate he had no way of understanding.

"So, um, Empress...are you asking me to be your heir?"

Skrack made a grating sound from deep within his shell, a sort of scraping and clicking, and it took Harvard a moment to realize this was the creature's laugh.

No, my child, the Empress said, *A human is not fit to rule the desert. Surely you understand this.*

"Yeah, I mean, sure, I just...I don't understand what you want from me, then."

I have an heir. His name is Mryk. He was taken from me not long ago.

Harvard felt his stomach sink. He did not consider himself to be very smart, but he had enough foresight to understand where this was going.

"By humans?" he ventured a guess.

At first, I did not know to why my Mryk was taken. Guardians and I gathered what information we could, and we discovered my heir has been transported to your human city in the name of research. He is still alive—I can feel his presence, just as I can feel yours. But he is in great pain.

"Okaaay," Harvard drew out the word, mentally scrambling to comprehend everything he was told. "So you want me to bring you to Bastion? So you can get him?"

No. You will get him.

"*Me?*" Harvard gasped. "But I...I mean, I wouldn't even know where to start! I don't...How would I even—"

There is another option, Harvard felt Skrack's heavy voice in his mind, *and that is direct action.*

"I...I don't—" Harvard stuttered.

Skrack, Kryaka explained, *is not a proponent of human engagement. He believes we should take matters into our own pincers.*

"You mean, you want to attack Bastion?" Harvard gaped.

No, I do not. Skrack does. I believe there is a solution in which no crab blood—and minimal human blood—will be spilt. And that is why I have chosen you for this task. Should you fail, Skrack's...direct strategy will be our next resort.

"Okay, okay, okay," Harvard struggled to organize his thoughts into words and phrases. "I don't want you to declare war on humans. I mean, that would be bad. Definitely bad. I'll help. But I don't even...I mean, I can get us to Bastion. But once we're there, I wouldn't even know—"

That is where my investigation into the human scientist serves us, Kryaka explained. *Humans of your city have a gathering in which they share what they deem scientific achievements, and in which they are given compensation for their research.*

"Yeah, the Galvin Conference," Harvard said with a bit of pride for understanding something the crab was talking about.

It is soon. We expect Mryk will be there. You will attend. You will find him. And you will bring him to me.

"I can do that," Harvard said with absolutely no confidence that he could, in fact, do that. "Sure. Yes. I can...wait, won't there be guards though? Like, the Delian Group? You guys know about the Delian Group, right? They probably won't let me steal a crab. Keeping people from stealing, is, like part of their whole thing."

That what is rightfully reclaimed is not stolen.

That didn't help Harvard very much.

"Um. Okay. Sure, I can figure it out. I can do it."

You must. Time is short, young Harvard. We must begin—

"Wait!" he interjected. "Not yet. I mean, I can't go back to Bastion without my crew."

Your crew?

"My friends," he said. "They're still with O'Neill. You saw them, Kryaka! They're good people! We need to rescue them before...before...he does whatever he's going to do them!" Harvard remembered with a shudder O'Neill's words as he ran away from the pod, all fear and adrenaline. *Your friends are dead.*

How dare you presume we deign to do you any service in return! Skrack boomed. *You are a mere human, pawn for our devices—*

Silence, Skrack, the Empress interrupted. *I remember the other humans you speak of, Harvard. They were not kind to you. They spoke of abandoning you.*

"They...they did?" Harvard asked. That couldn't be right. They would never. Would they?

They left you, sickly as you were, for their own selfish desire. They are worth nothing to you now.

Harvard weighed her words. Had they really intended to leave him forever? Was that the reason they were gone for so long? And to think, he'd even gone after them, hoping to save them.

No, he couldn't believe that was true. Yale would not do that. He was certain of it.

"I want to help you, really, I do, but if you want me to just leave my friends to die..." This was a stupid idea, wasn't it? "...then I guess you'll have to feed me to the hatchlings. Because I won't do it."

Harvard hoped he would get a quick refusal from the Empress, that she would say, *Don't be silly, Harvard, we can't lose you!* Instead, she turned to face Skrack. Harvard waited for the two to begin deliberating, but they merely stared at each other, clicking noises emanating from beneath their shells. It took a long moment of crab-noises for Harvard to realize they *were* deliberating, by desertwalker communication. He watched helplessly as the two creatures discussed his fate in a language he could not understand.

Finally, the Empress turned again to face him.

Your compassion does you great credit, she informed him, *and is much of the reason you endeared yourself to me in the first place. But do not allow it to make you weak. Compassion, like many things, will not always serve you well.*

"I'm not letting it make me weak," Harvard said weakly. "I just want my friends to be safe."

And safe they will be, the Empress promised. With a flick of her claw, a cohort of baby scuttlers fled from the den.

My Guardians To Be will see to it no harm comes to your friends, she vowed, then added, *for the most part.*

"For the most part?"

Be thankful, you disgusting little ingrate! Skrack commanded. *The Empress has done you a great kindness!*

"Oh! Of course! Thank you, Empress!" Harvard blurted out.

No thanks is needed, the Empress said. *Your loyal service is thanks enough.*

Harvard swallowed, wondering what his "loyal service" would entail.

Come, Skrack demanded, leading Harvard out of the den, *We begin our journey at once.*

* * *

Harvard had never been on a mission for crabs before. He didn't have much idea of what it would entail. Much to his surprise, it was a lot more walking than he would have expected. He was at least thankful the hatchlings had provided him with a new dustscarf and goggles from the depths of their den, but he wished he didn't have to wonder how scavenger gear—with no scavenger attached—had made it into a scuttler den.

With the Empress again tucked away in his pocket, Harvard trudged behind Skrack in the hot desert sun, countless hatchlings scurrying alongside. There could have been ten or there could have been hundreds. Every time Harvard looked down, he saw a different number of crabs flanking him.

"You little guys must be so tired," Harvard mused. He pulled at the bottom of his shirt so as to make a little pouch, then picked up a few of the hatchlings. They were docile in his hands, almost eager to be handled. He found six would fit in his makeshift pocket.

"Now some of you can take turns having a ride!" he exclaimed. "Hopefully this will give your little legs a rest."

He looked back down at the train of crabs extending behind him and picked a few more out of the lineup with the hand not holding his shirt. He placed a few on his shoulders, and even one on the top of his head.

What in the name of the Great Serenity are you doing, idiot boy child? Skrack asked when he saw Harvard adorned with tiny crabs, trailing behind him.

"I figured your hatchlings must be getting tired of all this walking," Harvard explained, "so I'm giving them turns to take a little break."

And what of you, human child? Are you not tired of walking?

"Well, I mean, yeah, but it hardly makes any difference to me if I have a few crabs on me, while I bet it makes a whole lot of difference to them."

If a crab could shake its head disapprovingly, Skrack would have done so. Seeing as he didn't have a head, though, he didn't. He simply grunted from somewhere deep in his shell and continued forward.

Harvard looked down at the crabs in his makeshift pouch. He worried they would be clambering to get out, but instead they folded their legs under themselves, hopefully enjoying the respite.

"I like your shell," Harvard said to one of the hatchlings with a particularly striking black and yellow pattern along its chitin back. "It reminds me of a honeybee. Can I call you that? Honeybee."

Harvard had no idea if the creature understood him, but it made no move to protest the name. Harvard smiled.

"And what about you?" he said to another. "The gray reminds me of a stray cat I used to see visiting the garden at my parents' house. They kept trying to have the gardener catch it and kill it, and I was so scared he would, but I think the cat was always too quick. I named it Speedy. Yeah, I know it's stupid, but I was only, like, eight. Do you want to be Speedy? I bet you're pretty fast!"

A thought struck Harvard as he studied the interweaving patterns on the creature's shell.

"Wait a second," he said. "I know you! You're the little guy I helped into the building. You were hurt!"

Gingerly, Harvard flipped the crab over to check if its leg was still bent awkwardly. To his relief, the crab's legs seemed entirely healed. Perhaps this was a different scuttler? But he knew those markings. He'd seen them right before...well, right before everything happened.

"I'm glad you're all better, Speedy," Harvard turned the crab back over, gently petting its carapace with a finger.

Are you naming them? Skrack demanded.

"Well, sort of," Harvard looked up. "I mean, they can't tell me their real names. I guess it's 'cause they're still babies? But I want to call them something! So, I'm giving them brand names, just like the one I have. That way I have a name to call them, but we both know it's not their *real* name."

Brand names?

"Yeah! Like Pepsi or Taco Bell."

I do not understand.

"Okay so way back before the Earth got hungry and ate humanity and all that—you know those stories? About the Quakes? Like they talk about in the Earth's Mercy Prayer."

I was present for their making.

"Oh. Yeah. Right. Well, way back before all that, there used to be humans all over the place. And they had these big companies with brand names. There were, like hundreds of them. But now that we have Bastion they're not around anymore."

And why does Bastion render these... "brands" obsolete?

"Well mostly they're obsolete because they sunk into the ground. And people were like, 'hey, remember these brands?' so they told stories about them. But then the Founders of Bastion made human life anew, so there was no need for brands or companies anymore, just the big six corps. And they don't need to compete with each other or anything cuz they signed an agreement. Now those old brands are just names that we say."

"Made human life anew?" Skrack repeated incredulously.

"Yup. That's what they teach us in school. The Founders of Bastion made human life anew. Now there's no need for big evil companies, because a smaller population means fewer people to manage, so Bastion can be the perfect city."

Harvard hoped it wasn't obvious he hadn't attended school after the age of fourteen, so that's where his knowledge of Bastion history came to an end. He remembered the basics that they were taught as children, as well as the bullet points laid out in the Bastion Pledge of Fidelity, but when he ran from his home, he also ran away from any hope of pursuing studies.

And you really believe this? Skrack asked. *That this city of Bastion is perfect now? So much better than the civilization that sunk into the Earth all those centuries ago?*

"Well, I don't think any civilization can be perfect," Harvard felt his face flush as Skrack challenged him. He'd never been much of a philosopher, and certainly not one for debates. "But, I mean, I think it's pretty good. People are happy."

Were you *happy?* The question caught Harvard off-guard.

"I was...different."

You were forced to become a scavenger.

"I chose to become a scavenger," Harvard admitted. A partial truth. *I chose to run away,* he thought, *and that choice made the decision for me.*

This made Skrack stop in his tracks.

You...elected to be a filthy little scavenger.

Now Harvard really felt his face burn.

"Well, I mean, not entirely. I'm just saying..." he looked down at his feet, kicking up dust. "I'm just saying I had a good life. And I chose to leave it. No one forced me."

But you left because you were not happy.

"Yes. But that's not Bastion's fault."

Whose fault is it, then?

Harvard felt an unexpected flare of defensiveness in his chest, though what he was defending he was not sure. His family? The corps? Humanity on the whole?

"No one's! It doesn't have to be anyone's fault! Sometimes people just get sad!"

Hm. How peculiar. Skrack began his thunderous walk again.

"What?"

Crabs are not the same.

"Crabs never get sad?"

Of course crabs are capable of feelings your insufficient human tongue might categorize as "sadness." Grief, disappointment, remorse. But we do not simply "get sad" as you seem to claim that humans do.

"Well," Harvard grumbled, looking out into the dusts, "I guess humans are different."

Undoubtedly, Skrack agreed, with no small amount of acid.

* * *

Harvard did not know how many hours they had been walking through the desert.

His legs had begun to drag, his trembling so violent it made every step a trial. His mouth was so dry it felt as though it were full of crumpled paper. But he didn't want to complain, lest he incur Skrack's wrath. Or rather, Skrack's incessant complaining about him, and the fact that he would be much more useful as meat than as a living person. He got enough of that from Princeton already, and he didn't enjoy getting it from a giant monster that could make good on his threats with no moral qualms. So, he kept his mouth shut.

However, it became increasingly difficult to hide his fatigue as the journey bore on. Even the crabs riding his shoulders had leapt off, not wanting to add extra weight, as he could hardly carry his own.

Halt, the Empress commanded from Harvard's pocket. She leapt out and began crawling toward Skrack. *The human boy is tired.*

This is because humans are weak and disposable sacks of meat, Skrack explained as though this were basic science. *A human child was not meant to do the work of one of our kind.*

"I'm not a child," Harvard protested. "I'm, like, nineteen or something."

You know a human is necessary for our purpose, the Empress chided, *and this is a fine one.*

Harvard couldn't help but smile at that. No one had ever called him "fine" before.

And he is of no use to us if we allow him to die here.

Harvard stopped smiling.

Let him rest, she commanded, *and find him something to eat.*

Fine. For our purpose alone.

For our purpose alone.

Every time Harvard thought someone might like him—every time!—he was wrong. In the end he was only *useful* to them, and only by virtue of being there at all, and that was the only reason anyone tolerated him. It was funny, really, because he so desperately wanted to be useful, but every time he actually *was* useful it felt like a slap in the face.

The Empress turned to face him.

Rest, she commanded.

Harvard didn't realize how weary he was until he sank to the ground. He fell to his knees, and before he could catch himself flopped face-first into the sand. The dusts were hot against his skin, but he didn't care. His aching muscles had a brief moment of respite, and that was all that mattered. He passed out immediately.

* * *

Harvard awoke from a dreamless sleep to the sensation of a crab leg ungently prodding at his shoulder.

What do you eat, human boy?

Harvard rolled over and groaned, but Skrack did not let up.

Speak. What do you eat?

"I don't know," Harvard mumbled.

How is this possible? Are you not aware of what you consume?

"I just...I mean...lots of things," he pulled himself up to a sitting position, rubbing his eyes blearily. It was dark. Had he really slept until past sunset?

I require specificity if I am to feed you, idiot boy. It's not as though I'm in the habit of keeping a human as a pet.

"I'm not your pet!" Harvard objected.

Fine. Then feed yourself.

Harvard thought, *I never knew crabs could be so petty.*

"Okay, fine, um..." he thought for a moment, "most of the rations we take with us are dried fruits and nuts, I guess."

So I will find you fruits and nuts.

"But I guess come to think of it, some fruits are poisonous to humans. And probably some nuts too."

So something different.

"We also have some dried meats?" Harvard suggested.

I can hunt you meats.

"Well, we'd have to cook it first. Otherwise, the bacteria and stuff could make me sick."

Skrack groaned. *Your feeble little human body is so fragile.*

Harvard rubbed the back of his neck, somehow embarrassed by this.

"Yeah, yeah, I know."

So no fruits, nuts, or meats.

"Um. There's beans, I guess?"

Beans?

"Yeah. We, um, we cook them, usually, but I don't have to cook them."

What kinds of "beans?"

"Oh. Well, um, I guess I don't know, honestly. Brown ones?"

You want me to search the desert...to find you brown beans?

Harvard flushed bright red.

"Sorry, is that too much to ask?"

It is no wonder humans are so easily killed. If you ingest anything that disagrees in the slightest with your delicate innards, your body rebels against itself. What primitive creatures you are.

Harvard felt he should be offended by this, but admittedly, Skrack was not wrong.

I shall search for—what is this?

Skrack turned his hulking body to the side, and Harvard followed his gaze. Near where he lay, the hatchlings were marching in a line akin to ants bringing food to their hill. Each carried a morsel in its pincers, dropped it on the ever-increasing pile of scraps, then scurried away.

I suppose, Skrack grumbled, *the hatchlings have seen to your nourishment without me.*

For the most part it was crumbs of indeterminable origin, though there were larger chunks that were from the packs of scavengers: a chunk of dried meat, a few almonds, a whole dried apricot. Harvard was wary, though, of sifting out inedible pieces, after nearly breaking his tooth on a screw that one of the hatchlings had mistaken for food. Luckily, one of the hatchlings was wise enough to drag along a water skin, pinched in its little claw. Harvard drank greedily.

The little feast was surprisingly satiating. By way of thanks, Harvard went to each hatchling—though they numbered in the hundreds, if not thousands—and gave each a little pet on the shell and a word of thanks.

Skrack muttered about how this was excessive sentiment, a flaw found in mankind. The Empress made no such remarks. Harvard liked to think she appreciated his show of gratitude, but perhaps it was just wishful thinking.

You should have a proper rest, the Empress announced. *You are not at your most vigilant after eating. Now is the ideal time for you to sleep.*

Harvard was certainly not going to refuse another nap. The Empress and Skrack argued about something, though it was all in clicks and claw gestures. Skrack must have lost the argument, because he grunted churlishly and laid his massive torso on the ground, producing a *thump* and a small cloud of dust. His claws rested in front of him, and his legs curled under his shell almost like a cat. He gestured with one large claw to the crook of the opposite leg.

You will sleep here, he announced begrudgingly.

"Oh," Harvard murmured, not entirely thrilled at the prospect of sleeping cradled in the arms—legs?—of a creature that clearly thought he was better off dead.

Skrack's body will shield you from windborne dust, the Empress explained, *and protect you from potential predators.*

"That's very kind of you, Skrack," Harvard did his best to sound appreciative and not terrified. "Thank you."

Skrack did not respond, so Harvard cautiously took his place nestled between Skrack's claw and torso, sheltered under the lip of his shell. Admittedly, it was quite comfortable. Harvard reclined against the cool chitin, laying one hand delicately on the claw. Despite his initial apprehension, it was easy to slip into sleep once again. For the first time in a long while, Harvard felt safe.

* * *

The Empress scurried through the sands on her own. Though she cherished the constant presence of Skrack and his many hatchlings to guard her and tend to her, a bit of solitude was always welcome. Afterall, solitary contemplation was a core value to any desertwalker, especially one with such a high station. The only way to achieve Serenity, after all, was to prepare oneself for the great union. Her seclusion was not only a luxury, but a necessity.

At least, for these brief moments. She was strong and she was quick, but all the same, she was small. She could not survive long without the aid of her trusted Guardian.

Trusted. Hm. Skrack was trusted, it was true. But as of late, he'd become increasingly...resistant. The Empress did not fear his betrayal. She knew his loyalty to the Lineage of the Southwest Plains—she could feel it, the way she felt the earth beneath her claws. But there was an uncertainty in him—no, a fear in him—that he had to resolve. Unfortunately, the Empress could not help him in this quest. This she knew. A desertwalkers' journey is always taken alone.

The Empress wondered if perhaps Skrack would take this opportunity to kill the boy as he'd wanted to do from the beginning. Perhaps she'd left as a sort of test. But no, she knew Skrack was too loyal to betray her, despite his hatred of mankind.

When she returned, he was watching the boy he cradled with his claw sleeping peacefully. His expression was something approaching wistful. The moment he became aware of her presence, he looked away from the slumbering human and out into the distant sands.

He gave my hatchlings names, he grumbled.

And this vexes you? the Empress asked as she scuttled toward the pair.

My hatchlings already have names.

But he does not know them, the Empress pointed out, *And they are too young yet to speak their names to him.*

He has no right to name them, Skrack insisted. Despite his foul disposition, he still extended his free claw to the Empress so she could scurry onto his shell, safe from the dangers of the dust.

He was not naming them, the Empress explained. *He was giving them names, which is a different thing entirely.*

Skrack was silent.

I do not trust him, he finally said.

No. I knew you would not. But what other choice do we have?

We do this without a human. Flesh is no match for claw.

No, the Empress said, settling herself atop Skrack's shell for her nightly respite. *There are too many of them. This way is best.*

He is human, my Empress.

He is. And he is a good one, I believe.

There is no such thing.

You have not studied them like I have.

And what have you found in your studies, O Empress?

Humans are not all as primitive as we have come to believe.

Interlude Nine: Jasmine

Jasmine was never fond of the way she was always ignored, but when she finally did receive attention, it was even worse. As the Aptitude Exams came closer and it became clear to the Academy students that she was their collective rival, she went from being a meek nobody to a target. It was so subtle at first that she hardly noticed it was on purpose—doors by her dorm room slammed late at night, textbooks disappeared, her painstakingly-written notes vandalized, her assignments shredded the day after she completed them. She was losing sleep thanks to all the extra work she had to do to make up for it, and to make things worse, losing precious study time.

The sabotage she could ignore, but then they started staring. It wasn't enough, apparently, to try and break her. They had to know if it was working. She could feel their eyes on her in the cafeteria, in the library, in the courtyard. She even identified their ringleader by the way he studied her: an Upper Bastion student named Carter Vik; the kind that came from wealth and would be sorely embarrassed if Jasmine took his spot at university. She didn't *want* to take anyone's spot. She just wanted to go to school, just like everyone else.

The attacks culminated one day at lunch. She sat with her friends in their usual spot in the Academy cafeteria, where no other students dared join them—except Simon, in his more brazen moments.

"You need to do something about that boy," Avi had muttered to Chavi as she grew increasingly irritated at his cloying presence.

"What? He's not bothering anyone!" Chavi had defended, who obviously ate up the attention without once considering what would happen to Simon when he discovered his pining was for naught.

"He's bothering me," Avi grumbled, with the veiled meaning: *and your failure to do anything about it is bothering me too.*

Thankfully, today it was only the three of them, as Jasmine preferred.

"Jasmine? How's it going?" Avi asked tentatively.

"I'm fine," she said abruptly, her head snapping up.

Chavi, as usual, was oblivious to Jasmine's struggle. It wasn't that they didn't care—they did, a lot. Too much, even. But they often didn't pick up on signals that something was amiss until it was too late. They continued their conversation with Avi as though Jasmine hadn't said anything.

"I *wasn't* exaggerating."

"You can't have *never* seen a fish," Avi rolled her eyes.

Chavi shrugged. "Just haven't."

"You've never, like, been to the aquarium?"

"Why would I? I already have to learn things at school. Why would I learn more things in my free time?"

"Actually, you make a big point of not learning anything at school."

"Yeah, exactly! Besides, the idea of aquariums freaks me out. I hate water."

"How do you *hate water*?"

"I just do!"

The conversation faded to a fuzz as Jasmine felt her eyes fluttering closed and her consciousness slipping away.

She jolted awake as a hand caught her shoulder, and realized with a start she was falling out of her seat. She looked up into Chavi's worried face, who was now properly concerned.

"You good?" they asked in a tone that indicated they were well aware she was not, in fact, good.

"Yeah," she lied, hurriedly standing up. "I'm just gonna go to...I'm gonna go..."

She felt her cheeks burn, embarrassed at having been caught falling asleep. She wasn't *like* this. She didn't *make* mistakes.

"I'm gonna go...um, to the library, I think," she stammered, lifting her backpack with a jerk.

There was a sickening pop, and a split-second later Jasmine felt moisture on her fingertips, leaking onto her arm. She looked down to see a red stain spreading across the fabric of her backpack, seeping into its contents. She tore the bag open to look inside. *Cranberry juice*, she thought as she saw the red liquid soak into the papers she'd spent all night penning, rendering their text illegible. But that theory was dispelled when she caught a whiff of the sharp, sour odor.

"It's *vinegar*," Chavi observed aloud. They stood, oddly placid, next to Jasmine, looking into the destroyed bag. "Someone put a bag of *vinegar* in here?"

Jasmine Reyez had had enough.

She often wondered how things may have gone differently. If she had decided to confront her tormentors before it had reached this point. If she had lifted the bag just a bit later. Or if she'd been able to hold it together a little longer. But in that moment, the fragile thread holding her together snapped, and the valve that had been welded shut burst open, as she gripped the soaking bag in her balled up fists and sobbed. She shook as the red liquid ran down her arms, meeting her elbow and dripping onto the floor.

For a brief, shocked moment, her friends only stared at her. So, it seemed, did the rest of the Bastion Academy of Arts and Sciences. The top student was having a breakdown right in the middle of lunch, after all. Who would want to miss this?

"What is this?" Chavi asked, turning the bag over in their hands. There was so much latent anger in their voice Jasmine felt a surge of panic, fearing they were mad at *her* for some reason.

"I...I'm sorry..." she stammered. Chavi's head snapped up.

"Why are *you* sorry?" they asked, not unkindly, placing a gentle hand on her shoulder.

"They...they're keeping me up at night and—and ruining my textbooks and—"

"*Who*?" Chavi demanded, firmly but again not unkind.

"I don't...I don't know," she whispered, but they must have seen her eyes flicker to the other students in the cafeteria.

"How long has this been happening?"

Jasmine couldn't bring herself to answer. She just sniffled.

Chavi turned, and Jasmine felt a wave of horror as it dawned on her that the cafeteria was completely silent, and every pair of eyes was trained on the two of them. Chavi walked away from her, lifting the still-dripping backpack over their head.

"Who," they demanded coldly, "did this?"

Silence.

"No one wants to admit it?" Chavi swiveled abruptly, and students cowered away. It had been a long time since the "incidents" from childhood that had landed Chavi in detention, but the memory was still salient.

Chavi glanced back at Jasmine. Involuntarily, her eyes flickered to Carter Vik, who was sneering at the scene from a table with his friends. Jasmine cast her gaze down at the floor, guilty.

Chavi held out the bag to Carter.

"Did you do this?" they asked calmly.

"Does it matter?" Carter sneered.

"Do you have a problem with my friend, Jasmine?"

"Look, she's got an unfair advantage, being born smarter than the rest of us. Someone's gotta level the playing field."

There was a murmur of agreement across the cafeteria, and Jasmine felt her stomach sink. Chavi whirled around and the whispers of assent fell silent.

"You all agree?" they asked. No response.

"Okay. Good," They turned back to Carter.

"Listen, you benefit too," Carter reasoned, "we all know you're not getting into a university if someone doesn't flatten the bell curve. You're dumb as shit. So why do *you* care?"

"Me?" Chavi smiled sweetly, tossing the bag aside. "Oh, I *don't* care. You're so right. I'm so sorry to have bothered you. Please, go back to your lunch."

Carter gave them a confused sideways glance before hesitantly turning back to his table, unsure if he'd won the conversation or not. As soon as Carter's back was fully turned, Chavi grabbed a fistful of the boy's hair and slammed his face into his cafeteria tray, silverware clattering at the impact. The whole cafeteria recoiled, students too close for comfort leaping backward as the boy lifted his head out of a now-bloody plate of potatoes, his nose at a different angle than before.

A gasp rippled through the cafeteria as Carter slowly stood, back still turned on Chavi. He wiped away blood and white mush with the back of his hand. Chavi waited patiently, arms crossed, for Carter to turn and face them.

"Well?" they asked. Carter whirled around and gripped them by the lapel of their school uniform. He swung his fist into their cheek. Chavi's head snapped to the side, but they were grinning wildly, and a giggle escaped their lips. That was the only permission they needed to unleash the ever-simmering rage beneath their surface.

Everything after that was a blur of violence and blood in Jasmine's mind. She couldn't tell who was involved in the fray and who was attempting to break it apart. She couldn't tell who was on Carter's side and who was on Chavi's—if anyone. She was frozen to her spot, watching in abject horror with her hands clasped over her mouth. The world seemed to morph into grisly shapes, bending to encase her. She felt a hand on her back guiding her away, and she found herself complying, allowing herself to be led back to the kitchens, guided by a gentle hand on her shoulder, and comforting words spoken in her ear.

When she came back to reality, she found herself seated in a room of the Academy kitchen, Rivka Chakrabarti kneeling by her side.

"It's all okay," she was saying, rubbing Jasmine's back. "Everything will be fine."

"This is...all my fault," she squeaked, her vision blurring with tears.

"No, it's not," Rivka insisted. "You didn't do anything wrong. You did nothing. You were the victim."

Jasmine nodded, sniffling, though admittedly she wasn't processing anything she was told. She was just seeing the violent scene in her mind over and over again. Still, Rivka's warmth and soft voice slowed her pulse. Somehow, she *was* being convinced that everything was alright, even though her mind refused to believe it.

"How about a cup of tea?" Rivka suggested, standing.

Jasmine whimpered her assent, putting her face in her hands. She heard the sound of water being poured, and a stove being turned on.

"There you are!" she heard Avi's voice from the doorway. She looked up to see the girl rushing to her side. "I should have figured you'd be here."

Avi placed a gentle hand on Jasmine's shoulder, at a loss for words. Avi was never particularly good at comforting people—she didn't have much experience.

"How...are you?" she asked hesitantly.

"Not good," Jasmine laughed feebly. Rivka placed a cup of tea on the counter next to Jasmine.

"Sweetheart, I know you're blaming yourself," she said in a voice that felt like warm cotton, "but my child makes their own choices, as misguided as those choices may be."

Jasmine took a sip of the steaming tea. The kitchen door opened and a meek-looking boy appeared in the doorway.

"Um...Ms. Chakrabarti? They want you in the principal's office."

Rivka stood, untying her apron. "Yes, I imagine they do," she sighed. Before leaving, she turned back to Avi and Jasmine.

"You girls wait here, okay? I'll be back in a few minutes."

Avi and Jasmine waited, but Rivka Chakrabarti did not return.

CHAPTER THIRTEEN

Pilgrimage

The creature wailed sound above them, and Yale backed away.

"How are you so calm about this?" Princeton whirled on the old man, still sitting amidst the remains of his labor. He shrugged.

"I figured we were going to die the moment the pod got knocked into the canyon. The *pod* is *life*. No pod, no life. And this"—he gestured to the liquids spilling into each other, shards of broken plastic and glass, scuttler legs and pincers and eyeballs once so pristinely preserved—"this was my life. So if I'm going to be eaten by a venomous lizard, well...now would be the time."

Yale and Princeton stared at him in amazement and horror. The beast's claws penetrated the metal just above O'Neill's head.

"We're not just gonna leave you here with a...a poisonous lizard!" Yale protested, "I mean, that's...that's insane!"

O'Neill shrugged.

"You were going to kill me yourself a moment ago."

"Yeah, that's when *I* was going to do it! We're not just gonna leave an old man to—"

"Hey!" Columbia called from outside the pod, extending a hand through the opening. "I think the hole is big enough now. Yale! Princeton! Come on!"

Princeton looked to Yale, who waved him forward. He nodded, and made his way to the hole, gripping Columbia's hand as she pulled him to safety.

Yale heard a shrill screech and leapt backward, looking up to see the lizard peeling back the metal of the pod as easily as one peels and orange. Yale extended a hand to O'Neill.

"We can talk about all the Harvard stuff later, okay?" they said. "Get up. Come with me. Now." They gave a wary glance up to the new hole in the pod, where a scaly black-and-yellow snout poked its way in sniffing for food. Its forked tongue shot out, and Yale ducked to avoid being smacked in the face with a rope of wet purple flesh. They glanced behind them to see Princeton struggling to squeeze out of the hatch, Columbia pulling him through on the other end.

"C'mon!" they said again. O'Neill looked up at them forlornly. Then with a sigh, he extended his hand to Yale's.

Only he didn't take Yale's hand. Instead, he placed in it a thick black leather-bound book.

"What the hell...what are you doing?" they demanded, examining the beaten old notebook they'd just been handed. "We have to leave! Now!"

"Yale!" Princeton called behind them. They turned to see that he'd finally made it out. They turned their attention back to O'Neill.

"That there," he said lifting a finger, "is the record of everything I've learned after thirty years in the desert. If you kids ever make it back to Bastion, I want you to take that with you."

Yale looked from the book down to the old man, then back at the book.

"You can't be serious," they said. O'Neill grinned, and it was a grin Yale was learning to despise.

"I'm dead s—"

The lizard wriggled through the hole, stretched its head into the pod, and clamped its jaws around O'Neill's torso.

Yale had never seen someone be eaten before. They hadn't known how much blood comes from being impaled with fifty pointed fangs. Despite claiming he was ready for death, O'Neill gave a strangled cry as the beast crushed his body, and Yale heard his rib cage collapse with a sickening crack. They wondered how O'Neill was screaming, then they realized that *they* were the one screaming, as the beast attempted to pull its gory prey out of the pod. Someone else was screaming too.

"Yale!" Columbia shrieked on the outside of the pod. "What's happening in there?"

Yale barely registered her voice, scrambling away from the monster. They tripped over the scattered equipment and fell heavily on the metal ground with a painful clang. They couldn't tear their eyes away from the morbid scene as the monster tore at its quarry, spraying the pod with blood. A hand gripped their shoulder and yanked them through the jagged metal portal, scraping their arms and legs.

"C'mon! C'mon!" Princeton said, helping them to their feet, but they couldn't seem to look away from the pod. Columbia grabbed them by the wrist and pulled them after her, leading them further down the canyon, under the cover of the haphazard rock formations jutting out at every angle.

Only when the Ivies had put a few miles between them and the ravaged research pod did they pause to catch their breath. It was only then Yale realized they were still clutching O'Neill's black research log.

* * *

While the other two caught their breath, Princeton took this opportunity to relieve himself behind a boulder. Sweet release.

"We can't stay down here," Yale advised when the three finally had enough presence of mind to speak. "We don't know what kinds of creatures live down at the bottom of this canyon."

"Well, we have a bit of an idea," Princeton commented, though he quickly recoiled after a glance from Columbia.

Yale looked up at the rocky slope above them, and Princeton saw the thick black book they hugged to their chest.

"What's that?" Princeton asked, pointing at the book.

"Oh, it's..." they looked down at it, leafing through the warped pages. "O'Neill gave me his research. He wanted us to take it back to Bastion."

Princeton stared at them. "And, um...are you?"

"I don't know," they flipped through the pages, and Princeton could see the splatter of the owner's blood adorning the edges. "He was using us. And when he was done, he was going to kill Harvard. I don't see any reason we should have to respect his dying wish."

I mean, yeah, Princeton thought, *but does anyone deserve to get crunched by a giant lizard?*

"We might get some use out of it," Columbia suggested, holding out her hand for the notebook. Yale handed it to her readily. She flipped through the pages and frowned.

"What?"

"It's just...well, most of it is not legible, actually."

"Really?" Princeton peeked over Columbia's shoulder. She was right—nothing but funky scribbles in that thing.

"It's like it's written in some kind of code," Columbia said. "Maybe some bits will be useful... the drawings, maybe. And maybe there will be a few notes here and there we can make out. But most of this? I can't understand any of it."

"Why would he write his research in a code?" Yale asked. "Afraid someone would steal his work?"

"Who's gonna steal his work *out here*?" Princeton gestured to the entirety of the desert.

Columbia shook her head.

"It doesn't make sense. Any of it, really. I mean, what was he doing out here to begin with?"

Yale cocked their head quizzically.

"Research? I mean, do you not believe him?"

"I do, but...Science doesn't just make people evil. I know scientists can get passionate about their work—" she hazarded a glance at Yale, "—but this doesn't seem like he just really cared about the work. He had some other reason."

Princeton nodded. "The real question is, who was paying him?"

"What?"

"That's what you mean, right?"

Columbia fell silent, considering this.

"It's getting late," Yale said. "We can camp here for a night, then we should try to climb up first thing in the morning."

"Works for me," Princeton shrugged.

"No one happened to remember to bring the tent during all that, did they?"

Columbia gave Yale a proud little smile and tossed them her pack.

"Thanks," they said, turning toward some of the more inviting overhangs of the twisting canyon. "I'll start setting this up."

"Wait," Princeton held up a hand, then glanced back at Columbia as if to ask, *Are you gonna back me up on this?*

She raised an eyebrow as if to say, *Depends on what you're about to say.* Yale turned, watching the two of them expectantly.

"What?" they asked.

Still eyeing Columbia in a plea for aid, Princeton took a deep breath.

"I was just wondering...are we gonna talk about how you, like...lost your shit?"

Yale's face was stony as they took a step forward. "I don't know, Princeton. Do you want to talk about it?"

Princeton scratched the back of his neck. "Um...I guess not. Okay. Cool. I guess not."

Yale nodded, then turned around again to go set up the tent.

"Believe it or not," Columbia leaned into Princeton, "They used to be like that all the time."

"All the time?" Princeton gaped.

"Well, not *all* the time," Columbia admitted. "But they've always had issues with impulse control. It took a lot less to...make them upset."

Princeton watched their captain construct their shelter for the night.

"Like what?" he asked. Columbia bit the inside of her cheek.

"Like—" she started, but cut herself off. "It doesn't matter. They're better now," she shook her head, then gave Yale another sideways glance.

"Mostly."

Once the Ivies were safely—*relatively* safely— hidden in their tent and lying on thin sleeping palettes, Princeton overheard Yale murmuring the Earth's Mercy Prayer.

"Why do you do that?" he asked. Their words stopped abruptly, and they shot Princeton a withering look, like he was intruding on something that wasn't his business.

"What do you mean?" they asked, lying back down and wrapping the thin blanket around themself.

"I mean, you can't actually believe that the Earth is listening," Princeton said. It was like the names thing all over again. Princeton wanted to trust the captain, but they kept putting their faith in things that didn't make any sense to Princeton. Didn't they realize by now that all the stories about the Great Quakes were bullshit?

"No, I don't think that the Earth is listening," Yale snapped. "But the prayer is not for the Earth, Princeton. The prayer is for me."

Princeton held up his hands defensively. "I'm just—"

"Have I gotten us killed, Princeton?" they cut him off.

"Well—"

"Answer the question," Yale demanded.

"No," Princeton sighed.

"Then maybe the prayer is working."

* * *

The climb back up from the Crags was not so much dangerous as it was arduous. The Ivies could only make it so far before they needed to catch their breath on one of the stone shelves.

"So...we're headed home, right?" Princeton asked when they finally made it to the surface. "I mean, we've got barely any supplies, one vapor canister—hell, I'm not even sure we really know where we're going—"

"We have to look for Harvard," Yale said.

"I mean, I think that would be...a really cool thing for us to do," Princeton tread carefully. "But, like...logistically...it might not be the wisest..."

"You want him to die?" Yale asked.

"No! Obviously that is...that is the opposite of what I want. But like, I also don't want *us* to die, ya know?"

He looked to Columbia for support, but her face was unreadable. He wished she'd give him *something*. He sighed before attempting his last resort.

"Listen, I know we're not supposed to talk about stuff back home, but..."

"It's fine, Princeton. What is it?"

"Look, I'm not saying we should just forget about Harvard or anything...like, we're a team and all, but...I've got people back home. I, um, I have four sisters, actually. And our dad is sick. And...I mean, that's kinda the reason I'm a scavenger. So it's not like I don't wanna find Harvard—I really do—but...but the dusts are huge. And there are people back home waiting for me. Like, *relying* on me. I know we don't have a lot to show for this trip, but if I die out here...well, that's the end of it for my family."

He wrung his hands together, shifting his weight from foot to foot.

"I mean...you guys have people too, right? People you wanna get back to."

Yale and Columbia shared a glance, and Princeton could tell it was a silent exchange he was locked out of.

"Yes," Yale finally responded. "I have people."

"I have someone too," Columbia nodded.

"So you guys get it, right?" Princeton felt a wave of relief wash over him; he hadn't realized how worried he'd been they would chastise him for suggesting that they go home.

"Harvard is just one guy. But I've got five people at home to think about. I don't wanna seem selfish—"

"You don't seem selfish," Yale shook their head, looking out at the setting sun over the dusts. "You make a good point. But..." they turned back to their team, "not good enough to convince me not to go looking for Harvard."

Princeton scratched the back of his neck. He hazarded another glance at Columbia, but her face was stony. Did she really not care? Or was she hiding her true feelings?

"I think..." he ventured, all too wary of the rage he could incur beneath Yale's placid surface, "that's a bad idea."

"Of course you think that," Yale said. "But I'm doing it anyway. That being said, I can't force the two of you to come with me seeing as you do have," they shot a wary glance to Columbia, "people waiting in Bastion. So, you can go home. I wish you the best of luck making it back. As your captain, I, er...I release you."

"You release us?" Princeton repeated.

"Yeah. You're, uh, released from service. To the Ivies."

With that, they started to unfasten the buckle of the leather band on their wrist.

"You should...you should probably take this back to the Commission. So they can give you a new captain and everything."

Columbia wrapped her hand around their wrist, impeding them from unbuckling the latch.

"Stop it," she commanded. "I'm not leaving you."

She looked back to Princeton. Though she was silent, her message was clear: *It's up to you. I won't be mad if you leave. Neither will they.*

Princeton froze. He'd never had to make a decision like this before. Well, that wasn't true. He had once. And he worried he might have made the wrong one.

"Um," he said.

Yale nodded, as though this were all the answer they needed.

"I understand," they said. "We'll see you back in Bastion, Princeton."

And just like that the other two walked away from him, Columbia's hand resting on Yale's shoulder, leaving Princeton alone. Princeton sighed. He ran his fingers through his golden hair. He kicked the dust in aggravation. He thought about the last thing his sister said to him before he left.

"Shit. Damn. Quaking fuck," he said to no one.

He leapt into motion, trailing the other two Ivies and waving his arms.

"Wait! Guys! Wait up! I'm coming too! I'm coming too!"

They paused to allow him to catch up. He was breathless by the time he arrived.

"I'm coming too," he panted, bent over with his hands on his knees.

Yale raised an eyebrow. "Are you—"

"Yeah, yeah, I'm sure, I'm sure. I wouldn't...it wouldn't feel right, ya know? It just...it wouldn't feel right."

Yale nodded, and Princeton thought he saw a shadow of a smile on their lips.

"Alright," they said. "Ivies. Let's move."

Part Three: The Guardians

Excerpt from Legends of Bastion

The next most circulated story amongst Bastioners is the Creatures of Ruin. Children in particular enjoy this story because, too young to grasp its true meaning, they enjoy imagining a world full of animals without claws and shells and wicked intentions.

The story takes place when the Quakes first began—roughly four hundred years ago, though it's difficult to pinpoint an exact start. Just as the Earth devoured humanity, it began to devour its other creatures.

The birds took to the sky. The bugs took to the air. The fish took to the ocean. But the crabs ruled the land. Where could the remaining land-dwelling creatures go?

"What will we do?" the brown dog asked the black cat.

"Do not worry," said the black cat. "I know how to survive. I will keep you safe."

"I will run away," said the horse.

"It will not work," said the black cat.

"Hmph! What do you know?" said the horse. And so the horse ran off, but the dusts were cruel. Its hooves slipped on the cliffs, and the horse fell to its death.

And the black cat watched.

"I will hide in the trees," said the squirrel.

"It will not work," said the black cat.

"I'll show you!" said the squirrel. And so the squirrel searched for a tree, but the dusts were cruel. It could not find a tree growing in the heat of the dusts, and unprotected the squirrel was swallowed up by hungry crabs.

And the black cat watched.

"I will dig into the ground," said the rabbit.

"It will not work," said the black cat.

"You know nothing," said the rabbit. And so the rabbit burrowed into the ground, but the dusts were cruel. The rabbit found that these sands were not made for the dens of furry things, and it was crushed as its new home collapsed atop it.

And the black cat watched.

Some versions of this tale go on and on in this manner. The cow, the pig, the chipmunk — while the creatures vary, all meet a similar fate. The end, however, is always the same.

The crow landed next to the black cat. It did not often dare to land in the dusts, for fear of the desertwalkers, but curiosity compelled it.

"Why do you look on while those around you die?" the crow asked.

"There is nothing I can do," the black cat replied. And the crow had to admit, this was correct.

"What will you do to survive?" the crow asked.

"Come. I will show you," the black cat said. So the crow followed from above as the black cat found the human.

"May I live with you?" asked the black cat.

"Of course!" said the human. "I will protect you! And your friends, if you've got any left."

"I have my friend, the brown dog. And though the crow can fly, he would like a place to land every once in a while to rest his wings."

"Then they are welcome," the human said, "in this, the Final City."

From then on out, every child in Bastion has been raised knowing that they live in the last beacon of humanity. Because who else could possibly have survived?

Moral: Trust in humanity is the only assurance of survival.

CHAPTER FOURTEEN

Princeton's Risk

With hardly any food, weapons, or sense of direction, the Ivies wandered through the desert in search of their fourth member. The dusts were expansive, but Harvard couldn't have wandered far, so the Ivies did their best to retrace their steps. Columbia, as usual, was silent, lagging behind the other two and watching for desertwalkers, her last vapor canister in a holster at her hip. Yale and Princeton were up ahead, walking silently.

"So...four sisters, huh?" Yale ventured, worried Princeton would bristle at their bringing up the topic. Instead, he only smiled fondly.

"Yup," he looked down and ran his hand through his hair. "I miss 'em."

Yale laughed to themself, trying to imagine Princeton wrestling with four little girls. Oddly enough, it wasn't as strange an image as they expected. It almost felt natural.

"And you're a scavenger..."

"To support them. Yeah."

"That's a lot of...responsibility," Yale said, which felt like a stupid thing to say. Yeah, of course it was a lot of responsibility.

Princeton scoffed, not unkindly. "Sure quaking is," he agreed.

"Do they know? What you do?"

Princeton looked up at Yale, taken aback. "Uh, yeah. Of course they...wait, does your family not know that you're a scavenger?"

"What? No...I mean, yeah, she knows."

Princeton nodded slowly, then pushed a little further. "She?"

Yale sensed they'd made an error and turned away.

"Let's stop talking about this."

"Hey, you're the one who brought it up!"

"I was just...trying to make conversation."

Yale quickened their pace, walking up ahead of Princeton. They glanced back in time to see Princeton glance at Columbia, and she raised an eyebrow as if to say, *"What'd I tell ya?"*

* * *

The vapor ran out. The Ivies had known they were on their last canister, but when it barely managed to squeeze out a pathetic cloud of gas to ward off a curious baby tortoisecrab, Princeton knew they were in danger.

"We should do another dig," Princeton proposed when they were settling in for the night. "We're gonna run out of food and vapor if we don't."

"I don't know," Yale shook their head. "It seems like an unnecessary risk to me."

"But digs are what we *do*."

"Yeah, when we're going out and back. Usually we do a few digs, get enough to surpass the quota and make a profit, then we head for Bastion. Staying out in the desert like this is risky enough as is. We don't need to add to that."

"That's even more reason to go digging! We can't go back to Bastion to get more supplies. *Or*," he raised his eyebrows at the other two, "we could go back now, restock—"

"No," Yale dismissed the suggestion outright. "We can't risk wasting that time. Harvard is out here on his own. We have to find him before it's too late."

"Right. Yes," Princeton nodded, shrinking, but the unspoken sentiment was still in the air: *it might already be too late.*

"A dig would waste time *and* put us in danger we don't need to be in. We're not doing it."

"It doesn't matter how long we can survive. What matters is we have no vapor. If any kind of desertwalker tries to give us trouble, we're dead."

"That's not true."

Princeton gaped. Yeah, they were the captain, so yeah, they wanted to save the whole crew. But could that blind them to the danger staring them right in the face? Was Harvard really worth killing the whole crew? Not for the first time, Princeton wondered if Yale's weird obsession with Harvard had made them delusional.

"Have you ever been in the dusts without vapor?" he asked. "'Cause Founders know, I haven't! We're naked, Yale!"

"We're not—"

"What's the plan if we get attacked? What's the plan, hm? Do you have one?"

Yale set their jaw, which satisfied Princeton a little. They didn't have a response, so maybe he was winning.

"What's the plan if we go on a dig and encounter something unfriendly?" Columbia unexpectedly countered. "You're right, no vapor is a danger. So why put ourselves in more danger?"

"You really think we're more likely to encounter something *down there* than *up here*?" Princeton asked.

"Down there is where they live, Princeton," Columbia said. There was no derision in her voice. Just simple, scholarly precision. "Up here is only where they hunt. We at least have some sense of the desertwalker population above ground. Under? We still don't know their density down there. We still don't know anything about the depths or the numbers of their burrows. Besides, we can't tell how old a building is before we go down. What if it predates the invention of vapor? We will have put ourselves in harm's way for nothing. I don't like this feeling either, Princeton. But the truth is, we are still safer up here than we are underground."

Princeton hated being bested, but since it was Columbia he was arguing with, it was no surprise that she had verbally pinned him.

"Then why," he spoke slowly, picking each word with precision, "don't we go back to Bastion?"

"You know why," Yale glared at him. "And this argument is over."

"But," Columbia added, and Yale turned to her. The argument wasn't over until Columbia said so.

"Once we run out of food, we *should* go back to Bastion. If we're starving, we're not going to find Harvard anyway. All we'll do is get ourselves killed. Okay?"

She looked to Yale for approval. Princeton had never seen Yale counter one of Columbia's proposals, but this was the closest they'd ever gotten. He thought he could see the battle between emotions and their better judgment happening behind their eyes.

"Fine," they finally agreed. "If we stretch, we should have enough for three days. After that, we go back."

Columbia nodded her assent. Princeton did too, hoping he put on a big enough show of agreeing that they wouldn't suspect his reservations.

It wasn't that Princeton didn't respect Yale's authority. He recognized on teams like this, someone has got to be the leader, and that leader wasn't him. He also recognized the leader could make mistakes, especially when they were not thinking straight. And if the whole incident in the pod was any indication, Yale was definitely not thinking straight. So if he took direct action, who could it hurt? The way he saw it, Yale's plan was a death sentence —they'd be pushing the team to exhaustion everyday, and without enough food, they wouldn't be alert or strong enough to fight off any scuttlers that came their way. But if Yale wasn't going to step up and get the team more food and supplies, then Princeton would.

Anything for the team, right?

He waited until he was certain Yale and Columbia had finally fallen asleep. After scavenging long enough with the Ivies, Princeton got to know their bedtime habits to a tee. Columbia fell asleep almost instantly. Yale would spend about twenty minutes rolling over and groaning a bit, but eventually they would murmur the Earth's Mercy Prayer when they thought no one could hear them, and after that they were usually out in a few moments. Princeton waited for the breath of both his crew mates to steady, then he crept out of the tent.

He didn't have a map. That was going to be a bit of an issue. Admittedly, Harvard was always the best one at navigating. Now Princeton felt guilty for giving him grief about it earlier. He could really use Harvard's expertise here. It took him a bit of wandering before he found a marble pediment jutting out of the sand.

"Bingo," he said aloud, whipping out his paddle to start excavating the ruin. He stopped short when he saw someone had already done exactly that. A depression in the sand revealed a window, clean of broken glass. Had this one already been hit?

Princeton shrugged. Scavengers always missed things. They weren't as *thorough* as him. Even if the place had already been swept, he could probably find a few canisters or cans they had missed. Maybe even pre-quake tech, though admittedly that wasn't priority number one at the moment. He scurried up to the opening, hurriedly slid his rubber grips onto the soles of his shoes, and leapt through.

Princeton had not been to many museums in his life, but he was still able to recognize one. Sometimes his sisters wanted to go, and he was dragged along. They couldn't afford to go to the fancier museums, but occasionally the Rubira Association would open a free one in Lower Bastion in the name of "charity." Princeton was never one for "culture" stuff—seemed like a waste of time, to be honest. But he'd at least taken in enough "enriching culture" to recognize the once-white walls, covered in scuttler-bitten frames and streaks of dirt. Shattered glass littered the floor like confetti.

Princeton couldn't tell what had once been displayed here. Art? History? The descriptions were too marred to read anything, canvasses now hole-ridden and faded. Not that any of it mattered. All that mattered was a museum was not a great location for scavenging since it wasn't likely to have anything useful.

But museums have cafes, Princeton remembered, having spent much of his childhood in museum cafes while his sisters did the whole culture thing. Maybe if he could find the—

A sound echoed off the marble ceiling. Princeton froze in place. It was subtle, airy, like the wind. But even Princeton knew there was no wind underground. His eyes darted around, looking for signs of movement, but he was alone. He heard it again, this time a distinctive fluttering sound that he could recognize—a laugh. Someone was already here.

Should he just leave?

Nah, that'd be a waste, right? He'd come all this way. Besides, if it was another group of scavengers, they'd probably be happy to meet him. He was a pretty chill guy, after all. He could give them a hand scoping out the place, and in return maybe they'd give him some supplies to take back to the Ivies. Especially if he explained the whole situation with the little dude gone missing. Surely, they'd have some sympathy, right?

He tracked the voices to a slanted marble stairwell. Whoever was here must be downstairs. He crept down the stairs, the echoes growing louder, though he still couldn't make out any words. He could, however, make out two distinct voices. They sounded like they were arguing. The higher voice was pleading—gently, not desperately. And the lower voice was starting to get angry.

At the base of the stairs, Princeton could see the wall ahead of him flickering with the glow of orange light— a fire being reflected in the next room. He pressed his back against the wall and inched slowly toward the doorway. Now he could make out a few sentences.

"—just saying that we can't keep this up forever," the higher voice was saying.

"We're not going to!" the lower voice shot back. "We only need a few more and then we're like, set."

"No, we're not 'set,'" the girl—probably a girl—dissented. "We'll have enough for a little while, but—I mean, Snickers, you really wanna stay here?"

Princeton laughed to himself. Snickers. What a stupid name.

"No one is talking about staying here! But until we go back—"

"We could go back now. We could cut our losses and go."

Snickers laughed derisively, the same sound Princeton had heard atop the stairs.

"Cut our losses? We didn't do all this *shit* just to give up now, when we're so close to finishing."

Princeton was tempted to swagger up and introduce himself. He was a pretty charismatic guy, right? Besides, most groups of scavengers were pretty kind to each other. There was a shared sense of camaraderie. He'd never come across another group out in the dusts, but he couldn't imagine it would be all that different. If anything, wouldn't they be more likely to want to team up if they were in a bit of a rut?

His instincts, however, were stronger than his airtight logic. Something told him to stay put. A fraction of that something came from the sound of that voice— Snickers, he'd gathered. There was something about the guy he just didn't like. He chalked it up to bad vibes coming off this Snickers guy, that's what it was. He decided to not mess with them, and instead check out the room across the hall, which—hell yeah! It looked like this was the cafe.

Sure enough, there were some decent finds in there. Lots of old fruit cans, some packets of nuts and chips, even some bottles of water that still looked sealed. No vapor, though. Columbia had been right. This museum must have dated back to before the stuff was distributed mid-Quakes, which meant he really didn't have any hope of finding useful supplies. Princeton set his jaw. He was determined not to make this trip a *complete* waste. He hurriedly stuffed as much as he could into his pack when he heard shuffling in front of him. He froze.

Princeton stared wide-eyed ahead of him. A young girl stared back. Could she really be a scavenger? She had the clothes for it—the goggles, the scarf, the boots, curly hair pulled up in two tight buns, but damn! She must have been, like fourteen years old! He smiled at her encouragingly, and raised his finger to his lips, as if to say, *"Don't mind me! We're just playing a fun little game where I sneak around and you don't snitch."*

The little girl nodded knowingly and trudged back toward her camp. Princeton breathed a sigh of relief. Good kid.

"That's not the point!" Snickers was saying to his counterpart. "The point is it's a quaking waste to—"

"Snickers? Twix?" the little girl interrupted, her tiny voice echoing in the grand hall.

"Not now Milky! I told you, don't interrupt us when we're—"

"There's a guy over there listening to you. You should kill him, I think."

That little fucking snitch.

Princeton stepped out from the shadows, hoping to make the best of a not-so-great situation.

"Whaaaat?" he feigned surprise. "What are you guys doing here? I thought...I thought no one was here. Oops! My...my bad, guys. This one is all yours. I'll just...I'll just be on my way..."

The other scavengers were impossible to read. As he'd suspected, a boy and a girl stood over the fire, watching him with stony faces. A fourth scavenger, a diminutive girl with cracked round glasses, warmed herself by the fire. For a moment that dragged out far too long, they stared at him.

"I'm just...gonna go?" he said. They launched themselves at him.

"WHAT THE FUCK?" he cried, bounding back up the stairs. "I haven't done anything to you! I'm minding my own damn business. I'm actually a really cool guy once you get to know me and...STOP TRYING TO KILL ME, OKAY? WHAT THE FUCK IS YOUR DEAL?"

He clambered up to the entry level, the sound of two—three?—pairs of booted feet echoing on the stairs behind him.

"I'll leave you alone! I promise!" he screamed as he ran up the slanted marble floor toward the entryway in which he came. Something slammed into his back, making him stumble forward. *I've been shot!* was his first thought, until he realized that a bullet *probably* didn't feel like a really pointy rock. *Shit. That girl threw a rock at me!* he thought.

He made it to the door, but of course, he hadn't come in through the door, he'd come in through the window on top of it, and the quaking thing was higher than he remembered. He jumped, arms outstretched, hoping to grip on to something that he could use to pull himself up.

His hand closed around one of the iron bars left in the window, which also meant closing around broken glass. He cried out, but a few cuts on his hand were better than being torn apart by deranged scavengers. Painfully, he pulled himself up and out of the sunken museum, onto the dust plains. The sand stung his sliced palm as he hit the ground, but at least he was out.

As he propelled himself out of the window, the remaining shards of glass ripping at his skin, he heard the thud of a massive foot, and his muscles seized up. He'd been so eager to get inside the ruin, he hadn't bothered to scout out the area, and didn't see the creature waiting just out of view.

He looked behind him to see the largest desertwalker he had ever seen—a reptilian beast, scaly skin loosely hanging in wrinkles around its body, two massive claws extending from the base of its neck, four pairs of legs. It pointed its long snout at Princeton, and he could see its nostrils were as big as dinner plates. The creature let its forked tongue fly out at him— it was a curious action, not an aggressive one, but the force was still enough to knock Princeton off his feet and tumbling into the dusts.

He picked himself up as the lizard lifted one clawed foot, lumbering toward him. It stopped short, giving a little whimper as something pulled it back. Only then did Princeton notice the leash. A rope tied around the beast's neck kept it from wandering any further.

Founders, he thought to himself, *they keep a pinchdragon as a pet? Who the hell are these people?*

As if on cue, he heard his pursuers emerging from the sunken building.

Okay time to go, he thought before turning around and sprinting into the night. He arrived back at camp *nearly* unharmed, and laden with extra food. He furtively slipped a few of his treasures into each scavenger's pack, hoping spreading the wealth would make his transgression less obvious. He removed some bandages from Columbia's pack and wrapped his sliced hand. He'd worry about whatever hit him in the back later. It still throbbed— maybe they hit him with something harder than a rock. What's harder than a rock though?

It didn't matter. He was tired from all the good deeds he did today. With the fruits of his labor safely stowed away, Princeton slid under his thin blanket and let out a relieved breath. Even though no one would know if his act of heroism, he still felt a bit of pride swell in his chest. *Dusts, I'm a good teammate*, he thought to himself, before instantly passing out.

CHAPTER FIFTEEN

The Remains

Boy, Harvard awoke to Skrack's booming voice in his mind.

"Yes?" he sat up, rubbing his eyes.

I have decided I will not kill you.

He stared up at the beast that now held him in the crook of its claw. "Oh. Um. I thought you'd already decided that?"

No. I was merely refraining from killing you because my Empress willed it. Now I have decided.

"Oh. Well. Um. Thank you?"

Let me be very clear, boy child: you are not strong. You are not brave. You are not fast. You are not particularly clever. You are only available.

"So do you still want me to—"

Yes, naturally we still require your aid. I'm just saying. Do not think you are more special than you are. Do not think you have been chosen by any force other than sheer chance.

"No, I mean, I definitely get that. Why would you choose me, right? I've got...I've got nothing to offer."

Exactly. You understand well.

"Yeah. A little too well, actually."

Good. We understand each other.

"Yes."

Excellent. Onward, then.

"Right," Harvard agreed uneasily. "Onward."

* * *

Harvard squinted, holding up a hand to shield his eyes. He could see heat radiating off Skrack's shell. The hulking creature was unaffected by the harshness of the desert. Not the heat, not the wind, nor the dust could leave so much as a scratch on—

Wait.

"Your injury," Harvard observed, pointing up at Skrack's shell.

Hm?

"The place where O'Neill shot you. It's already healed!"

Only the other day Harvard had pulled the harpoon from the chitin, leaving a gaping hole that poured sticky blue blood. Now the chitin had completely reformed, leaving in no indication that there had ever been a gash there.

Yes? This surprises you?

"Well...I mean it just happened..." Harvard blushed, feeling as though he'd asked a stupid question though he wasn't sure why.

It happened over a day ago.

"But it's completely healed!" Harvard marveled.

Humans are fragile beings of soft tissue and pliable bone. Your bodies betray you.

"So crabs just...heal that fast?" Harvard thought of Speedy, the injured crab whose legs had righted themselves so quickly Harvard wondered if it was even the same creature.

Yes. And the fact that you do not is further proof of your evolutionary inferiority.

"Huh," Harvard considered. "Yeah, I guess so. Humans are pretty inferior, aren't they?"

You...believe this?

"I mean, I don't think crabs are better than humans in every way, but I guess evolutionarily," he slowed a bit to get the unfamiliar word out, "crabs are better. I guess that's what O'Neill was studying." He frowned. "Or maybe not. Maybe it was all just a lie."

The research was no lie, The Empress confirmed. *And in truth, he was making great strides toward better understanding our capabilities.*

Skrack made a noise like the crab equivalent of an indignant harumph.

"You don't think humans should be able to heal just like crabs?" Harvard asked. "I mean, you said yourself that or fleshy bodies are what makes us inferior, but if we learned to be stronger, like through science and stuff—"

You cannot understand with your small human mind the secrets of the desertwalkers. No human can understand the secrets of the desertwalkers, and no human should seek them.

Skrack shuffled forward faster than Harvard could follow, putting an abrupt end to the conversation.

"I didn't mean to hurt his feelings," Harvard said to the Empress, who still rode in his shirt pocket.

Pay him no mind, she assured him. *He is a Guardian by nature. He guards. And that includes secrets.*

* * *

As the caravan of crabs and human trudged their way through the desert, a familiar shade of green caught Harvard's eye. All the Commission supplies were standard issues.

"That's a scavenger camp!" he said aloud, pointing out in the distance where he saw a scavenger's tent poking up over the horizon. "Can we go by?"

And why would we do something so foolish? Skrack asked, his voice dripping with condescension. *So that they can attack me, and harm the Empress? I think not.*

They may prove helpful, The Empress mused. *We are lacking in supplies for our human counterpart. It would save the hatchlings some scrounging to find human food for Harvard.*

Or they may prove hostile, Skrack retorted, *and kill him on sight.*

"Scavengers aren't like that!" Harvard laughed, though, admittedly, he'd never encountered any scavenger outside the Commission. He was warned that scavengers, once out in the dusts, become more protective of their own people. "The dusts changes people," Yale had said on Harvard's first day as a scavenger. But all of the scavengers he'd met back in Bastion seemed perfectly friendly. Surely being exposed to the elements couldn't change someone that drastically, could it?

You are more than capable of defending us, the Empress reasoned, *so it is worth the negligible risk. We will approach the camp in hopes of their generosity.*

Fine, Skrack said laconically, and pivoted his thick shell toward the camp.

"Scavengers are generally good people," Harvard piped up, feeling as though it was his responsibility to clear the besmirched name of his brethren. "We all have a sort of...group bond."

I'm sure that's why your crews tend to eliminate each other when there's limited resources, Skrack grumbled.

"What...what do you mean?" Harvard asked.

You do not live as long as I have, Skrack explained, *and remain ignorant to the hostile nature of mankind. I have seen scavengers much like you destroy each other over scraps out in the dusts.*

"Well, that's weird," Harvard said incredulously. "All the scavengers I know are really cool. They would never do stuff like that."

And you, Harvard, are well acquainted with all humankind? Then I suppose I must be mistaken despite my centuries upon the earth. All humans must be, as you say, "cool."

Harvard frowned. "Well, you don't have to be mean about it," he grumbled. "I'm just saying—"

The words caught in his throat. He surveyed the scene in front of him. They had reached the edge of the scavenger camp, but no friendly face came to greet them. The only thing that greeted them was the stench of decay. Sprawled outside the tent was a human form, partially buried by the dust that had blown over it, a gaping gash in their back. Little scuttlers gathered at the site of the wound, gorging themselves on the rotting flash.

And what do you think happened here, Harvard? Skrack asked the dumbstruck boy. *Too much kindness? Too much group bonding?*

"That...that's not...humans didn't do this!" Harvard stammered. "They were attacked by something. A desertwalker. Like *you*." He hadn't intended to wound, but the words fell out of him before he had a chance to stop himself. Skrack did not seem particularly wounded.

Seems unlike a desertwalker to leave its pretty rotting on the ground, wouldn't you say? And come to think of it, don't scavengers usually come in groups of four? Where are the others, Harvard? Where—

Skrack, The Empress' voice cut through, cold and commanding. *Stop this. We will gather what is useful to us and then we will leave this place. Any speculation serves no purpose. Harvard, search the tent and see if anything is of value to you.*

Harvard did not search the tent. He wobbled, paling, and felt as though he might vomit. He lifted a shaky hand to put his dustscarf over his nose to shield himself from the odor. The Empress watched him, then turned to have a silent exchange with her Guardians To Be.

I have reconsidered, The Empress declared. *Sit aside, Harvard. The hatchlings will bring you a selection of items they deem valuable.*

"Th...thank you, Empress," Harvard sputtered, willing his trembling legs to bear him away from the carnage. He lowered himself down in the sand, facing away from the site of the camp hoping that Skrack would not follow.

He wished he could scrub the whole scene from his mind, but it was indelibly plastered there, every time he closed his eyes. What *had* attacked that scavenger camp? Skrack had a point, for all his cynicism. A scuttler wouldn't have left fresh meat out like that. It would have brought the carcass to its den for the hatchlings to feast upon. But wouldn't a run-in with another scavenging team mean more bodies? Had it been a mutiny? If it were a mutiny then—

Harvard stood up abruptly, running back toward the skeleton of a camp. He braced himself for the sight of the gore, willing himself not to look at the bloody gash in the person's back, and dashed for the corpse. Holding his breath, he knelt and picked up one of the limp wrists. As he'd suspected, it was fastened with a leather band, complete with a gold plate screwed into it. He fumbled with the clasp until the thing came loose, then sprinted back to his safe haven a few yards over.

Once he had put some distance between himself and the camp, he examined his find.

Computers - Captain.

"Scavengers didn't do this," Harvard said definitively.

And what makes you so certain of that? Skrack lumbered over in his direction. Harvard held up the strip of leather.

"This is a captain's band," he explained. "All scavenging captains get one so they can recognize each other. When you come across a dead captain, you're supposed to take the band back to the Commission to prove that something happened to the crew."

And you're convinced that a group of killers would follow this rule?

"Yeah, actually. Because if you bring in a captain's band, no one will suspect you killed that captain. No one can prove anything out in the dusts. If you say you came across a dead body and there's no one to contradict you, then yeah, you came across a dead body. Bringing in a captain's band would be the best way to prove your innocence. And if it was a mutiny, the remaining crew *definitely* would have taken the band. That way they could prove to everyone else they had a new captain. This is, like, a really important custom for scavengers. They wouldn't just leave it."

Skrack was silent for a moment, apparently considering this.

I suppose humans are very attached to their customs.

Harvard nodded vigorously. "We are. I know it's possible a scavenger would break custom, but…I really don't think they would. Humans are attached to their customs, like you said. Like our brand names. I think something else came and attacked them and…didn't take one of the bodies, I guess. I don't know. Maybe it ate three of them and wasn't hungry anymore."

Skrack didn't seem convinced, but at least he was no longer taunting Harvard about the dead humans.

Perhaps, Harvard. Perhaps.

At this point the hatchlings gathered at his feet, presenting him with offerings. Most of it was garbage— a wrapper, a torn shirt, an empty canister— but a few articles caught Harvard's interest. As the Empress had predicted, there were a few packs of food that would keep him from starving during the journey, and some water skins. The hatchlings had also brought him a worn satchel, which was a welcome gift since he'd left his own pack in O'Neill's pod. He inspected it and found it contained a slender switchblade, which he decided to keep. The hatchlings brought him a hunting knife that reminded him of Yale's. He didn't like wielding a knife, but figured he should take it just in case.

The hatchlings also brought him a sandstaff, a scavenger weapon that he'd had a little training with back at the Commission. The things scared him too much. Sandstaffs were aluminum rods filled with rocks to make quick work of cracking scuttler shells. The idea sickened him.

He wondered if there'd been any full vapor canisters in the tent, or if the hatchlings didn't dare touch them. He didn't bother checking himself—it would be rude, he imagined, to carry canisters of scuttler vapor amongst scuttlers.

One of the hatchlings dropped a shard of glass by Harvard's foot, glinting in the setting sun.

"Hm," Harvard said aloud, stooping to pick it up. It was a piece of a mirror, a bit larger than his hand, edges jutting out at awkward angles.

As he examined the shard of glass, he froze, catching a glimpse of his own reflection. His skin was a shade darker than usual, thanks to sun exposure and the layer of dirt that coated his body. His freckles, which were once the defining feature of his face, were now hidden under the grime. He had cuts on his face he didn't remember receiving, and bits of dried blood speckled his forehead and cheeks. His hair, usually wild and bright red, was a rusty hue, matted and stringy.

The vanity of a human is a thing unparalleled, he heard Skrack's voice behind him.

"I'm not using the mirror," he said indignantly, whirling around to face the creature. "I just...I don't know. It could be useful." He took one of the scraps of cloth the hatchlings had brought him and carefully wrapped it around the shard, shielding himself from its jagged edges.

"It could be a good weapon," he justified, slipping it into the tattered pack. He wondered if that was the reason the scavenging team had had it in the first place. Scavengers had no use for a mirror—there's no point in fussing over your appearance before having it ruined by the wind and the dust, especially not when your only audience was a handful of desert creatures. But what a strange weapon to keep when you had knives, sandstaffs, and vapor. What was the point of keeping an improvised weapon when you've got far more effective ones at your disposal? Maybe one of the scavengers *was* using it as a mirror. Harvard shrugged and slung the pack over his shoulder.

"I'm ready," he announced, pointedly not looking back at what remained of the Computers. "Let's go."

Interlude Ten: Ronan

At first, Ronan didn't realize anything was amiss. The shop had a few patrons in today, so he figured he could slip in unnoticed and pocket a few carrots and tomatoes. It was only when he moved to leave that he noticed the door was locked. He glanced around and saw he was the last one in the store. How had everyone left so quickly? And why was he—

"Five thousand three hundred and sixty-eight," said a voice behind him. He whirled to see the grocer, hair wild, glasses slipping down his nose, stalking toward him with his arms crossed.

"Hm?" Ronan asked innocently.

"That's how much you owe."

"Sorry. I don't understand." He felt his stomach begin to churn, and suddenly his knees felt weak.

"No, you do. You've been coming here for years now because you thought I was an easy mark, and you thought I didn't notice. But I did notice, and I kept careful track."

He held up photographs. Ronan knew about photographs, but other than the occasional family portrait, he wasn't used to having one taken of him. How did this man, struggling to keep his business afloat, have a camera?

"I've got evidence and I've got records. At first, I let you get away with it, sure. Then I thought, alright, this kid has stolen a few hundred points of meat from me. And yes, I knew it was a kid. I said to myself, okay, let's let him think he's in the clear, then we'll get him. By the time I had my evidence, I figured, eh, let's wait. Cuz when a few hundred turns into a few thousand, it goes from being a petty crime to a quaking felony."

"You let me rob you for thousands of points?" Ronan asked, feeling himself start to tremble for the first time in a long, long while. "Why?"

"I knew once it got past a certain point, I could get it all back."

Ronan cocked his head, confused.

"Are you going to turn me in?"

The man stared at Ronan, dumbfounded.

"Why in the name of the Founders would I do that?" he asked. "You steal thousands of points. If you're wasting away in a Delian cell, you're not gonna be making up that money for me, now are you?"

"But...but how can I ever make that money back? I can't...no one would ever pay me that much. I'll be in debt to you forever."

"Oh, you'll be in debt forever, sure. Not to me, though."

"What?"

"I'll sell it."

"I don't understand!" Ronan cried, getting frantic.

"I'm going to *sell* your *debt*."

"Who would buy debt?"

"The biggest debt-buyer in Bastion."

He grabbed Ronan by the arms and pulled him toward the door. "C'mon," he said. "Move."

"Where?"

"I'm taking you to the Commission. And I'm gonna get my quake-scourged money."

Ronan felt like an idiot for not realizing it earlier. He was just as stupid as Kathy had always said he was, wasn't he? Letting Ronan steal vegetables that would probably never sell was an investment, and one that was about to pay off.

Kathy was right. He really couldn't handle a business. He couldn't even handle himself.

CHAPTER SIXTEEN

The Chocolates

"This isn't ours," Yale noticed almost immediately when they sifted through their pack the next morning. "Where the hell did this come from?" They lifted a packet of nuts.

Princeton shrugged. "I got it from the apartment building with the squid dude," he lied.

"No, you didn't," Yale responded matter-of-factly. "I took stock of everything we got on that dig. This wasn't in it."

"Well then I don't remember where it's from," Princeton said with what he believed to be a casual and nonchalant swagger, "but it's from somewhere."

Yale looked like they were going to protest, so Princeton continued, "Unless you think you prayed *so hard* that the Earth decided to *reward you* with a nice bag of nuts."

"Shut up," Yale snapped, throwing the nuts back in the pack. It made them bristle, but it worked. They didn't bring up the mystery food again, and they four set off into the sands.

"What's that on your back?" Columbia asked after they had been trekking along for a few hours.

"What?" Princeton's hand flew to the place where one of the other scavengers had struck him the previous night. The spot was still raw.

"Oh. That. I...um. I hurt it when we fell into that crevice. Like, in the pod. There was—"

"No, that's not what I mean." Columbia approached Princeton and put a hand on his back. Her fingers traced the edges of the injury, then he felt a sharp sting as she jerked her hand away.

"Dusts!" he shouted reflexively, "what did you—" he whirled on her, stopping himself mid-sentence. In her hand she held a slender metallic needle, Princeton's blood glistening on it in the desert sun.

"This was in your skin," Columbia said.

"Oh, I mean...it's probably nothing," Princeton said in a voice that indicated it was most definitely something.

"It just looks like a needle," Yale observed.

Columbia examined it closer.

"It's not," she determined. "There's something blinking on the end here. It's small, but I think it's some kind of...device?"

"Device for what?" Yale asked. Columbia ignored them. Her attention was focused on Princeton.

"And this was from the lab? You're sure?" she asked. Princeton felt himself begin to sweat.

"Yes," he lied.

Columbia pocketed it. "Maybe we can take it back with us to Bastion, see if anyone could identify it. Who knows? It might end up being useful."

"A blinking needle?" Yale asked skeptically. "It's probably just, like, a weird thermometer."

As the other two consulted, Princeton's mind was racing. *Those guys from the dig. They stuck me with something. I mean, that must have been on purpose, right? But like, what is it? Did they inject me with something? Is it a drug? Is it—*

He became aware of the approaching figures on the horizon. Perhaps if it were just another band of scavengers he wouldn't have been able to make them out, but he saw the unmistakable shape of a pinchdragon.

"Um, guys?" he squeaked, pointing into the distance.

They tracked *me? Why?*

"What the hell?" Yale said when they followed Princeton's gaze. "Is that a group of scavengers riding a desertwalker? How is that possible?"

"Maybe we should ask," Columbia suggested, "looks like they're coming our way. If they're friendly they might give us a ride."

"Or," Princeton countered, "maybe we shouldn't talk to them."

"They might need help," Columbia pointed out. "We can't just ignore them."

"Uhhhh yeah I think we can," Princeton said.

"Or they could help us," Yale proposed. "They could have extra food, canisters...we could add a few days to our search if we're lucky."

"I don't know about that, guys," Princeton laughed nervously.

"Princeton. What's wrong?" Columbia asked. It was less of a question and more of a command, the subtext being: *you know something. Spit it out.* Such urgency—and such authority—was a rare thing to see from Columbia, and it took Princeton aback.

"I just am getting...bad vibes from these guys," he explained unhelpfully. *They tried to kill me possibly I think,* he added internally.

"They've got a *pinchdragon*," Yale observed in awe.

"Which means—" Princeton started, meaning to finish sentence with: *they could be dangerous.*

"Which means they know how to tame desertwalkers. That's huge."

Princeton glanced toward the encroaching team of scavengers. They were closing in fast. He shifted nervously, which wasn't lost on Columbia.

"Princeton!" she repeated, and this time there was no disguising the edge in her voice. "What is happening?"

"Why would Princeton know—" Yale started, but when they turned to see Princeton and Columbia sharing a tense moment of eye contact, they stopped.

"What...is going on here?" they asked slowly.

"Can you guys just trust me? Please?" Princeton begged. His pursuers were almost up on them.

"I would like to trust you," Columbia crossed her arms, "but I'm getting the feeling that you're hiding something from us."

"Princeton," Yale asked, "are we in danger?"

"I—"

By the time Princeton started to speak, it was too late. The pinchdragon already towered over them. The front rider pulled on the reins, which were in fact thick ropes tied to the top half of the lizard's skull, and the creature gave a screech as it pulled up short, its thick claws skittering on the sand. Princeton swallowed when he saw just how big those claws were up close—each one was thicker and longer than a human arm, curved like a scythe.

The rider atop the lizard's head stayed put as one behind leapt off, producing a cloud of dust as they hit the sand.

Yale glanced back at their team. Princeton shook his head. Yale nodded an acknowledgement.

"We are going to discuss this," they hissed, taking the tone of a peeved parent, "but not now. First, we figure out what this is about."

They turned back to the rider—the boy Princeton knew as Snickers. Now that he saw him in the light, Snickers was a muscular guy, his head topped with shaggy dark hair that desperately needed a trim.

"We're the Ivies," Yale announced, displaying their captain's band. Snickers reached into his bag. Yale continued. "We—"

Snickers pulled out a gun.

Princeton seen them on occasion if he was unlucky enough to stumble across a Delian Group officer. But he had never seen one in the hands of one his age, and certainly never had one pointed at him. All three of them tensed, instinctively putting up their hands, as the captain leveled the barrel at them.

"On your knees. The three of you. Now."

Dumbstruck, Yale did as commanded, so Columbia and Princeton followed suit.

"Your bags. Toss them over."

Yale removed their pack from their shoulders and tossed it to Snickers. Again, Columbia and Princeton mirrored them.

"Can we go now?" Yale asked. Snickers only laughed.

"Your wrists," he commanded.

"What?" Yale asked.

"Give me your wrists," he said, producing a length of black cord from his satchel. Yale recoiled.

"What the hell is this?" they asked. "You have our shit. Leave us alone."

"We don't care about your shit," Snickers sneered, kicking Columbia's pack aside. "Now give me your quaking wrists. All of you."

"What do you want with us?" Yale demanded.

"You'll find out, okay?" Snickers handed the cord off to Twix as he cocked the gun. "Now I'm getting impatient."

"You're not going to *take my crew prisoner*," Yale growled.

Snickers bent down where Yale was kneeling, wearing a smug grin, and in the same patronizing voice one would speak to a hurt child he whispered, "Yes, I am."

What happened next was so quick that Princeton could hardly process it. Yale jerked their shoulder back and their sledgehammer fell from its holster. They caught it right below the head and jabbed it into Snickers' stomach. He staggered back with a grunt, discharging the gun. Princeton heard Columbia scream behind him. That pulled him out of his daze. He leapt forward, taking Snickers by surprise and knocking the gun into the sand below. As someone's hands closed around his arms, pulling him away from the captain, he planted one good kick on the gun, sending it hurtling in the air and out of anyone's reach. *At least that's one thing taken care of*, he thought as he something heavy slam into his ribs.

* * *

By the time Yale got to their feet, Princeton was already engaged with a scavenger just a few feet away, a girl wielding a sandstaff glimmering in the desert sunlight. Once the other captain straightened, he lost no time in loosing his hammer as well, swinging it up to catch Yale under the jaw. They parried with their own hammer instinctively, and the handles clashed with a discordant clang. Holding the handle with one hand and the head with the other, Yale jerked their hammer back, hoping to yank the other captains' hammer out of his hands, or at the very least destabilize him. Instead, he thrust his forward, catching Yale in the shoulder. It wasn't a hard blow, but it had enough force behind it that they grunted and stumbled backward, letting go of the hammerhead and letting it swing behind them.

Yale had always known there was a possibility they'd have a confrontation with other scavengers out in the dusts, but it had never actually happened. Until this point, the captain's hammer was only for smashing in windows or breaking down doors. The only enemies they ever came across in the desert were scuttlers, and those were easily disposed of with vapor, or, if they weren't, your next best hope of survival was to flee and pray to the Earth that you run fast enough. Their next attack was clumsy and easily pushed aside by the other's expert block. Again, the hammers met with a metallic ring and fell away again.

Maybe, Yale thought as they circled the other captain warily, *now is the time to run away.* After all, that strategy had always served the Ivies well in the past. Snickers lunged forward, making it clear that wasn't an option.

* * *

Columbia was just about useless in a fight. She also knew this wasn't going to stop her from laying down her life to help Yale. If she could just find some way to be helpful without being beaten down immediately. She scanned the scene as she pulled herself to her feet. The two captains dueling, Princeton grappling with the girl holding the black cord who wielded a sandstaff—those things were dangerous, Columbia knew. One good crack from a sandstaff could easily shatter bone. There were two more of them still lurking by the pinchdragon. The smaller one jumped into action, leaping for Princeton. The other, a meek looking girl with cracked glasses, hung back. This was the one drew Columbia's attention.

Columbia lurked around the periphery of the fray, trying to get a closer look at the fourth scavenger. She was young, standing with her hands clasped against her chest—no, she held *something* against her chest, and she cowered behind the pinchdragon's massive haunches, watching her compatriots attempt to bring Princeton down.

Columbia was not a fighter. She had never attacked anyone in her life. She never so much as tripped anyone, let alone engaged them in battle. She took a deep breath, and she leapt on the girl from behind, hands outstretched to grab whatever she was holding.

* * *

Princeton was pretty sure he could handle a single scavenger, even if she was trying to hit him with a metal pole. Well, trying and succeeding *occasionally,* but he was fast enough she only managed to land a couple glancing blows. It'd leave some bruises, sure, but overall, he'd say he was winning. Or, at least, not losing.

That was, until the little girl jumped onto his back.

"Stop that!" he shouted, as if that would stop her from wrapping her legs around him and sticking her fingers in his eyes. Stumbling blindly, something hard jabbed him in the stomach and knocked him to the ground.

* * *

He's done this before, Yale observed as they continued to block the other captain's swings with their hammer. He raised his hammer above his head, and Yale prepared for a heavy blow. Instead, he went low and hooked the hammerhead around Yale's boot, pulling, pulling their feet out from under them. They landed heavily on their back, air knocked from their lungs. Before they could scramble to their feet, he planted a booted foot on Yale's stomach, and they gave a pained grunt. He bent down and yanked at the leather strap on their wrist, reading the inscription.

"Listen up, Ivies!" he shouted, dropping Yale's arm. Princeton and Columbia froze where they were—Princeton entangled with the two girls who were fighting to keep him from running off, Columbia wresting something from the hands of the wide-eyed fourth scavenger.

"This is how it's gonna go," the captain announced, hefting his sledgehammer over his shoulder. "You're gonna come with us willingly, or you're gonna watch me bash in your captain's skull."

* * *

The Chocolates, as Yale soon learned they were named, lined the Ivies up on their knees as they bound their hands. The girl called Twix had since retrieved the gun, so any hope of fleeing unharmed was dashed.

"Thanks buddy," the captain named Snickers patted Princeton on the shoulder. "You were a big help."

"What," Yale hissed, turning to Princeton, "was that supposed to mean?"

Snickers grinned. "I'm sure your friend here can tell you."

Twix, the girl with the sandstaff who seemed to be second in command, ordered the Ivies to climb onto the back of the pinchdragon, behind the seats the Chocolates had rigged to it.

"But like, do we get seats?" Princeton asked.

"No."

"What about seat *belts*?"

"You get *ropes*. So don't try and jump off, unless you like the idea of getting dragged through the sand."

It was far from comfortable, being fastened to the back of a giant lizard as it lumbered across the desert, but Yale had to admit they were at least relieved they weren't dead. They'd heard rumors of scavenging crews who'd gone crazy in the desert and started killing each other wantonly. They worried briefly that was the kind of crew they'd stumbled into. At least there was *some* reason these scavengers wanted to keep them alive, though what that reason was they couldn't fathom.

"Princeton," Yale seethed, "what did you do?"

"I didn't do anything!" Princeton retorted.

"He did!" the feisty little girl, Milky Way, chimed in. "He found our secret hideout! I said we should kill him but Twix said not to because he would lead us to more. And he did! You guys!"

"Milky, shut up!" Snickers groaned from the front of the lizard.

"Princeton!" Yale snapped.

"Okay, okay," Princeton admitted, "I went rogue a little..."

"You can't go rogue 'a little'! You disobeyed direct orders!"

"Yeah, cuz you're fucking insane, Yale!" Princeton whirled around to face them. "You wanted us to go three more days in the dusts when we were already running out of everything! We were gonna die!"

"We had an agreement!" Yale reminded him.

"You guys weren't listening to me!" Princeton defended. "What was I supposed to do?"

"Not that!"

"You have *lost your mind*!" Princeton punctuated each word with a gesture of his bound hands. "Either that or you're an *idiot*."

"Oh. *Oh*!" Yale feigned offense. "You think I'm stupid? Are you calling me stupid?"

"I mean, yeah, kinda! Face it, between the four of us, Columbia is the only one who ever knows what the hell is going on half the time."

You have allowed the fact that you are friends with two brilliant girls to convince you that you, too, are brilliant, they remembered one of their teachers saying. *You are not.*

"That's not fair!" Yale protested. "I've been keeping this crew from getting killed for years!"

"Oh, wow, good for you, making sure we don't die," Princeton drew out the words, loading them each with spoonfuls of sarcasm. "What a big accomplishment that is!"

"It is, actually!" Yale countered. "Not like you would know."

"Could you guys shut up, please?" Twix asked from her seat on the saddle. "You're, like, by far the most annoying prisoners we've had yet."

"Oh, I'm so sorry that we annoy you," Yale shot back. "Admittedly, we were pretty annoyed that you took us prisoner at gunpoint."

Twix shrugged.

* * *

"You guys are weird," Twix observed to Columbia. "Usually by this point they're begging us to let them go."

"Would it work if we begged you to let us go?" Columbia asked.

"Nope."

"Then it doesn't seem like there's a point, is there?" She hazarded a glance back at her crew mates, whose squabble had escalated to childish shoving. If they weren't both tied to the lizard's torso, they would be in danger of knocking each other off.

"I don't think any of us would beg. I don't think it would be in character," Columbia sighed.

Twix shrugged again and turned back around.

If they were really thinking, they would have tied our hands behind *our backs*, Columbia thought. *I guess they're banking on the fact that we're too scared of them to try anything. They're right—I'm definitely not going to risk getting the other two hurt. But still...*

She leaned forward, toward the saddle where the Chocolates sat. In front of her was the girl she'd wrestled with—Mars, she was pretty certain—and in the back pocket of her worn jeans was the device that she'd clutched to her chest.

Everyone knows not to keep something important in your back pocket, Columbia thought. Then again, not everyone had grown up in Lower Bastion. She waited for the pinchdragon to come across particularly rough terrain and feigned falling forward as the creature bumped underneath her. She extended her hand and brushed against the girl's pants, knocking the device out of it and into her outstretched palm.

"Hey!" the girl whirled around, and Columbia feared she had been caught. "Watch it!" she reprimanded, though her youth made what should have been a command more of a petulant complaint.

"Sorry," Columbia murmured in the meek voice she had practiced all too much growing up. "I've never ridden one of these before. It's hard to sit up straight."

This seemed to soften Mars' frustration.

"Just hold onto the rope or something. It's kind of annoying when you keep bumping against my ass."

It's kind of annoying you forced us to ride this stupid thing, she thought, and pointedly did not say. Yale, she knew, would not have had such restraint, but she prided herself on the things she did *not* speak aloud.

Though she didn't want to give herself away, she hazarded a glance at the item she had stolen before deftly slipping it into her boot. It was flat and circular, with a needle like a compass. However, it didn't have the telltale directional markings a compass would have. It simply pointed forward. Columbia surreptitiously slid the little circle into her sock as the creature scuttled forward. Though the Chocolates were likely not taking them anywhere pleasant, she could take comfort in the fact she had taken something from them. Something, she imagined, quite important.

It was a few hours before Snickers yanked on the pinchdragon's ropes, and the creature skidded to a halt.

"We're here," Snickers said gruffly.

Columbia lifted her head to see where the Chocolates had steered them. She felt the sinking sensation of recognition.

Behind her, she heard Yale say, "Oh *dusts*."

CHAPTER SEVENTEEN

The Bath

I imagine you might want to bathe, the Empress addressed Harvard on their second day trudging through the desert. *It is my understanding that most mammals like to bathe regularly, and humans are not equipped to do this without the aid of an external water source.*

The possibility was tantalizing to Harvard. He felt he had accumulated a new layer of skin of dust and sweat since they first left the den. He would give anything for the sweet sensation of being able to scrub that filth away, especially in some cool water—

Impossible, Skrack interrupted. *Finding such a water source would take us too far off course.*

But without proper hygiene, the human is liable to contract diseases.

He is welcome to contract diseases at his leisure once the mission is complete.

If he contracts any diseases prior to the completion of the mission, we will find ourselves short a human.

Alright. Fine.

Skrack turned his hulking body toward Harvard.

How do you bathe?

Harvard found himself flushing.

"Well...um...I mean, normally, it involves a lot of water and soap. Water's kinda scarce around here so, um, when we go out for a dig we usually bring these special sanitizing wipes, but, uh, I don't have any..."

Then we will find water. Maybe soap as well.

"I mean...won't that be hard?"

There were occasional pools of water scattered around the dusts, but they were few and far between. The Ivies had only stumbled across a water source once in their time digging together. It was one of the few joyful memories he had as a scavenger. They were all so thrilled to find the small pool they'd leapt in, fully clothed, just to experience that rare sensation of being completely submerged. They'd played like children, splashing and dunking each other under the surface. Sometimes water in Bastion felt almost as rare as it was in the desert—water from the showers at the Commission came out in a dribble. Harvard hadn't actually had a proper *bath* since he'd lived at Bell Manor.

Keep in mind the Guardians To Be know this desert well, and they know its secrets. They will guide us to the nearest water source. It is no difficult task.

"Oh. Then, um, yes please! That would be great."

Skrack gave a disgruntled huff, or, at least, a sort of grating noise.

You must be quick, he warned.

"Yes. Of course."

Follow me, Skrack lumbered away, following the hatchlings.

* * *

The hatchlings gathered at the edge of a glistening pool, just underneath a rocky overhang. It was shadowy enough a passing scavenger likely wouldn't have even noticed.

Harvard removed a shoe and dunked his toe in the water. It was enticingly cold. He looked up to see Skrack still standing behind him.

"Are you...gonna watch?"

I find it prudent to ensure that you do not slip and fall unconscious, accidentally killing yourself, as humans are wont to do. Since your survival is our utmost priority at this moment, I think it wise to ensure this does not occur.

Harvard found he didn't mind this so much. It wasn't like having another person watch him bathe—just a megacrab protecting him. This didn't really feel invasive, or even uncomfortable. In fact, if Skrack hadn't made his clear hatred of Harvard known, it would almost be sweet. So Harvard shrugged and peeled off his dirty clothes, which were now all caked with grime. He didn't relish the idea of putting them back on, but to his delight he noticed the hatchlings had dragged a new shirt and pants to the edge of the pool for him. The delight was short lived, as wondered where the clothing had come from. He comforted himself by imagining that they were simply stolen from a scavenger's pack.

As Harvard descended into the pool, he turned to Skrack's black marble eyes still watching him.

Fascinating, the creature mused.

"What?" Harvard asked.

You were born a female.

Harvard blinked. This certainly wasn't news to him, but it was a fact he rarely thought about these days. He wondered why Skrack felt the need to verbalize it. Did this come as a shock to him? Was it a problem?

"Um, yeah," was all Harvard could think to say as he started to wipe the layers of dirt and sweat from his body.

So was I.

Harvard stopped his scrubbing and looked up at the crab towering over him.

"Really?" he asked, then immediately felt stupid about it. Had he given it a moment's thought, he would have been able to piece this together. Skrack had hatchlings, after all. Of course he must be a female crab. It simply never occurred to wonder about the role of sex and gender in crab society, so he'd never really examined the issue further.

I was not aware that humans were capable of separating the psychological from the physical, Skrack continued. *I did not believe that human society was...advanced enough to understand that dichotomy.*

Harvard did not want to let on how little he comprehended what Skrack was saying.

"Yeah, we're advanced enough for that," he said, again feeling oddly defensive about human society.

Skrack watched him silently for a moment, though Harvard had a feeling he wasn't watching him at all, simply contemplating.

This gives me...much to consider, Skrack said, then was quiet.

After the brief exchange, Harvard focused on the simple pleasure of washing his hair, feeling the cool water on his face, wiggling his toes in the wet sand. He even giggled a bit as the tickle of the water lapping against his stomach. A few of the hatchlings joined him in the water, paddling delicately around him as though they, too, wanted to guard him from harm. He laughed as he watched the chitin flaps churning the water like little wings.

"You look like a butterfly, Speedy!" he cupped the creature in his hands.

Human, Skrack boomed abruptly. *Clothe yourself. Now.*

Harvard figured Skrack had gotten bored watching him splash around in the pool, so he waded to the edge of the pool at a leisurely pace.

Now! Skrack repeated, and this time Harvard could hear that there was urgency in his voice. He scrambled over to the small heap of clothing the hatchlings had brought him, fumbling to find armholes.

"What's wrong?" he asked, as he pulled the strap of his goggles over his still-soaking red hair.

A predator approaches.

At the very thought, Harvard began to shake. He whirled around, searching for the source of Skrack's sudden wariness. However, the dust plains looked barren. The wind was low today, so there was very little airborne dust obscuring Harvard's view. He could see for miles in every direction, and there didn't appear to be any enemies in sight. He listened for the telltale clomping of heavy legs, but he heard nothing but the gentle whisper of the wind, and the lapping of the water in the pool.

"I don't see any—"

An explosive cracking sounded behind him, and he instinctively dove to the ground, covering his head with his hands. He felt his back pelted with sand and stone, and heard a roaring, unlike any sound he'd ever heard a desertwalker make. Hunched over, he used trembling hands to pull his goggles over his eyes, shielding them from the debris that rained down on him. He flipped over on his back to get a better look, only to find something big and gray hurtling down at him. He rolled out of the way, narrowly avoiding being crushed as the thing slammed into the ground, kicking up a cloud of dust. Harvard fastened his dust scarf to avoid choking, eyeing the thing for the fraction of a second it was on the ground.

It looked a bit like a massive ridged gray bullet, rounded on one end, and the other end—Harvard followed the other end to see this was only the tail of a long, long creature, the front of which was currently dealing with Skrack's claws in its face.

The tail lifted again, ready to strike, but this time Harvard was ready for it. He was on his feet before it could come down on him, and he sprang out of the way. This time, however, it did not rise. Instead, it barreled toward him, knocking him off his feet and leaving him sprawling in the dust.

Scrambling to his feet, Harvard finally had enough distance to get a good look at the thing. It was big, five times the length of Skrack at least and twice as tall. Its ringed serpentine body slithered around the crab, aided by thousands of tiny legs. Harvard could now see the hole where the thing had erupted from its subterranean tunnel, able to approach nearly undetected.

If there was one thing Harvard's brain was good for, it was remembering images. As soon as he saw the thing in its entirety, he placed it based on the notes that O'Neill had shown him: this was a netherworm.

But what had the *notes* beneath it said? They'd been in that strange script Harvard couldn't understand. He turned to run, putting distance between him and the creature, but his path was blocked by the thing's tail crashing down in front of him.

Dual-brained. Harvard remembered O'Neill saying that. While the front half of the worm was focused on warding off Skrack, the back half had a mind of its own—literally—and it was intent on killing *him*. This worm did not care for the quest of the Empress of the Southwest Plains. This worm saw prey.

The tail slid toward him like a tidal wave, fencing him in, forcing him to run *toward* the fray.

"Skrack!" he cried out. Using one claw to wallop the worm's head—which was now bearing its circular mouth and throat full of churning teeth—Skrack pivoted, reaching down the other claw to grasp Harvard. For a brief moment Harvard was afraid the pressure of Skrack's grip would crush his rib cage, but Skrack stopped on the threshold between a *firm* grasp and a *deadly* one. He hoisted Harvard up to keep him out of the way of the thrashing tail, but this left him with only one claw to defend himself. The worm headbutted him and he stumbled backward, only to be thumped by the tail, which left him skittered across the sand, Harvard flopping all the while in his claw.

"Put me down!" Harvard screamed, his head aching from being whipped around so violently.

You will be crushed.

"Not on the ground!" Harvard explained, "Put me down on your back!"

You will not ride me, human.

"I'm not asking to ride you. I'm only asking you to carry me."

That is demeaning.

"I don't want to demean you, Skrack. I just want us both to not die!"

It wasn't as elegantly put as he'd hoped, but Skrack obliged. He dropped Harvard onto his shell so abruptly Harvard yelped and began to slide down the creature's smooth back. He scrambled up to wrap his fingers around the front edge of the shell, gripping tightly as the crab charged the worm again, both claws at the ready.

Skrack jabbed at the base of the worm's mouth, a move that resembled an uppercut. Focused on the worm's front, Skrack paid no mind to the rogue tail. Harvard saw it careening toward them with enough power to knock Skrack flat on his back, leaving him defenseless.

"Tail to the right!" he shouted.

Without turning to the side, Skrack lifted a sharp leg to the right, allowing the tail to impale itself on it. The worm gave an unholy cry and dove toward Harvard in an attempt to scoop him up in its toothy mouth. Harvard looked up at that circular mouth, like the tip of a funnel, but deep within it he could see the gnashing of its internal teeth, hungry for meat. He gripped the edge of Skrack's shell, paralyzed, as the mouth came bearing down on him. Then the worm's tongue lashed out at him. It was silvery and sharp, like a fluid sword, and it was aimed directly at his chest. Just as the tongue was about to skewer him, a claw gripped him by the waist and yanked him out of the way, placing him right at the edge of Skrack's shell. The tongue only sliced into his right arm, eliciting a yelp from Harvard as it slid across his skin like a cold knife.

As the worm's head shot over the crab's shell, Skrack pressed his claw into the worm's flesh and pinched hard. The worm cried out in pain, ripping its head away, and as Harvard clambered back onto Skrack's shell, he could see a sizable portion of worm skin still remained in Skrack's closed claw. Green bile spewed from the hole below the worm's mouth, and writhed in agony, screeching.

Skrack dropped the worm gore and backed away, giving the worm a wide enough berth to make its retreat, slithering back into its hole, its cries of agony fading away as it descended back into the depths.

Then there was silence. Harvard clung onto the edge of Skrack's shell as though it were the only thing keeping him alive. He was trembling so violently he could barely keep his grip. He wasn't sure if he wanted to cry, puke, or pass out.

A claw reached up behind him, gently plucked him from off Skrack's shell and set him daintily on the ground. Harvard's legs were too wobbly for him to get his footing and his knees buckled. Before he could hit the ground, the opposite claw came up to catch him. Harvard expected some kind of admonishment from the creature, a tirade about how his weak human form had almost gotten them killed, or about how he was a burden to all of crab kind.

Instead, Skrack said, *You did well, human.*

"I...I did?" Harvard stammered, allowing himself to be lowered to the ground. He settled into the crux of Skrack's leg, just the way he'd slept. This time, Skrack showed no reluctance to let him lie there. In fact, he laid his other claw comfortingly across Harvard's body, like a weighted blanket.

You did. You protected me from harm. For that, I thank you. After a moment of contemplation, he added, *You were correct. Upon my shell is the safest perch for you, come danger. It was a wise choice and I should have known sooner it was a prudent move.*

"Oh," Harvard felt his cheeks flush. "Um, thank you. I...thanks."

You tremble violently.

"Yeah, I...um...I have a disorder. It makes me shake when I get scared."

But the danger is gone.

"It, um, it doesn't work like that," Harvard laughed nervously. The claw that covered him pressed into him a little harder, forcing him to relax muscles that he hadn't realized he was holding so tense. He allowed his legs to go limp, and with a sigh he released the tension he was holding in his shoulders. The quivering did not cease, but it subsided somewhat, hindered by the weight of the claw.

No more danger will come to you this day, Skrack said as hatchlings began to crawl over the edge of his claw and fuss over the cut on Harvard's arm.

Allow yourself to rest.

Harvard leaned his head back against the chitin that held him, and without meaning to, he fell into a dark, dreamless sleep.

Interlude Eleven: Chavi

Shortly before the end of their fourth year, Chaverim Chakrabarti was expelled from the Bastion Academy of Arts and Sciences, following an "irreconcilable incident." That, at least, was what the official report said. The official report also said Rivka Chakrabarti's employment at the academy would be terminated as a result. It was immediately after their expulsion that Chavi informed their mother of their intentions to make up for the sudden and immediate loss of income.

Rivka Chakrabarti's Lower Bastion basement apartment was barely big enough to house two people. For the past four years, Chavi had been living in the dorms at the Academy, only staying in their old room on weekends. Now, however, they had no place else to live.

But Chavi was not a child anymore. They couldn't possibly live with their mother, especially when their mother's only source of income was gone. Thanks to them.

"I didn't...I didn't mean for this to happen," they sat at the kitchen table, staring down at their clasped hands. "I didn't know this would happen. I mean, if I knew you would lose your job..."

"You still would have done it," Rivka nodded. Chavi stared at her. She gave a fond chuckle when she saw her child's disbelief.

"I know you," she said, "and I know that you want the kids at school to think you're cool and tough and that you don't care about anything. But I know you care, especially about Jasmine. I know the child I raised."

"So...you think I did the right thing?" they asked hopefully.

"I didn't say that," Rivka held up a finger, "but I can't imagine you doing anything else."

Chavi sighed, stood, and made their way to their room so they could begin packing. They didn't have many possessions, after all, so it shouldn't take too long.

"You don't have to do this," Rivka said as she moved to stand in the doorway.

"I do."

Chavi could not lie to their mother. At school, they were tough—no, more than tough. The Chavi the students of Bastion Academy knew was invincible. Fearless. Carefree. Only Rivka Chakrabarti knew they still awoke in the early hours of the morning gasping for breath, petrified by nightmares of being trapped beneath the earth's surface, consumed by dust. Only their mother knew how scared they truly were.

"I think, in a way...I think perhaps the reason I've been so afraid of the dusts is that somewhere, deep down, I always knew I was going to end up there. That I was just...postponing the inevitable."

Chavi could see their mother's lips grow tense as she fought to hold back tears.

"Don't say that," she whispered.

"No, I think it's better this way," they said. "If I look at it this way, then...then it's like I'm finally facing the things that's always haunted me? I don't know, maybe it sounds stupid...but it's easier for me to do this if I pretend—" they cut themself off, looking down at the backpack they gripped in their hands.

"If I pretend like I never had a choice."

Rivka nodded, losing the battle against her tears. She pulled her child into a tight embrace. Chavi gently pressed their lips to her forehead.

"Will you be careful?" she rasped.

"Of course."

"Will you come back?"

Chavi smiled sadly, pressing their face into their mother's dark hair streaked with grey.

"Of course."

CHAPTER EIGHTEEN

Sandheads

Columbia registered exactly where they were within a matter of seconds. It was not the billowing white tents that clued her in, nor the rows of pews lined up meticulously in the sand. It was the black robes, hooding pale faces. The Congregation of the Earth's Mercy. Sandheads.

Columbia puzzled over this as she was roughly pushed off the pinchdragon and onto her knees, Princeton to her left, Yale to her right. Sandheads famously hated scavengers. So why were they being brought here?

"Ten vapor canisters," Snickers commanded. "Ten water skins. Five oxygen tanks. Twenty sets of dried rations. That's our price."

This only deepened Columbia's confusion. They hadn't just been brought to the Congregation. They were being *sold* to it. But why? Labor? She didn't see any indentured scavengers working around the camp. This didn't make any sense. But the Chocolates commanded their due as though this were a time-honored practice.

A robed man came to the front of the crowd of acolytes, and a silver chain with a little globe on the end signaled his station: a priest. His eyes were hidden under his black hood, but Columbia could tell he was surveying them. The bottom half of his face creased with dismay.

"There are only three," he observed.

"This crew is three," Snickers confirmed.

"There are always four."

There are always four. So she was right. They were not the first crew of scavengers the Chocolates had sold to the Congregation. But *why?*

"Not *always*," Snickers snapped, and she could tell he was growing impatient.

"Five vapor canisters," the priest counters, "Ten water skins. Ten sets of rations. *One* oxygen tank."

Snickers turned to Twix. She nodded curtly.

"Fine."

The priest produced a pen and paper from the folds of his robe, scribbled something, and held it out for Snickers to take. He snatched it eagerly, pocketing it.

A receipt?

The priest nodded to two robed acolytes, and they rushed off to a tent at the edge of the camp. Snickers stalked over to Yale, grabbed them at the bicep, and thrust them forward.

"This one's the captain," he said. Columbia watched Yale's head turn slowly up to face the scavenger, and her stomach bottomed out. For a brief moment, she was almost thankful that Yale's hands were bound, because she knew that unrestrained, they would not hesitate to go for the throat. She had seen that rage on their face before. She had seen it twice.

Two acolytes came forward and grabbed Yale's arms on either side, dragging them to their feet. A third appeared in front of them, a white belt tied around his robe. He nodded to the first two indicating they should follow, and guided the two sandheads toting Yale deeper into the camp. Yale was not corralled so easily.

"Don't *touch* me!" they shouted, yanking their shoulder so violently that one of the acolytes stumbled, but did not let go.

The white-belted acolyte whipped around. He pulled his fist back and struck Yale with surprising force. Columbia yelped in horror as Yale's head whipped to the side. A few dots of blood spattered the sand. Yale's body sagged. Columbia lunged forward, but Twix grabbed her gruffly by the shoulder and shoved her down. As Columbia and Princeton were roughly guided to their own tent, all they could do was watch as the acolytes dragged Yale's inert body away, their feet dragging in the sand.

* * *

Columbia and Princeton were seated on the bare ground, back-to-back, bound to the central pole of the tent. Columbia eyed the wood up and down—scratch marks, teeth marks, dried blood. They were not the first people to be tethered here, and the previous prisoners had fought tooth and nail to escape.

"And what if I have to piss?" Princeton was asking the acolytes peevishly. "What am I supposed to do, hm?"

This was answered with a swift kick in the ribs. He wheezed, doubling over, which made the ropes tighten on Columbia's end.

"What are you doing with Yale?" she demanded of another one of the acolytes. He lifted a pale hand to silence her.

"The fate of your captain does not concern you," he said, his eyes hidden under the brim of his hood. "Concern yourself with your own."

"It very much *does* concern me," she shot back. "Tell me now or I'll—I'll bite at your legs!" It was a weak threat, and she knew it. She was not accustomed to making threats.

The acolyte was not amused by her feeble attempt at intimidation.

"The preparations for the ritual have already begun," he said.

"What does that mean?" she demanded.

"Yeah!" she heard Princeton chime in from behind her, who had since recovered from the kick, "what does that mean?"

"It *means*," the acolyte snarled, "you will never see your captain again."

* * *

Yale awoke with a mouth like rust. They could feel the train of blood where it had dried dripping from their nose onto their lips. They moved to examine their injury only to find that their arms were restrained. They were tied to a wooden chair, thick layers of rope pinning their arms and holding their back flush with the chair. They were full of questions, but it all really boiled down to one.

"What the hell is this about?" they said aloud.

"This," said a voice, "is about penitence."

Yale's head swung up to see the priest, the globe pendant swinging from his neck, standing at the tent's entrance. They turned to survey the rest of the tent—two other acolytes, pale faces similarly shielded, stood on either side of them, giving the appearance of two black stone pillars.

"Look," Yale said, "I'm not super religious, if I'm being honest. I don't really feel the need—"

"You don't get a say," the priest snapped. He took a step toward Yale, his black robes billowing.

"Where is your fourth?" he demanded.

Yale bit the inside of their cheek, contemplating. If they knew Harvard was still out there, would they go after him? What did the sandheads even *want* them for, anyway?

"There is no fourth," Yale lied. "Just the three of us."

"There is always a fourth," the priest insisted, just as he had before.

Yale shrugged as best they could with their bonds.

"I don't know what to tell you," they said with attempted casualness. They were finding it difficult to be casual given the circumstances.

The priest stepped closer, and Yale flinched back, thinking they'd be struck again. Instead, the priest got down on one knee so he was level with Yale, and while his hood still shielded his eyes, Yale could see a pale mouth full of crooked teeth.

"The ritual only proceeds," he said, "if we return all four."

Ritual? Return? What in the name of the Founders was he talking about?

"I don't understand," Yale said with a nervous laugh, and they hated how small they sounded.

The priest put one hand on either arm of the chair and jerked it forward. Up this close, Yale caught the scent of the man's robes. They smelled like...rot.

"If we do not have your fourth," he hissed, "then we will find them."

Now Yale's heart really started racing. Would they really do that? Search the dusts for Harvard, so that they could do their "ritual?" And what would they do to him once they found him? Dusts, what were they going to do to *them*? In their moment of fear for Harvard, they'd forgotten they were the one tied to the chair facing down the robed priest.

"He's dead," they lied, casting their eyes down for fear their face would betray them. They heard rustling fabric as the priest stood.

"Good," he said. "That is acceptable for the ritual to proceed." He nodded to the acolytes at the perimeter of the room, and they drew closer. Yale suddenly had the sense that the tent was slowly constricting.

"Do you regret your transgressions against the Earth?" he asked.

"What, you mean...you mean scavenging?"

"Yes."

"You're asking me if I regret being a scavenger?" They glanced at acolytes that flanked them, searching for a hint as to what they were supposed to say. They priest snapped his fingers in front of their eyes.

"Answer!" he demanded.

"I...I mean, it's not like I had any other choice," Yale sputtered the best non-answer they could manage.

"Do you regret it?" he persisted.

"There was nothing else for me to do!"

The priest sighed heavily, his face creasing in what looked like genuine disappointment.

"You have rejected your last opportunity to repent. You have lived in sin, so you will die in sin."

"Repent?" Yale asked. "Wh...what are you talking about? Just let us go!" They struggled against their bonds in vain.

The priest shook his head. "It is too late. The ritual has already begun."

"What ritual?"

The priest did not answer. Instead, he nodded to one of the other acolytes, who disappeared from Yale's view and reappeared a moment later with a steaming stone cup. The acolyte handed it to the priest.

"Drink this," the priest commanded as he held the cup out to Yale. Yale could smell the steam rising from the cup—like lavender and honey. They knew that scent. It was the same stuff O'Neill had used to knock Harvard out when he was in pain.

"No," Yale said.

"Drink it," the priest repeated.

Yale spit in his face.

All at once, three acolytes converged on them. Two on either side to hold them in place, and one behind them to tilt back their head and pinch their nose, forcing them to open their mouth. The priest grabbed their jaw and yanked it open, eliciting a pained cry. He poured the steaming liquid into Yale's mouth, allowing some to dribble down their neck. Then he pushed their jaw shut and clasped his hand over their mouth, forcing them to swallow.

Having lost the fight, Yale swallowed obediently, and they were released. They gasped for air as one of the acolytes wiped some of the excess tea from their face.

"What...what are you going to do to me?" Yale asked, their body already heavy with the soporific effects of the concoction.

The priest grinned.

"Holy matters are of no concern to a heretic," he said through a tight smile.

"Tell me," Yale struggled to say.

"Cleanse you."

Yale was already slumping over, fading into oblivion.

* * *

The moment Yale awoke, they weren't quite sure if they *had* awoken, because they were standing in complete darkness. They blinked a few times to ensure their eyes were in fact open, then put out a tentative hand. It stopped against a hard surface only a few inches from their face—wood. They pushed against it and it hardly rattled. There were wood panels to the sides as well, trapping them in a cramped little box. Only a few streams of sunlight fought their way through the front of the box, which looked as though it had been boarded shut long after the rest of the box had been constructed. As they dragged their hands along the wood, they could feel it had once been polished, but over the years had chipped away.

"Hey," they said, quietly at first, then louder, "Hey!"

They banged on the wooden panel in front of them. The panel didn't move, but the whole box began to sway dizzily, and it occurred to Yale their box was suspended upright at the end of a rope.

From their confines, Yale could hear the priest beginning a sermon, "Today we gather for one of our most sacred duties as servants to our earthen mother: to feed her when she hungers."

"*What*?" Yale screamed, banging on the wood.

"Dear Lady Earth," the priest intoned, "we offer you this sacrifice: a scavenger, your most wicked enemy, to be forever entombed in your cold and your darkness. May you take this scavenger's living spirit and snuff it out, as testament to the way they have wrong and defiled you."

"Do *not* do this!" Yale begged, their heart hammering in their chest as they began to grow frantic. "Let me out! Let me out now!"

No response came to their pleas. Instead, the priest continued, "We hope this humble sacrifice pleases you, and you will grant us more sacred time upon your surface. For the Earth's Mercy, we pray."

A crowd echoed, "For the Earth's Mercy, we pray."

"Let! Me! Out!" Yale punctuated each word with a fist against the wood. The only answer was jolt as the box was slowly lowered toward the ground, toward the ground and into it.

They were being buried alive.

Interlude Twelve: Seven

The whole thing passed like a surreal nightmare. Ronan could hardly convince himself it was really happening; the shopkeeper dragging him down the steel steps to the Commission, evidence and paperwork being exchanged, numbers tossed around—numbers that represented *him*, his value, the amount he would need to work off before he was free again. Lastly, they took his name.

"We don't do outside names here," the Commission man—Herman— explained. "You leave all that behind when you come down here. You're not a person anymore, you understand. You're a scavenger. You don't ever let your old name cross your lips, you understand? You're the seventh new one we had this week, so until you get your brand name, you are Seven."

Ronan's—newly named Scavenger Trainee Number Seven's—training group was made up of nine kids around his age. Some older, maybe in their mid-twenties, and a few as young as fifteen. It reminded him of the crowd assembled at Founders' Square. At least those kids had a choice. Well, sort of. In a way, he'd had a choice. If he'd just stayed in Bell Manor, he wouldn't be here.

The trembling had started—of course it had. Looking at these other trainees, most of them bigger and more intimidating than him, how could he avoid feeling vulnerable? No one else seemed nervous. If they were, they were hiding it well. Number Four was doing stretches. Number Two was braiding her hair. Number Nine watched from the corner, sullen.

The door slammed so suddenly Number Seven jumped, which made Number Six laugh. He couldn't help but gawk at the newcomer, who might have been the most beautiful human he had ever seen. They wore a simple undershirt revealing muscular arms and a generous amount of brown skin. They wore their hair in a tight black bun, shaved on the sides, and had small, square frameless glasses that gave their dark eyes a kind of intensity. Seven guessed they must be about his age, but their jaded expression made them look tired beyond their years. Number Seven swallowed and willed his shaking to go away. It got worse.

"Alright, listen up," the newcomer commanded. "You don't wanna be here. I don't wanna be here. So let's just get this over with, okay? I'm going to be your Instructor for scavenger training. You can call me Instructor. And I will call you: One, Two, Three, Four, Five, Six—" Their eyes lingered on Ronan for a moment, and he felt himself shrink.

"Seven," they finally said, almost uncertainly, "Eight, and Nine."

What was wrong with him? What had he already messed up that he was getting negative attention already? Were his faults really so egregious that someone could tell just by looking at him? Seven felt himself shrivel, blushing, and only when Instructor looked away did he realize he'd been holding his breath the whole time they were looking at him.

"This is not going to be easy," they addressed the group at large. "I'm sure you know the dusts are dangerous. But it's not just that. The dusts change people. And I'm going to do my best to prepare you for something you can never truly be prepared for. We're going to meet here every day for a week and we're going to train the entire day. Then you'll have a final evaluation, and you'll get placed with a scavenging crew. From then on," they shot another glance at Seven, "you're on your own. So you better pay attention now, if you want to live."

The training was, as Instructor had said, brutal. Seven was woken at five each morning by an alarm bell, blearily stumbled to the training room, and submitted himself to Instructor's exercises. Some of the training made sense to him—they did a whole lesson on the best way to dodge a scuttler's pincers and how to wield a sandstaff, a weapon unique to scavengers. Some lessons were a little more baffling, like the hand-to-hand combat tutorial.

"Why do we need this?" Number Six asked. "There's not going to be anyone out there except me and my team."

"You don't know what's going to happen," Instructor said sternly. "You might run into people. And people in the desert get weird. Haven't you heard of sandheads?"

Seven shuddered at this. He couldn't imagine what "weird" meant, and he didn't want to know.

Whether it was vapor canister practice and desertwalker defense, Seven found he was useless at everything Instructor told him to do. It wasn't for lack of trying. Each evening his muscles ached so much he could barely walk, and he was so exhausted he nearly didn't make it to his cot. At every turn, he feared infuriating Instructor. He could see the frustration in their eyes every time he slipped on the mat or couldn't lift a weight or shook too violently to shoot a vapor canister properly.

One of the worst days was hunting knife training. Seven jabbed at the air tentatively, and Instructor shook their head with a deep sigh. Seven could feel the eyes of the other trainees watching him, all gaining proficiency with the hunting knife in the eyes of Instructor. Seven was the only one left, desperately trying to copy the form of his fellow trainees and failing miserably.

"You're not gonna be able to pull back like that," Instructor explained. "Whatever you're stabbing, whether it's human or scuttler, it's gonna have guts."

Seven recoiled at the word "guts."

"And the thing about guts is that they constrict. No one likes getting stabbed, yeah? So you're gonna have a hard time pulling that thing out. And if you've been practicing like it's not a big deal to stab a scuttler, then suddenly your knife is stuck and you're defenseless, you're gonna have a moment of panic. And a fraction of a second is all it takes for one of those things to get ya."

Seven cringed again at the phrase "get ya." He did not want to be got, yet he felt painfully aware that it might be inevitable. How could he train to defend himself in only a few days? He was nothing but fresh meat for the beasts out there, and he knew that. His whole class of new scavengers knew that. He was as good as dead.

CHAPTER NINETEEN

The Massacre

"Columbia! Princeton! Help!" Columbia could hear Yale's muffled cries from outside the tent. In all the years she had known them, they had never once called for help. Not like this. Not with this level of panic in their voice, not with this kind of sheer terror.

"Yale!" she responded in vain, pulling at the ropes in vain. "We have to do something. They *need* us!"

"I know! I know!" Princeton hissed, furiously pulling at the ropes on his end as well.

"We're coming for you Yale!" he shouted, despite a) Yale probably could not hear him and b) they were decidedly not coming for them.

"Dusts!" Princeton shouted, waggling his arms impotently. "How are we supposed to—*Look! Columbia! What the quaking fuck is that*?"

"What?" Columbia asked, still fighting uselessly against her bonds.

"In the back! Look!"

Columbia whipped her head around to the back of the tent to see a procession of tiny yellow-and-purple crabs making their way toward them like a miniature battalion.

"*Columbia!*" came Yale's ragged cry from outside the tent, now more muffled than before, "Please! Please don't do this! Please!"

"What the hell are they *doing* to them?" Columbia wondered aloud.

"Columbia, I'd really like to find out, but I really think we're going to be *eaten alive by crabs right now*."

Columbia watched the line of crabs draw nearer, splitting neatly into two lines: one crawling up her legs, and the other crawling up Princeton's. She gave an involuntary cry, shaking her legs in an attempt to dislodge them. The crabs held their ground. She could hear Princeton behind her fighting the same battle.

To her surprise, the crabs did not bite her. They seemed much more interested in the ropes that held her in place. Using their little claws and even smaller mouths, they bit into the fibers of the ropes, snapping them.

"Princeton!" she cried, "Princeton, they're helping us!"

"What the *fuck*?"

"I don't...I have no idea...Look! They're breaking the ropes."

"I repeat: *what the fuck*?"

Columbia resumed her tugging with renewed vigor now the baby scuttlers were weakening the ropes, but they were not yet thin enough for her to break free. Yale's cries outside were fading. Something was blocking them out.

* * *

Yale jerked as the bottom of the wooden crate hit the ground, and as the sound of voices became distant overhead, they heard dirt pour over them. A few streams of dust drizzled in between the slats of wood above them, sand pooling at their feet like a grotesque hourglass.

"Please let me out! Please!" they cried, pounding on the wood directly above them. The few slivers of sunlight that managed to squeeze their way into the box were already being blotted out. The wooden panel above their head wasn't loosening against their punches, and the sand pouring into the box was already nearing their knees. They lifted their feet to stay on top of it instead of being buried by it.

Desperate, they began to claw at the wood, their fingertips tearing and bleeding. Slowly chunks of wood began to fall and blood trickled down Yale's hands. They couldn't hear the sound of their own screaming over the pounding of blood in their ears. They couldn't even feel the pain as splinters dug themselves into their fingers and the palms of their hands. They inhaled particles of dust with each breath, coughing violently, bumping up against the walls of the box.

Now in complete darkness, they blindly clawed at the invisible barrier above them, feeling like they'd been here before in a nightmare, like they somehow knew that this was how they would die.

* * *

Screams erupted from outside the tent. Something was happening. She could hear the sound of bodies falling, of weapons clashing, and some kind of animalistic screech.

"What's happening out there?" she asked aloud.

"Like I know!" Princeton shouted, his eyes fixed on the crabs that were strangely not devouring their captive prey, and instead working at the ropes that held them in place.

"They're fighting," Columbia guessed.

Princeton gave one final pull and the ropes snapped. He stood, crabs falling off him. He pulled Columbia to her feet, and both made for the entrance of the tent. Already, everything outside had fallen quiet.

Before them was a scene of carnage. Fallen bodies of acolytes lay scattered across the dirt, limbs broken at unnatural angles. Only on those with lighter colored robes were the blood stains visible, wide gashes in their chests and stomachs.

"What...the fuck," Princeton murmured, surveying the gory remains.

* * *

Yale wiped the dust away from their eyes, their mouth, their nose, but it only served to cover them in more of the fine sand and leave scratches on their face from the splinters in their hands. The sandheads hadn't been merciful enough to let them keep their dustscarf or goggles, so they squeezed their eyes shut as they took breath after painful breath of dust particles, stinging their throat and nose.

They thought about Harvard. They would survive this, if only to find him.

Do not cough, Yale pleaded with themself, *cough and it's over*. They knew once they gave into the temptation, the tickle in their throat, their lungs would keep spasming, gasping for air, and they would be helpless to stop the dirt and grime from getting in. But it was already in their mouth, they could feel it on their tongue, and it was already coating their throat. They held their breath to avoid taking in anymore grime.

Keep digging, they thought, *keep digging*. The wood was breaking underneath their fingers, but they weren't going fast enough. They were now crouched atop the sand that had already poured in, but swiftly running out of space.

I'm not going to make it, they thought, their face pressed up against their hands as they desperately tore apart the wooden paneling, and warm blood from their fingers mixed with the dust on their lips. Blood roared in their ears, and they began to feel weak just as their fingers broke through the lid of the box.

They drew a ragged breath before they could stop themself, and a coughing fit set in, each gasp taking in more and more dust and flakes of wood. Blood began to wet their dry mouth as they swallowed splinters.

Sand covered them, like an insect slowly trapped in amber, as they thrust upward with one arm, gasping, until they were consumed by darkness.

* * *

"Yale!" Columbia cried, frantically searching the fallen bodies to see if one belonged to her friend.

"This is all my fault," Princeton murmured to himself, numbly. "I'm the reason we're here. This is all my fault."

Columbia ignored him, scouring the bodies.

A hand shot out of the dirt, bent claw-like, plastered with sand. Princeton was the first to arrive and start pulling, revealing forearm and elbow, then another hand not far below it. After a few moments heaving, the two pulled a barely conscious Yale from the wreckage of the casket they had been buried in. The two stumbled to the side, gently lowering Yale to the ground. They were coated in dust and bits of wood poked out of their hair like a crown of splinters.

"Princeton!" Columbia barked. "Go to that tent. Get me an oxygen tank and a waterskin. Now!"

Princeton nodded obediently and ran for the tent Columbia had pointed at.

Yale was on their hands and knees, hacking up dust with every breath. Columbia ran her hand in circles along their back.

"Breathe," she murmured soothingly. "You're okay. Just breathe."

She doubted her encouragement was helping them any—in fact, she doubted they were even present enough to hear her voice.

Once it seemed they'd emptied their lungs of dust, they began to take ragged, wheezing breaths. Princeton returned with the oxygen tank. Columbia turned the valve to start the gas flow, then gently placed the mask over Yale's face. As their breathing steadied, Columbia readied the waterskin Princeton had provided. He knelt down on the opposite side of the captain, glancing to the hole they'd pulled them out of.

"Holy shit," Princetin murmured, seeing the broken wooden casket lodged in the ground, "they really dug their way out of *that*?"

"Princeton," Columbia snapped, her hand still placed protectively against Yale's back.

"Columbia, look," Princeton insisted, indicating the top of the box where Yale had clawed the wood away. He took Yale's hands in his own, and sure enough, the dust concealed a layer of warm blood, still leaking from their fingertips. Columbia poured some water over their hands as Princeton gently massaged the dust away. Beneath, the two found Yale's fingertips a bloody mosaic of wood splinters. Princeton stood.

"I'll get some bandages," he said, running back off toward the supply tent. Columbia nodded, though both knew it would take a lot more than bandages to heal their captain's utterly ruined hands.

Yale's breathing seemed to have stabilized, so Columbia removed the mask. They attempted to speak the moment the mask was off their face, but they were still too weak. Columbia hushed them, pulling them into her.

They made one more feeble attempt to speak.

"Motherfuckers," they rasped, "tried to bury me alive."

"They're all dead now," Columbia said comfortingly.

"Nice," Yale gave a weak thumbs up, then fainted in Columbia's arms.

* * *

Columbia stood amidst the carnage. She did not bother to inspect the bodies further, or to organize them into some kind of burial. They'd like to be buried, wouldn't they? She didn't want to give them that honor, even in death. She'd studied them enough to confirm some desert beast had made quick work of dispatching them, and they'd been caught in the midst of their ritual unprepared. Now she stood at the edge of the encampment, looking out onto the sand. She heard the flap of a tent behind her, and Princeton wordlessly appeared next to her.

"They're doing okay," he reported. She wasn't going to ask, but he knew she wanted to hear it.

"How many scavengers do you think are buried here?" she asked. The thought of it made her sick, but she couldn't help but wonder how many decaying bodies, bodies of people she knew, were under her feet.

"I don't know," said Princeton. For the first time since she'd known him, he made no joke, no poorly timed attempt at levity. He was more somber than she'd ever seen him.

"How many more camps do you think there are?"

"I don't know," he repeated.

She turned back to the red horizon.

Princeton made a sound like he was going to speak, but instead only muttered to himself. She had a sense this was a private moment, but she snuck a glance in his direction. His head was bowed, his eyes closed, and his lips were moving almost imperceptibly. He was murmuring the Earth's Mercy prayer.

* * *

When Yale awoke, they were in a cot in one of the sandhead tents. Their head pounded and their hands ached, though when they examined the damage, they found their hands had been tightly bound in layers of bandage, so thick they could hardly move their fingers.

They heard rustling next to them and turned to see Princeton sitting in a chair at their bedside, arms crossed, head drooping, snoring lightly.

"Princeton?" they asked gently, happy to discover that their voice was more or less back to normal.

At the sound of his name, Princeton's head shot up. He made brief eye contact with Yale, then threw his arms around them, clasping them in a muscular embrace. Princeton began to shake imperceptibly, and Yale, stupefied, realized that he was crying into their shoulder.

"This is all my fault," Princeton sobbed, clutching Yale tightly. "I'm sorry. I am so sorry. This is all my fault. I'm sorry. I'm sorry."

Yale didn't know what to do except lay a gentle bandaged hand on the boy's back.

"It's okay," they said into the crook of his neck. "We're okay."

Interlude Thirteen: Jasmine

Jasmine knew if she considered her decision she might change her mind, so she didn't consider it at all: she chose to follow Chavi to the Commission and decided never to rethink her choice again. She told them she'd failed the Aptitude Exam, that she didn't have any other options, and maybe they were just so desperate for her company that they believed her. It was her fault that they had to brave the dusts, so she wasn't going to let them do it alone.

Jasmine was nothing if not studious. If she had been a student of books, then she could be a student of the body. Through her rigorous early-morning and late-night sessions with Chavi, she built up enough muscle to be a passable scavenger, despite her small form. She could even be convinced, on occasion, to spar with them, preparing for the off chance they encountered some kind of human threat out in the dusts. She would not be satisfied until she knew how to exist in the desert, and how to hold her own in a fight. The one thing that brought Jasmine comfort more than anything else was *knowing*. She knew she'd never be as strong as Chavi, but she was a quick study, and soon she was able to dissect a fight into discrete pieces and work through it like a puzzle. Once she *knew* how to approach it, she was able to beat them in nearly every fight.

"Reputation is a powerful tool," they told her. "We should tell people you've been here longer than me. When they see that you have seniority—that *I* defer to *you*—they'll respect you more."

Jasmine struggled in training, but her supplemental work with Chavi kept her from standing out as a weak link, which she was thankful for. After a week of intensive lessons, Chavi and Jasmine were placed on the Cookies crew together.

"You're letting us stay together?" Chavi asked, incredulously, when Herman gave them their team assignment. "I just kinda figured you'd split us up."

"Oh, don't get sentimental about it," Herman waved a dismissive hand. "Scavengers who know each other already work better together. It's a technique. We didn't do it out of pity."

The rest of the Cookies, however, did not seem to work well with Chavi and Jasmine.

The captain was Oreo, a diminutive but intense boy with piercing eyes and a permanent scowl. Chavi was renamed Nilla and Jasmine was renamed Lotus. Last was Thin Mint, or as he had dubbed himself, Minty. Jasmine had never seen a weasel in real life, but if she had, she imagined it would look a lot like Minty. There was something imperceptibly slimy about that boy, the crooked grin he always wore on his rodent face, the way his nasal voice dragged out of his mouth, the way his eyes darted manically.

Chavi scoffed at the nickname.

"That's stupid," they complained. "This whole brand thing is stupid. Can't we just have normal code names?"

"What's a normal code name?" Lotus asked.

"I don't know. Birds. Colors. Types of snakes maybe. Cookies? It's ridiculous. No one will take us seriously."

"They're not supposed to take us seriously. They're not even supposed to know we exist," Lotus pointed out.

"There's a reason for the brands," Oreo said, his voice dripping with condescension. "It hearkens back to an era—"

"I don't need a history lesson, Oreo," Chavi—Nilla—rolled their eyes. "If I was any good at learning, I wouldn't have become a scavenger."

"That is not true," Oreo frowned. "Becoming a scavenger has nothing to do with intelligence—"

"Sure. 'Minty' here is living proof of that, huh?"

Minty grinned devilishly, his gaze fixed on Chavi.

"Oh yeah," Minty teased. "I'm an evil genius."

The two stared at each other for a long uncomfortable moment, Minty all the while wearing that sideways smile.

Lotus knew that her time as a Cookie was going to be fraught, because her best friend had already made an enemy. Minty would knock Nilla over during training exercises, and then feign innocence.

"I didn't see you there! I just didn't expect you to be *in my way*."

"You better not keep this up in the desert" Nilla grumbled.

"I would never," Minty said, wearing an expression of exaggerated hurt.

It turned out Minty wouldn't *have* the chance to pester Nilla out on digs because Oreo insisted on putting Nilla on lookout regularly.

"This is a waste," they complained, as the rest of the Cookies descended beneath the ground. "I'm useless up here."

"Not if a scuttler shows up."

"But—"

Oreo already knew the unspoken question: why can't Minty do it?

"Minty has been at it longer," Oreo explained.

And Minty gave a sweet smile and wave before disappearing deeper into the cavernous hallways of the sunken building.

Every time Chavi complained, a little voice in Jasmine's mind would pipe up unbidden. *This is all your fault, Chavi,* it would say. *You have no right to whine. If it weren't for you, neither of us would be here.* She didn't want to say it aloud, of course. She was not the kind of person to make biting comments openly. Chavi was, of course, and she'd seen that very habit land them in detention countless times. "Don't you ever think before you speak?" Avi had once asked them. "Yeah, I think, 'oh, I should totally say this,' and then I say it!" came the reply. Avi put her head in her hands in mock agony.

Jasmine couldn't silence the nagging little voice saying, *I could have left you. You could be on your own. But I sacrificed everything, and you're here complaining like you're not the one who got yourself kicked out of the Academy. Like you're not the one who can't behave.* Each time these thoughts crossed her mind, she felt a pang of guilt for even letting such hateful thoughts even enter her head. But the more Chavi's rivalry with Minty flared, the more these thoughts began to crop up.

"It's like he doesn't take this shit seriously!" Nilla complained, and Lotus bit down a remark about how *they* had never taken *anything* seriously for the past sixteen years. This was different, of course. This was not the Academy. This was life and death. The Chavi she'd known was gone forever— this was Nilla, and Nilla took more responsibility. Nilla took this very seriously, because two people's fates were riding on their success as a scavenger: Lotus, and Rivka Chakrabarti, whose cascade of black and silver hair now felt like such a distant memory. Warm, gentle Rivka, who always welcomed Lotus into her home like she was her own daughter. Lotus wondered if she would ever see her again.

"Can't you just let it go?" Lotus asked one evening, sitting at the foot of their bed as they braided her hair in preparation for the dusts.

"No, I can't let it go," they shot back. "We're all putting our lives on the line here, and he acts like it's a big joke. He's a quaking psychopath!"

"He is not." She hated it when people used that word. It was unscientific and didn't get at the heart of the matter. Anyone who was "crazy" must have something else going on, and she didn't want to speculate about Minty.

"He put spiders in my shoes."

"You don't know it was him," Lotus pointed out. "There might have just happened to be spiders in your shoes."

"The next morning he said 'hey, did you like the spiders in your shoes?' I don't even know how he got in! The door was locked! The little shit!"

Lotus sighed. "He's targeting you because you targeted him."

"Why are you defending him?" Nilla snapped.

"I'm not! I'm just saying, don't act like you don't have a role in this."

"I didn't ask for any of this, Jasmine! I didn't want any of this to happen!"

"And I did? Do you think Minty did?" She immediately regretted the amount of indignation that had tinged her voice. She *had* chosen this.

"I just—" Nilla began.

"And you're not supposed to say Jasmine anymore. Lotus."

"Okay. Lotus. I...I just hate this." They sat heavily on the bed next to her.

"I don't love it either."

"But I'm happy you're here."

"Yeah. Me too."

She turned to face them.

"We're gonna make this work, okay?" she reassured them, echoing the promise they'd made to her as the two first made their way to the Commission's door. It couldn't have been more than two weeks ago, but it felt like years had already passed.

Nilla sighed.

"Yeah," they agreed. "We're gonna make this work."

"Just be patient with him," she urged.

They groaned.

"I'm horrible at being patient with people. And that's saying something. I'm only bad at two things. Paying attention, knowing things, and being patient with people."

"That's three things."

"Okay, well add math to the list. Whatever."

"And what do you mean 'knowing things'?"

"I don't know."

"Just don't put anyone else in the hospital, okay?"

Lotus had meant it to come as lighthearted, a gentle reminder, but instead it came out like a barb. She could see Nilla tense, and she immediately regretted the comment, worrying it had done some unintentional hurt.

"I'm sorry, I—" she started, but Nilla cut her off.

"No. It's fine. You're right."

They buried their face in their hands, and Lotus felt paralyzed, unsure of what to do. The closeness between them had always been one of mutual understanding. In this moment, she *didn't* understand what was expected of her, and it made her feel like she was balancing precariously on the point of a knife. She wondered if they were about to cry, and the thought made her stomach twist. She had never seen them cry, and she hated to think of what it would take.

"I felt it when it happened," they lifted their face, staring blankly at the ground. Before Lotus could ask for clarity, they continued. "Honestly, I don't remember much of it. I don't even remember feeling pain. I was having fun, almost. Not almost. I was. I was just so mad, I think—at everything. At the world. At the Academy, for making me feel like a failure. At myself, for *being* a failure. But I didn't know where to take it out and then finally, I did. But then in the middle of it, I felt his skull crack. And then suddenly I wanted to puke. I thought, Founders. I killed him. All these words I must have learned from spending too much time around Avi popped into my head—like 'blood brain barrier' and 'grey matter' and 'blunt force trauma' and stuff like that. And for a second it felt like everything fell away, and I saw myself for what I really was…a monster."

"You're not a monster," Lotus said.

Nilla shook their head. "I never…I never wanted to kill anyone."

"And you didn't," reminded them.

"I almost did."

"But you didn't."

"Don't jinx it," they laughed sardonically, shaking their head.

"You did what you thought was the right thing," Lotus said.

"Did I?" their brow knit in contemplation. "Or did I just do what I *felt* was the right thing?"

"Aren't those the same thing?" Lotus asked.

"Definitely not."

Lotus felt herself once again at a loss.

"I'll try harder to be...different than what I am," Nilla said.

"Don't say it like that," Lotus chided.

"But it's true. That's what you want, right? For me to be different."

"I want you to grow up. Everyone grows up. I'm not trying to change you. I think change is going to happen no matter what."

They sat in silence for a long moment.

"It's your turn," Lotus said abruptly, standing. "Your undercut is about ready for a trim. I'll grab a razor."

As she headed for the little cabinet in the bathroom, a wave of sadness washed over Lotus. She had become accustomed to understanding Nilla as well as historical texts she'd read at the Academy. She could read every one of their expressions and gestures as easily as she read her textbooks. This was still true, for the most part. But ever since the incident with Carter, something in them had shifted and Lotus wasn't able to place it. And that mystery terrified her more than any monster in the desert.

She shaved their hair in silence.

CHAPTER TWENTY

The Message

When Harvard awoke, his arm was completely bandaged. The Empress was perched on the edge of Skrack's claw, waiting patiently for him to come to.

Harvard, he felt her silken voice in his head, *Skrack tells me you encountered a netherworm, and you suffered an injury. I am sorry to hear of it.*

"It was nothing," Harvard mumbled blearily, rubbing the sleep from his eyes. Well, that wasn't entirely true. The encounter with the netherworm was the single most terrifying thing Harvard had experienced in his life. The injury, however, was dressed so neatly he couldn't even feel it. It would have been a lot worse had Skrack not pulled him out of the way in time, but Harvard pushed away the thought of his body impaled on a worm tongue like a gory kebab.

Still, the whole situation haunted him, a persistent needling in the back of his mind. He'd escaped alive, sure, but not unscathed. And they were sure to meet other obstacles like that on their trek through the desert. Would he be so lucky next time? And what about the rest of the Ivies?

As the three began walking again, Harvard pressed the Empress for information about his friends.

The hatchlings have reported back, she declared from her perch atop Skrack's shell, facing Harvard where he walked behind the giant beast. *Your friends are not in danger.*

Harvard breathed out a sigh of relief.

Anymore.

"Anymore?" he looked up at her.

Yes. The hatchlings called upon one of our allies in the north for assistance.

"What ally?"

Vyrak.

"I...um, I don't know who that is," Harvard admitted sheepishly.

I believe humans refer to her species as "crabsnake."

"The hatchlings got a crabsnake to help my crew?" Harvard asked in disbelief.

Yes. However, I am told another danger approaches them. The humans are not yet aware of the presence of this danger, but it follows.

"What is it?" Harvard asked, thinking of the netherworm he'd just barely escaped from. And *he'd* had a megacrab on his side.

The Guardian's To Be cannot tell.

"How can they not tell? Isn't the point of them, like, to see things?" Harvard demanded, a little bit of impatient anger at the edge of his voice.

Yes. They saw the creature, but they do not know what it is.

"So an *unknown monster* is following my friends?"

Yes.

"We have to go to them!" Harvard ran out in front of Skrack.

"Stop!" he shouted. "We have to go find my crew and save them!"

Time will not allow for it, Skrack protested, pointedly taking no pains to hide his annoyance at having to navigate around Harvard. *The time of the conference fast approaches.*

"I don't care!"

Skrack stopped in his tracks, and Harvard immediately sensed he had made a mistake.

"I...I mean...I do care. About the mission. But...I also care about my crew. And besides! They can help!" Harvard looked up toward the Empress, since he expected she would be more amenable to his pleas.

"I mean, really, what am I going to do on my own as one human? But four of us? We'd be, like, unstoppable! Let's go get my friends out of danger, and then we can all go to Bastion together and save your heir."

Child, do you know how many days out from Bastion we are? Skrack asked.

"Um, I'd say three?" Harvard ventured a guess.

That is correct. And do you know how many days there are before the conference?

"No."

Three.

"Oh."

If we waste our time upon these humans of yours, we will miss our opportunity. All our efforts will have been in vain.

Harvard crossed his arms.

"I'm sorry, Empress. And I'm sorry Skrack, too. And I'm sorry, hatchlings. But...but this is where I draw the line. Either we go help my friends, or...or I'm out. I'm not going to leave them when I know something is out there trying to hurt them, something even the Guardians can't recognize. They're in danger and they don't know it, and we can help. I can't know that and just not go to them. I can't."

Fine. Then we will find another human for our purposes while my hatchlings feast upon your flesh.

Harvard suspected that at this point this was an empty threat.

"Empress?" he appealed. However, the Empress was silent. "Empress?" he asked again, a little more feebly this time.

We had an agreement, Harvard, she said ruefully. *The Guardians were to watch over your human companions. We were to go to Bastion. Your proposal is not part of the agreement.*

"But—" Harvard began to protest, but she cut him off.

I am aggrieved for you, Harvard. Truly, I am. But if you are to fail to meet the terms of our contract, then yes, Skrack is correct.

Harvard sighed. This is just how it was supposed to go, wasn't it? Everyone tolerated him until he wanted something for himself. Then he was too much of a quaking burden, wasn't he? *Literally* quaking. Then again, was this *really* for himself? Maybe the Empress had a point...the Ivies hadn't exactly been kind to him. They were going to leave him in O'Neill's pod! They abandoned him with a murderer! Really, it was only fair—

No.

He couldn't think like that.

Yale would never abandon him. And he couldn't abandon them. Or Columbia, who had never hurt him and always known what was best for the team. Or Princeton, cruel as he may be. He'd never been kind to Harvard, but when Harvard was shaking too much to defend himself, Princeton was there, vapor canister ready, to stand by his crew mate. He didn't have to do that. But he did.

Harvard inhaled deeply, facing down the beast in front of him, knowing Skrack could easily crush him with one blow of his claw. He crossed his arms. And he said, "Fine."

I'm glad you will be reasonable.

"Your hatchling's can eat me."

What?

"I'm not leaving my friends when they're in trouble. I just can't. So if those are the two options, then yeah, your hatchlings can eat me."

He grinned, a glint of mischief in his eye. "If they can catch me!"

With that, he sprinted off into the desert.

* * *

The hatchlings could catch Harvard. In fact, they could catch him very quickly, he discovered.

That was impressively stupid, Skrack said, standing over Harvard as he was held to the ground with the weight of hundred of tiny crabs that had ambushed him. They weren't eating him, luckily. Just holding him down.

Where would you have gone? How would you on your own fight off an enemy even the Guardians cannot name? Did you really believe you could escape from our contract?

"No," Harvard admitted, gingerly picking crabs off of him. He lifted Speedy and gently placed him on the ground. "I didn't. But I owed it to my crew to try."

He waited for the hatchlings to begin biting at him, but they did not.

"Maybe they're not hungry," he mused aloud.

They do not want you, Skrack said, and Harvard almost felt offended.

They see you as an ally, the Empress corrected.

Your meat disgusts them.

They have grown to see you as one of their own.

You are not worthy of their consumption.

Harvard gave the two crabs a puzzled look. "I'm getting mixed messages here."

Empress Kryaka gave the crab equivalent of a sigh.

Rise, Harvard.

The hatchlings instantly parted, leaping off his body and scurrying in the sand. Harvard stood, dusting himself off.

Though your loyalty is misguided, it is clearly stronger than the bond of your vow. We will help you find your friends, on the condition they help us. If they should refuse, they will be devoured.

"They won't refuse," Harvard assured his carcine compatriots with a smile.

You are confident.

"I mean, if the alternative is being devoured, like...that's not great. But they won't refuse. They're good people, Empress. You maybe didn't see them at their best, but they are."

They had better be, Skrack grumbled. *Let us move. We waste more of the precious little time we have left. We must find a way to make up for this delay, Empress.*

Patience, Skrack. We will re-evaluate once Harvard's companions are safe. I have faith we will find a way.

You have more faith than I, Skrack grumbled.

"Hatchlings, take us to my friends!" Harvard declared.

You do not give them orders, boy. I give them orders.

"Oh. Sorry."

Hatchings. Take us to...take us to Harvard's friends.

Interlude Fourteen: Seven

There was still time to prove his parents wrong, Seven had decided. He might have failed at his business model, but that didn't mean he had to fail at this too. The night after the knife training, he remained in the training room long after most of the other scavengers had gone to sleep, practicing what he had been taught over and over again. It was so easy for him to see something and draw it, or to play a song once his fingers had learned it, but for some reason to watch someone do something and then *do* it was a completely different endeavor. Why was it so hard to get his body to move like everyone else's? He thrust forward with the practice knife again and again, each time losing his balance thanks to his own momentum.

"Your stance is wrong," a voice said. Seven yelped, nearly dropping the practice knife.

Instructor sat on one of the benches, pack dropped between their feet, watching him closely.

"Do it again," they commanded, "and spread your feet this time."

"What...what are you doing here?" Seven asked, suddenly shaky. Instructor shrugged.

"I like going for walks at night," they said. "This is about the only place in the compound that's empty after dark. *Usually* empty after dark."

Seven looked down at his shoes, oddly guilty for ruining Instructor's solitary time.

"So," Instructor said, "let's see you fix your form."

"I can't...I mean, I'm nervous when you're watching," he shrunk, feeling his face start to burn. The Instructor nodded.

"And you'll be nervous if you're facing down a huge desert creature," they said, crossing their arms. "So do it again."

Seven nodded, spreading his feet like he was told. It didn't help. The Instructor sighed, and Seven got that usual sinking sensation he got in his stomach when he knew he had failed.

"I know I'm the worst one," he said, staring down at the mat, unable to meet their eyes. "I mean, for what it's worth. I'm at least aware. And I know it's a huge pain for you and—"

"It's not," they cut him off. They sighed again, then stood, walking over to the edge of the mat. "Listen. Do you know why I'm so hard on you?"

"Because you think I'll make a terrible scavenger."

"No. Well, kind of," they admitted. "I just don't want you to die."

Seven cocked his head. "Really?"

"I mean, I don't want anyone to die, ideally. But...look, I know you're scared. Everyone is scared when they join the Commission. That's just how it is. You're not alone. But you're so scared you're letting it stop you from learning. You can survive out there. Anyone can, if they know how. But if you don't stop getting in your own way, you'll never be able to. Is this making any sense?"

Seven scratched his head self-consciously. "Um...a little."

"Like, look at the way you're standing right now," Instructor gestured to Seven's stance. "Your feet are together, your arms are together, your shoulders are slumped—you're afraid to take up space."

"I don't...I mean, I don't wanna get in the way."

"Get in the way!" the encouraged. "It's good for you. I love to get in the way. I do it all the time." They seemed to take pride in this.

"So how do I...I mean, I can't take up more space. I'm just the size I am."

"No, you're not. Here, let me show you."

They walked up behind Seven and kicked his feet apart. He would have fallen if they hadn't grabbed his hip with one hand and his wrist with the other.

"Square your hips like this. This foot angled forward. This one to the side. Don't lock your knees. Bend them."

"Sorry—"

"Don't be sorry. Your grip on the knife is wrong. We went over grips, remember?"

"Sorry!"

"Don't be sorry. Use this leg to push forward. The power comes from your leg, not your arm. Did you get all that?"

"I...I think so."

"Good. Let's practice together. Take a step back with this foot so we can go through the whole thing."

Seven thrust the practice knife in the air, Instructor guiding him through the motions from behind. He froze. He actually felt...strong. Powerful, even. Like he really could survive out there on his own.

"How did that feel?" Instructor asked from behind him.

"Um...good," Seven stammered.

Instructor laughed. "I meant, did you feel more stable? Or did you feel like you got more power behind it?"

"Oh. Um. Yes. I did."

"Good. I guess I'm doing my job, then."

The two lingered there for a fraction of a second longer, the Instructor so close to Seven that he could feel their breath on his neck. Seven swallowed.

"I should go," Instructor said abruptly, releasing him. "It's late, and, uh, I have stuff to do in the morning—"

"No, right, yeah," Seven could feel his face betraying him as it began to burn. "I should probably...it's late..."

"I'm gonna go," they ran for their pack, scooped it up, and left the training room without another word. The heavy double door slammed behind them, and the sound echoed in the empty practice room.

Seven found himself baffled by the interaction. There was something swelling inside him he didn't understand. Instructor had intimidated him so much when he'd first arrived, but their closeness...it had made him feel warm. And not just physically warm, but there was this kind of burning on the inside, a pleasant burning. He'd never felt it before and scared him.

But why had they left so abruptly? Had he done something wrong? Had he hurt them in some way? Here he was thinking maybe they were starting to like him, and he had just done something to ruin the whole thing, and worst of all, he didn't even know what it was. He let the practice knife drop as he fell to his knees on the mat, wrapping his arms around himself.

CHAPTER TWENTY-ONE

The Parting

Yale knew they should sleep, but their thoughts wouldn't let them.

They thought of Harvard.

They didn't let themself imagine finding him—it was too painful to entertain the possibility when they knew full well Princeton was probably right, and he was long dead.

Instead, they replayed every interaction they'd ever had with him, thinking of all the ways they'd gone wrong.

They'd hurt him.

That day in training, when Harvard had disobeyed the orders—the same thing Yale had done when they were a crew member of the Cookies—everything that had happened with Minty was still too fresh, and it all bubbled to the surface. They'd grabbed his wrist, and maybe their grip was too tight or maybe they twisted his arm, but they'd *hurt* him, and when they realized what they had done the shame felt like it was drowning them. They had promised they would never hurt him again, and now he might be dead because of their negligence.

They thought back to that day they'd trained him late at night, the day they showed him how to take up space. His closeness had been so unexpectedly pleasant that it had scared them, and their mind had started racing with all the things they could do next now they stood behind him, one hand pressed on his hip.

What scared them was not the idea that he might have rejected them. That, they could deal with. No, it was the opposite question that taunted them: what if he'd gone along with it? What if he'd welcomed it? They would have melted. They wouldn't have been able to resist the temptation. Back at the Academy, they rode just about every impulse they'd ever had. But this was different. They were the Instructor and he was their trainee, soon to be crew member. And for scavengers, getting entangled with a crew member could have life-threatening consequences. And they would not allow their emotions to take over again, causing someone else to get hurt. Not after Carter. Not after Minty. Caring about people made Yale do stupid things. They knew this, and

Columbia knew it too. No, they couldn't risk what would happen if they got too close to Harvard, so they'd run away.

Resisting his pull was one of the hardest things they'd ever done.

But had they gotten too close anyway?

They tried to convince themself that they were chasing Harvard because they were a good captain, because they wouldn't leave a crew member behind, and because they needed to atone for what happened to Minty.

They weren't sure if that was true.

Yale thought of the last time they'd seen Harvard, when everyone told them he was going to die and they'd stubbornly refused to believe it, as though sheer willpower alone would bring him back to health. He'd wanted to tell them his name. They'd refused, out of the same obstinance that kept them from comprehending Harvard's impending death.

They regretted that now.

Not that they cared what name he was born with. He was him, and that was all that mattered. But his pleas to share his name were one final attempt at closeness, and Yale had brushed it aside in the vain hope Harvard would be okay.

If Harvard was really truly dead, then their last moment together had been Yale's rejection, a rejection borne out of headstrong selfishness.

Every chance they'd ever had to be something more than crewmates with Harvard, they'd squandered it.

Yale finally fell asleep, with that knowledge causing an ache in their chest.

* * *

Princeton packed their scavenged equipment while Columbia checked Yale's bandages.

"How are you feeling?" he heard Columbia ask.

"Well, I could certainly do without all the fading in and out of consciousness," Yale grumbled. "I would like to *stay* conscious this time, if it's all the same to you all."

"Believe me, Yale, we would be more than happy with that," Princeton said.

Yale had been able to find a replacement sledgehammer—the sandheads had the stored hammers of the scavengers they'd disposed of. There were four. They tried not to think about the previous owners. It made them nauseous.

The Ivies were also able to find vapor canisters, water skins, oxygen tanks, sand paddles, food, and a few weapons; Yale and Princeton both helped themselves to new hunting knives, and Columbia took a sandstaff—she said she preferred it to a knife anyway.

"It's definitely not great the Chocolates took everything we had," Yale reflected as the three started their trek away from the camp, "but with all this, we can probably extend our search by a few days."

Princeton froze in his tracks.

"What?" Yale asked.

"Oh. I mean...It's just...I thought..." he stammered.

"What?" Yale repeated. Columbia shot them a look but said nothing.

"We agreed to search for three days, and, I mean, it's the third day," Princeton said. "Not to mention that we all just barely survived that whole thing—"

"We said three days because that's all we had supplies for," Yale said. "We have more now—"

"We almost died!" Princeton reminded them. "*You* almost died! And you seriously want to stay out here? After all that?"

"I don't *want* to stay out here," Yale informed him levelly, "But if Harvard is still out there—"

"He's dead!" Princeton blurted out, then immediately regretted it and walked it back. "Or if he's not dead, he's gone back to Bastion. Do you really wanna die out here when he could be waiting for us back at the Commission?"

Yale considered this for a moment, staring fixedly at Princeton, before saying, "You're right."

Princeton let out a sigh of relief.

"You should go back."

"What?"

"I promised three days, and I'm sticking to that promise. But I also promised I wouldn't give up. I'll stay out here a few more days and if I still can't find him, then I'll go back. But you should go now. You too, Columbia. You shouldn't be alone."

"But—" Columbia started, but Yale cut her off.

"You've got your sisters," they nodded to Princeton. "And Columbia, you've got—"

"I know who I've got," she interrupted, "but you've got people too."

"And I'll be back for them. But not without Harvard."

She shook her head. "I just don't get why you—"

"You don't have to get it. I'm just asking for you to listen to me."

A pained look crossed Columbia's face. She pulled her bag up higher on her shoulder.

"Just don't...don't be stupid, okay?" It was a strangely direct command, coming from her. Yale just nodded somberly. Columbia turned to a dumbstruck Princeton.

"C'mon, Princeton. Let's go."

* * *

It's better this way, Yale decided as they trudged alone through the desert. *I never wanted Jasmine out here anyway.* It was the best possible solution, really. Jasmine would be safe for at least a little while, before heading out for another dig, this time fully stocked and well-rested. And soon, Harvard would be safe too. They were *going* to find him. They felt that with iron-clad certainty. That's what a captain is supposed to do, right? Keep the team alive.

Yale fought the urge to glance over their shoulder, knowing it would just make the whole situation more unbearable, but the voice in their head telling them this could be the last time they would ever see their crewmates won out.

They turned, just one last time, to see Princeton and Columbia heading back toward them.

Are you quaking joking? they thought to themself. *It's been, like thirty seconds.*

Yale sighed, readying themself for the inevitable "we simply couldn't bring ourselves to leave you" and "we love Harvard too much to ever give up on him."

Instead, Princeton approached looking sheepish, scratching the back of his neck awkwardly.

"So, here's the thing," he said. "We don't actually know which way Bastion *is*."

"Are you fucking *kidding* me?" Yale asked.

"I mean, I never really thought about it, but Harvard was always the one to keep us on track. We got really turned around in the Crags, and then with the Chocolates, and then with the sandheads…We're lost without Harvard. Literally."

Princeton flushed when he said this, and Yale guessed he was embarrassed to admit Harvard had been an asset.

"You haven't been keeping track of directions?" Columbia asked quietly—not accusatory, only a gentle inquiry.

"How the hell would I have been able to do that?" Yale snapped. "The Chocolates stole all our shit—including our compass."

"And you didn't think to grab one from the sandheads?" Princeton demanded—accusatory this time.

"I doubt they even had one! What would they use it for? They spend all their time *burying people alive*. Did you notice? Did that happen to you? Oh, right, no, it didn't. It happened to *me* though. So, excuse me if I didn't think to look for a *quaking compass* while I was busy *choking* on *dust!*"

Princeton recoiled. "I just…I mean, I'm just sayin'…"

Columbia held up a hand. "Stop. This is pointless. It doesn't matter why we're lost, but we are lost. Now we just have to figure out how we're getting back."

"*I'm* not going back yet," Yale said.

Columbia furrowed her brow, giving them a pitying look.

"What's your plan? Really?" she asked. "The dusts are expansive—more so than we can possibly imagine."

"You were willing to let me go a few minutes ago."

"No, I wasn't. I was willing to bring Princeton back to Bastion to get him to safety, then come back for you."

Princeton whirled on Columbia, wide-eyed.

"*That* was your plan?" he gaped. "You were just gonna dump me at the Commission and then turn around?"

"What does it matter to you?" Columbia shrugged. "You'd be safe."

"Yeah, but if I'm the only one who makes it back to Bastion…I mean, I just look like an asshole."

"Is that really what matters to you, Princeton?" Yale seethed. "Not looking like an asshole? That's your priority here?"

"Well, I mean, it's just...you gotta admit it doesn't look great for me if I'm the only one to make it back when my team is stumbling around in the dusts—"

"I would have stocked up and come back for you the first chance I got," Columbia cut in. "Now it looks like that's not an option. So splitting up doesn't make sense. It makes sense for us to try and find our way back *together.*"

"What are you not getting, Columbia? *I'm not going back without Harvard.*"

"*You have to!*"

Never in all the years that they had known each other had Yale heard Columbia yell. Both Princeton and Yale flinched, startled by the sudden outburst from a woman they'd assumed was not capable of anger hotter than a low simmer.

"Look," she hissed, "back when I thought I could come back for you, things were different. I let you dream whatever you wanted to about Harvard because I know I could search for you with the Commission behind me. But now? Now I need to be honest with you, Yale. Harvard is gone. Princeton is right—he's probably dead. And if he isn't, he will be soon. If you want to come back out and look for him after we've made it back to Bastion, we can—"

Yale shook their head, looking down, "It'll be too late."

"It's *already* too late! You know what's gonna happen if we find him, Yale? We'll find *bones.*"

A heavy silence settled upon the Ivies. Yale didn't look up from where they stared into the dusty ground. Columbia finally softened.

"I didn't...I didn't *want* to say those things to you," she murmured, back to her usual soft-spoken self, "but I'm not going to sit back and watch you sacrifice yourself—sacrifice all of us—on a dream that won't come true."

Yale was motionless, head still down, hands balled into fists at their sides.

"I know what you're thinking," they heard Columbia say. "I don't think this is really about Harvard, is it? You still haven't let go—"

"Don't say it," Yale whispered, without lifting their head. "Please. Don't say it."

Columbia sighed ruefully. "I don't have to. You already know."

Yale clenched their teeth. She was always so certain she knew everything about them. And sure, she understood *some* of the reason they were so committed to getting Harvard back. But she didn't understand all of it. In fact, they weren't sure if they understood all of it themself. They willed themself to look up and found Columbia's stare still boring into them.

Princeton's head ping-ponged back and forth between the two of them.

"What," he said, "the hell, are you two *talking about*?"

No answer came from either. They just stood there, Columbia staring at Yale levelly, Yale refusing to meet her gaze. Silence descended upon the Ivies like a thick wave of saltwater, heavy and churning.

Then Columbia did something she promised never to do when she joined the Commission.

"Chavi," she whispered, "people need you at home." Yale felt themself start to tremble. Before they could respond, Princeton's voice snapped them back into reality.

"Hey *guys*?" he asked, a note of terror in his voice that sounded out of place. "What the *hell* is that?"

Both whirled to face him, expecting to see the usual desertwalker barreling toward them, or perhaps even another team of rogue scavengers coming to brutalize them. But Princeton wasn't pointing out into the dusts. He was pointing *up*.

CHAPTER TWENTY-TWO

The Creature

Skrack stopped abruptly, and Harvard, anxiously following, nearly crashed into him.

"Do you see it?" Harvard asked, following the crabs gaze over the horizon.

I can sense it.

"What is it?"

Skrack considered this, shifting his claws on the sand. *I do not know.*

"Can we fight it?" Harvard asked eagerly, his confidence inflated after the victory against the netherworm.

I...do not know. This creature...it troubles me.

"Yeah, it troubles me too!" Harvard agreed impatiently. "According to the Guardians To Be, it's going to kill the rest of my crew!"

That is not why it troubles me. It should not be here.

"Of course it shouldn't—"

Silence, child. It should not be here. It is not of the desert. It is something new.

"I mean...look, don't take this the wrong way, but have you ever considered there may be something in the desert other than crabs?" Harvard ventured.

Skrack turned his hulking body toward Harvard, and even though his eyes were black and unreadable, Harvard could still sense his righteous rage.

I have lived more life than you could comprehend. I know this desert better than you will ever know yourself. I have communed with the land in ways you could never dream of. I know who my brethren are and that. Is. Not. One of them.

"O...okay," Harvard shrunk away, "but maybe we can still fight it? Just like we practiced!"

We did not practice.

"You know what I mean."

I do not.

"Like with the worm! Me on your back, you…ya know, fighting and stuff." He gave the air a feeble punch as if to illustrate his point.

That puts you in unnecessary danger.

"I can help!" Harvard insisted indignantly. "Remember how I saw that worm tail coming and you, like, totally stabbed it?"

That was one time.

"You have to admit it was pretty cool, though."

I suppose it was "pretty cool." But it was an aberration.

"But it could happen again! We're a team, Skrack!"

No, we are not.

"Look. I know you don't want me getting hurt cuz I got a job to do. And I'll still do that job! But if there's any way I can help my friends from getting killed by that…that thing, then I'm gonna do it. So please. Let me get on your back."

Harvard expected that a word from the Empress would be needed to help convince the headstrong crab, but she stayed silent. Instead, Skrack wordlessly lowered his shell so Harvard could clamber on. Grinning wildly, Harvard fastened his dustscarf, lowered his goggles, and climbed aboard.

* * *

Yale looked up to see what looked almost like a bird—or, no, a bat seemed to make more sense, from the way the sunlight showed through the skin of the wings. It circled the crew from above, like a vulture circles carrion. It was too far to make out any features, but it must have noticed that the Ivies had noted its presence, because it gave a shriek and dove.

"Move!" Yale shouted, and the Ivies scattered in different directions. Distance distorted its size, so Yale couldn't be certain of how large the thing was until it planted its hefty claws on the sand, a cloud of dust billowing away from it. Only then did Yale see that this was not a bat, and definitely not a bird—it was about twice their height, and its wingspan must have been at least three times that.

The next thing Yale noticed was the beast's fur. Though its claws were reptilian, like those of the Chocolates' pinchdragon, most of the creature was covered in burnt orange fuzz, interrupted with white stripes along its serpentine tail. It stretched its neck toward Yale to what seemed like an impossible length, and they backed away, nearly tripping over their feet in the process. It gave another screech, revealing two rows of pointed teeth, and this time so loud they felt the vibration of it in their bones. They reached instinctively for their hunting knife. It seemed almost silly, like pulling a butter knife on a dragon, but it was the only thing they had to defend themself from the thing now pointing its leathery snout at them.

Princeton opened his mouth to speak, then closed it, then opened it again to say, "Hey, what the *fuck*?"

The creature took one step forward, claws digging into the sand, and snapped at Yale, nearly catching them in its jaws.

Then Columbia was there. Sandstaff clutched with hands on either end, she shoved the metal rod into the thing's mouth, and it caught on its jagged teeth. For a moment they stood locked there, creature and girl, like two sword fighters pressing their blades together. The creature craned its neck forward, pushing both Columbia and Yale back. It snapped, but with the sandstaff caught in its teeth, it couldn't catch anything in its jaws. Infuriated, it unhooked itself and retreated.

Princeton fumbled with his pack, pulling out a vapor canister they had recovered from the sandheads camp. He called out, and the creature's serpentine head whipped toward him. He pumped the lever on the canister furiously, the white vapor dissipating in the hot desert air. Once he'd emptied an entire canister toward the creature, he pulled out another, backing away as the thing advanced. It must have inhaled some vapor, but nothing happened.

"Hey guys?" Princeton said shakily. "I think we're totally fucked."

* * *

Harvard felt like he was in a fairy tale, a brave knight riding his steed into battle. Except he wasn't very brave, and Skrack was far from a steed and would surely resent the notion. Still, he couldn't help feeling a swell of pride as he gripped Skrack's shell, wind blowing back his curly hair, ready for action. Well, as ready as he could be. But if he could help his friends even a little bit, then he would do it.

All of that melted away when Harvard saw the thing they were up against. Instantly he understood why it had felt so unfamiliar to Skrack—it resembled a bird more than it did a crab, which made it unlike any desertwalker Harvard had ever seen. What kind of desertwalker had wings? And could fly? Harvard's instincts told him he should leap off the crab's the first chance he got. But his friends were in danger, and no matter what, he would not abandon them. Would Yale abandon him? No. He gripped the hilt of his hunting knife with one hand and the edge of Skrack's shell with the other, steeling himself for battle.

The beast was so focused on the Ivies it didn't hear Skrack's approach. The crab barreled into it. It stumbled, but caught itself, giving a cry of surprise and rage.

"Speak to it!" Harvard suggested. "You can communicate with other desertwalkers, right?"

I...I cannot reach this creature. Its Essence is alien, Skrack said, raising his claws defensively.

"What do you mean?"

I do not...I do not understand this beast. It is not...one of us.

"It's not from the Southwest Plains?" Harvard guessed.

No. It is not a desertwalker.

"But...all beasts that walk in the desert are desertwalkers," Harvard puzzled, watching the bird-thing regain its footing. "That's like, the whole definition."

This beast, Skrack said as the creature spread its wings in preparation to charge, *does not simply walk.*

Skrack rammed into the beast, sending it reeling. For a few precious moments, the Ivies were forgotten. In a fury, the beast charged the scuttler, which batted at it with its claw. The bird monster bit Skrack's leg, and he gave a pained cry. Harvard gripped Skrack's shell as the crab reared backward, the beast's jaw clamped onto his leg.

Do something do something do something, Harvard told himself. But what could he do? He was just a tiny human caught in a battle between two titans.

Desperate to help, he pulled out the knife he'd taken from the abandoned scavenger camp. He used what little upper-arm strength he had to pull himself to the top of Skrack's shell. There he could clearly see the beast's head only a few feet below him, trying to rip Skrack's leg from its socket.

This is going to be stupid, Harvard thought, before leaping off Skrack and landing on the bird creature's neck. He wrapped his legs around the furry beast to avoid being bucked off, then jammed his knife into the monster's eye.

The bird let out an anguished howl, releasing Skrack and throwing its head backward. Harvard's head whipped back as the bird attempted to shake him off, and he gripped the fur with his fingers, squeezing his eyes shut and using all his strength not to be thrown to the ground.

A claw gripped him gently around the waist, and he released his hold on the bird monster as Skrack placed him back on the shell. The bird monster still wriggled in agony, Harvard's knife lodged in its eye, now dripping blood.

Harvard felt a stab of guilt for having harmed the creature, even though it had been going to kill Skrack. He couldn't let that happen. The creature steadied itself, focused back on the enemy—on him. Harvard's pulse quickened as the creature locked eyes with him, burning with pure, animalistic fury. He gripped Skrack's shell in preparation for the bird's attack.

Its striped tail shot at him from the right, wrapping around his body.

"Uh-oh," he said, just before the tail flung him out into the empty desert.

* * *

"No way," Princeton murmured as he watched the struggle. "There cannot be a *person* riding that crab. It's not possible."

"They're working together," Yale breathed, transfixed.

"We should still go," Columbia suggested. "It's not safe for us here."

"We can't just leave them!" Yale protested.

"Um, they seem to be doing pretty fine on their own," Princeton observed as the human figure in the distance leapt on the neck of the beast.

"This person...I mean, they saved us. We can't just—"

"Yes, we can," Princeton cut them off. "They probably bonded with the scuttler over, I don't know, a love of eating human flesh, and once they kill the bird thing they're gonna split us fifty-fifty. The dusts make people insane, remember? Or did you forget about how we got sold to religious psychos who tried to bury you alive?"

Yale looked to Columbia, who was watching the battle intently. They were completely paralyzed and needed her advice more than ever. She gasped, and Yale whipped their head around to see the human thrown off into the sand.

* * *

For one terrifying, weightless moment, Harvard hurtled through the air, anticipating the moment he would hit the ground. He didn't so much "hit" the ground as violently scrape up against it, his skin burning as it slid along the sand. One side of his body would be completely scraped. His brain registered that he was hurting but there was so much pain he couldn't entirely tell what part of him had gotten hurt. All of him, maybe?

He pushed the pain away as he picked himself up off the ground, dazed. He stumbled as he tried to regain his footing, feeling as though the earth were pitching under him like a fishing boat out on the Infinite Ocean. He sank to his knees, took a deep breath, and tried again to rise. This time the ground had settled. Where was Skrack? Where was the creature? He turned to see the two beasts in the distance—how far had he been thrown?—still locked in combat. But Skrack kept turning to where Harvard had fallen, and the bird creature used these moments of distraction to snip at him.

Please protect them, Harvard willed. *Don't worry about me. Save them. Please.*

But Skrack could not hear Harvard's silent plea. He disengaged with the bird in favor of moving toward his human companion, abandoning the rest of the Ivies to check on Harvard.

* * *

"We need to see if they're okay," Yale declared. Columbia grabbed their arm.

"Listen," she said. "I know you always think you can save everyone. But you can't. If we stay here, all of us will get killed. We need to go. Now."

Yale gritted their teeth and nodded, giving in to Columbia's pulling.

"I think maybe we should start, like, running, actually," Princeton suggested, pointing toward the fray. The scuttler had given up on the fight in favor of its fallen human, and the bird monster swiveled its rope of a head to focus on the Ivies.

* * *

"Skrack, no!" Harvard said aloud, but the crab was still too far away to hear him. He watched helplessly as the monster gave a hungry cry, pursuing his friends. He'd come all this way to save his team, and now he was about to see them massacred, just like those scavengers from the abandoned camp.

The abandoned camp...had they been killed by this creature too? Or at least, the one who still remained? How had the rest survived?

Terror knotted in his stomach as he watched the way the avian moved toward his crew, greedily, just like...a crow. An image crystallized in Harvard's mind, one he hadn't thought about for many years: the garden of Bell Manor. This creature, though alien to Harvard, was familiar in shape—he'd seen it thousands of times. He'd fed peanuts to that shape on the edge of the Bell property, much to his mother's chagrin.

A super messed up crow, Harvard thought, looking at the claws, the whipping tale, the bent beak—*but still a crow. And I may be a failure of a scavenger, but I definitely know things about crows.*

* * *

Running away from monsters was something the Ivies did frequently, but it was beginning to look like this would be the last time. The bird monster spread its wings and beat them twice, lifting into the air to land behind the three scavengers. It took long strides with its scaly legs, and Yale knew this was a foot race they were destined to lose.

Then the footsteps stopped.

* * *

Harvard reached for his pack, rifling through the food rations for the little bundle he'd stored away. He pulled out a knot of fabric, concealing the shard of mirror he'd found in the abandoned scavengers camp. He thrust the thing above his head, catching the glint of the sun, and angled it toward the avian.

Its head swiveled around nightmarishly, like an elastic owl, and it gave a squawk of glee when it saw the bright, winking light. It padded heavy feet in Harvard's direction.

Harvard realized he should have planned this better.

He lifted the mirror hard high above his head, angling just right to reflect the sunlight toward the monster. It was a gamble, but one that seemed to be working.

"I'm right here!" he shouted to the creature racing toward him, though it probably cared much more about the glimmering object in his hands than his shouts. What would he do when it reached him? Run? Fight?

No, he would probably just stand there and let it eat him, like the last remaining scavenger of the Computers, who'd had their flesh picked away by the time Harvard found them. By the time the Ivies got to his body, they wouldn't even realize it was him who had saved them. But despite the creature growing larger and larger, wings flapping eagerly, eyes wide, jaw snapping, there was no way he would rather die than protecting his team.

When the beast was mere centimeters away from him, a fraction of second from crushing him in its jaws, he screamed. It was less a scream of fear than an unrestrained outpouring of emotion, the last cry of a boy who had made peace with his impending violent demise. The sound tore itself out of him like a spirit releasing his body after years of possession.

Then the beast was pinned to the ground, skewered by a massive crab leg. Harvard expected the beast to cry out, but the bird monster died in silence. Skrack had completely shattered its spine.

Harvard let out a shaky breath and collapsed to his knees. Only then did he realize he had been gripping the shard of mirror so tightly blood had begun to trickle down his arms. He stared absently at the beast that had almost killed him, now bloody and motionless in the sand.

He was only pulled out of his daze when Skrack asked, *Shall we go see your friends?*

* * *

"No, no!" Princeton held up a finger. "Before you even say it, no!"

"I mean, they might have just saved our lives..." Yale said.

"Might have?" Columbia asked.

"Yeah, and now they're riding toward us on a *giant quaking crab!*" Princeton gesticulated wildly to the desertwalker and human who were making their way toward them.

"Crab that's been protecting them," Yale pointed out. "That's not normal."

"Yeah, that's not normal! It's weird! Too weird! We should get the hell out of here."

"It would be fascinating to understand how someone tamed a scuttler," Columbia mused.

"Um, hello? Do you not remember the Chocolates? And how you guys were like, 'oh maybe they'll be our friends! Maybe they're nice!' and then they sold us? Did you forget about that?"

"Did you run off and secretly piss off *this guy* too?" Yale shot back. Princeton seethed and crossed his arms.

"Okay clearly someone has not forgiven me as much as they say they did," he grumbled.

"We'll be careful," Yale assured him. "We'll stay on our guard. We have vapor, remember."

"Yeah, if our vapor even works anymore!"

"It does," Yale assured him. "That bird was...something else. At the first sight of danger, we'll run away. Trust me."

* * *

Harvard felt a pang of disappointment when he saw the Ivies take up defensive positions. Did they not recognize him? Or worse, did they recognize him and not want him back? Then he remembered he was still wearing his goggles and dustscarf, and his telltale red hair was caked with dust and sand. What reason would they have to expect he was even still alive, much less had saved them?

Harvard's stomach fluttered at the prospect of seeing his crew again. He hadn't dared let himself linger on the thought because he wasn't sure he would ever make it back. How would they feel about him? Would they be mad at him for abandoning them with O'Neill? Would they feel betrayed he had befriended a desertwalker? He couldn't help but wonder about all the reasons they might be mad at him, all the things they might yell at him about when they saw his face.

Skrack came to a halt in front of the Ivies. Harvard peered down at them. From this height, they looked so...small. So scared. Even with Yale putting on what must have been the bravest face they could muster, he could tell. He understood a little better why Skrack had so little respect for humans. Compared to him, they were just so...temporary.

Harvard slid down Skrack's back and landed awkwardly in the sand, cautiously approaching his team. When he was close enough that they could see him, he ripped off his dustscarf and goggles, gave them a friendly wave, and shouted, "Hey guys!"

Interlude Fifteen: Seven

The final evaluation reminded Number Seven of a game children played in school. He'd had no experience with such games, but he was aware children who'd gone to normal school had the opportunity to play games quite frequently. The training group was split into two teams, and each team was given four rings. The normally empty training area was covered with stacks of crates to serve as obstacles, obscuring the teams from each other. Each team hid their four rings on their respective side of the training room and tried to steal the other side's rings without being caught. And "caught" did not just mean tagged. It meant tackled and wrangled until the team got their ring back.

Number Seven, for once, felt he might be in his element. He might not be smart or strong, but he was excellent at going unnoticed. Much to his chagrin, his team captain, Number Two, had assigned him to defense. He began to protest, but Number Two quickly shut him down.

"You're tiny, Seven. Even if you could find a ring, you couldn't keep it."

Number Seven shrank at this. He couldn't deny it was true. So he slunk around his team's territory, watching for invaders. It wasn't even his job to attack them. He was assigned to call out to Number Six if he saw anyone cross the line.

Instructor watched the game—no, exercise—pacing, arms crossed, evaluating each of the players.

Seven was left to stew in his own emotions as he stood at the line separating him from enemy territory, watching his teammates sneak behind crates and wrestle with opponents. He had hated the training— he hated the way his body felt like it was about to give out, he hated the constant embarrassment, he hated the exhaustion. More than anything, though, he hated his impotence. He hated the way everyone looked at him, like they knew he would never make it.

He saw a ring.

The other team had hidden it just beyond the dividing line, right under an overturned crate. It was a smart move, admittedly. Seven's team would never have thought to look so close to their own side of the room. Seven glanced around. Everyone seemed to be focused on his teammates across the line. He furtively stepped over the line and reached for the ring.

A hand grabbed his wrist before he could reach it.

"What's your job?" Instructor demanded from where they appeared next to him.

"I...I was on defense," Seven admitted.

"Is this defense?" Instructor asked.

"It was right there!" Seven exclaimed. "No one else was going to see it."

"I don't care!" Instructor snapped. "Your captain gave you orders, and you listen to your captain!"

Seven became painfully aware the entire game had stopped so the other trainees could watch this altercation.

"But I...I want to help!" Seven said in a voice that verged on pleading.

"I know, I know, and you think that's so selfless of you, to try and help your team. But it's *selfish*. You wanna feel like a hero but you *don't get to*. Not at the expense of your team."

"It's just a game," Number Two grumbled from where she stood by the crates.

"It's not a game!" Instructor shouted. "Shit like this? This is how people die out there! And if you don't believe me, then you'll go out there and see it for yourself. But it's slip ups like this that could cost your whole team their lives."

Seven nodded vigorously.

"You listen to your captain, alright? That's how you survive in the desert. You don't survive by being brave, you don't survive by being smart. You listen to your captain and you do what they say. Got it?"

"I—" Number Seven stammered, the maelstrom of shame and humiliation welling up inside him and threatening to burst. He felt his throat tighten and tears welled up in his eyes unbidden. *Not now*, he begged himself, *please don't cry now.*

Instructor's grip on his wrist constricted, and he yelped as they pulled him closer, twisting his arm. Pain shot up his wrist and he wondered if it was bruised.

"Got it?" they repeated, and for the first time, Seven was *scared* of them.

"You're hurting me," Number Seven whispered. Instructor released him immediately, looking oddly shaken, and Number Seven backed away, massaging his wrist.

"Training is over for today," Instructor said abruptly, still staring at Number Seven with an expression he could not quite place. There was annoyance in it, but also a hint of shame. "Everybody get out."

No one moved. They just stared at the two, dumbfounded.

"Get out!" Instructor shouted, and this time the cohort hurriedly departed. Number Seven glanced over his shoulder as he hurriedly exited the training room. He saw Instructor burying their face in the heels of their hands.

That night, Number Seven stayed in the training room long after the lights were shut off. It was useless, of course. He couldn't build up the muscle he'd lacked for seventeen (eighteen?) years in one night, or the stamina, or reflexes. He was going to be dead weight on his team, and pretty soon, he would just be dead. He laid into a punching bag, his hands unwrapped because no one had given him anything to wrap them in. His wrist still hurt from where Instructor had unwittingly twisted it. He thought it might be sprained. He hit the bag until his knuckles were bloody. He could hardly make it swing. He screamed in frustration and pain, but he did not stop.

Number Seven did not wake up to the bell the next morning. Instead, he woke up to the sound of shuffling in the hallways, scavengers greeting each other and shouting from room to room. He shot up out of bed. How late had he slept? He threw on clothes and stumbled out of his room toward the entry hall.

"You're late," Herman grumbled. "Most teams met an hour ago."

"I know. It's just I—"

"I don't care what your excuse is. I guarantee you I've heard it before. Just get in there, okay? Your team is waiting for you. You're with the Ivies. Your brand name is Harvard."

"R-right. Sorry."

Seven—Harvard—rushed into the training room, already blurting out his apologies as he burst through the door.

"I'm so sorry, so sorry. I know I'm late. I was just...I..." he stopped abruptly when he had a moment to look at the team. Two unfamiliar faces, a girl with dark skin and round glasses and a tall tan boy with dyed blond hair stared back at him. But beyond them was the face that made

Harvard's stomach twist: the person Harvard had once known as Instructor, who now wore a leather band indicating they were his captain.

"Harvard," they said, adjusting their frameless square glasses and gesturing for him to come forward, "meet your team. This is Columbia," they gestured to the girl, "and this is Princeton." They nodded their head to the boy.

"I'm really so so sorry—" Harvard repeated. The captain held up a hand.

"You can stop apologizing," they said in a tone that Harvard couldn't quite read. Were they mad?

"You can call me Yale, now," they said, giving Harvard a careful nod.

"Oh, so he's like...a little guy," Princeton observed, looking Harvard up and down, which made him about ready to curl up and die right then and there. Yale's head snapped to the side to face Princeton.

"Did I ask for your opinion?" they demanded. Princeton shriveled, which gave Harvard a bit of guilty satisfaction. He couldn't help but feel grateful to his captain for shutting down the discussion of his body so quickly.

"No, captain," Princeton muttered, chastened.

"Didn't think so. Now, the two of you can head to equipment storage. We're late, so most of the other teams have already taken the good stuff, but still. See what you can scrounge up for us, alright?"

"Sorry," Harvard murmured again. "I know it's my—"

"Stop," Yale cut him off, "apologizing." Definitely annoyed this time. Harvard was certain of that. There was something else, though, and he couldn't quite pick up on what that was. Yale turned to their other two crew mates.

"Get going," they commanded, "before everything is gone."

Harvard followed the other two toward the door, but Yale's voice stopped him.

"Not you, Harvard," they said. "I want to have a word with you."

Harvard felt a sharp stab of panic. Hadn't they already had enough words with him already? What else could they possibly have to say? The door slammed shut as the other two scavengers left the room. Harvard turned around, making his way back meekly, preparing himself to be scolded. His new leader placed a hand on his shoulder and leaned in, but to Harvard's surprise they said, "I'm sorry."

Harvard blinked. "What?"

Yale sighed.

"I've been going through some stuff and I took it out on you. I shouldn't have. So, I'm sorry."

For a moment, Harvard was so taken aback that he didn't know what to say. Then he stammered, "Do you...do you wanna talk about..."

"No," Yale snapped. "And don't ever ask that again. Everything we did before we were the Ivies — we leave that behind when we join a team. Understand?"

Harvard nodded meekly. Yale sucked in a breath.

"I'm sorry," they said again. "I...I'll be better. I promise."

"It...It's okay," Harvard found himself saying.

"No, it's not," Yale insisted. "I was a bad instructor, but I wanna be at least a half decent captain. So if I'm ever that mean to you again you can, I don't know, slap me."

"I'm not gonna do that," Harvard laughed awkwardly.

They gave a crooked grin. "I know. I'm just saying. I shouldn't have embarrassed you like that, and I shouldn't have hurt you. No one should. And you shouldn't let them."

"Oh. Okay." Harvard realized belatedly that this was the first time in his life anyone had told him how he should be treated.

"How...is your wrist?" they asked.

"It's fine," Harvard lied. "It doesn't even hurt anymore."

Yale sighed, and Harvard was sure they knew it wasn't true. For a fleeting moment, they looked as though they might cry.

"I know it's more than I deserve," Yale continued, "but...can we just forget about this whole week? Pretend it never happened."

"Yes. Please," Harvard agreed instantly. "I would...I would very much like that."

"Okay. Good. We're starting fresh then."

"Yeah. That, um, that sounds good."

"Thanks."

Harvard cast his gaze down. "Um. I mean for what it's worth, you weren't...I mean you weren't wrong," Harvard admitted, shuffling his feet. "I'm gonna drag down the team. And I know that."

Yale inhaled slowly. "Look, Harvard, there's this misconception that being a scavenger is about being big and strong and whatever. But that's not true. It's not even about being smart, or fast. It's about listening to each other."

"I'm a good listener," Harvard said. And it was true. He was.

"Then I think you'll be a good crew member, too."

They gave Harvard a firm pat on the shoulder and his heart fluttered. As they made their way to the door, Harvard called out to them.

"Instructor! I mean, captain. I mean—"

"Yale," they corrected without turning back around. "You can call me Yale."

"Yale," Harvard repeated, as if testing the name out. "You've been out there in the desert, right?"

A moment of silence. Yale stood in the doorway, one hand on the door frame, still not turning to face Harvard.

"Yeah."

"Is it really as dangerous as they say?" Harvard asked.

"Yeah."

Another moment of silence, then Yale glanced over their shoulder. "But hey, that's why you have a team."

That night, Harvard imagined being out in the dusts with the Ivies. Perhaps it wouldn't be so bad. He imagined Yale saving him from a wild animal, some kind of crab. Or better yet, he imagined himself saving Yale. The fantasy paled, however, when he remembered how unrealistic it was. He couldn't save anyone. He didn't even know how to save himself.

CHAPTER TWENTY-THREE

Reunion

At first, the Ivies were frozen, staring at him wide-eyed. Finally, Princeton said, "Harvard?"

Then suddenly he was being hugged. He wasn't exactly sure who was ruffling his hair, or rubbing his back, or cupping his face, or wrapping their arms around his waist and lifting him off the ground. And he wasn't sure who was saying, "You're okay!" or "We missed you so much!" or "We thought you fuckin' died, bro!" (though he was pretty sure that last one was Princeton.) All he knew was that he was entangled in a ball of limbs and there were tears falling down his face, and there were tears falling down everyone else's faces too, and they were *happy* to see him, they were *happy,* and *he* was happy.

In fact, it was the happiest moment of Harvard's life.

Once he was set back on the ground and the Ivies gave him a bit more space, he realized he had no idea what to say.

"So, uh," he ventured, "what's up with you guys?"

Columbia and Princeton just stared at him, and Yale laughed.

"Not much. Don't worry about it," they smiled, waving a bandaged hand. Harvard made a mental note to ask about that later. He couldn't take his eyes off them. They looked exhausted, disheveled, and on the verge of collapse. And yet they were even more beautiful than Harvard remembered. He wondered if it was just because he'd been away for so long.

"Forget about us. What happened to you?" Princeton asked.

"You were out in the dusts all on your own," Columbia added. "We didn't know...we didn't know if you'd make it."

"Yeah, I mean I didn't either," Harvard laughed. "I totally would have died, if it hadn't been for, um..." he looked over his shoulder and Skrack trudged up behind him.

"Dude, you keep a scuttler as a pet?" Princeton marveled.

"No, no!" Harvard said in alarm before Skrack could make an indignant comment. "He's not a pet. He's my..." Friend? "...associate."

Yale nodded slowly. "So you became *associated*...with a desertwalker?"

Harvard could feel himself blushing.

"Look, I know this is gonna be hard to believe," he held up his hands defensively, "but there's so much more to desertwalkers than we ever knew. They have their own society and factions and rules..." he cut himself off, wondering how to word the last bit. The Ivies stared at him, and he couldn't tell if it was amazement or disbelief—or worse, concern.

"And, they can speak. They, um, started speaking to me?" Harvard squeaked.

Yale took a deep breath. "What do you mean," they said levelly, "that the crab is speaking to you?"

"Um. Okay so what I'm about to tell you is gonna sound really weird."

"What you're *about* to tell us is weird?" Princeton asked incredulously.

"Scuttlers can speak *directly into your mind*. But! Before you say anything, I can prove it. This is Skrack and he and I have been traveling together for days. Skrack, show them!"

Skrack was silent. Still the Ivies stared, and Harvard felt his pulse quicken.

"Um...Skrack?" he goaded. Skrack shifted his claws awkwardly.

I cannot do what you ask, Harvard.

"Why not?"

They cannot hear me.

"Yeah, but why?"

They have not yet gained the Empress' trust. We can only communicate with those the Empress deems worthy. There is no way to change this.

Harvard turned to his crew. "Um, just a second," he held up a finger. "We're having, um, technical difficulties. Empress? Where are you, Empress?"

Skrack extended a claw with the Empress perched atop it. Harvard scooped her up to show her to his friends.

"This is, er, Empress Kryaka of the Southwest Plains. She's kinda a big deal." He turned to face the little crab in his hands.

"Please speak to them," he begged. "Otherwise, they're gonna think I've totally lost it."

I'm afraid I cannot do that, Harvard, the Empress said.

Harvard felt a hand on his shoulder.

"Harvard," Columbia said sweetly, "you've been on your own for a long time. And it must have been really scary for you. We understand if you felt lonely and—"

"N...no!" Harvard stammered, "It's real, I swear! This is the Empress and she rules all the crabs—well, I mean, not all of them, just, just some of them—and, and this is Skrack and he protects her, and—and his hatchlings. They're training to be Guardians. And—"

"Harvard," Yale said, "you don't have to prove anything to us. We're just happy that you're alive."

"But it's true!" Harvard insisted. "Please, Empress. Help me."

Trust is not a choice, Harvard. It is not given freely. It must be earned. It can only *be earned. You must understand this.*

"Okay, yeah, sure, but I mean, how can they earn your trust?"

The same way that you did. You proved yourself to be of good heart. If they do the same, only then will they be able to speak to me.

Harvard turned his head up to face his team.

"So, um, here's the thing," he explained, rubbing the back of his neck self-consciously. "She said she can't talk to you cuz she doesn't trust you, and uh, Skrack can't either, because, well...okay so they have this thing going on where if the *Empress* can talk to you, then they all can, but if she can't...basically you just have to prove to her that you're good, and then you'll hear her and you'll see what I mean."

Yale nodded, their face stony, and Harvard wondered what they must be thinking.

"Look, I know this sounds crazy. I thought...I thought they'd be able to talk to you, and then you guys would just, like, believe me!" Harvard explained.

"Hey guys?" Princeton asked. "Group meeting. Sans Harvard. No offense, Harvard."

"N...None taken," Harvard stammered. He wasn't offended—no, he was *afraid*. After everything, he was finally reunited with the Ivies—what would happen if they thought he'd simply lost his mind? Would they leave him again?

Princeton shuffled the others off to have a furtive tete-a-tete, and Harvard was alone with the crabs.

* * *

So, good news and bad news, Princeton figured. The good news was that they'd found Harvard. The bad news was that when he was alone in the dusts, Harvard had lost his mind.

"Okay, so, uh, when are we gonna break it to him that he's not actually talking to crabs?" he asked.

Yale gave Princeton a stern look. "We don't."

Princeton blinked. "Excuse me?"

"Listen, Princeton. I'm just as confused as you are right now. I don't know what to make of Harvard's claims the crabs speak to him. But whatever delusions he is under—if any—something is happening here. I mean, have you ever seen a scuttler let a human *ride* it like that? Whether or not you believe a word coming out of Harvard's mouth, that thing saved us. And not just so it could get to us first. No, for some reason, that creature wants us to live. And it has...I mean, it has a relationship with Harvard. Look at them!"

They all turned to see Harvard "conversing" with the massive creature, laughing at something the smaller one had apparently "said" to him.

"Whatever is...happening right now," Yale gestured vaguely at Harvard and his carcine companions, "it saved Harvard's life out there. Founders, it just saved *our* lives." They turned back to face the other two in a conspiratorial huddle.

"So whatever Harvard says, we believe it. Or at the very least, just act like you believe it. As far as he knows, we believe every word. Got that?"

Princeton stared at Yale wide-eyed before whirling on Columbia.

"Okay so clearly Yale has lost it too. What do *you* think?"

"Actually, Princeton, I agree with Yale," Columbia admitted.

"Oh, Founders. Oh, *Founders.* I'm the only sane one left on the crew. Does that mean I get to be captain now?"

"Shut it, Princeton," Yale snapped. "I'm still captain, and you're still taking my orders, alright?"

"Look," Columbia reasoned, "I don't know if I believe that Harvard is really *speaking* to them. But..." she tapped her finger to her lips, glancing over to the small crab in Harvard's hands. Her face lit up. "Carcine creatures *must* have some kind of communication system beyond our understanding!"

"Um," Princeton said. "I feel like I'm missing something here. Please explain."

"Think about it," she said. "When we were on board O'Neill's pod, the desertwalkers never bothered us."

"Yeah, because the pod looked like a crab," Princeton said.

"If that was really why, then a crabsnake never would have bothered us!" Columbia continued. "There must have been another reason the desertwalkers left O'Neill in peace. And what had changed by the time we got back?"

"Harvard was gone," Yale said.

"Yes, and he took *that crab* with him," Columbia pointed at the so-called Empress cupped in Harvard's hands. "O'Neill thought he was safe because the scuttlers were stupid enough to think he was one of them, but that's not true at all. As soon as his crab—*that* crab—was not on board, they were hostile. They *knew* there was something in that pod to protect, and they *stopped* protecting it as soon as it was gone. I mean, I don't know anything about an Empress, but there must be *something* special about that crab, and the other scuttlers know it."

Princeton nodded slowly, chewing on all this. Finally, he said, "Yeah that settles it. You're all crabshit crazy."

"Princeton!" Yale snapped. "Regardless of what your smooth little potato of a brain is telling you, you are still a member of this crew and we are going to act as a team. We are going to go along with Harvard whether you like it or not, and if you call him crazy one more time—and this is a promise—I *will* punch you. In the face."

Princeton held his hands up as if to prove his blamelessness. "Have it your way, cap," Princeton said. "I'm just saying that if we're crab food— that's on you."

"Sure," Yale grumbled, "that's on me."

They turned back toward Harvard and motioned for the others to follow. He translated—or so he claimed—the creatures' demands. He told them an implausible story about the Empress' heir, and how if they didn't save the scuttler in two days, the desertwalkers would attack the city.

"Except we spent a bit of extra time finding you guys," Harvard admitted, looking down and wringing his hands, as though his act of bravery was somehow an embarrassment for him. "So, um, honestly I'm not really sure how we're gonna get there in time."

"I know how we can get there in a day," Columbia said, casually, as though this should have been obvious. All faces, including those of the crabs, turned to face her.

* * *

"We'll need Skrack's help," she continued, "but he can't come with us. We'll have to go on our own."

This is foul deceit and trickery, Skrack complained. *I will not be party to it.*

Allow the girl to speak, the Empress admonished.

"We can take the Empress with us, if you'd like," she continued, "to ensure we follow through as promised."

I will not leave my post as your Guardian, Empress, Skrack complained. *I cannot allow this plan to be realized.*

Let us hear it, the Empress said, silencing her Guardian.

"They wanna hear what it is," Harvard translated.

So Columbia told them.

"Founders," Yale murmured, "I always knew you were a genius, but I mean—that's brilliant."

Columbia shrugged, though her cheeks rouged at the compliment, "I didn't think it would come in handy until we were back in Bastion, but now it looks like it's our best choice."

I cannot allow it, Skrack repeated.

I can, the Empress said. *Harvard, I will allow your friends to bear me to the city, where I will wait outside the city walls for the return of my heir.*

Empress, they seek to destroy you. They are untrue. I can sense it.

Do you truly believe Harvard to be untrue, Skrack? After everything you have witnessed? After his willingness to die for his friends?

His friends are human. Humans are loyal to other humans. They will not be loyal to us.

"That's not true!" Harvard protested. "I'm loyal to everyone! We'll save your heir, I promise! And I'll protect the Empress the whole time. I'll guard her with my life. You have my word."

"Mine too," Yale added, and all heads, human and carcine, turned to face them. "What?" they asked. "If they need to trust us, then damn it,

I'll give them a reason to. Empress, you're going to be safe with me and my crew. I'd stake my life on it."

Harvard wanted to hug them, but he resisted the urge, shuffling in the sand. After looking Yale up and down calculatingly, Columbia turned toward the creatures.

"You have my word as well," she said. "No harm will come to the Empress while she is in the care of the Ivies. That's a promise."

The two turned to Princeton, who was watching all this with his arms crossed. He rolled his eyes, then shrugged.

"Fine. Whatever. I promise to protect the 'empress' or whatever."

Yale clapped their hands. "Does she trust us yet?" they asked.

No, came the Empress' definitive answer, *but the terms of the agreement are favorable.*

Fine, Skrack grumbled, *but if you are to fail...if the Empress does not return safely, if the heir is not retrieved in time...we will have our vengeance. Do not think that the city will protect you, humans. The city is only safe because we allow it. If you err—*

"We won't!" Harvard said, though he couldn't mask that the threats already had him trembling.

See to it, Skrack said with finality.

Your friends should rest, the Empress observed. *There is an empty den not far from here. I sense it in the earth. It should be sufficient shelter for the night.*

Harvard nodded. His wariness of scuttler dens had faded long ago.

"Lead the way, Empress!" he smiled.

You do not give the Empress commands! Skrack admonished petulantly. *Empress, at your leisure.*

And with that, the strange caravan made their way to safety.

* * *

Princeton stared at the hole in the ground wide-eyed.

"In there?" he asked. "There's no way. This is the long con, guys. They just want us in there so that they can feed us to their young or whatever."

"Princeton," Columbia groaned, "don't you think that if they were going to kill us, they would have done it already?"

Princeton shifted indignantly. "Maybe they're just not *hungry* right now," he suggested.

"There's not even anyone in there right now," Harvard said. "It's an old den. Besides, Skrack says he won't eat you because your flesh is unworthy—though honestly I think he's just grumpy so you can ignore him. There'll be plenty of room for all of us, and Skrack and the Empress. Go inside. It's fine. I promise."

Harvard's promises meant little to Princeton. He shook his head vigorously.

"Nuh-uh. No way. No way in *hell*. You're crazy, Harvard. You're *insa*—"

He didn't have a chance to finish, because Yale decked him in the face.

CHAPTER TWENTY-FOUR

The Den

The den seemed to extend infinitely into the red ground, illuminated only by the sparse light of the glowing fungus, full of little branches and nooks. Each of the Ivies picked a crevice where they would sleep for the night. Skrack and the Empress remained in the central node, just below the entrance, in case any predators made an appearance.

Harvard crept into the cavern where Skrack lay, the Empress perched on top of his shell.

What do you seek, Harvard? Skrack's booming voice in his skull made him jump.

"Um...did you see Yale leave the den? I can't find them anywhere," he asked.

One of the humans left the den, yes. I do not know which. I cannot tell them apart.

"Well, I mean, you can tell me apart," Harvard said. "You just said my name."

Yes, well...you have...very distinctive hair.

Harvard couldn't help but grin a little at Skrack's evasion. He "cannot tell humans apart." Sure.

"I'm gonna go look for them, okay?" he said.

Don't be out too long, Skrack cautioned. *It would be a shame if you were to be devoured by desertwalkers just before you complete your mission.*

"I *won't* get devoured by desertwalkers, Skrack!" Harvard reassured the Guardian, like a child insisting to their mother that they will, in fact, be making good choices.

I'm just...I'm just saying.

Harvard climbed up the sandy incline out of the den into the desert breeze. Only a few paces from the den entrance was Yale, sitting on the sand, changing the bandages on one of their hands.

"You shouldn't be doing that on your own," Harvard said as he approached.

"It's fine," Yale dismissed him without looking up. Harvard knelt by their side.

"Let me help you," he said.

"I said it's *fine*," Yale repeated, still staring fixedly at the bloodied hand they were wrapping. Harvard placed a smooth hand on their injured one.

"Please."

Yale looked at him. They looked so, so tired.

"Okay," they complied. Harvard took their hand in his and began wrapping it the way he'd learned to at the Shack whenever one of the other kids hurt themselves running through the city.

"What happened?" he asked, knitting his brow as he turned Yale's ripped fingers over in his hands. Yale avoided his gaze, staring fixedly out into the desert.

"You missed a lot, Harvard," came their evasion.

"How did this happen to you?" he pressed.

Yale was silent, eyes still fixed on the horizon.

"Oh. I see," Harvard amended. "It's okay. You don't have to talk about it if you don't want to. Sometimes it's hard to talk about things that are scary."

He cringed at his own words.

"Ugh. Sorry. That sounded so stupid. I have a hard time picking words sometimes, I guess. 'When things are scary.' I mean, like, you're the captain. You're probably not scared of anything."

"I was scared," Yale said abruptly.

"What?"

"I was scared. That was the most scared I've ever been in my life. Hell, it probably would have done me a lot of good if I'd been a little more scared earlier in my life, but well—ya know."

They glanced down at their hands and Harvard nodded.

"I wish I could have been there," he admitted, then winced. "Sorry, that sounds weird. I just mean—"

"I know what you mean," Yale cut him off, and though he couldn't be sure, he thought he saw a whisper of a smile on their face.

"Huh," Harvard said quietly.

"What?" Yale eyed him.

"It's just. Funny. You're so brave, and, like, you were the most scared you've ever been. But for me, I feel like this is the most *brave* I've ever been. I mean, I guess that makes sense. I've got a megacrab protecting me. Sorry, I don't, like, mean to brag about that. It probably seems like while you were having a terrible time I was just playing in the sand with crabs—"

"No, Harvard," they touched his shoulder gingerly with their other hand. "I'm glad. Really. It's good to know that you were in good hands. Or, claws, I guess. With you out there in the desert on your own...you know, I was worried—I mean, we were worried—we feared the worst."

"But..." Harvard hesitated. He'd been dreading asking this. "I mean, if you thought I was dead, why didn't you go straight back to Bastion?"

"Because we hoped for the best."

Harvard felt something swell in his stomach, something warm.

"Oh," he squeaked.

"Princeton and Columbia, they wanted to go back. Nothing against you, of course, but you know...they have people back home to think of. But I wasn't gonna go back without you. I wasn't gonna leave you out here on your own."

Harvard couldn't help but blush, even though he felt so stupid doing it.

"Thank you, Yale. You're...you're a good captain," he stammered, his cheeks burning.

"Heh. I disagree. But thanks." They looked as though they would say something more, but then decided against it, shaking their head.

Harvard edged a little closer, finishing the wrapping on Yale's hand. Something about this closeness felt dangerous. And yet he wanted to be even closer. He'd never felt this kind of magnetism before, an invisible force urging him to close the distance between them, bathing in their warmth. It scared him, a bit. But it was nice, and he never wanted to leave. He realized with a flutter in his stomach he could stay by Yale's side forever, if they would only let him.

"How does that feel?" Harvard asked abruptly, lifting the hand he'd finished bandaging.

"Better, actually. A lot better. Where did you learn how to do that?"

"When I was younger and...yeah," he cut himself off. Now wasn't a great time to delve into everything from Bell Manor to the Shack. In fact, with any luck, he'd never have to tell Yale any of that. All of that had happened to Ronan Bell, after all. Now he was Harvard.

"It's hard to talk about things that are scary, huh?" Yale grinned. This time they didn't try to hide it.

"Yeah."

"Well, thank you, Harvard."

The two stared at each other for a long, silent moment, and Harvard felt like maybe they were waiting for something, but he didn't know what. He felt like he should say something, but he didn't know how to put it into words.

"You should get some sleep, okay?" Yale finally said.

"Sure," Harvard said, disappointed. He didn't want this to end. He refused to let it end. "Um. Yale?" he ventured.

"Yeah?"

"You know, I helped you with the bandage. I...I could help you with other things too."

Yale's smile faltered. "What other things do you mean?"

"Remember when we first met? And you said you were going through something but you wouldn't tell me about it. I just...I wanted to let you know that if you ever—"

"Sure," Yale agreed, but judging by how they promptly resumed staring into the empty desert, Harvard assumed they didn't mean it.

"Um."

He wrestled with himself, unsure of whether to flee now or to push the topics further. They just seemed so *sad*. Maybe he could...If he could just...

"Go to sleep, Harvard," Yale stood up, trudging out into the dusts. Harvard scrambled to follow.

"You really shouldn't walk out here on your own at night, ya know! It's not—"

"Go to *sleep*, Harvard," Yale repeated, that cold firmness in their voice. Harvard leapt back, his face rapidly flushing with embarrassment.

"R...right. Sorry. Okay. Yeah. Sorry. I...I'm sorry," he stammered. He practically sprinted back into the den, kicking himself for having pushed too hard. *Idiot*, he told himself, *stupid stupid stupid*. He dove into his own little corner of the den, put his face in his hands, and curled his fingers into his hair.

"I'm so *stupid!*" he said aloud into his palms. Ever since the Ivies had left him, he'd hoped of their reunion. He thought about the feel of Yale's hand on his when he had been sick, and he had wondered if he would ever feel their touch again. Now he felt like such a child for spinning his indulgent little fantasies, for thinking for *one moment* that *any* of the Ivies would be happy to see him again. He was still a burden on them, and that was never going to change.

He fell asleep that way, curled up in a little ball of remorse and shame.

* * *

"Knock knock," Princeton appeared at the entrance of the little den where Columbia planned to sleep for the night. "I mean, you know, there's no door, but like, you get the idea."

"What's going on?" she asked. He looked down sheepishly.

"Can I, uh, sleep in here tonight? With you? Is that okay?"

Columbia gave him a quizzical look, but she couldn't see a reason why not, so she scooted over to make room for him. He gave her a grateful smile and dropped his pack next to hers. He laid out on the ground next to her.

"So what, uh, what brings you here?" she asked tentatively.

Princeton flinched, laying out his sleeping mat. He flopped down on it and sighed heavily before giving her an answer.

"It's just...I imagined the inside of scuttler dens so many times. I thought...I thought this was going to be the last thing I saw before I died. I mean, I was certain. Ya see, some scavengers, they think they're gonna get out, eventually. They think they'll make enough to get a new job. I never thought that. I always assumed I would be a scavenger for life. And the only way I could imagine dying was getting dragged down into one of these, waiting for baby scuttlers to tear me apart."

Columbia said nothing, just surveyed Princeton with an expression of wonder. This was the first time he'd ever shown her any kind of vulnerability, and she wasn't going to let it slip away without giving it some good long analysis.

"Are you scared?" she asked. "Right now?"

He scoffed, and it was the most unconvincing scoff Columbia had ever heard.

"Like, no," he said. "As much as I think this whole plan is, like, totally fucked, you guys have a point, I guess. If these guys were gonna eat us, they would have already. So, I mean...yeah. I guess we're safe here."

His eyes still darted around the den, scanning the opening for movement.

"You're a bad liar, Princeton," Columbia informed him sweetly.

He scoffed again, but this time it was a shy, embarrassed kind of laugh, like a boy caught halfway through pulling a prank.

"I don't actually have to lie that much," he admitted, "so I'm kinda out of practice."

Columbia smiled. She wasn't sure if Princeton had ever made her smile, actually, so this was a welcome change. She stood—or, at least, stooped —and took a few steps over to the entryway of the den. She planted herself there and curled up.

"What are you doing?" Princeton asked.

"Well, let's say a scuttler does try to come eat us," Columbia postulated. "This way, it'll get to me first. Figured it would help you sleep easier."

Princeton rolled his eyes. "Columbia, this is stupid. I'm...I'm not sacrificing you to a hypothetical crab."

She shrugged. "No, you're not. I'm choosing to sleep here because I think it'll make you feel better, even if you won't admit it. I'm not in any *real* danger, you know. I just wanna make sure you feel...protected."

Another rarity: Princeton blushed.

"That's...thanks." He curled up abruptly, refusing to meet her gaze. She tossed her used shirt over the den's only glowing mushroom, sending the alcove into darkness.

"Princeton?" she asked as she lay her head down in the dirt.

"Hm?"

"I know that lately Yale has been...*focused* on Harvard. But this whole thing about being a team? That applies to you too, okay? We *all* protect each other. That's what it means to be on a scavenging crew."

"Yeah, yeah, whatever," Princeton grumbled from where he was lying. "All for one and one for all and all that."

He fell silent for a long moment, and Columbia thought he fell asleep until she heard him call her name in the darkness.

"Columbia," Princeton murmured. "Can I...ask you about something?"

Columbia sat up. Princeton had never come to her for advice. He'd never come to her for anything, really. Until Yale's episode in the pod, Princeton hardly spoke to her at all.

"Um, yeah," she said. "Sure."

She heard him sigh in the darkness, and the sound of his clothes rustling as he flipped over to face her.

"I keep saying I need to get back to Bastion for my sisters. And, I mean, it's true. I do. But that's not the only reason I want to get back."

"Okay. So...what is the other reason?"

"Honestly?" Princeton took a sharp breath. "I just don't wanna die."

"Princeton," Columbia said, "I'm pretty sure that's normal."

"I know, I know but like...sometimes I just feel like it's wrong? Like, selfish. I mean, Yale is so ready to jump into danger for other people. I mean, think of all the shit they were willing to do *just* for Harvard."

Columbia wrapped her arms around her legs, choosing the right words. "That's not necessarily a good *thing*, Princeton. I know it may look all heroic and selfless but honestly, sometimes it is good to have self-preservation instincts."

Princeton laughed. "It seems so obvious when you say it like that."

"I mean, it *is* kind of obvious," Columbia smiled to herself. "I think," she said, "it's okay to do things for yourself."

"Do *you*?"

"What?" The question caught her off guard, and she turned to face in the direction of Princeton's voice.

"Do you? Do things for yourself? I mean, like, yeah, sometimes it seems like Yale is doing *everything* for Harvard but like...it also seems like you're doing everything for Yale."

"I'm not," Columbia shot back immediately.

"Okay," Princeton said, and though Columbia couldn't see him she *knew* he was holding up his hands defensively and eyeing her skeptically. "I'm just saying."

"You wanted my advice, so I gave you my advice, okay?" Columbia snapped. "I don't remember asking you your opinion."

"Oof, alright," Princeton grumbled. "I was just, like, pointing it out I guess."

"Good night, Princeton," Columbia curled up demonstratively, as if to signify. "This conversation is over."

"Good night," Princeton said warily, and Columbia could hear him lying back down as well. The two lay in silence again for another long moment.

"You're not...the first person to have said that to me," Columbia finally said. "And...it's not good. I know that."

"Mm hm," Princeton said, hesitant to give any further observations.

"That doesn't mean I'm wrong, though. It just means...I guess I'm not great at taking my own advice, sometimes."

"That's okay. I don't think anyone is, honestly. I mean, Yale is always telling me to stop going off on people, and yet..."

The two laughed, and Columbia realized it was the first time she had laughed with anyone for a long while. She heard Princeton inhale sharply, and she knew he was about to ask her something that scared him.

"What...happened with the two of you?" Princeton asked quietly. "I know we're not supposed to talk about it, but...I mean there's a lot of things we're not supposed to do that we've totally done. So...?"

"What do you mean?" Columbia asked. There was too much there for her to ever tell, let alone in one night.

"On your last scavenging crew," he clarified.

"Oh," Columbia said, her stomach fluttering at the thought.

"Oh?"

"Someone died," she said laconically.

"I sorta figured," Princeton admitted. She was shocked by the softness of his voice. Maybe it was listening to him in the dark. Or maybe he was really trying to be gentle with her.

"And Yale, they think it was their fault?" he guessed.

"Yeah," Columbia sighed.

"How'd it happen?"

Columbia stared into darkness, breathing out slowly.

"Yale didn't obey the captain's orders. And...they probably should have."

Princeton was silent for a long moment, and they two floated in darkness together.

"So, it was their fault?" he finally said.

"Yeah. It was," Columbia sighed, even though she'd spent countless hours assuring Yale of the contrary.

"That makes—I mean, a lot of things make sense now, I guess. Like, the whole Harvard situation, and everything."

"Yeah," Columbia repeated. At this point it felt like it was all she could say.

"Why did they let them be a captain after that?" Princeton asked. Admittedly, she'd wondered the same thing herself many times.

"It's...it's a long story." Truth be told, she was fairly certain that after the ordeal with the Cookies, Yale *did* make a better captain than they would have otherwise. Being confronted with the fragility of their own crewmates sparked something in them, a protectiveness that wasn't there before. They'd always been protective of *her*. Now they were protective of everyone.

"I mean, didn't they get punished?" Princeton pressed gently.

"Yeah, of course, but...they won't tell me." Columbia hated to admit it to herself, but this was the part that ate at her the most. Not Minty's gruesome fate, but the fact that her best friend was keeping secrets from her for the first time.

"What do you mean?" Princeton asked.

"They had a disciplinary hearing, and, I mean, I presume they got some kind of punishment but...they won't tell me what it was."

"Why not?"

"I don't know," she admitted.

"I mean, I thought the two of you—I mean, you just seem like—"

"Yeah. I know. That's why it bothers me. It's the one thing they won't tell me."

It's not like I've been completely honest myself, she wanted to say, but didn't. Yale was still under the impression that she'd failed her exam, landing her here.

"Damn," Princeton murmured. "Damn."

"Yeah," she repeated one more time, definitely marking an end to that line of questioning. Maybe she shouldn't have told Princeton anything, but she felt a little lighter letting someone else know the truth. A little strange that "someone else" was Princeton.

"I'm sorry, Columbia," Princeton whispered.

It wasn't much, but somehow, it was enough. It was all he could have said. She only nodded, even though she knew he couldn't see her. Then she heard rustling and knew he had curled up to sleep.

It felt like she was caught in a time loop, fated to repeat the same moment of her life over and over again. She'd watched that creature come for her the same way she'd watched Chavi pummel that boy in the Academy years ago. They'd come to her rescue when the truth was, she wasn't entirely sure if she had needed rescuing. And it ended up getting them in trouble, and due to the twin chains of friendship and guilt she always went down with them. Would the cycle ever stop? When? When Chavi died? When *she* died?

She reminded herself of what Rivka Chakrabarti had told her as she placed a steaming cup of tea in her hands. *You are not responsible.*

But she still felt responsible. For Chavi. For Harvard and Princeton. For everyone.

Interlude Sixteen: Lotus

"Listen up you little shits, I'm gonna need you to act like you actually like each other for this one," Oreo instructed before their next dig. "There's an old computer store not far from here, one of those fancy ones—"

"Don't you think it's already been hit?" Nilla asked.

"Yes. Many times. Which is why no one will check it again for something that got missed," Oreo explained.

"Fancy" no longer described the shattered glass, smudged once-white surfaces, one-pristine synthetic wood now splintered and cracked, once-clear glass staircase now webbed with cracks and caked with dirt. Nilla, as usual, had been posted outside while Lotus, Oreo, and Minty explored the sunken shop.

"Careful on those!" Oreo warned as Minty tested the glass stairs to the floor below.

"Seems fine to me," he shrugged, and with a little salute descended to the floor below.

"What are we even looking for?" Lotus asked, carefully turning over broken screens and keyboards that littered the ground.

"Show me if you find anything that looks like it might be useful. I'll let you know."

Lotus frowned. She didn't like feeling out of her depth, and when it came to knowledge, that was a rare feeling for her.

"What are we looking for?" a voice behind her said. She jumped, dropping the device she held, its screen further shattering as it crashed to the floor.

"What are you doing here?" she whirled on Nilla.

"Scavenging. That's, like, the whole job."

"You're supposed to be over there," Lotus pointed toward the hole they'd broken in the wall to get it.

"We have better chances of finding something if we're all looking."

"Shit!" a voice cried from across the room. Both turned their heads to see Oreo examining the ground. "Everyone out!"

"What?" Lotus asked.

"There's—" Oreo cut himself off when he saw Nilla standing behind Lotus.

"What the hell are you doing here?" he demanded.

"Helping out!" they smiled congenially, holding up a half-eaten tablet computer. They turned their back on Lotus and took a few paces deeper into the shop, rifling through the scattered devices.

"Stop!" Oreo shouted. "No one move!"

Nilla froze.

"What's wrong?" Lotus asked.

"This building's got steelmites," Oreo explained.

Lotus gave him a quizzical look. She still hadn't learned all the dusts vocabulary.

"The floor," Oreo clarified, "it's unstable. Minty!" he called. There was no response.

"Minty!" Oreo called again. No response from below. He cursed under his breath.

"What...are we supposed to do?" Lotus asked.

"Get out," Oreo glanced at the hole in the wall they'd first entered through. "And hope Minty puts it together and gets out of here before everything falls on him. We just—"

The light shining into the building was eclipsed as a silhouette passed in front of the ragged entrance. Thin legs began feeling their way through the gap, snuffling.

Oreo's gaze shot to Nilla.

"This," he exclaimed, jabbing a finger toward the creature, "is why you stay out *there*."

Nilla, however, didn't seem to hear his words. They were transfixed by the creature breaking its way into the building. Though Lotus and Nilla had both heard of the creatures that roamed the desert and seen them from afar, neither had seen one up close before. Nilla raised the vapor canister they had stashed in their pack. Oreo held up a hand.

"No one move," he cautioned again. "We can't risk—"

The megacrab crashed down, and the floor shook on impact, and with a horrible grinding sound, the right edge dipping a foot. Oreo stumbled backward, catching himself on a splintered table. The sound of shattering glass drew Lotus' attention for a fleeting moment from the beast to the back of the store—the floor's sudden downward movement had completely decimated the already frail glass stairs. She turned her attention back to the creature.

It was not as large as those she'd heard rumored, creatures the size of buildings or cars, but it was still an intimidating animal, barely shorter than Lotus and at least a meter wide, claws snapping, legs scraping the cement floor. The beast swiveled, the pure black orbs of its eyes fixed on Lotus. She gasped, and she felt her body tense as it shifted toward her. She heard something below her creak. Out of the corner of her eye, she saw Nilla move, but Oreo shouted, "Stop! Don't do anything."

He glanced toward the staircase again.

"Minty!" he screamed, inching toward the exit. This time there was a shouted response from down below, but it was muffled. He knew something was happening up above, the lack of stairs left him trapped.

Lotus' impulses told her to follow Oreo toward the hole, but the beast that approached her was standing in her way.

"We've gotta do something about this thing!" Nilla shouted behind her.

"Leave it! It won't hurt us!" Oreo commanded.

"It's staring right at Lotus."

"It won't harm her," Oreo assured them. The creature advanced on her steadily, as though trying to prove otherwise. The three stood in a slowly shifting triangle—Oreo by the makeshift entrance, Nilla by the back of the store, and Lotus by the left wall. The megacrab in the center was lumbering one hulking footstep at a time toward her. Lotus had never looked a monster in the eyes before. She always thought that in the face of danger, real danger, she would be able to think fast, but here she was, petrified.

"If it were going to kill, it would have done it already," Oreo reasoned. "Lotus is safe."

"Bullshit," Nilla said. "I'm gonna stop it."

"Nilla!" Oreo held up a hand. "Stay where you are!"

"My crewmate is in danger!" they protested.

"Your crewmate is in danger below you!" Oreo pointed down. "Steelmites are no joke—"

The scuttler inched forward. It made a sort of clicking sound from deep within its shell. Lotus flinched.

"I'm the one with the vapor," Nilla said. "It's my job—"

"It's your job to keep your crew safe."

"That's what I'm gonna do."

"Nilla!"

They bounded off a splintered table, drawing the attention of the lumbering creature that had sidled up toward Lotus. Before it could so much as raise a pincer in defense, Nilla gave a sharp spray of vapor. The creature squealed in dismay but didn't go down like Lotus had hoped. Instead, it swiped its lower pincer upward, catching Nilla by surprise and knocking them across the concrete. They landed heavily, and the whole floor jolted.

"Nilla!" Oreo scolded. "Stay down." The scuttler however, was not going to back down so easily.

Lotus took her opportunity to scurry away, carefully climbing over debris without shaking the floor too much. The megacrab's heavy footfalls rattled the ground as it lurched toward Nilla.

"Don't!" Oreo shouted, but even he knew it was a lost cause. It was either vapor, or the crab would tear them apart. Nilla gave another sharp pulse of vapor when the crab was above them, again eliciting cries of pain. The creature's legs scratched at the ground as it writhed in agony. Nilla attempted to stand, but a crab leg caught them in the stomach and slammed them to the ground. The blow looked as though it could have impaled them, but the moment their body hit the concrete, the whole floor dropped from below them. It descended around three meters, landing on the floor below with a sickening thud. Oreo screamed.

Lotus gasped sharply, bracing herself against the wall. *Minty*, she thought. He would have been crushed into paste below them. As much as she hated him, no one deserved that. Her stomach lurched.

Nilla scrambled to their feet, pumping the vapor with abandon, spraying the creature that refused to die, until it shuddered and lay still.

A moment of stunned silence followed. Lotus watched the scene from her hiding place amidst the rubble. Nilla stood, breathless, above the crab carcass. Oreo stared in silent horror, until he finally brought himself to speak.

"You *idiot*!" He cried, his voice dripping with pure, fiery rage. "You killed Minty! You *killed* him! He's dead!"

Before Nilla could open their mouth to speak, Orea launched himself at them. It all happened so fast that Lotus barely had time to respond. One moment her captain was across the room, and next he was clambering over a crab carcass, tackling her crew mate.

"You killed him!" Oreo continued to scream, fists swinging, as Nilla struggled to push him off of their already bruised and battered body. "I *told* you! I told you not to!"

Recovering from her shock, Lotus forced herself into action.

"Oreo! Stop it!" She cried, climbing over the rubble. She wrapped her arms around her captain's waist and pulled. He resisted like a feral animal, his fingernails leaving bloody scratches on Nilla's throat as she finally managed to drag him away and deposit him heavily in the corner.

I'm glad Chavi made me work out, she thought morbidly, wondering if Oreo would have killed Nilla had she needed the upper arms strength to pry him away. She looked down at him with a mix of revulsion and pity as his anger turned to violent sobs. He beat the ground with his fist.

"Fuck!" He shouted. "Fuck!"

She willed herself to turn back around and look at Nilla's crumpled form. The twisting in her stomach was painfully familiar, like she'd lived the whole scene before—and she had, hadn't she? This was not the first time she'd seen that face bloodied in an attempt to protect her, and even though she didn't ask for it, maybe didn't even need it, she was still the reason that her friend lay at her feet.

They remained motionless on the ground, and for a moment Lotus wondered if Oreo had badly injured them. She laid a hand on their shoulder and rolled them onto their back, their eyes staring absently into the distance.

"Jasmine," they rasped, "I think I fucked up again."

CHAPTER TWENTY-FIVE

Columbia's Plan

"I figured the device she was holding must have been the one she used to track Princeton. So I jabbed her with the needle when we were fighting," Columbia had explained. "But I couldn't get the device from her. So I slipped it out her pocket when we were riding the pinchdragon and hid it in my boot."

"How did you think to do that?" Yale asked in awe. "I mean, how did you know—"

"I didn't," Columbia shrugged. "I just figured once we got out of there—if we got out of there alive—we would want a way to find the people who had done that to us. Besides, now they'll have a way more difficult time finding new targets."

"Maybe we should keep them from finding new targets ever again," Princeton suggested darkly.

"No, no, we're not killing anyone," Yale declared. "That's not what we're about."

"But they tried to kill *us!*" Princeton protested.

"Do I really have to give you the whole 'if we kill them then we're just as bad' spiel?" Yale asked.

"I mean, no," Princeton sulked, "but like, we don't know who else they're gonna go for. By killing them we could be saving, like, tons of other scavengers."

"Or we can turn them in when we get back to the Commission," Yale proposed. "They'll get arrested or whatever. That way there's no blood on our hands—hopefully, there's no blood at all."

"Yeah, yeah, I guess. Whatever," Princeton grumbled.

"Do you really wanna have a quadruple homicide on your conscience?" Columbia asked.

"Okay, yeah, I mean, like, I guess not," Princeton threw up his hands in defeat. And so it was decided.

The Chocolates were camped out due south of the sandheads camp, surely staking out another unlucky scavenging crew to sell. When the Ivies approached them—or rather, when Skrack approached them, flanked by the Ivies and the Empress in Harvard's caring hands—they were gathered around a fire, their tents casting pointed shadows onto the desert floor, listening to some plan that Snickers was spinning.

Twix was the first to see the looming desertwalker in the sparse moonlight. She screamed, tripping over her own feet to back away. Snickers did not take his cue.

"What's wrong with *you*?" he demanded, just as a claw closed around his torso and lifted him into the air. He gave a horrified shriek, his legs kicking wildly.

"Get the vapor, you idiots! Get the vapor!" he cried when he saw the beast that held him.

Yale stepped out from behind Skarck's leg and held up a cautionary hand. "If you get the vapor, he's dead."

The Chocolates froze, petrified, noticing the Ivies for the first time.

"You guys are supposed to be dead!" Twix pointed.

"Oh, we're well aware," Yale crossed their arms, sauntering between Skrack and the terrified Chocolates. Well, Twix was terrified, and Mars' eyes were wide behind her cracked glasses. Milky Way seemed amused. She gave Skrack a friendly wave, which went ignored.

"How is this possible?" Twix demanded.

"Wouldn't you like to know," Yale sneered. "We're not actually here to kill you," they admitted, "as nice as it would be, after everything you put us through. But if you don't do what we ask, our crab—"

Harvard coughed meaningfully.

"Our friend—"

Cough. Harder.

"Our *associate* who we *do not own* and who is working with us *completely out of his freewill* will crush your captain in his claw."

"It'll be gross!" Princeton interjected unhelpfully. "You'll all get sprayed with blood and guts and bone bits and you'll have nightmares about it forever!"

Snickers gave a horrified squeal.

"Then what do you want?" Twix asked, her eyes still fixed on the desertwalker that held her captain aloft.

"Just give us the lizard," Yale demanded levelly, cocking their head toward the captive pinchdragon, "and no one gets hurt."

"Fine! Fine! Take whatever you want!" Twix lifted her hands in a show of supplication.

"Whatever we want?" Princeton raised an eyebrow.

"Princeton—" Yale warned.

"Give us the gun!" Princeton demanded.

The rest of the Ivies were silent. It wasn't a bad idea, Yale had to admit.

Twix hesitated. "We need it. It's for...self-defense."

"Oh? Were you *defending yourselves* when you sold us as human sacrifices to the sandheads?" Yale spat. Twix bit her lip. Yale held out a hand expectantly.

"Gun!" they demanded. Princeton gave a silent fist pump of victory. Twix scurried back to one of the tents, holding the gun far away from her like one might hold a particularly offensive fish. Yale guessed she was not usually the one who handled it, and she didn't enjoy it. She dropped it in Yale's waiting hand.

"Alright!" she said. "You have what you want. Will you—" she cast a worried look up at the dangling Snickers, "will you let him go now?"

"Yes, please!" Snickers shakily agreed.

Yale nodded.

"You can put him down now, please," Harvard requested politely, and Skrack dropped Snickers none too gently to the ground. He landed gracelessly on his side. Twix helped him to his feet, brushing off the dust and checking him for injuries.

Yale turned to go, but Columbia moved up next to them.

"Hold on. I have something I'd like to say, if it's alright with you," Columbia requested. Yale gave her a befuddled glance, but still nodded apprehensively.

Columbia turned on her heels and marched up to Snickers. She looked as though she might be about to give him a lecture about the impropriety of his actions, or perhaps about the proper upkeep of desert creatures.

"Whaddayou want?" Snickers demanded.

Columbia pulled back her fist and swung it into Snickers' lower jaw. Yale gasped. The Jasmine Reyez they'd known all those years ago could never have landed a punch, but Columbia the seasoned scavenger managed to knock the boy off his feet. When did she get so strong? Did she even have any idea she was that strong?

Standing over him, fist still clenched, she said simply, calmly, "Don't hurt my friends."

Then she strode back toward Skrack.

Princeton started clapping. Harvard was quick to join in, his face a delighted mix of astonishment and admiration. Stunned, Yale found themself joining in the round of applause. Princeton started chanting, "Co-lum-bi-a! Co-lum-bi-a!" and doing a little dance.

She blushed.

Now *there* was the Jasmine Reyez they knew.

* * *

Harvard had never felt the sensation of power, of freedom, that he did when riding atop the pinchdragon.

She couldn't speak to Harvard the way the Empress and Skrack did, but once the Ivies removed her bonds and the saddle that the Chocolates had forced her to carry, she was already eager to help them. The Empress assured Harvard that she'd been given an explanation of the mission, and the creature, Fallah, an ally from the Northeast Plains, was happy to be of assistance.

I could have called upon any one of my quicker allies once Skrack agreed to leave me in your hands, she explained, *but once you told me of Fallah's plight, I was committed to freeing her. She is thankful we came to her aid, and more than willing to help.*

Riding the gargantuan reptile without a saddle was nearly impossible— though the Ivies had tied themselves to her abdomen to ensure that they wouldn't fall off, they still clung to each other as the lizard glided across the terrain. Princeton took up the rear, then Columbia, then Yale, and in the front, Harvard, giving Fallah directions as he gently petted her head.

He'd never felt so empowered in his life—sitting atop a huge beast, wind whipping his hair back, leading his team. He didn't want to admit it, but the feeling of Yale's arms around his waist played no small part in his elation. He'd never particularly liked being touched before; now he didn't want them to stop.

For the first time in—well, he didn't even know how long—Harvard felt like he was doing something right.

The trip only took a few hours. By the time Bastion came into view, Harvard felt his heart sink, disappointed the ride was over. His moment of euphoria had been so fleeting.

The four leapt off the creature's back, landing heavily on the dust just outside the city gates.

"Do you want to come with us?" Harvard asked, removing the Empress from his pockets and holding her out in the palm of his hands.

Leave me here, she commanded. *I will wait for you with the Guardians to Be. In a few days' time, Skrack will be with me. And here we shall wait for the return of my heir.*

"Okay," Harvard said reluctantly, placing her on the ground. It just seemed too dangerous, leaving a creature so tiny exposed to the elements. It occurred to him to wonder if anyone had ever felt that way about him.

As if sensing his apprehension, the Empress reassured him, *Do not worry for me, Harvard. Your concern is appreciated, but unwarranted. I have survived many ages, and I will survive many more if I so choose. Your mortal flesh should be your concern, as it is much more delicate than my chitin armor. By safe, and do well.*

With that, she scurried into the sands, disappearing across the windswept plains.

Part Four: Bastion

Excerpt from Legends of Bastion

While not a cautionary tale, the most ubiquitous tale in Bastion is that of the city's origin.

Many Bastioners conceptualize the Great Quakes as one discrete event. After all, we speak mainly of history in terms of "pre" and "post" Quake, like two sides of a token. In actuality, evidence suggests the Quakes lasted for decades, maybe even centuries, prior to the founding of Bastion. Their exact origins are unknown, but their effects are known all too well. In a series of earthquakes lasting for generations, the Earth began to cave in on itself. Some continents crumbled like cookies, while others jammed into each other to form new land masses. Tectonic plates shifted with impossible speed, reshaping the surface of the planet over the course of decades, a process that should have taken thousands of years. Some claim the Great Quakes were a result of humanity's moral failings. Those people, if we may be so bold as to claim such a thing, are idiots. * A few individual humans may bear the ethical weight of the Quakes, but those individuals are long dead, records of their lives lost to history.

While we can't say for certain what caused the Earth to devour its own creatures, we do know humanity had capabilities far surpassing what we have today. They had metals sourced from caves in far off lands, lands they flew to with flying machines, and they used those metals to make communication devices nearly everyone on the planet possessed. This is why scavengers are crucial to Bastion—they provide us a glimmer of what was once known, and some useful materials that no longer exist in our natural environment.

But how did Bastion emerge from the barren dusts, scraping together what humanity once knew? Nothing is certain, but stories passed down and evolved over the years.

This is the tale.

When the Quakes first began, scourging the Earth, humans splintered into competing communities to see who would last the longest. There was the City of Glass, the City in the Sky, the City of Dust, the City of Wood, the City of Ashes...

And the list goes on.

Bastion was the City of Concrete and Steel, and the people of Bastion were wiser than all the others. The City of Glass shattered. The City in the Sky fell. The City of Dust blew away. The City of Concrete and Steel, however, remained.

And when the people of Bastion learned that they were the Final City, they did not mourn. For they knew they outlasted the rest due to their superior intellect, and those other cities had no one to blame but themselves. So, the people of Bastion basked in the glory of the knowledge they'd won an impossible race.

Moral: Practical wisdom reigns supreme.

That is the legend.

A legend that, admittedly, doesn't hold up to scrutiny. Why, in the midst of centuries of earthquakes, would anyone choose to erect a city of glass? And yet, the fabled City of Glass has captured the imaginations of countless storytellers. More baffling yet is the City in the Sky. How is such a thing possible?

What is truly known is this:

Bastion, before it was Bastion, was founded as a community of scientists flown in from all across the world in an effort to stop the Quakes, or at least discover their cause. It was not the only such community, but it is the only one we have extensive records of. As the Quakes tore apart their buildings and desertwalkers harassed them, quickly their objective shifted from research to survival. Generations passed, and centuries worth of research and progress was lost as the descendants of the original inhabitants focused more on simply evading death.

Then came the First Bastion Summit, generations after the city was founded. Leaders stepped forward, ostensibly the six "smartest" and "kindest" of them. The progeny of great scientists, they approached their situation logically. The only way forward, to rebuild the city and achieve the greatness mankind once knew, was to specialize. So each of the six committed to pioneering a different sector of city life: Technology. Education. Infrastructure. Administration. Health. And most importantly, Security.

Only the identity of the First Enforcer is unknown. According to the documentation of the First Bastion Summit, they believed justice was too serious a job to be influenced by common people. Thus, the Enforcers of justice should remain more or less anonymous, and receive no great wealth for what they do, as it is for the good of the people. The First Enforcer was lauded for their selflessness and bravery, going nameless into the annals of history. Some call the first Head Enforcer the keystone of Bastion, holding the city together for no praise or glory.

While this is the part of the story that falls loosely under the category of fact, even this story of the Founders strays into the realm of the fantastical. Surely you have heard people evoke that name of the Founders as if to deify them. The Founders have ascended to godhood—almost. The people of Bastion are rational, unlike the Congregationalists who split from them at the city's founding. They are far too rational to believe in anything but the power of science, and that is the value the Founders passed along to their children, so that their children would rebuild the human race.

And they are rebuilding to this day.

The City of Steel and Concrete lives on.

Footnote: My collaborator has noted above her opinions on those who blame humanity for the Great Quakes. I take a slightly more nuanced view. People, by their very nature, search for someone to blame. It is much easier to sling that blame upon the humans of the past and be done with it than to contend with the ways humanity has failed to grow since then. My humble plea to you as a reader is to introspect, to look at Bastion as it is now, and wonder, "What path are we on? And why?"

CHAPTER TWENTY-SIX

The Commission

There was no fanfare upon their arrival. No other scavengers who said, "Hey, you guys have been gone a while. What happened?" They seamlessly slipped back into the bustle of the Commission without so much as turning any heads. People disappeared. Sometimes they came back. That was just the way of the dusts.

Yale went straight to their room, thankful to be back in a place with a bed and running water—though cold and weak—and no monsters except the occasional rats and roaches. They found a small pile of papers by their door—letters from their mother. One for each day they had been gone. They had let her know in their last letter, of course, they would be going on a dig and she wouldn't hear from them for a while, but they had been gone two weeks longer than expected. It felt like it had been an eternity, but in truth their time away had only been extended by about a week. Still, a week of uncertainty about where her child had disappeared to must have been agony for her. Usually, they were very prompt in communicating with her, so their silence must have been terrifying. They'd make sure to write to her the first chance they got. But first— well, there was business to attend to. They went to the front desk to make some reports.

The Ivies didn't have much to show for the extended time they'd spent in the desert since the Chocolates had taken what little they managed to collect during their stay with O'Neill, but they had everything they'd been able to carry away from the sandhead camp. Herman had scrutinized all of it, muttering to himself about the quality and prices, then said, "Alright. We'll take it."

Yale held out a hand expectantly.

"And...the money?"

"Not enough to pay you anything."

"I gave you our finds. Give us the money."

"You didn't make quota, Yale."

"You still have to pay us."

"You know the by-laws as well as I do."

"Yeah, so we both know damn well that you have to pay us."

Yale knew that this was a game Herman was famous for playing. If he managed to convince you that you weren't owed anything, then you walked away with nothing. But if you could be enough of a nuisance that it was worth it to pay you off, you'd get a fraction of what you were due. Yale was fine with a fraction, and they were well-versed in the art of being a nuisance from their younger days.

"How's the kid?" Herman deflected.

"He's not a kid. Don't change the subject."

"Look. I can't give you anything for this. You spent way too long out there and didn't come back with half the shit you were supposed to. You got some food, great, but you know pre-tremor tech is the only thing that brings in the points."

"I know. And we had some, but our shit got stolen—"

"Stolen?"

"Crew called the Chocolates came and abducted us. Sold us to a bunch of sandheads so we could be their human sacrifices."

Herman was unimpressed. "Okay," he drawled, as if to say, "And this is relevant how?"

"So I'd like to report them."

"Alright."

"You'll take punitive action?"

"Sure."

Yale slammed a palm on the desk, but Herman didn't flinch.

"You can't just let this go! I mean, they beat the shit out of us! And they were ready to have us killed!"

Herman held up a hand as if that would calm them. "Listen, kid, if the Chocolates come back to the Commission, sure, we'll whip up some kind of punishment. Jail, probably. But this ain't the first time I've heard about scavengers going rogue and trying to sell each other to sandheads. And this is definitely not the first time I've heard about the Chocolates. Haven't been back in years, Yale. They're gone. They belong to the desert now. So my advice to you? Let it go."

"*Let it go?*" Yale fumed, who had never been able to let go of anything in their entire life.

"Yup. Now if you're done here—"

"No, I'm not done!"

Herman looked deeply disappointed.

"Alriiiiight," he drew out the word, "what else could you possibly want?"

Yale wasn't sure how to broach this next subject, but they figured it was their responsibility to tell someone.

"Has anyone reported...um, a giant bird?"

"What?"

"A creature out in the dusts. It's not a scuttler, it's...well, it flies, but it's got a tail. And its wings are more like a bat. It's orange and furry and—"

"You're saying you saw a giant furry orange bird?"

"Something like that. Yes."

"Nope. No one's reported anything like that."

"It almost killed us. And there could be more of them. It might be a new species of desertwalker. But we figured out—well, Harvard figured out—that it's attracted to light, or anything shiny. It might be worthwhile to invest in—"

"I'll bring it up with the guys in back," Herman dismissed them, making a shooing gesture with his hand.

"But you don't even—"

He waved Yale away more aggressively.

"I said I'll talk to them, alright? Calm down—you made it back in one piece. We'll talk about your bird and maybe we can do something about it."

"I *know* what you can do about it. You can equip scavengers with—"

"Damn it, kid, you just don't shut up! We'll deal with it. Now get out of here."

Yale knew when they were beat. They hadn't always, but it was a skill they'd developed over the past few years. They crossed their arms, bit down a retort, and made their way back toward the barracks. Herman's voice stopped them in the doorway.

"So that Harvard kid's still alive, huh?" Without looking back, Yale knew he was reclining in his chair, fiddling with a pen. "Never thought he'd last this long. Did you?"

Yale fought the impulse to whip around, swallowing ten different responses they desperately wanted to shoot back. They forced themself to take a slow, deep breath before responding, "I think, after some practice, I make a pretty good captain."

"Hm," Herman grunted skeptically, "maybe you do."

As Yale stalked away again, Herman added, "You seem a little wound up. Take it easy, will ya?"

Without turning back, Yale flipped him off.

Interlude Seventeen: Harvard

Harvard lifted hand weights in the feeble hope that he would be able to bulk up his arms. He hadn't managed it yet, but every night when he wasn't too exhausted, he went to the training room in an attempt to, well, train.

He heard the heavy double doors slam shut, and he dropped the weight, narrowly missing his foot. Unable to suppress his childhood instincts, he hid behind a punching bag, even though he hadn't been doing anything wrong. He peered around the edge to see Yale stumbling onto the practice mats. Were they alright? It looked like they were having trouble walking right. Harvard suppressed the instinct to go help them—maybe they'd be embarrassed. They fell awkwardly to their knees and took a swig from what looked like a water bottle, but Harvard guessed that maybe it wasn't water. In their other fist he noticed they grasped a piece of paper, gripping it so tight it was crumpled in the palm of their hand.

Yale bent over and wept.

They sobbed into the blue plastic of the mat, their shoulders heaving. Harvard felt painfully voyeuristic, knowing he was seeing something he was never meant to see. Should he try to sneak away? Surely, they wouldn't notice. He crept toward the door, his eyes focused on the prostrate captain to ensure they weren't looking up—and collided with the rack of hand weights, which clattered noisily to the ground.

Yale's sobbing ceased abruptly as their head shot up, looking in Harvard's direction. Harvard cringed, preparing himself to be chastised. Instead, Yale asked quietly, "Harvard?"

He nodded meekly. They reached an arm out for him, inviting him closer.

"Come here."

He did as commanded, unsure what was happening. He knelt beside them.

"Harvard," they said again, drawing out his brand name and staring into his eyes. "Haaaarvard."

"Are you...okay, Yale?" he asked tentatively.

He saw tears spring up in their eyes again and they shook their head. Then they held out the bottle to him.

"One of the Computers distilled this. Apple, I think. It's terrible." They took another swig, then pushed it into Harvard's chest. "Try it."

"No, I...I don't think I'd like that very much."

Yale shrugged, and went to drink more, but Harvard caught their wrist.

"Um, actually, I will have some!" he blurted out, grabbing the bottle from them and placing it out of reach. When he turned back around, Yale was staring at him.

"Harvard," they said again, their hand flew up to his cheek. "You're so good, Harvard. You're so, so good. How d'you do it? You're so good, Harvard. So good."

Harvard felt himself blush as Yale stroked his face.

"Um, you're good too, Yale. You're a good captain."

They shook their head, looking as though they were going to burst into tears again.

"No," they said. "No no no. I'm bad, Harvard. I'm so bad." They glanced at the crumpled paper they grasped.

"What's that?" Harvard asked, gingerly touching their balled fist.

They jerked away, almost cowering, wrapping themself around the crumpled page as if to protect it.

"No!" they cried. Harvard shied away, worried he'd done something horribly wrong. Yale softened a bit, inching back toward him. "I don't...I don't want anyone to see it. She wrote it for me. But I...I'm letting her down."

They let out another sob, and Harvard felt a stab of jealousy. He didn't know who "she" was, but the idea that Yale might have a girlfriend outside the Commission made him nauseous. He didn't know why, but he felt strangely possessive over his captain. He put a hand on their shoulder.

"You *are* good," he assured them. "I promise. You are a great captain, and...and you make me feel happy to be on the Ivies. You make me feel safe. And..." he struggled to choose his words, and just landed on, "You're a good captain."

Yale sniffled, wiping their nose with the back of their hand.

"Do you really mean that, Harvard?" they asked.

"Of course I do."

Yale embraced Harvard with such intensity that it forced the air out of his lungs. They clung to him, sobbing into his shoulder.

"Thank you, Harvard. Thank you. You're so good. Thank you. Thank you."

Still gripping him, they started rocking back and forth. Harvard couldn't tell if he liked this or not. On the one hand, he was proud he was able to comfort Yale, and the hug, while it threatened to crush his bones, was actually pretty nice. Then again, they were drunk, so...it didn't really mean much of anything, did it? By this point they were repeating the phrase, "so good, so good," into the crook of his neck.

"Let's get you to bed, okay?" he suggested. Yale pulled back and nodded morosely, sniffling. With some difficulty, Harvard helped Yale to their feet and guided them toward the door of the training room. His strength was woefully inadequate to support their weight, but he still slung their arm over his shoulder to half-guide, half-drag them toward the door to their quarters. He tried the door. Locked.

"Do you have your key?" he asked. By this point Yale had passed the sobbing-drunk phase and reached the sleepy-drunk phase, and their eyelids were fluttering. Harvard jostled them a little.

"Do you have your key?" he repeated. Their head lolled to the side.

"Pocket," they grumbled.

Harvard sighed and plunged a hand into their pocket, fishing around for the key. It wasn't in the first one, so he reached around to the other side.

"Harvard!" Yale gasped, laughing. "What are you doing in my pants?"

Harvard flushed.

"I—I'm looking for your key!" he stammered.

"Oh yeah. Right." Yale rolled their head to the side again and closed their eyes. Harvard's fingers closed around the key and he withdrew it hastily, eager to open the door and finish with the whole awkward night. After some fumbling with the lock, he managed to get the door open and pull Yale inside.

He pushed them onto the bed, but they were still gripping his shirt, so they pulled him down with them. He fell gracelessly on top of them, an alarmed squeak escaping his lips.

"You...you have to let go of me," he said, but Yale was already passed out. He carefully unhooked their fingers from the fabric of his shirt and extricated himself from their unconscious embrace. Standing, straightening his clothing, he watched them sleep. They looked so beautiful, even with their glasses askew, their hair a mess, and tear tracks still glistening on their face. Harvard felt his face burning at the thought. But somehow, after this whole night, they were even more beautiful than before. Because the captain of the Ivies had seemed invincible to Harvard, and now he saw that they were human, and that they hurt, hurt somewhere deep down, and they'd showed that bit of themself to Harvard—though unintentionally—and it made them feel more real than they'd ever felt. And the way they'd stroked his cheek, and told him how good he was...did they really mean that? Or was it all just drunken ramblings? And what did it really *mean,* that he was "good?" He wasn't a good scavenger, that was certain. So did Yale see in him that he didn't?

He felt something in him stir looking down at Yale in the bed, snoring peacefully. Someone in the world thought he was good, even if he didn't understand it, and even if no one else in the world would believe it. Someone who he thought was the most competent, caring person he'd ever met. Before he knew what he was doing, he bent over and placed a gentle kiss on their cheek. Yale smiled in their sleep. Harvard darted away, guilty, feeling as though he'd committed some horrible crime, and closed the door behind him.

The next morning the Ivies were scheduled to discuss their next dig, but the captain was late.

"Can we turn off the lights, please?" they asked, squinting.

"What'd you do last night? Anything fun?" Princeton grinned, tipping his chair back.

Yale sat heavily, burying their face in their hands. "Honestly, I don't remember anything. I must have totally blacked out."

Harvard's stomach sank.

"You don't remember anything?" he asked. Yale shook their head.

Harvard tried to pay attention for the rest of the meeting, but all he could think about was last night, about how accidentally vulnerable the captain had been. Now they didn't remember any of it. Part of him was thankful. He was feeling terribly embarrassed about how the night had ended, and maybe it was a good thing that they didn't remember him fishing around in their pockets for their key, or clinging to him when they passed out, or his impetuous peck on their cheek which he'd immediately regretted. So probably it was for the best. Still, he couldn't help feeling like it was a waste. He'd done his best to care for them and they really didn't remember a thing?

When the meeting was over and the team filed out, Yale's voice stopped him.

"Hold on, Harvard."

He turned to face them. They looked away, oddly sheepish, which was an alien look on them. When the door closed behind the other two, they said, "I remember...a little bit of last night, actually."

Harvard's stomach fluttered.

"I remember, um, that you were there, and um...I wanted, to know, uh..."

"Yes?" he asked.

"Did I..." their eyes darted away, "do anything embarrassing?"

He shouldn't be feeling disappointed. He had no right to feel disappointed. But somehow, he did.

"No," he said, hoping he didn't like crestfallen. "You just...fell right to sleep."

Yale smiled and breathed a sigh of relief. "Whew. Okay. Great. I was really worried there."

Harvard frowned. "Yeah, well, glad I could help." He turned to leave, his chest feeling tight.

"Harvard?" Yale said as he reached the doorway. He turned back around.

"Yeah?"

"Thanks. For being there last night."

The corner of Harvard's mouth quirked up in a half-smile. "Yeah. No problem." He scurried away, uncertain how to feel.

CHAPTER TWENTY-SEVEN

An Old Friend

The common spaces in the Commission were often referred to as "lounges," though there was very little about them to suggest the title. They were cramped little rooms, rarely cleaned, containing a table, rickety wooden chairs, and a few storage cabinets. These rooms were almost never used for "lounging," but for teams to discuss their next dig's plan. While they were not forbidden from meeting in each other's rooms, most tended to avoid inviting others into what little private space they were allotted. For scavengers, privacy was a luxury, and they were fiercely protective of it. All scavengers' rooms were identical: a constricted, cave-like compartment with a twin cot, a single chair at an entirely unused desk, and alcove with a shower stall and metallic toilet. It was no wonder the rooms were never used as shared spaces—there was barely enough space for the person who lived there, let alone enough to share it.

Harvard, Columbia and Princeton all sat around the table with Yale standing at the head. They seemed to have more of a semblance of a game plan than the rest of them. Harvard had already told the crew what the Empress had given him, but it wasn't much to go off.

"Look," Yale said, crossing their arms, "we can't very well wander into the Galvin Conference as we are and try to steal a crab. It would be way too obvious something was amiss. I doubt they'd even let us in."

"So we're gonna break in?" Princeton interrupted eagerly, a menacing grin already spreading across his face.

"What? No," Yale cocked their head in confusion. "Why would...how would we do that?"

"Well, I was thinking—"

"We just have to look like we belong," Yale clarified.

"Okay, but how do we do that?" Princeton asked.

Yale placed their palms on the table and smiled, and Harvard guessed that whatever plan they had come up with, they were very proud of it.

"We go in as presenters."

The other three were silent for a moment. Columbia looked as though she was considering this. Princeton's mouth hung agape.

"Yale, buddy," he finally said, "we don't know shit about science."

"No, we don't," Yale conceded, then dropped a book on the table with such a loud thump that it made the other three jump. "But this guy did."

Harvard's stomach fluttered as he recognized the tome in front of him: O'Neill's research book, the one he'd flipped through the day before he'd made his escape. The sight of it made him nauseous, reminding him of the old man's devilish smile, and the brush of the needle against his neck. He didn't want to look inside that book—it would only remind him of the man who wrote it.

Columbia had no such associations with the thing. She picked it up and flipped through, examining the worn pages.

"It's a good idea," she admitted, and Yale beamed. A compliment from Columbia, especially about intelligence, was rare. "But I'm not sure how feasible it is."

Yale's face dropped.

"What do you mean?" they asked. "That thing must be full of, like, groundbreaking scientific information."

"I'm sure it *is*," Columbia agreed, "but can you *understand* any of it?"

Yale's face flushed almost imperceptibly. "Well, no," they admitted, "but I thought you would—"

"I could probably make out some of this, sure," Columbia agreed, looking through the diagrams and charts, "if it weren't written in code. But even then, I don't have enough context. How much of this is new information? How much was proved years ago? I could probably tell you what most of this means, but how much of it would make a convincing presentation? Convincing enough to present at the *most prestigious scientific conference in Bastion*? We don't have enough information."

"Okay, okay," Yale nodded, crossing their arms as they pondered Columbia's points. "So we just need to find out...everything about contemporary science."

"Unfortunately, yes," Columbia said, dropping the book back on the table.

Yale's eyes widened. They turned to Columbia and raised their eyebrows, sending a message that was entirely lost on Harvard.

"*No*," Columbia responded firmly. "We can't."

"What else can we do?" Yale asked.

"We're not supposed to make contact with people outside of the Commission."

"I know, I know," Yale waved a dismissive hand. "We're not supposed to, yeah, but—"

"Because it's dangerous. For all of us."

"Can you think of anything else we can do?"

Columbia bit the inside of her cheek.

"Okay, fine," she conceded. "But I'm not going. And you better be fast, okay? And don't let anyone see you. And—"

"I know, I know," Yale said, grinning wildly.

"What...what are you talking about?" Harvard asked quietly. Yale held Columbia's gaze.

"I'm gonna go consult someone," Yale said, "and I'm gonna make sure we have a presentation. A good one. I'm going out tomorrow. I'll be back."

* * *

Simon Foster pored over the display for the—thirteenth? fourteenth time? Avi had lost count, admittedly. Once she'd put her stamp of approval on it—her "stamp of approval" being a solid, "Yeah, looks good to me"—she didn't bother looking at the thing. Simon, however, seemed somehow convinced they had made a mistake somewhere, and that mistake would be found, and when it was found they would be publicly mocked or burned at the stake or even worse: banned from academia. So Avi indulged him by joining him in the lab for one last review, more interested in her book about the evolution of worms than his mutterings.

"We missed a citation," he jabbed his finger at the poster.

"Okay. Then add it," Avi said without looking up from her book.

He shook his head. "I don't like cutting it this close."

"We're not cutting it close."

"It's tomorrow!"

Avi shrugged. "And we're ready."

"We have to reprint. Who knows if the university word processor is even free."

"Then don't add it."

"That's plagiarism!"

Avi closed her book and placed it on the lab desk.

"You really think someone's gonna notice? It's one paper we didn't cite. An obscure academic article. Who is possibly going to notice that?"

"Someone might!"

Avi sighed. She shoved her book in her backpack as she prepared to head back to her dorm.

"How are you...I mean how are you not nervous about tomorrow?"

She continued shoving stray papers in her bag before zipping it.

"I guess...I just kind of feel...underwhelmed?"

Simon gaped. "Underwhelmed? You're presenting at the most important conference in the world, and you feel *underwhelmed*?"

She put a hand on his shoulder.

"It's gonna be fine," she assured him.

"We can't all be as naturally confident and charismatic as you," he complained, adjusting his glasses self-consciously.

Yes, that was the problem. She was just so bold and fearless. That was why she felt this emptiness in the face of the most important research conference in the city. She was simply...just too competent. That was likely it.

"True, but you're pretty smart, so that counts for something," she wrinkled her nose affectionately, gave him a pat on the back, and left the lab.

"You can reprint if you want," she called over her shoulder. "Or don't. I don't care. It really doesn't matter."

A part of her felt guilty as she strode down the university halls back to her room. Simon had been an excellent research partner and, over the course of the past four years, a genuinely good friend to her. It wasn't fair to him that she wasn't feeling the same kind of thrill he was about presenting tomorrow. Then again, maybe it was for the best that she wasn't. He'd never dreamed he'd get to do something like this. She, on the other hand, had practically been raised for it. For him, this was a dream come true. For her, it was...she didn't know. It wasn't that she didn't like the research, of course—she loved it more than anything. Significantly more than she loved trying to sell it to people. That was a prospect she hated.

Avi unlocked her dorm door and tossed her bag on the floor by the door. Admittedly the word "dorm" undersold the student lodgings at Bastion University of Sciences. It was more of an apartment, with the caveat that it was owned by the school. She put on water for a cup of tea and removed her shoes.

There was a knock on the door.

Avi groaned. It was probably another student from the class she was an assistant in, looking for a little extra homework help. Didn't they know what was happening tomorrow? Couldn't they give her a moment's peace? Begrudgingly, she opened the door.

Avi gasped, staring wide-eyed. Her childhood best friend, whom she hadn't seen in four years and she let herself believe she'd never see again, Chaverim Chakrabarti, stared back at her.

* * *

Avi made a sound that was a half-scream, half-cry as she launched herself at Chavi, wrapping her arms around them. Stunned, Chavi slowly hugged her back. What had they expected she would do, upon seeing them again? Only now that she was in their arms did they realize part of them had been anticipating she would be angry, abandoned. But Avi showed no signs of ill will toward them, just unadulterated relief to see them alive, standing at her door.

"You're back," she squeaked, pressing her face into their neck and squeezing them tighter.

"Yeah," they breathed. "I'm back."

When Avi's face came away, Chavi saw it was wet with tears. She grabbed their hand and pulled them into her apartment.

"Sorry, it's...I didn't think anyone was...it's not particularly nice."

Chavi couldn't help but laugh because if Avi had seen the place they had been living for the past four years, she would surely have a new definition of nice. The entire back wall of the apartment was glass, facing Midtown Bastion down below. Houseplants lined the area in front of the window—Avi had always had a knack for keeping things alive. The place was small, but there was still room for a pristine kitchenette, a leather couch, and a double bed.

Avi ushered Chavi onto the couch, but she was too full of nervous energy to sit herself.

"Founders...how did you get here? I mean, how did you find me? What have...are you okay? Did you get hurt? How did you...I mean, what are you doing here...sorry, I just have, like a million questions, I just...Don't you *dare* leave me like that again!" she said in a low growl.

"It hasn't exactly been fun for me either," Chavi laughed sardonically. They knew they should address the task at hand—they didn't have long to put together what was becoming an increasingly elaborate plan. But it was easy just to fall back into old rhythms, and the temptation to abandon it all and spend time with their old friend was difficult to resist. Perhaps Jasmine had the right idea in staying back.

"Jasmine!" Avi exclaimed, as though just realizing that her other friend wasn't there, "Is she—"

"She's fine, she's fine," Chavi reassured her, "she just...she thought it would be more discreet if I came alone."

"Discreet?" Avi gave them a quizzical look. "What do you—"

"We're not...we're not back yet," Chavi struggled to find words that fit the unique situation the Ivies had found themselves in.

"What do you mean? You're here. Of course you're back," Avi protested.

"But we're not...we still have our debt. To the Commission. Besides, I'm sure I haven't sent back enough for my mom—"

"We can work it out!" she waved a hand. "You're back, and Jasmine's back and—"

"Avi, I need you to listen to me," Chavi insisted. "We are in a complicated situation and I can't explain all the details right now."

"Why not?" she asked.

"For one thing, you wouldn't believe me. For another thing, we don't have time."

"Time?"

Chavi sighed. Now to business. Here they were, having the reunion they had dreamt of for years, and it had to be ruined by a promise made to purportedly talking crabs.

"I need you to help me put together an entire presentation for the Galvin Conference. Right now. Or if we don't...we could die."

Avi stared at them for a long moment.

"You have to present at a conference...or you'll die?" she repeated back.

"Yes. We have to...um, we have to steal a crab?"

Avi looked at the window, contemplating. Chavi expected her to press them further on the request, but maybe she knew that pushing was futile.

Avi was always one to care more about the "how" and less about the "why."

"Well, you need a slot, obviously," she said, turning back to Chavi. "They don't just let anyone off the street present."

"Oh. I, uh, I hadn't thought of that, actually."

"Chavi!"

"I don't know how these things work!"

"It's fine. You can just take mine," she said too quickly. Chavi paused.

"Are you...are you serious?" Chavi asked. "I mean, you've been preparing for this thing your whole life. Ever since I met you. You're really okay with just giving away your slot like that?"

She shifted uncomfortably, adjusting her headscarf, her eyes darting to the window.

"I mean, you said it's important, so yeah, it's cool. I can present next year or something. It's not a big deal."

Chavi stepped forward, gingerly placing a hand on her arm. She turned to face them.

"Avi, never once have I ever asked something of you and you just said, 'yeah that's fine.' And this is the biggest thing I've asked of you. Ever. And that's really okay?"

Avi sighed.

"I...I don't want to present."

"You what?" Chavi gaped.

"And I didn't want to tell you because I knew you'd respond exactly like that!" Avi waggled an accusatory finger.

"But...I mean, why not? You love, like, science and shit!"

"The Galvin Conference isn't science," Avi crossed her arms. "It's people desperately trying to sell science. Which feels...wrong, somehow. I like research. I don't like being forced to sell my research just because that's what everyone expects of me."

"Well, um, here's a wild idea: don't do it?"

Avi scoffed. "Like I could ever get away with that. A Taheri given an opportunity at the Galvin Conference and turning it down? I'd never hear the end of it."

"But they'll be...okay with you giving your slot to me?"

"I'll come up with something. I'm sick," she decided. Chavi fixed her with a skeptical look.

"I'll make it work," Avi waved a hand, and it was hard to deny. When Avi Taheri said she was committed to something, she would certainly do it.

"You need something to present," she said.

"Can I just present your research?"

She shook her head.

"You can have my slot, but you can't use my research. The university knows what I've been working on. If they see you got it, they'll know I helped you. And if something goes wrong…I'd really like to avoid getting in trouble, if possible. If we do this right, it'll look like you stole my slot without my knowing."

"Can we use something…from this?" Chavi held out O'Neill's black notebook, hoping she wouldn't think much of the blood staining the edges a dark brown. Avi's eyes widened as she flipped through the pages.

"Founders," she murmured to herself. "Some of the creatures…I mean some of them are just legends, some of them are absolutely unheard of. As in…as in I don't think anyone knew they even existed." She turned her frantic eyes to Chavi. "Have you seen these things? In real life?"

"I mean, some of them," they shrugged, a bit of pride welling up in their chest. "Some of them have definitely tried to kill me."

"This is…I mean, this is incredible."

"Can you read it though?" Chavi asked, indicating the scribbles that painted the page. "I mean, the code he wrote it in—"

Avi gave a sharp laugh. Chavi knew she hadn't meant it to be derisive, but it still stung.

"Code?" Avi asked. "You thought this was a code?"

"Is…is it not?"

"This is *research shorthand*, Chavi. Every researcher writes their notes like this."

Chavi breathed a sigh of relief.

"So this is good, right? There's tons of stuff in there we could present on!"

"No, it's not that simple," she said without tearing her eyes away from the page. "Most of this is field research. If you go in presenting stuff like this, data from the dusts—I mean, considering how young you are—"

"They'd assume we're scavengers trying to pass off our experiences as field research?"

"Yeah. And when they figure out you're impersonating someone, you'll get in big trouble. And if they managed to figure out *why* you're impersonating someone...you'd be in bigger trouble."

"Well. Shit."

"Whatever you present, it has to be something you could have researched here, in a lab in Bastion."

Avi was a marvel in many ways, and two were evident simply in the way she'd received Chavi. She was presented with a challenge and she accepted it without question, eagerly even, because a challenge was all she ever wanted. The second was that she was enjoying it thoroughly. As she pulled apart the puzzle in her mind, Chavi saw a wide smile crack her face. Chavi had not seen Avi's smile in four years, and the familiarity of it made their chest ache.

"Oh! That reminds me! I, uh, got you a gift," they said, reaching for their boot.

"You? A gift?" Avi laughed.

"Yeah. I just...I thought you would like it."

Chavi produced the vial containing the remains of the crabsquid tentacle. Avi's eyes widened. She held out a hand reverently, and Chavi placed the glass container in her outstretched palm.

"What is it?" she asked.

"Crabsquid. I, uh, don't know what the scientific name for it is—"

"Big monster, predatory, tentacle and claws, lives in subterranean water deposits?"

"That's the one."

"*Lligo cancer*. Those things only exist in legends. The last time someone had a sample from one was...I don't know if anyone has ever gotten a sample from one."

Chavi sat back down on the couch, reclining with a self-satisfied smile. "Well, you'll be the first."

"How did you get it?"

"Oh, it tried to eat me."

Avi snorted. "No, I'm serious!"

Chavi leaned forward to pull up the bottom of their jeans and reveal the scabs from the spines piercing their skin. Avi stared in horror and wonder.

"No way. How did you survive?"

"Jasmine. If it weren't for her, I'd be dead. I mean, she's saved my life probably thousands of times out there."

Avi shook her head in awe. "I can't...I can't even imagine what it's like."

"Neither could I, until I was living it."

"It really is as dangerous as they say."

Chavi couldn't help but laugh. "Oh, it's worse."

Her eyes lit up hungrily. "You must have thousands of stories you could tell me."

"I do. And I want to, but...Avi, my crew is depending on me here. Jasmine is depending on me. If we don't get into this conference—I mean, then we're fucked."

"Right. Conference first. Then, maybe after...we could catch up? Jasmine too, of course. The three of us. Just like old times."

"Just like old times," Chavi smiled.

* * *

For a large part of the day, Avi worked on her own, glancing at the pages of the notebook, muttering words of admiration, then scribbling down notes.

"So, what's in there?" Chavi asked.

"A lot," Avi said. "But I think I've found something you could in theory have researched here at the university instead of out in the field."

"What is it?"

She looked up from the book, grinning wildly as she always did when she'd made a particularly juicy discovery.

"Okay, so you know how desertwalkers have conditional immortality?"

Chavi wanted to groan at hearing the phrase again. "I am aware, yes."

"Well, um, *maybe they don't,*" she said conspiratorially, as though someone could overhear her new scientific secret.

"What?" Chavi thought O'Neill had been studying something about finding conditional immortality for humans. But was he *disproving* conditional immortality the whole time?

"It's...it's hard to explain," she looked back down at the book "But I'll give you the rundown best I can while we put this thing together. It's honestly not far off from what Simon and I have been researching, but—"

"Simon? Simon Foster?" Chavi interrupted.

"Yeah. He's my research partner."

Chavi felt a pang of something, but they didn't understand what. Why should they care if Avi and Simon were working together now?

"I just...I didn't think the two of you were friends. I mean, you didn't even like him—"

Avi laughed, and a little bit of hurt crept into her voice. "We *weren't* friends. Then the two closest people in my life disappeared. So I made do."

Chavi couldn't help feeling a bit defensive at the notion they'd just "disappeared." As if they'd had a *choice*.

"He's, what, your replacement friend?" they needled.

Avi closed the notebook pettishly. "He approached me after you left. Everyone else was too scared to, but he wasn't. He said...he was just really nice about it, okay? He's *actually* a really sweet guy."

"I know, I was the one who liked him!" Chavi reminded her. She rolled her eyes.

"Oh please, you didn't even know him! What was he studying?"

"Ummm," Chavi tried to remember back. "Science?"

"Engineering!"

"Oh," Chavi said, crestfallen.

"Listen, you don't get to be jealous—" Avi chastised.

"I'm not jealous—"

Avi fixed them with a skeptical look. "Really?"

"I—" Chavi began, but cut themself off. They stared at her for a moment. She looked older. The confident, fiery, young girl that had once been their best friend was now a young woman, and they'd missed that transformation. They'd been off having a transformation of their own— but had it done them any good, really? Here was Avi, blossoming in the life she'd always dreamed of, and here they were, cold shell of the menacing kid they used to be. Did Avi look at them and see a stranger?

"Avi, are you mad that we left?" Chavi asked quietly.

"Yes, of course I'm mad!" Avi exclaimed, before averting her gaze and reeling her words back. "Not mad at you, just...just mad. Just mad my two best friends got taken away from me."

Chavi exhaled softly, unsure of what to tell her.

"I'm sorry," they murmured. Avi somberly opened the notebook again and turned a page.

"Yeah. Me too."

Chavi watched her reading. "You know we had to, right?" they asked.

She swallowed. "Yeah. I know. That doesn't make it hurt any less."

The two sat in silence before Avi finally said, "I think...there is a part of me that thinks—and I know this is not true, but...I think there's a part of me that thinks you took Jasmine away from me."

The words hit Chavi like a blow to the stomach.

"But...she didn't have a choice," Chavi reminded her.

Avi stared pointedly out the window. "Yeah. I know."

She turned back around abruptly.

"Simon's been a really good research partner. You know, after everything. He's not as good as Jasmine but, you know, he tries. He's a people-pleaser, that guy. And he thinks I'm a genius, which helps."

"You *are* a genius," Chavi said.

Avi was not one to deny a compliment, especially one she believed, so she only shrugged. She glanced at the notes the two had been compiling.

"You're actually not bad yourself. We could have worked together, maybe."

"Yeah, if you gave me a chance!" Chavi said, an unhealed wound from years ago beginning to fester.

"You didn't give *yourself* a chance," Avi shook her head. "You were always sabotaging yourself."

"I was not...okay, a little," they admitted.

"Have you stopped doing that, by the way?" Avi asked with a sly grin.

"What's left to sabotage? I live in the desert. Oh, I *am* captain now, so I guess that's cool."

"Congratulations," Avi nodded approvingly.

"It's not really an accomplishment."

"I bet you're a good captain."

They shrugged. "I'm okay."

Suddenly Avi reached for their hand, squeezing it tight as though she worried they would run off again if she didn't hold them down.

"Don't go back," she commanded. "Stay in the city. We'll figure something out, just...don't go back. You'll die out there. I know it. I've always known it. *Don't go back to the desert.*"

Avi was a hard woman to say no to. And of course, the prospect of staying in Bastion was a welcome one. Never having to set foot in the Commission compound again. Never facing down another desertwalker. Never worrying thirst or hunger would get them before a creature would. But there were other considerations, ones Avi couldn't understand.

"I don't...I mean, I don't know," Chavi admitted.

"Your mom misses you," Avi pleaded. It was a cheap shot, but she must have known it would work.

"You've been going to see my mom?" Chavi asked quietly.

"Of course. Every week."

"And how...how is she?" It was a dangerous question, but they couldn't stop it before it was out.

Avi shrugged. "Fine. I mean, relatively. Still doesn't have a steady job, but I find her things when I can. She hates it. She doesn't like that she needs my help, but she's not stupid, so she takes it. She misses you. A lot. She talks about you all the time."

It wasn't as though they expected she would have forgotten about them but still, the information tugged at their chest with an unexpected ache.

"You should see her," Avi suggested. "While you're here."

"I...I don't know. It wouldn't be fair." They weren't sure if they meant it wouldn't be fair to her or to them, but the prospect of seeing their mom only once before returning to the dusts was too painful to entertain.

"I can't see her just to leave again."

"Then *don't go back.*"

Chavi laughed, and the sound felt hollow in their throat.

"I mean, I don't *want* to go back. I almost died, like, so many times it's a miracle I'm still here."

"So don't go back. It's not worth it," Avi said with the sort of cold, logical tone that only someone who works with numbers all day is able to master.

"My mom—"

"Will be fine," Avi reassured them.

"I have my team to worry about," Chavi explained. "Harvard—"

"Who's that?" Avi cut in.

Chavi pulled their hand away from hers, rubbing the back of their neck trying to figure out how to explain this to her.

"He's...he's one of my crew members. He's not like me. I went to the Commission voluntarily, so most of the money I make I get to send home. I only keep a little debt to the Commission for food and equipment and everything. Harvard...he was already in debt to someone else. He was bought."

Avi considered this "So...he's an indenture?"

"Yeah, basically. And he...I can't leave him."

Avi laughed, and Chavi could hear that she was losing her patience. "Of *course* you can."

"No, Avi. You don't understand. I *can't*. I...I won't."

Avi held their gaze for a long moment, a silent understanding passing between them.

"Oh," Avi finally said. "I see."

"Yeah."

Avi sighed.

"I wish I could help him. And you and Jasmine. I would pay your debt. All of it. Even your fourth crew member, too, if you wanted. If I—"

"If you had your own money. Yeah, yeah, I know."

"And I will," Avi reminded them, though it sounded more like she was reminding herself. "One day."

"Let's just see if we can all stay alive that long."

"Don't pay your debt. None of you. Can't make you pay if you never go back."

"It doesn't work like that, Avi. You have to pay your debt in order to leave the Commission. If you don't, you're in violation of the Bastion Law Code, which puts you in the Delian Group's hands. And the Delian Group..." they locked eyes with Avi. "I mean, they're not famous for being gentle with people."

Avi nodded. Her family was in charge of land allocation, after all, so she would know just how much of the city was dedicated to Delian detention centers. But even she wouldn't know what happened inside them. That was something most could only speculate on, because once someone's fate belonged to the Delian Group, they weren't often seen again.

"How many scavengers do you know who have really been able to do this?" Avi asked. "To pay off their debt and actually come out ahead?"

In truth, Chavi wasn't sure. Most of the scavengers they'd met during their time were still there. Some died or disappeared. Others were rumored to have paid their debt, but in truth Chavi couldn't be sure. They'd just disappeared one day, and everyone would circulate the rumor they'd gone back to their normal life. But how many scavengers really did achieve normalcy again? Chavi had no way of knowing. They'd merely clung on to the dream that it was something they could do. A few years, they'd always told themself. A few years and I'll be out of here.

"We'd be hiding from the Delian Group. Forever."

"Maybe that could be okay. Better than nearly being slaughtered by monsters. We could figure something out."

"I...I'll think about it. For right now, we just have to get through the conference."

"Right. The conference." Avi sounded disappointed, but she swallowed her feelings with the practiced precision of someone who has had to do it many times. Chavi felt a little guilty nudging her back to planning, but they had the Ivies to worry about.

Avi placed a floor plan for the convention center on the desk in front of them, alongside an itinerary of events.

"These are part of the presenter kit. Everyone gets a map and a schedule." She pointed to a timetable on the itinerary.

"There are always demonstrations at the conference. Usually, researchers with the big corps who want to show off something they've been working on, mostly Satsuki and Zuri since they're the ones with all the flashy progress. It's a lot of pomp and circumstance, usually nothing special, since most of the real progress is super boring. But if your crab is gonna be anywhere, then it's there."

"What group would it be with?"

"I'm not sure. But even if you knew, they don't release the demo order in advance. If you want to get your crab, you're going to have to do it before the demo starts. Once the show starts, well, the show must go on. You'll be screwed. Besides, whatever they're testing on it is probably going to kill it. Unless you want a dead crab, I suggest you find a way to grab it before the demos begin."

"How can we do that?" Chavi cocked their head.

Avi beamed. "I've got an idea."

* * *

While Avi put the finishing touches on their presentation, she sent Chavi back to the Commission armed with a measuring tape.

"You'll need to go in wearing something suitable," she explained, "but I can have that taken care of. Just get your team's measurements and drop them off with my tailor before the workday ends. Ill-fitting clothes at an event like this would be a dead giveaway."

"Your tailor...?" Chavi repeated.

Avi scribbled an address on a scrap of paper and handed it to them.

"Go here. Say it's an order for Taheri and it needs to be done by five AM tomorrow morning."

"That seems like a tall order. You really think they'll—"

"Yes," Avi nodded. "For me? Of course they will."

Chavi whistled quietly to themself.

"I don't get the point of this," Princeton complained as Yale took his measurements.

"The point of this," Yale said, "is so we don't look like shit."

They stood up. "Alright, you're done. Go get your bag. Harvard, get over here. Let me take your measurements."

"Oh!" Harvard flushed. "Um. Okay."

Princeton left, grumbling about dress codes, to go fetch his bag of possessions.

"If things go poorly," Yale had warned, "we may not be able to return to the Commission. If there's anything you don't want them selling to other scavengers or just trashing, I'll drop it off where Avi can keep it for us."

No one really wanted to discuss what "things going poorly" could mean, but the stakes were clear: if they were caught, they'd be in the hands of the law. Stealing from a corp was a major offense, especially one of the big six. But if they failed, there was always the looming possibility of annihilation at the claws of the desertwalkers. Now they were back in Bastion, Skrack's threats felt like a distant dream. Still, they didn't dare let themselves get too comfortable back in the city, lest it meant risking an attack in the name of the Empress.

Princeton deposited his backpack on the table along with the other scavengers' belongings—Yale's sledgehammer in its harness, the Chocolates' gun wrapped discreetly in a shirt, Harvard's worn satchel. Yale didn't recognize it. He must have salvaged it while he was alone in the dusts. Despite knowing he'd been accompanied by carcine guardians, the thought of Harvard on his own in the desert, scavenging for food and supplies, gave Yale a pang of remorse. Someone as good and kind as Harvard didn't deserve to suffer that way. He should never have had to go through that. And if they'd been a better captain, he wouldn't have. If they'd been a better captain, they wouldn't be in this situation at all.

While Yale laid the tape measure against Harvard's back and scratched down numbers, Columbia pored over the notes Yale had brought back.

"You should be the main presenter," they said when they handed off Avi's summary. "You have the best chance of seeming like you know what the hell you're talking about."

Columbia opened her mouth to protest but didn't. They both knew it was true.

"So basically," she said while Yale struggled to get an accurate measurement of Harvard's chest, "we're presenting about how desertwalkers aren't actually immortal."

"Yup," Yale nodded, kneeling down to take Harvard's pants measurements. "Turns out most of O'Neill's research on crab immortality pointed to the fact that it *isn't* a thing."

"How much longer is this gonna take?" Harvard fidgeted with his shirt collar.

"Not long, just...it's kinda hard to get an accurate measurement with you shaking this much."

"Sorry."

"No, it's fine, it's just...I'll try to go fast, okay?"

"Okay."

Columbia adjusted her glasses and leaned back her chair.

"But there's still no cause of death for some of these creatures," she said, perplexed. "Some of them just...stop."

"Yeah, sorta like humans," Yale shrugged.

"No, not like humans," Columbia shook her head. "Humans always die because of something—organ failure, a stroke, a heart attack. After a few hundred years, some of these crabs just...end."

Yale stood, rolling up the tape measure. "What does that mean?"

"I don't know. Maybe there's some kind of disease that we haven't identified yet or...or some kind of parasite."

"Is this useful information? Is this impressive?" they asked.

"Yeah, I mean, I think this might be huge," Columbia marveled as she flipped through the pages.

"A crab parasite?" Princeton wrinkled his nose, doubtful.

"I mean, I don't like to say it, but a lot of corps would jump at the idea of finding a way to kill scuttlers quickly and easily," Columbia said.

"You think...some of these guys might want to wage biological warfare on the crabs?" Yale asked.

She shrugged. "It's a possibility."

"That... feels wrong," Yale said.

"We can't do that!" Harvard exclaimed. "Skrack and the Empress...they're our friends! We can't sell them out like that!"

"Um, *hello*?" Princeton said. "Did you miss the part where they're gonna *kill us if we mess up*? Did you miss the part where the baby crabs are gonna eat us? They're not our friends!"

"This is why the Empress doesn't trust you," Harvard grumbled, face flushing.

"We don't have anything solid," Columbia assured him. "All we have is...a trend."

"But is a trend enough to present?" Yale pressed.

Columbia looked over the notes one last time.

"I think so. Yes."

* * *

"What do you mean, you're canceling? You want me to present on my own?" Simon asked. And to think he'd only been worried about a missing citation. If he was the only presenter, they'd have to change the entire layout of the—

"No! There's no way you're presenting without me," Avi looked indignant at the very thought.

"Then what are you trying to say?"

"That we can wait until next year."

Simon gaped at her.

"What the hell are you talking about? We've been preparing for— I mean, *you've* been preparing for your whole life. And you just said you weren't nervous. Now suddenly you can't do it?"

"I lied. I am nervous. I am so, so nervous," Avi asserted, "and I think I will feel better next year. So let's just wait, alright?"

Simon set his jaw. "No," he crossed his arms.

Avi looked taken aback. "No? What do you mean, no?"

"I mean, no. Avi, I've dedicated everything to this research specifically to present it tomorrow. We're not just gonna give up on that because you're having a bit of stage fright. I mean, that's—"

"Simon," Avi pleaded. Pleading was not something Avi made a habit of—she rarely needed to—so Simon found it jarring to see her so suddenly vulnerable. His good nature got the best of him, as it often did. Even in a situation like this, when it meant the world to him, when every fiber of his being told him he had to stick up for himself—he just couldn't tell her no. No one could tell Avi Taheri no.

"Do you promise to tell me what's really going on?" he asked.

Avi looked deflated, as though she were disappointed her feeble deception had not worked.

"How did you know?" she asked.

He found himself smiling, and he realized with all the research and figure-checking and late nights reviewing articles, he hadn't let himself smile in a long time. Had he been holding all this tension in his shoulders for months? When did he last take a deep breath?

"Because I know you, Avi," he said, "and I know how much you hate it when someone tries to...to buy you."

Founders knew he'd certainly seen it enough. The Zuris were constantly courting Avi for internships and fellowships, and while it was work she loved, he knew how much she couldn't stand feeling like a commodity. He'd seen her face every time one of those offers arrived in the campus mail. She'd wrinkle her nose and stow the paper in a pile on her desk that she always claimed she would sift through but never did.

"Besides, I've known you for years. Obviously, I can tell when you're lying to me. I just feel like there's something I'm missing here, and...I want you to let me in."

She sighed. "I can't tell you everything right now," she said, "But I promise I will. Eventually."

"Okay," he said. "I'm going to hold you to that, you know."

And he meant it. He would. He couldn't refuse her requests, but he could at least demand the truth. But he cared for her enough to wait until she was ready to tell it.

CHAPTER TWENTY-EIGHT

Shared Burden

Harvard leaned in to get a better look at the convention center floor plan.

"Avi says they'll have everything for the demos stored here," Yale said. "That means one of us has to go in while the rest of us are at the display, grab the crab, and then get out before anyone notices."

"You really think no one will question that?" Princeton asked, reclining in his chair, arms crossed.

"No."

"Why?"

"We've got these."

They put two nametags on the table. One bore the name, "Avi Taheri," and the other "Simon Foster."

"We're impersonating presenters?" Columbia asked, her brow furrowed with worry. Harvard knew he could hardly lie about anything without his trembling giving him away. Then again, he trembled when he told the truth, too.

To his relief, Yale shook their head.

"We don't need to impersonate anyone. A bunch of researchers vying for spots at big corporations are not going to know two university students. The Taheri family is big, so chances someone who actually knows Avi will be there are slim."

"And you think just because we have nametags, they'll let us do what we want?" Princeton asked.

"I mean, not exactly," Yale conceded, "but we'll be a lot less likely to get asked questions. As long as they think we have a right to be there, no one will bat an eye. I mean, until we steal the crab, but hopefully by the time they notice we'll be out of there."

"One other thing," Princeton held up a finger. "There's only two. Last I counted, there are four of us."

"It's normal to bring a guest or two to help you set up. This one is for Columbia," they placed Avi's badge into Columbia's hand, "And *this* one is for Harvard."

Yale slid the badge that read "Simon Foster" across the table so that it laid in front of him. He felt his stomach churn at the idea of wearing someone else's name. It wasn't the lying he cared about; it was the idea of pretending to be someone smarter, someone more successful than he was. Wouldn't it be obvious? Wouldn't people read the name of some accomplished university student, and know the person who wore it was a fraud? How could he pretend to be the very thing he'd failed at pretending to be his entire childhood? He had never been a refined child, so how could he be a refined man?

Yale placed a plastic portfolio case on the table.

"You'll go into the back room with this. You'll look like a regular student with some kind of internship. Assuming the crab isn't, I don't know, huge, it'll probably fit in here."

"Wait, why Harvard?" Princeton interjected. Harvard wished he hadn't been wondering the same question.

"Columbia has the best shot of passing off as an academic. Harvard has the best shot of grabbing the crab without anyone noticing."

"I do?" he asked.

"You're small, fast, and discreet."

You mean, I'm easy to ignore, he thought bitterly. Still, part of him was touched by the compliment, if it was a compliment. It was nice to know Yale thought he could make himself useful, even if his *use* was simply being near invisible.

"Listen, I don't mean to be a nay-sayer here," Princeton put up his hands, "but—"

"Really?" Yale cut him off, "Because you seem to be saying 'nay' a lot."

"I just think," Princeton continued, "maybe *I* should be the one with the name tag."

"Are you joking?" Yale asked. "You think *you* get the name tag? After everything that went down with the Chocolates?"

"That was different!" Princeton said. "This is just stealing a crab—"

"Which is why Harvard can do it."

"Yeah, but..." Princeton gave Yale a look that was clearly supposed to mean something.

"But what?" Yale asked.

Princeton rolled his eyes. "The shaking, dude! We can't have him steal something. He'll drop it."

Harvard's face flushed. He opened his mouth to bow out, but Yale spoke first.

"That's not his fault," they hissed.

Princeton held up his hands defensively. "I'm not saying it is. I'm just saying that I'm not about to put my life in his hands if they shake that much. C'mon, we were all thinking it." He looked to Columbia for support.

"No, we weren't!" Yale shot back.

"Harvard is the reason we're in this mess in the first place," Princeton pointed out, and Harvard felt a stab of guilt. He was right, of course. If Harvard had just died in the desert like a good boy, then none of the Ivies would be roped into this.

"Maybe it shouldn't be me," Harvard admitted tentatively. "I mean, I—" He desperately wanted to say, *I don't have the best history with stealing things*, but he didn't.

"I can go with you, if you like," Yale offered. "As long as one of us has the credentials, we should be fine."

This put his mind at ease, a little. The pressure of the whole plan riding on him was lighter when he imagined Yale by his side, carrying that weight with him.

"So you're saying both of you go while I just...what? Do nothing?" Princeton demanded.

"You'll be with me at the booth," Columbia interjected, but Yale spoke over her.

"This isn't about *you*!" they shouted, which made Harvard jump. "I'm sorry if all your fuckups in the desert ruined your self-esteem, but this is not about salvaging your pride. This is about keeping Bastion from being overrun by crabs."

"Oh, I know!" Princeton laughed derisively. "Which is why I find it funny you trust *Harvard* more than you trust *me*."

"I've already explained—"

"I know you've explained, and I'm saying, I think you're wrong. Harvard was the reason we met O'Neill in the first place, and if that hadn't happened—"

"You can't blame Harvard for that!" Yale cut in.

"Oh, I *don't* blame Harvard for that!" Princeton stood, his chair clattering to the floor. "I blame *you*!"

A heavy silence fell over the Ivies, like a suffocating blanket.

"What?" Yale finally asked. Harvard realized that he had been clenching his fists. He willed his fingers to relax, but they wouldn't oblige.

"If you hadn't kept him on the team when I told you to get rid of him, then none of this would have happened," Princeton said.

"Don't talk about him like he's not here," Columbia chastised, but again she was ignored.

"Oh, so you think everything *Harvard* has ever done is *my* fault?" Yale asked.

At the first hint of anger in their voice, Harvard felt the instinct to run. He was back in his parents' home, being scolded. He was back in scavenger training, being harangued for some stupid mistake that would have gotten his crew killed out in the dusts. He hadn't seen this kind of rage from Yale since before they were captain, since they were the Instructor gripping his wrist and telling him never to *ever* disobey a captain's orders again. Princeton was not cowed. Instead, he met that anger with anger of his own.

"Uh, yeah! Cuz you're the reason he's still here! You didn't trade him in when you had the chance."

"You wanna know what Harvard is still here? Do you really wanna know?" Yale seethed.

"Yeah! I do!"

"Because I can't trade him in! He's my *punishment*!"

Columbia gave a small gasp. Princeton's mouth snapped shut abruptly. He opened it to say something, closed it again, then finally asked, "What?"

"Do you know what you have to do to become a captain, Princeton? Do you think there's some kind of test? Or you have to give them your resume? No, being made captain is a disciplinary measure. It's what they do to make sure you don't fuck up again, because this time, you're responsible for more than just yourself. So when I fucked over the Cookies so royally, they said, 'Congratulations! We're making you captain! And we're sticking you with the worst kid we have, and he's so in debt you will *never* get rid of him. And if he dies, you're kicked out *for good.*' So don't blame me for keeping Harvard, because I didn't have a tremor-scourged choice!"

"Yale!" Columbia shouted, but it was too late. The damage was done. Harvard stared at them, tears burning his throat.

"Is that true?" he strained to ask.

Yale sighed. "Harvard, I—"

Before they could finish, Harvard rushed out of the room, door slamming behind him.

* * *

The remaining three stood in silence.

"I...I'm sorry," Princeton finally said. "I didn't know."

"No, you didn't," Yale spat.

"I—"

"Go away, Princeton," Yale commanded, and Princeton gave a nod so deferential it almost looked like a bow and made a hasty retreat.

"I...didn't know that," Columbia murmured.

"I know. I didn't want to tell you," Yale pulled out a chair and sat down heavily, their face in their hands.

"Why not?" Columbia sat down next to them.

"I think...I was embarrassed? I already blamed myself so much for what happened to Minty and I...Harvard was meant to be a constant reminder of what I had done. A reminder it could happen again. And if you knew that too...you would look at me differently. You would look at *him* differently. And I... didn't want that. If you thought that the Commission had just left me off the hook, well...maybe you would let me off the hook, too."

"You know I don't blame you," she reminded them.

Yale lifted their face and gave a sad laugh. "I don't believe that," they smiled grimly. "I think *you* might believe that, but I sure don't."

"You don't have to believe me. But I still want you to know."

Yale nodded. "I'm sorry I kept it from you. I know we agreed to share everything. And I let you down."

Columbia gently placed a hand on their back and inhaled sharply.

I lied to you too, she wanted to say. *And my lie is much, much worse. I'm here because of you. I did this for you because I think you hate yourself, and I think you're worth more than you know. I did this for you because I can't imagine life without you. I did this for you because you are worth it.*

She didn't say any of that. All she said was, "I don't think it's possible for you to let me down."

"Are your expectations for me really that low?" they scoffed.

She shook her head, grinning despite herself.

"You're a good person, Chavi," was all she could think to say. "And I don't think you've ever been able to see that, but you should at least know that someone does."

They didn't agree with her, but they didn't protest, either, which was a good sign. They just exhaled slowly, turning something over in their mind.

"Jas..." they began, and Columbia realized with a shock they were actually blushing, something she'd never witnessed before.

"I thought for a long time that the only reason I was so angry Princeton wanted Harvard off the team was because I knew it wasn't possible. Maybe that *was* why in the beginning. But at some point...at some point that's not what it was about anymore. And it's not about feeling guilty about Minty. And...and it doesn't have anything to do with being a good leader, either. I don't know what it's about. It's just...I stopped being afraid of what would happen to me if I lost Harvard. I was afraid of losing Harvard because it was *him*. And for a really long time I didn't want to admit it to myself because I thought it was stupid, but...it's about him. Maybe it's always been about him. I don't know. Shit."

They looked up at the metal wall, avoiding her gaze.

"Oh, Chavi," Columbia said gently, placing a hand gingerly on their shoulder, "I know."

Yale turned to face her. "You do?"

She gave a fond laugh. "I told you! I know you. You can't hide anything from me as well as you think you can."

"I didn't even realize it myself, to be honest," they admitted. "And then he was gone, and suddenly nothing was more important than him."

Their face flushed even more, and they turned away again, looking down at their mud caked boots.

"What...what do I do?" She'd never heard this kind of helplessness in their voice before. The Chavi she'd once known at the Academy was so self-assured, so brazen and bold. And yet, she didn't mourn the loss of the old Chavi. Maybe a change was good for them.

"Talk to him," she suggested.

"He might hate me now," they laughed sadly.

"He doesn't," she assured them. "In fact, he's probably hating himself. He'll be happy to see you."

Yale met Columbia's gaze, and she could see a rare combination of hope and fear playing in their eyes.

"You really think so?" they asked.

She nodded.

"We might die tomorrow," she said. "Go talk to him."

* * *

A burden. That's what Harvard's parents had always said he was, hadn't they? It should really come as no surprise that his crewmates, even his captain—*especially* his captain—felt the same way.

He didn't cry. He was too exhausted. He just sat on his bed, hunched over, gripping his arms to his chest, his mother's words—word—swimming around in his head.

Useless useless useless useless.

Why had he left home if not to prove his family wrong? Had he not just proven them *right*? He'd always told himself, *They're wrong about me. When I'm on my own, I'll be a different person.* But here he was, completely and utterly the same. Small, stupid, and deluding himself into believing he could be anything but.

There was a knock on the door.

The childish part of Harvard wanted to scream "go away!" but he didn't indulge it. He took a deep, shaky breath, stood, and opened the metal hatch.

Yale stood in the doorway, looking smaller than Harvard had ever seen them. The way they moved had always seemed so bold and confident to Harvard, like they weren't afraid to take up space. Now they stood before him, shoulders slumped, wringing their hands awkwardly, and he almost felt like he was looking at a different person.

"Hey. Can I, uh, can I talk to you?" they asked timidly. Admittedly, Harvard wasn't in the mood to talk to anyone right now, but...well, if he did have to talk to someone, he was glad it was them.

"Yeah, sure," he stepped aside so Yale could enter the room. It was strange, having two bodies in the space meant for one. It felt close; almost too close. Yale grabbed the sole wooden chair in the room, the one each of the scavengers' quarters was outfitted with to match the useless wooden desk. They placed it facing the foot of Harvard's bed. Harvard shut the door and seated himself on his mattress, willing himself to look at Yale even though he desperately wanted to look away.

They bent over, hands clasped in front of them, and locked eyes with Harvard. His stomach fluttered with uncertainty.

"I wanted to say I'm sorry," they said.

Harvard blinked. "You have nothing to be sorry for," he found himself saying.

"I do," Yale insisted. "I shouldn't have said those things. Any of that. I gave you the wrong idea about your role on the crew and...and I'm really, really sorry."

Harvard was silent for a moment. He couldn't hold Yale's gaze any longer. He broke away, staring down at the cracks in the dirty cement floor.

"But it was all true, wasn't it?" he asked. "The things you said about me being your punishment?"

Yale sighed. "Yeah. But you shouldn't have found out like that. Not—"

"In front of everyone?" Harvard guessed, his face burning just at the memory of the whole scene.

"I was going to say so...directly. But that too. I...lost control. I used to do that a lot. Mostly I think I've gotten a handle on it but sometimes I make mistakes."

"It's okay," Harvard laughed sadly. He'd meant to sound comforting, but Founders, he just sounded pathetic, didn't he? "Really. I should be apologizing to you for being so...I mean, they wouldn't have made me a punishment for you if I wasn't the way that I am."

He felt his throat tighten a little at the end of the sentence.

Do not cry, he berated himself internally, *Not in front of them. Don't do this.*

"What do you mean?" Yale asked quietly.

"You know what I mean." *Don't make me say it. Please.*

"I want to hear it from you."

"Useless. I'm useless."

"Remember what I said to you that day when we were first put on the crew together? About how you'll make a good scavenger because you're a good listener?"

"Yeah, I think so," Harvard thought about the day more than he liked to admit. About Yale's comforting words, about their warmth, about their touch. About the feeling that for the first time since Harvard could remember, he felt like someone might truly be looking out for him. He pushed all of those thoughts aside, reminding himself the reason Yale was speaking to him in the first place: he was a punishment.

"Everything I said that day was true. It wasn't just to make you feel better, or to placate you so you would get along with the rest of the team. The truth is, I'm jealous of you. You're...soft in a way that I never learned how to be."

Harvard scoffed. "It's not exactly like 'soft' is a good trait in a scavenger."

Yale gave an affectionate grin. "Harvard, what are you talking about? You got those desertwalkers to *trust you*. And you didn't do it through strength or bravery or even intelligence. You did it simply by being the person you are. And that's...I mean, that's just incredible. And if it hadn't been for that ability you have to make people...hell, even crabs... trust you, then we'd all be dead. I'd hardly call that useless."

Harvard felt his face burn. He couldn't tell if this onslaught of compliments was something he had actually earned, or just another leadership tactic to keep him in line. But Yale seemed so *genuine*. No, it wasn't possible. They couldn't be serious. The Ivies had a mission tomorrow, after all, and they were just doing damage control before the conference.

"The Commission thinks I'm useless," he said, "otherwise they wouldn't have put me with you."

Yale laughed, but there was no derision in it. Only genuine fondness. "Harvard, why does it matter if you're useful or not? I just reminded you that you saved all our lives, and still you don't see your own worth. Look, I'm not...I've never really been great at the whole pep talk thing, if I'm being honest. But what I'm trying to tell you...what I'm trying to say...I mean that you're a good person. And it doesn't matter what the Commission thinks. It doesn't matter what Princeton and Columbia think. It definitely doesn't matter what *I* think. Hell, it doesn't even matter what *you* think, even though I'd certainly prefer it if you saw yourself a kindlier. All that matters is despite everything, you are still *kind*, and you are still *good*, and that's not true of many people in the world."

Harvard didn't want to cry in front of Yale, not now, not again. But he felt his throat burn. All he could do was keep himself from breaking into sobs. So he swallowed and allowed his tears to well up in his eyes and fall slowly down his cheeks.

"Do you...Do you mean it?" Harvard asked. Yale gave a warm smile, and it made Harvard's heart begin to race.

"Harvard," they murmured. "I have always meant what I say about you. That's always been the case, and it's true now. You are..." They struggled to find the right words. "You are very special, Harvard. And I want you to know that. Even if you don't realize it yourself..."

Tentatively, Yale lifted a hand and placed it on Harvard's knee. Harvard inhaled sharply, shocked by the touch, but also by the softness of Yale's skin against his.

"You're special to *me*."

Realization came crashing down on Harvard in one glorious and horrible moment. Harvard did the only thing he knew he was good at: he panicked. His breath quickened, as his body began trembling violently, like a frightening animal in a storm. Yale immediately retracted their hand, standing up so quickly the chair skidded on the stone floor.

"I'm sorry. I shouldn't have...I didn't mean to...shit. I'm so sorry. I should go."

They moved for the door, unwilling to meet Harvard's gaze, but he gripped them by the wrist and pulled them back.

"No," he said, his voice still quivering. "It's fine. Really, it is. I just—" he bit his lip, fighting back the tears burning in the back of his throat. Yale cautiously lowered themself back into the chair, eyeing him warily.

"I was just...I mean, I was surprised, I think. I didn't think—"

He squeezed his eyes shut and tears made their way down his cheeks. He hung his head, avoiding Yale's gaze, though he could feel them watching him.

"I didn't think it was possible for someone to want to be with me."

"Oh, Harvard."

Yale leaned forward to grip Harvard's hand where it rested on the bed and placed the other hand under Harvard's chin to lift his face to look at them. He kept his eyes shut, but he could feel their warm breath against his cheek as they whispered, "I do want to be with you."

Yale squeezed Harvard's hand and he shivered, goosebumps rising all over his body. He wasn't sure he'd ever been this close to another human being. He finally opened his eyes to see Yale's face mere inches from his own.

"Do you really want that?" he asked. Yale placed a hand against Harvard's cheek, and he gave a little gasp. They leaned in even closer, to the point where their nose and Harvard's were almost touching.

"I want nothing more," they whispered. Harvard expected them to draw even closer, but he realized they were leaving the next move up to him, giving him the choice to either accept or rebuff their advance. He inhaled shakily before he placed a quivering hand on the side of Yale's neck, then pulled himself forward to place his lips gently against Yale's. Harvard's mind raced with the impossibility of it all. Could this really be happening? But nothing had ever felt more real to him than the warm softness of Yale's lips against his own. They snaked their arm around his waist and pulled him closer, eliciting a little whimper of surprise from Harvard. Harvard could feel Yale's lips curling into a smile, and they chuckled quietly.

"You know, we could stop right here," Yale whispered, drawing a hand through his hair while the other arm was still wrapped around his middle. "You say the word and I'll be gone."

"No, I—" Harvard chuckled shakily, but he found he was no longer nervous. No, there was a different feeling churning around in his stomach now. Excitement.

"I'd like you to stay. I mean, if that's alright with you."

Yale pressed their lips against Harvard's forehead.

"Yes," they whispered, "that's more than alright with me."

"I just...um—" Harvard stammered. "I don't know what comes next."

Yale laughed quietly, and it put Harvard at ease. "I'll show you."

They tilted their head back down and kissed Harvard again, harder. Without breaking away, they pressed one hand against Harvard's shoulder, gently pushing him back against the bed.

Harvard had only ever known Yale first as the strict Instructor, then as the stoic captain of the Ivies. And suddenly here they were in his bed, desperately touching him.

The word that came unbidden to Harvard's mind as Yale pressed their weight against him was *hungry*. Perhaps it was only the isolation they had suffered for so long that made them seem so rapacious for the simple joy of touching another human being. But maybe it was *him*. Maybe this person, who Harvard viewed as all but a god upon Earth, truly wanted *him* and him *alone*. And that delicious idea, that sensation, was the real source of joy Harvard got as he ran his fingers through Yale's hair, feeling their breath on his neck, hearing their noises in his ear. He felt like they wanted him—no, *needed* him, like somehow, they always had. They grasped at his shoulders, his hair, his neck, his hips—gripping as though Harvard could be torn away from them at any moment. He felt a kind of lightness, a moment of perfect togetherness, like a scale played on a piano as it reached its resolution. For that fleeting moment, everything was perfect.

Harvard fell asleep curled up on his side, Yale pressed up against him, one hand placed possessively on Harvard's hip. He felt Yale's steady breath on the back of his neck and nestled his head into his pillow. His last thought before losing consciousness was a wish—a wish the morning would never come, and that he could stay in this moment forever.

CHAPTER TWENTY-NINE

The Mission

When Harvard awoke and felt Yale's strong arms clasped around him, warmth jittered in his stomach at the memory of the previous night.

That was real, he thought to himself. *That happened. Founders. That happened.*

Yale must have sensed he was awake, because they—regrettably—untangled themself from him and propped themself up on an elbow. They reached across Harvard for their glasses on the stool next to the bed.

"Good morning," they smiled. Harvard felt like he melted a little.

"Good morning. Um...what time is it?"

"Early. Around five."

"Oh. Good." Early meant more time together. Early meant this didn't have to end. Harvard could stay like this forever.

"I should probably get up," Yale said, and Harvard's heart sank. "I've got some, uh, things I need to prepare for today."

"Oh. Right," Harvard tried to laugh good-naturedly, but it was a poor facade. Did they *really* have things to do? Or did they just not want to be with him any longer? Yale seemed to sense Harvard's panic, so they wrapped their arm around his waist and pulled him close.

"Did you have a good time?" they asked, using their free hand to play with his hair.

"Yeah. I, um, I'd never done that before," Harvard admitted.

Yale grinned and laughed quietly. "Yeah, I kinda figured."

"Oh. Was it obvious? I...I mean, I hope I wasn't—"

"You were perfect," Yale planted a kiss on Harvard's forehead.

Perfect. Harvard wasn't sure if anyone had ever called him perfect before.

"Really?"

"Really."

They swung their legs off the bed and stood, and Harvard averted his eyes, afraid his stare would make them uncomfortable. When he looked up again, he found them watching him as they pulled on their shirt.

"What?" he asked.

"Nothing," they shrugged, but the whisper of a smile on their face implied it was definitely *something*.

"I'll see you in the common room around eight, alright?" Yale asked. Harvard nodded. "Try to get some more sleep before then. It's gonna be...well, it's gonna be a day."

"I'll try," he smiled weakly.

Yale bent over to ruffle his hair.

"Good boy," they said as they turned to leave the room, and Harvard's stomach did a little flip. For the first time in his life, he blushed for a reason other than embarrassment. Harvard knew he would not be able to fall back to sleep. All he could do was lie in his bed, extending a hand to the empty space where Yale had lain, remembering what it was like when they were there.

* * *

Yale was, in a word, confused.

They'd never wanted to be with anyone, not the way they wanted to be with Harvard. They'd never even had the desire to sleep with the same person more than once. But with him? They wanted to turn around, run into his room, scoop him up in their arms and say, "Let's get out of here, shall we?" Then they could run away with him, adopt a dog maybe, and never have to worry about being alone ever again. Of course they couldn't do that. They had a responsibility—to Columbia, to Princeton, and also possibly to some crabs who were threatening to wage war on mankind. So, it wasn't really the best time to have an impulsive romantic getaway. But the *impulse* was there, and that's what was so alien to Yale—an impulse to do anything *romantic*.

Well, the good news is, if I die today then I won't need to have an identity crisis, they thought bitterly. *And if that was the last night of our lives, at least we got to spend it together.*

They didn't want to *pity* him, to treat him like a little glass animal at risk of shattering. But that morning, the look on his face—Yale felt as though they could say one word wrong, and he would crumble in on himself. He was so damn *anxious*. Yale wondered if he'd been born this way, or if someone had done this to him. *If I ever meet the person who made him doubt himself all the time, I'll have some choice words*, Yale thought, *and also some choice acts of violence.*

Yale froze when they saw Princeton waiting outside their door. They braced themself for his questions—it wasn't exactly a logical jump to guess where they'd been the previous night. If Princeton had put the pieces together, however, he didn't let on. In fact, he didn't even question Yale was only now getting back to their room, wearing the same clothes from the previous day, now rumpled. The way he was rubbing his arms self-consciously, he almost looked as nervous as Harvard.

"Hey," he said, jumping to attention when he saw Yale approaching, "Can I...uh, can I talk to you?"

Yale sighed.

"Will it be quick? We don't have much time, you know."

"Yeah, no, totally, I know. It'll be fast. Promise."

Yale nodded, gesturing toward their room. Princeton entered ahead of them, seating himself awkwardly on the wooden chair. Yale fished around in a drawer for a fresh set of clothes and a towel so they could shower before heading out to meet Avi's tailor.

"What do you want?" they demanded, tossing a shirt and a pair of pants onto their bed.

"I, uh, wanted to say I'm sorry," Princeton said. "About yesterday. I shouldn't have pushed you to say all those things. I...I was wrong to blame you. And I know that now. And," he sighed deeply, "and I'm sorry."

Yale paused, still faced away from Princeton. They slammed the drawer shut.

"You should be apologizing to Harvard," they said, turning around, "not me."

"Yeah, um," Princeton rubbed his thighs anxiously, staring down at his feet. "You're probably right, huh?"

"I am right," Yale stared at him, waiting for him to return their gaze. "He's the one you hurt."

"I know, I know," Princeton groaned, "but like, it wasn't fair to you, either—"

"Why are you so afraid of him?" Yale asked, catching Princeton off guard. He stared up at them blankly.

"What?"

Yale crossed the room to start to water in the cramped shower stall. The faucet creaked in protest.

"You've apologized to me plenty. But you never go to him. Are you scared?"

"I am *not* scared," Princeton scoffed in the voice of a man wondering, *holy shit am I scared?*

Yale hung the towel on the peg outside of the shower stall.

"Then there's nothing preventing you from saying all this to *him* instead of me," they raised an eyebrow at Princeton, who nodded solemnly. Then they made a shooing gesture with their hands, and Princeton scurried out of the room like a chastised dog.

* * *

Princeton paced back and forth in front of Harvard's door. Yale's words had rattled him. Not because he was afraid of Harvard. No, obviously not. That was stupid. Laughable, even. But because he couldn't help but remember his sister's words on the day he left. *You just want to feel like the hero, but you don't actually care about being a hero.* Maybe she'd been right. Was he really a better crew member than Harvard? Or had he just wanted to feel like he was? Why was he *like* this? How could he try so hard to be good, and somehow still make everyone mad at him?

"I mean, he's probably still asleep now, right?" he said aloud. "Yeah, he's still sleeping. Wouldn't wanna wake the little guy. Especially not before the big day. I'll just tell him after. Yeah, that's a good idea. He'll still be around after."

Princeton nodded to himself as if in affirmation and made his way to his own room to get ready.

* * *

Harvard wasn't sleeping, but he still wasn't thrilled at the prospect of getting out of bed. Reality always came along and ruined the brief moments he got to play with fantasies in his head. This morning, he wasn't even fantasizing, not really. Just replaying the events of the previous night over and over in his mind.

Reluctantly, he pulled himself out of bed and washed up. He found a package at his door, wrapped neatly in brown paper. He brought it into his room and unwrapped a suit jacket, slacks, a white button-down shirt, and a slender black tie.

Scavenger quarters did not have large mirrors, since appearance is not the primary concern of someone who spends years of their life digging around in the dirt, but there was a small mirror in the bathroom he could use to see bits and pieces of himself if he stood at the right angle.

It had been so long since he had clothes that fit him properly. Ever since he left Bell Manor, he'd made peace with the fact that from then on, every other article of clothing would hang on him loosely. Most of his clothes before the Commission, after all, had been scavenged, so he couldn't exactly be choosy. Then once the Commission supplied his clothes, everything was used—and there were rarely scavengers as small as him.

He smiled at himself in the mirror, admiring the way the suit outlined the shape of his body. It made him feel...serious. No one ever took him seriously, not really. How could they *not* take him seriously in a suit like this? He was an *adult*. He was a *man*.

He almost wanted to cry.

"Damn!" Princeton exclaimed Harvard walked into the common room, "You're looking fine as hell, my man!"

Harvard blushed and smiled meekly, yesterday's quarrel apparently totally forgotten, and Princeton walked over to give him one of those high fives that turns into a thump on the back.

"Thanks," Harvard adjusted his tie self-consciously. "You, uh, you look good too."

"Oh, I know," Princeton grinned. And it was true. Princeton didn't *need* the help of a suit to look masculine, but it did accentuate his features—his height, his broad shoulders, his muscular arms and legs.

Harvard turned at the sound of the door opening, and saw Columbia walk in. She wore the exact same jacket and tie that Princeton and Harvard did, tailored to suit her form. She looked sleek and professional. A tailored suit, Harvard decided, probably looks good on everyone. Harvard swallowed, wondering what Yale was going to look like.

Just act normal, he told himself, *and pretend like everything is normal. And don't think about last night. And don't think about how you know what they look like under the suit. And don't think about how it felt to have their body pressed up against yours. And don't think about how they kissed you and you want them to do it again. And don't think about—*

Yale entered behind Columbia, and Harvard felt his knees get so weak he almost collapsed into Princeton's arms.

Unlike the other three, they weren't wearing their jacket. Instead, they had it hooked around their finger and slung over their shoulder.

"Ready to go?" they asked, surveying their team, pointedly not scooping up Harvard in their arms and carrying him away like he'd sort-of-kind-of hoped maybe they would.

Columbia nodded.

"Let's go."

The four of them filed into the hallway, where they would head to the desert hatch and exit the compound unnoticed.

"Hey Harvard," Yale said once the other Ivies were just a little bit ahead of them. "You look good."

This time Harvard's knees did buckle, and if he hadn't caught himself stumbling into Princeton, he would have collapsed to the ground.

* * *

Harvard adjusted his cuffs repeatedly as the group approached the convention, more to distract himself from his trembling than to actually straighten them.

"I still think it's not fair that you and I don't get nametags," Princeton complained, but his playful tone was measured, as if to indicate to the rest of the group that he'd moved on from the fight the previous night.

"We don't need name tags," Yale said sharply, as if to indicate they had definitely *not* moved on from the fight last night.

"So, we don't even get code names?" Princeton looked visibly disappointed.

"They're not code...fine, Princeton, if you want a fake name you can make one up. I doubt anyone is going to be talking much to the two of us anyway."

"My name is Felipe!" Princeton announced triumphantly. "And you will address me as such."

"Okay, cool," Yale grumbled, though they couldn't completely mask their amusement. For all his flaws, Harvard had to admit Princton had a certain skill for deflating tension. Had it not been for his presence and constant obnoxious commentary, Harvard's shaking would probably have become uncontrollable by this point. But thanks to the constant distraction, it was barely more than a tremor. *Maybe*, he wondered, *this would actually go okay.*

Thinking such thoughts, however, was often a fatal mistake.

CHAPTER THIRTY

The Conference

Columbia often wondered what the Galvin Conference might look like. She was told while growing up she would one day attend it with Avi, but she wasn't sure if she really believed that. She simply couldn't see herself presenting, *performing*. Avi had a natural sort of charisma about her—she could easily wheedle any corp representative into giving her funding, even if she didn't need it. The very idea of it made Columbia nauseous. She'd been happy to help Avi but was determined never to attend the conference herself.

Yet somehow, here she was, wearing Avi's nametag. Maybe it was the knowledge of how dire her task was, but it didn't scare her as much as when she was younger. Maybe she'd grown. Maybe she simply knew there was no way out. Still, she was terrified.

Despite her stomach fluttering, she couldn't help the feeling of awe washing over her when they flashed their identifications to the guards and were admitted into the main atrium. It wasn't just sleek glass staircases, the gold columns, the layers of balconies like a decadent cake, or the red walls that bent over the room like tidal waves frozen in amber. It was simply the *size* of it. The height of the ceiling, the undulation of the crowd, the wide expanse of displays—it was all just so...big. It was the biggest room she'd ever been in, the biggest crowd she'd ever been in. And she'd never felt so small.

"Wow," she murmured. She turned to see her companions were equally amazed. None of them had seen anything like this either, had they?

"C'mon," Yale said, eyes still pointed up at the levels of the building, all on display from the main room like honeycombs in a beehive. "Let's find our booth."

* * *

There were different kinds of wealth, Harvard realized. He was used to the marble, fountains, galas, and flowers painted on dishes for eating dessert. He wasn't used to the aggressive simplicity, and elegant grandeur of the room he walked into. Buildings, he supposed, send a message. His parents' house had sent the message, "We are rich. We want you to see that. We want you to be overwhelmed with delicate little beauties we can provide because we have that power. We want to pamper you and treat you because we can, and you won't forget it." This building sent the message, "We are here to do business. We also have loads of money, but that's beside the point. This is not about you. This is about the progress of humanity." Funny that just the space you exist in could tell a very different story.

The conference staff had already set up for them. It was only a tri-fold board, which paled in comparison to some of the scientific demonstrations and flashing screens around them, but it still looked sleek and professional.

"This is incredible," Columbia marveled, examining the display. "You and...the two of you, you did this together?"

"Sure did," Yale smiled, and Harvard could tell they were trying to keep a lid on their pride. Still, he couldn't help feeling a pang of jealousy. Who was this Avi girl that Yale spent so long working with? How long had Yale known her? What kind of relationship did they have? Did they like her? How much time did they spend with her? The thoughts made him feel queasy, and he worried if he lingered on it anymore he would be sick in one of those pretty golden garbage cans.

"Who knew the two of you would make such a good team," Columbia marveled, which made Harvard's envy burn even hotter. Yale shouldn't be allowed to make a good team with anyone but *him*. He knew it was unreasonable, but he couldn't push the feelings aside.

"So we just stand here and...wait for people to talk to us?" Princeton asked, scanning the conference hall.

"Pretty much," Columbia said. "You see all the people with the badges?" she indicated to the right of the ballroom, where a group of suits were mingling. "They're the investors. They're trying to decide which of these projects are worth their time and money. Each color represents a different level—green is for new companies, yellow is for established but small companies, blue is for big companies, and red is for the big six."

Harvard felt a stab of panic. Would a representative of Bell Enterprises be here, under the auspices of his own name? He didn't feel like it was *his* anymore, not really, but if the other Ivies knew he could have been heir to the one of the six largest corporations in Bastion and he gave it up to be a scavenger—would they see him differently? Would he be a traitor? What would Yale think?

"How do you know all this?" he asked Columbia. She froze, contemplating the best way to answer.

"I...wanted to present at the Galvin Conference when I was little," she explained. "I, uh, had a partner. And we worked on projects together. We thought...maybe we'd make it."

"Well now you're living the dream!" Princeton clapped Columbia on the back. "And I bet your old partner is probably here too, somewhere."

Columbia shook her head sadly. "She's not."

Harvard fiddled with his nametag, hoping that his trembling was not too noticeable. Would it give him away? Of course not. Anyone could have a tremor. But a *refined child*—a refined student, that is—wouldn't shake so much. He looked at the name tag. Simon Foster probably wouldn't be trembling like this, whoever he was. He was probably smart and sophisticated and put together. Harvard fidgeted with the zipper on the portfolio case. Pretending to be someone else only reminded him he could never escape who he *really* was.

* * *

Yale scanned the crowd of corp representatives, already perusing the booths of researchers pandering to them. They hoped the rest of the crew couldn't see how uncomfortable they felt. All of the judgment. At the same time, it made them want to laugh. What would their teachers from the academy think, seeing them here? Would they be proud— or only angry that they were wrong to have told them they'd never become anything? *Well, they weren't wrong*, they reminded themself. *This is all a lie. This whole thing is a lie.*

Yale furrowed their brow at a representative without a corp label. He was a skinny man with dark hair and a confident stride, drink in one hand and gesticulating with the other as he held an animated conversation with some medical researchers.

"Who is he?" they asked Columbia, discreetly nodding in the man's direction. Columbia shrugged.

"I don't know. Why?"

"He's got the red lanyard. Those are usually the really big companies, right?"

"Usually, yes."

"But he doesn't have a company label on his badge. At least, not that I can see. So what company is he with?"

"Maybe he's not with a company?" Princeton suggested.

"He must be with somebody. The whole point is that in order to be one of the viewers, you have to have *connections*," Columbia said.

"Well, let's hope he doesn't come talk to us," Yale said.

"Why?"

"I don't know. I don't like him."

Yale had caught a few glimpses of the man peering at their booth, and that had put them on edge. Were they just being paranoid, or had the man taken a particular interest in them? Had they prepared something truly innovative with Avi? How ironic, then, would it be that Avi's great scientific triumph would be presented by four fakes, two of her former classmates, no less. But Yale worried it was something else drawing the man's attention. They couldn't imagine what— they'd thought through every aspect of their disguises, and Avi had vetted the display for any potential errors. Aside from their young age, nothing set them apart from the other researchers.

"So... what's killing the crabs?" a short man with a blue lanyard asked as he looked over the display.

"We don't actually know," Columbia explained, her back ramrod straight and her voice touched with scholarly precision Yale remembered from their Academy days. "That's why we could use funding for further research. But if there is some kind of untraced pathogen—"

"We could use it against them?" the man ventured.

"I was...I mean I was going to say it could potentially be dangerous to humans."

"Doubt that!" he laughed. "We hardly have anything in common, us and those beasts."

Yale resisted the urge to step in front of Columbia and remind this man which of them was the *researcher* and which of them was the one *looking to buy research* so maybe he should shut up and listen to the person who knew what the hell she was talking about, but they figured that wouldn't be appropriate for an academic conference, so they simply fantasized about stepping hard on the man's gleaming black shoes.

"There's been talk about how we might finally clear those things out," the man told Columbia conspiratorially. Despite her facade of scholarly impassiveness, she allowed herself to raise a cynical eyebrow.

"That seems...unlikely, considering their number. And size. And lack of vulnerabilities," she said levelly.

"Well clearly they must have some," the man said, gesturing to the display. "Of course, I'm not scientist—"

No, you're not, Yale thought and fought hard not to say.

"But there has been discussion of expansion."

"Expansion? Expanding the city?" Columbia asked incredulously.

"Well, you can hardly expect us to stay here forever! It is the nature of humanity to want to conquer. To expand! And if you take a look at the other displays," he waved a hand at the conference at large, "you'll notice a theme. We've been cooped up in Bastion too long. Time to show those scuttlers who the apex predator really is!"

He shoved a fist into his palm for emphasis, and Yale saw Harvard visibly wince. In fact, now that they were watching him, they noticed he had been shifting uncomfortably for the whole conversation, as if it had put him in physical pain just to hear. Now he had this...connection with the creatures of the desert, how did it feel to hear someone talk so callously of wiping them out?

"I hear the Satsuki group may even be whipping up a plan to make creatures of their own," the man continued.

"Make creatures?" Columbia repeated.

The desert belonged to the desertwalkers and Bastion belonged to humans. That's just how it was. The idea of humanity somehow concocting creatures of their own...it seemed unnatural.

"Big mean things that'll wipe out the quaking scuttlers once and for all!"

"You'll never do it," Harvard blurted out, drawing a worried look from Columbia. "There's too many of them and they understand the Earth better than we ever will. Besides, they have the same right to live as we do—"

"And *we* have a right start picking 'em off!" Princeton interrupted, casually placing an arm over Harvard's shoulder. "Go humanity! Go innovation! Go *science*!"

This seemed to satisfy the man, and he gave Princeton a nod of agreement before moving on to the next booth. As soon as he was out of earshot, Princeton gave Harvard a shove. Yale fought down the urge to shove Princeton even harder into the next booth over, unleashing choice words about what would happen if he touched Harvard again.

"What's wrong with you, dipshit?" Princeton demanded. "These people love talking about killing scuttlers! It's, like, all they do!"

"People are scared of desertwalkers," Columbia agreed, "So fighting them is a...popular topic."

"I know, I know!" Harvard stammered. "I just...I didn't mean to say it. It just slipped out. I can't...I didn't like hearing him talk about them that way."

Defending himself seemed to make Harvard's nervous shuffling even worse—and of course, his ever-present trembling. Yale crossed the display and laid a hand on his shoulder. Harvard inhaled sharply, but the trembling subsided slightly.

"It's okay," they assured him. He nodded mutely, releasing a slow shaky breath. He looked like he was about to say something when his head snapped up. Yale followed his gaze to see that another investor was looking at their display—the man they'd seen earlier with the red lanyard and no corporation attached. A burly man with a thick blond beard hovered just behind him, hands clasped in front of him. When the smaller man saw that the Ivies had turned their attention to him, he flashed them a tight smile.

"Impressive stuff," he gave Columbia a reverent nod.

"Thank you," she gave a polite little bow, then extended a hand cordially. "I'm Avi Taheri. Pleased to meet you."

He accepted the hand gingerly.

"You can call me Devrin," he said.

"Is that a first name or a last name?" Columbia asked.

"Neither," he shrugged. "Just a name."

Columbia's smile faltered, replaced with a confused grimace. The man who called himself Devrin grinned.

"Names, names, names," he said. "So silly." He gave Yale a wink, as though it had a hidden meaning they alone would understand. The fact they certainly *didn't* understand left them feeling like they'd missed out on something very important.

"This is my assistant, Pierce," he gestured back to the sturdy man behind him, who gave a curt nod. Yale wondered what kind of activities the man "assisted" with, and they guessed it probably wasn't paperwork.

"Ms. Taheri, I must admit, you look different than when I last saw you," Devrin said.

The Ivies froze. Yale hazarded a glance at Columbia, who had managed to keep her composure. Good. If she could keep it together, then so could they.

"Of course, you were very young then, so it's no surprise that you've grown," he added.

"I, um, you'll have to excuse me," Columbia gambled, "but I don't actually remember you."

"Oh, that's not surprising," he smiled. "You were such a little thing. I was a friend of your family's, all those years ago. It's been a long time since I've seen any of the Taheris, admittedly. Tell your family I send my regards."

"I...I will. If you don't mind me asking, what...what corporation are you with? I see you don't have a—"

"Oh, this thing?" he waggled the lanyard playfully. "Seemed a little silly, honestly, putting a label on myself to say I belong to a corporation when in fact a *corporation* belongs to *me*."

It would be supremely uncouth to refute any corp representative, especially one who had been given the honor of a red lanyard, but this claim was an unlikely one. Most major figures in the big six families were well-known in Bastion. Even Yale, who didn't keep up with current events, had heard names like Azizi Zuri and Saoirse Bell before, and could probably pick out their faces in a crowd. If the man wasn't holding out solid proof of his societal significance in front of him, Yale would have immediately assumed he was lying.

As if sensing their confusion, he clarified, "The Delian Group, of course. We like to keep a low profile. Best not have the people in charge of your safety swanning around like celebrities, right?"

"You're...you're saying you're the Head Enforcer?" Columbia gawked.

Devrin nodded. "Have been for quite some time, as a matter of fact. It's nice when no one knows your face. It keeps you out of the *drama*."

He gave Columbia a knowing expression.

"There's always some kind of *drama* with these family corps. No offense, of course, Miss Taheri."

"No, I completely understand," Columbia responded sweetly.

"Anyway, I'd best be off. Lots of displays to see," he waved a finger in the air and gave a brief eye roll as if to say, *Work, amiright?* then disappeared into the crowd, his imposing chaperone shadowing him diligently.

Princeton glanced around the conference hall.

"So let me get this straight," he said, gesturing to the security stationed around the building. "*He* is *their* boss?"

Now that they were watching, the guards did seem to stand up a little straighter when Devrin passed, eyeing him cautiously.

"The real question is: why is his assistant totally jacked? Like, why do you need an assistant to be that ripped?"

Yale wondered the same, but they kept quiet, turning to watch Columbia's response. She was silent, looking out into the undulating crowd. Something about the interaction must have disturbed her. Something about it had disturbed Yale too—probably all of them—but they couldn't figure out what it was. Maybe it was the casualness with which the man flaunted his power, or the way he spoke like there was a hidden meaning behind every word. Maybe it was something else.

Time passed quickly as Columbia spoke with one viewer and the next. Most of the conference attendees used this time for mingling and networking, scraping their way up the social ladder, all conversations motivated by the poorly concealed question, *how could knowing you benefit me?* Columbia had convinced Harvard to slip into the crowd to mingle, as would have been expected of a university student trying to make his way in the world.

Yale watched Harvard from afar as he chatted with some minor corp representatives. They wondered how he could look so natural in an environment so different than the one they'd both come to know together. He looked as though he'd been trained for situations like this, not for the harsh world of the desert. They wondered what he could possibly be talking about—something that made the women he spoke to laugh. He smiled sheepishly, and Yale couldn't help smiling too. They thought back to the previous night. And now, watching him when they should be thinking of how they were going to manage this heist, they couldn't help imagining how easy it would be to grab a fistful of red hair and pin him against a wall and—

"I said *talk* to him," Columbia chastised sweetly.

"I *did* talk to him."

"Seems like you did more than talk to him."

"I just think the conversation went really...really well."

"Let's hope we get through this. I'm sure the two of you have a lot more to talk about."

Columbia looked as though she were going to say something else, but her mouth snapped shut. Yale gave her a quizzical look, and she only urged them forward.

* * *

Harvard's training from his days at Bell Manor taught him manners. It taught him how to put on a smile and listen attentively and nod at the appropriate times and say something polite and meaningless when the conversation allowed for it.

It had never taught him to dispel his panic, and he felt the anticipation of his upcoming task roiling in his stomach.

He worried everyone could see him start to sweat, that they could see him shaking, hear the tremor in his voice, and eventually someone would point out that this absolute wreck of a boy could not possibly be the esteemed scholar Simon Foster, and he must be up to no good. And even if he wasn't found out, he would still have to swipe the crab, and the thought of it made his sweaty palms even sweatier.

He glanced up at the clock on the back wall. It was almost time. He thought he might pass out.

He politely excused himself and ran to the bathroom.

He caught sight of himself in the mirror, looking so pale he thought he might be sick. He turned on the tap just to hear something that wasn't the din of voice outside. He gripped the porcelain of the sink until his knuckles were white, willing his legs to stop shaking.

I can't do this, he thought. *I can't do this.*

"Are you okay?" Yale's voice startled him so much it made him jump. They stood in the bathroom doorway, hands in their pockets.

"What? Yeah!" Harvard slammed a hand on the faucet and brushed a stray curl out of his face. "I'm fine."

"You don't look fine," Yale observed as they approached him. Harvard had a moment of panic.

"Is something...is something wrong?" He looked down to examine his suit. Yale laughed, which relaxed Harvard just a little.

"No, I mean, you look great," they said, "but not fine, is what I mean."

Harvard didn't know how to explain it all to them, other than to burst out crying, tell them he gave up and that it was too much pressure and they were just going to have to do this without him. Luckily, they saved him from having to answer when they added, "Actually, your tie's all messed up. Let me fix it for you."

They closed the distance between them and undid his tie. Harvard breathed deeply, but Yale's sudden closeness only made his heart hammer even harder. Their brow knit in confusion.

"I've...never done this on someone else before," they admitted. "Um...hold on. Let me do it like this."

They stepped behind him and reached around him to tie the tie from his perspective. With Yale standing behind him, Harvard remembered that day in training when Yale had taught him how to use a knife. They'd been pressed up against him just like this, but now...things were different. Now they'd been together. The tension that had once hung in the air between them, that had made Yale run away in what Harvard now guessed was shame, had evaporated. And he could tell Yale felt it too, by the way they allowed their fingers to linger on his neck as they tightened to knot at the base of his throat. They pressed their lips just below his ear, planting an achingly gentle kiss at the top of his jaw. Harvard inhaled sharply.

He knew Yale probably intended this to put him at ease, but only flustered him even more. He wished all of this—the conference, the desertwalkers, the Commission, everything—would just melt away, then it would only be the two of them, and he could lean back into them and really, truly relax.

But it wasn't just the two of them. Harvard had a job to do, and right now all Yale was doing was making him even dizzier.

"We should go," he whispered.

"I know," they said in his ear, and after a moment they released their hold on his tie. They placed a hand on his back to encourage him forward. "Let's move."

Harvard left the bathroom somehow more terrified than before, but with a renewed sense of purpose. He nearly collided with the man standing near the bathroom door, but Yale's hand on his shoulder held him back.

"Oh!" he yelped. "I'm sorry, I—"

"Where are the two of you headed?" the man said. Harvard realized he was the one who had been asking them questions earlier—Devrin, he remembered. Harvard felt a stab of panic, a cold sensation that dropped into his stomach. He reminded himself that no one could possibly suspect them of anything criminal. If anything bad were about to happen, Yale was right beside him.

"They're getting ready for the demos in there, I expect," he nodded toward the hall.

"We have academic viewing privileges," Harvard responded automatically. According to Avi—well, according to Yale, according to Avi—this was the best thing to say if anyone began to ask them questions. Technically Simon and Avi hadn't been awarded this privilege, as they were researched for students who were already interning with major corporations, but it was the kind of claim that would require a bit of digging around in the paperwork to disprove, and the Ivies were betting that no one was going to be willing to check up on that until after the crab had mysteriously disappeared. Still, Harvard was worried that this man would see past the lie and lay their plans before them. Instead, he nodded approvingly.

"I imagine it's good for students such as yourselves to get acquainted with the industries you're going into. After all, you're studying specimens from out in the dust, and I'm assuming the two of you have never been out there, have you?"

"No, sir," Yale answered too abruptly.

"It's a shame," Devrin said, "that so few people have. I think it would do them good, to see what's really out there. Most people, even researchers, believe all the fairytales they hear about the desertwalkers. Everyone could benefit from seeing the real thing."

"Have you been, sir?" Yale asked levelly.

"A few times, yes. It's a big world out there. It's a pity the experience is wasted on scavengers."

Harvard saw Yale wince at the unexpected mention of scavengers, especially one so full of derision. Harvard was no stranger to this kind of dismissive attitude, but it was the disgust in Devrin's voice that caught him off guard. It reminded him of his mother. He could tell that it wasn't lost on Yale, either.

Please don't say anything, he begged internally. *We have to go. It doesn't matter what he thinks. We have a job to do.*

But Yale could not resist responding to the barb, even if it was flung unwittingly.

"As the Head Enforcer, have you...arrested many scavengers?"

Devrin shrugged.

"We don't like to make a habit of it. But I will say, they do have a habit of getting into trouble."

This gave Yale pause.

"What do you mean?"

"Oh, I mean, too many scavengers and suddenly Lower Bastion is teeming with ne'er-do-wells. We've got to keep things in check down there. That is, if the sandheads don't pick enough of them off."

Something sinister passed over Yale's face. They laughed humorlessly.

"Why would the sandheads—I mean why would they—" they stammered.

"Haven't you heard? Scavengers are *sacrilegious*!" Devrin joked, smiling to himself. "It's the very core of their religion to punish those who disturb the Earth. That's why the Rubira group came up with it in the first place. Give the dregs of society something to cling onto while keeping each other under control. They keep each other in check. Sometimes the sandheads need a bit of help so, you know, we do what we can."

We do what we can. Harvard wondered what that could possibly mean. He knew that the Delian Group would occasionally arrest scavengers, but actively trying to kill them? He couldn't tell if the man was being serious or testing their gullibility.

"People do one of three things when they get desperate: religion, drugs, or jobs that don't pay them enough. Sometimes a combination."

Harvard resisted the urge to pull Yale by the hand, conscious of the time they were wasting. More than that, he saw the hard determination that Harvard knew too well meant that rage was simmering underneath. It was the same look they'd had when they scolded Harvard during scavenger training, when they'd shouted at Princeton to let Harvard go back when they first found O'Neill's pod. His worry about time slipping away from them was second only to the worry that this man would goad Yale into doing something regrettable, something that couldn't be undone.

Instead, they said with measured coolness, "And what would you, Enforcer, know about being desperate?"

Devrin looked satisfied, as though he'd caught them in the exact trap he'd laid out for them.

"You don't need to be desperate to observe it. In my job, I see enough desperation to know the shape of it."

Harvard touched Yale's arm gently, a subtle indication they should break away, but they shook it off.

"You look disappointed," Devrin observed, giving a little pout.

"I guess I just thought that the Delian Group protected all the people of Bastion."

"It does," he asserted, then with a self-satisfied smile added, "scavengers aren't *people.*"

"We should go!" Harvard interjected, gripping Yale's wrist in fear their hand might snap up and strike the man. "We, uh, don't wanna miss the observation period. Before the show starts."

Yale didn't pull away from Harvard's grip, but they didn't look at him, either. Their eyes were fixed on Devrin.

"Actually," Devrin purred, "I was hoping one of you could help me with a project I'm working on. A student like yourselves would be perfectly suited. If you don't mind missing the demonstration, I would love for one of you to discuss the details with me."

Harvard felt his stomach drop. *One of you. He* was the one with the nametag. *He* was the one holding the portfolio case. *He* was the one who was fast and stealthy and easy to ignore. Which meant—

"Simon, go ahead without me," Yale said, their eyes still fixed on the man. "I'll be with you in a moment."

"Um. Yeah. Uh...Okay," Harvard stuttered, easing his grip on their wrist. He hadn't realized how tight he'd been holding it. He wondered if he had hurt them.

"Right. Yes. Okay."

He scurried off before he lost his nerve, through the door that led to the back hallways.

Harvard forcibly slowed his pace as he made his way down the hall. As it was, he didn't look suspicious. He would if he was spotted sprinting into the backrooms, sweating and looking incredibly guilty. If anyone saw his nervous expression, he hoped they'd chalk it up to the pressure of presenting to investors. In truth, the only thing he could think was,

They were supposed to be with me. I'm on my own. I'm not good enough on my own. I'm going to mess it up on my own. The only reason he'd ever agreed to this leg of the plan was because he was going to have Yale by his side. Now he felt directionless, like he was lost in the desert all over again. The memory came crashing back down on him, the panicked frenzy as he fled O'Neill's pod, the vast emptiness of the desert, and then, of course, the dust catching in his throat. His breathing suddenly felt constricted, like he was choking on dust. He was alone again, alone alone alone.

But he *wasn't*. In fact, he was surrounded by people. He wasn't abandoned in the desert, lying unconscious in the sand. He was in a fancy convention center, wearing a suit and an official name tag. Yet, somehow, he felt just as invisible as he always had. Even surrounded by people, he still managed to feel like no one saw him. Would he ever feel like anyone could see him? Or would he always be a ghost?

If I'm destined to be a ghost, I can at least use it to my advantage, he thought, steeling himself as he navigated the back halls. He remembered the layout from Avi's floor plan—he could see it when he closed his eyes. *No one will notice me. I am a master of being unnoticed. I even have a name tag. This should be easy.*

He stopped in front of the door. If Avi was right, this should be where the corps and the other high-profile researchers would be storing equipment. If the crab was anywhere, it was in here. He could hear the bustle inside. Harvard took a deep breath. *You're a ghost. You're a ghost. You're a ghost.*

He pushed open the door and stepped inside.

He froze.

Directly in front of him, he saw his own face.

"I do hope our little behind-the-scenes tour has been of interest to you, Mistress Bell. If you ever find yourself wanting an internship, know that the door is always open."

Kathy.

CHAPTER THIRTY-ONE

The Demonstration

Yale turned their gaze from Devrin to watch Harvard disappear into the back hall. *At least one of us made it,* they thought. *Everything should still be fine. I just have to deal with this—*

They felt a tug on their wrist.

"Ivies. Pretty name."

Yale whipped around to see Devrin gripping their captain's band, which they'd neglected to remove from their wrist. He was studying the inscription with great curiosity. Yale instinctively tugged their arm away, but Devrin's hold was surprisingly strong, and he barely flinched. Their heart raced as realization settled on them like thick fog. They'd been found out. It was over. All because they'd *stupidly* forgotten the *obvious* thing that would give them away—

"Don't beat yourself up," Devrin seemed to predict Yale's course of thought, still examining the band. "Most scavengers are oddly attached to the thing. Won't give it up even when they have to."

Panicking like a trapped animal, Yale tried to break free from the man's grip, only to have him pull them in further. He smiled and murmured, "Easy there. Don't want you to dislocate anything."

He turned his gaze back up to Yale, but he did not let go. He had his fingers wrapped around it and his palm pressed over the clasp, so Yale had no hope of unbuckling the thing and fleeing.

"For what it's worth, I knew you were scavengers from the beginning," Devrin explained. "It's not exactly like a group of researchers this young is likely to be selected for the Galvin Conference. And of course there's the way you walk. There's a certain gait all of you people have. I think it comes from constant fear something is going to eat you. That stays with a person. And there's four of you, for Founders' sake. You might as well have walked in with 'scavengers' tattooed on your foreheads."

Finally, Yale found it in themself to speak, leaning in so they could not be overheard.

"What do you want?" they hissed.

Devrin raised both eyebrows, feigning shock. "Want? Nothing. You have nothing to fear from me. I won't tell. At least, not right now. Just consider me..." his eyes glinted devilishly, "an interested party."

"Okay, fine," Yale fumed, "then why don't you let me go?"

Devrin considered this. "Well, that hardly seems fair," he reasoned, "seeing as I'm doing you such a big favor by keeping your secret for you, especially after you messed up so badly, putting your whole crew at risk."

If they weren't so terrified this man would ruin the entire operation with a word, Yale would have used their free hand to punch him in the mouth.

"What brings me back to my original question," Yale said through their teeth, "what do you want?"

"How about this: tell me your name," Devrin said. "And don't just make one up. I'll know."

Yale hesitated. Their real name was something they held close to their chest, almost more precious than life itself.

"I...I...can't..." they stammered, beginning to sweat. "If I tell you that, you could have me arrested."

But their mind went elsewhere—if they were arrested for impersonating a researcher—and planning to steal from a corp—what would happen to their *mom*?

Devrin only laughed derisively. "Sure, I *could*. But I won't, I don't think. And if you don't tell me, a quick wave of my hand will have the whole security team coming down on your little band of scavengers. So it's either you, or all of them. What'll it be? *Captain*."

Yale stared into this man's deep gray eyes as if the information was being pried out of them.

"Chaverim," they whispered, "it's Chaverim."

Devrin's thin lips curled into a menacing grin.

"Chaverim," he repeated, and released the band. Yale yanked their hand back, reflexively massaging their wrist.

"Well, Chaverim, captain of the Ivies," Devrin said, "your secret is safe with me."

"Why...why do you want to know?" they asked, feeling as though they'd been beaten at a game they hadn't known they were playing.

"Don't you think it will be nice for me to know I've got a scavenger friend named Chaverim?"

Yale's head shot up.

"I'm not your friend," they spat. Devrin looked satisfied with himself as he turned his back on them.

"You will be."

* * *

Harvard knew he should stop looking at her, that he was only making himself more obvious by stealing glances at the young heiress, but he couldn't help it. Was it the fear she would spot him, or that he hadn't seen his own sister in six years? Who was she, now? Was she the Kathy Bell he had grown up with, who teased and taunted him and eventually pushed him out of the house? She didn't look it. She looked like a young professional, sporting a pale blue blazer and pearl necklace, her fiery hair pulled into a tight braid.

"We do hope you'll consider an internship with us," the man was saying to her. "There is, after all, a time-honored collaboration going on between our two corporations."

"I imagine there is a time-honored collaboration going on between all the corporations, or the city could not exist," Kathy pointed out, "though I agree the Zuri Institution is particularly intriguing to me. Anywhere that I can continue my studies. Admittedly I applied to the Rubira Association as well, but they didn't seem to think I had the credentials."

The man waved his hands, "A bunch of snobs," he said. "We would be honored to have a young woman of your intelligence among our ranks. Will you be staying for the demonstrations?"

"I don't believe so, no. I have business to attend to at home I'm afraid."

Harvard found himself transfixed by her. They still looked identical, and yet, somehow he felt they couldn't look more different. As he'd gotten smaller over the years, thanks to hunger and the constant desire to make himself disappear, she'd become larger than life. She commanded attention and respect, and the way she smiled left you with the impression she was always in control. She had grown into a woman, and here he was feeling like he was still a boy. He wondered what kind of person she'd become. Was she kinder, softer than she'd once been? Or was she cruel as always? If she'd met him now, as adults, with no memory of their past, could the two of them be friends?

Harvard forced himself to focus on the task at hand, difficult as it was to break away from Kathy. He felt utterly lost in a room full of equipment he did not understand. Synthetic food demonstration by one of the lesser corps, some sort of medical display, an engineering display with what looked like an engine, a computer chip wired to a variety of monitors, something with orbs and electricity — mostly devices that Harvard couldn't imagine the uses for. He'd never known much about technology. His family didn't even have a computer, but with the rarity of computer chips that wasn't necessarily a surprise.

He wished he'd asked the Empress for more information. What did Mryk even look like? Perhaps she'd assumed he would just know how to find him. The way that he could feel the presence of the Empress, of Skrack in his mind, perhaps he'd just—

He closed his eyes and drew in a long breath, focusing on that part of his brain where he heard carcine voices. Was anyone there? It was an art he had little practice with, but if he could just reach out with his mind—

Hello?

It was a voice unlike that of Skrack or the Empress. Small, tinny, and most of all, scared. Harvard was filled with an overwhelming urge to protect that voice, to hold it and take it away, to ensure no harm ever came to it. He was pulled to it—

And he knew where it came from.

Without even realizing what he was doing, he turned to one corner of the room, and there on a display table was a crab trapped in a round glass case with a metal base, like a grotesque snow globe.

The desertwalker in the case was unlike any Harvard had seen out in the desert. Its shell was small, like that of the Empress, but it glimmered an iridescent purple and green, reflecting the harsh glow of the lights above. Its legs were about a foot long, looking out-of-proportion with its miniscule abdomen. The glass case was so slender the creature didn't have enough room to fold its legs and rest. It could only amble around, poking at the glass with its spindly appendages, ramming its sparkling shell against the glass to no avail. Watching the helpless thing made him ache, the same ache when he saw the harpoon lodged in Skrack's shell.

I'll help you, he wanted to say, but he knew the creature could not hear him. It did, however, freeze, slowly turning to face him. Could the creature tell the Empress had placed her trust in him? Did it know why he was here? Harvard couldn't speak aloud to the creature without drawing attention, so he only thought, *I'm here to take you home.*

The crab did not seem receptive to his message. It clawed at the glass again, in his direction.

Hello? Hello?

He wanted to shush it, to assure it that he was a friend, but the crab seemed too befuddled by the presence of a receptive mind. The researchers whispered to one another, wondering what had agitated their subject.

Almost there, almost there, he told himself. Just wait for them to turn. *They won't see you. You're a ghost. You're a ghost.*

His fingers brushed against the glass. He wrapped his palms around it, lifted it off the table...

His eyes darted toward Kathy.

Perhaps it was just chance, or perhaps she felt his eyes on her. But she turned. Her eyes locked with his, and they held each other's gaze for an agonizing moment that seemed to stretch for hours. Kathy looked as though she was trying to parse exactly what she was seeing, how she could possibly be looking at some kind of illusory version of herself. He thought perhaps she didn't recognize him. All those years must have made her memory fade. Did she even remember she'd had a brother at all? How often did she think about him, if ever? He willed her to turn away, to forget him, to ignore him like she'd always done, like everyone always did, to treat him like the nothing he was.

He could not hear her speak, but even from across the room he could read her lips, *Ronan?*

His tremor hit him like an earthquake. The glass case slipped from his fingers and clattered noisily to the ground. He bolted. He wasn't certain, but he could have sworn he heard Kathy's footsteps pounding after him as he darted into the hallway.

* * *

Yale stumbled over to the refreshments table.

What the hell was that?

They searched for something they could drink. A glass of champagne. That would work.

Yale raised a shaky glass to their lips. *Now I know what Harvard must feel like all the time.* They took a sip, hoping to stop the trembling. No interaction had ever left them as shaken as this one. What did the man want? By taking their name, he had gained complete power over them—the ability to lock them away at any moment, to take away their mother's only source of income.

"What's wrong?"

Yale whipped around to see Columbia, her brow knit with concern. Should they tell her everything now? Or wait until it was all over? They took a deep breath, leaned over to her, and whispered in her ear, "I think we may be involved in something deeper than we expected."

She nodded solemnly. "We'll talk about it later," she said, and Yale relaxed just a little. Columbia understood. She wasn't panicking. And after this was all over, they could talk about what happened and what to do about it.

A frazzled-looking Harvard ran up to them, his face even redder than usual, looking like he was holding back tears— again, more so than usual.

"Where's the crab, Harvard?" they demanded, harsher than they'd intended.

"I'm sorry! I'm sorry!" he cried, and with a sinking feeling Yale realized he was apologizing to *them* personally.

* * *

"What's going on?" Princeton approached them, "And why does Harvard look like he's about the puke?"

Because he is *about to puke*, Harvard wanted to say. The world was closing in around him dizzyingly fast, and every step he took he had the strange sensation that the floor was trying to leap up and slam into his face.

He was furious with himself. He'd allowed Kathy to ruin everything. Again. Another heist he couldn't pull because she's been there, and she knew. Of course she didn't really know. She'd probably dismiss the incident completely. She didn't care about him enough, after all, to think anything of maybe seeing her long-lost brother at a science conference. But still. She'd somehow managed to ruin everything anyway, and Harvard discovered he would never forgive her. Now he wasn't just furious at himself—he was furious at both of them. Two identical twins who just kept ruining everything.

* * *

"Come with me," Columbia commanded, beckoning them to follow with a discreet wave of her hand. She led the three to a wooden door labeled "Family Restroom."

"How is this a *family* restroom?" Princeton asked. "There's only *one* toilet."

"What are we doing in here, Columbia?" Yale asked as she locked the door behind them.

"According to the floor plan Avi gave us, this is the only accessible place where we can talk without drawing any attention. I figured it might be useful to know where all the isolated rooms were, so I took note of it before we left. It was this or the janitorial closet down the south hall, but I think this is a little more comfortable."

Comfortable was a stretch considering they were all very tightly packed next to a toilet and an infant changing table, but it was probably a step up from the closet.

"Okay, so what's going on?" Princeton demanded. "Where's the crab, Harvard?"

"I couldn't...there was..." Harvard stammered, his eyes frantic.

"It doesn't matter," Columbia cut him off. Admittedly, she was just as curious as Princeton was about why Harvard had come back empty-handed, but clearly something had rattled the poor boy. She knew that expression on his face— she'd felt the same way standing frozen in the cafeteria while violence unfolded around her, and her only thought was that she had done this to herself, that she was the one to blame. Whatever had put Harvard in such a frenzy was not something he wanted to share, so she wasn't going to press.

"Plan A didn't work," she said. "That's okay. That's why we have a Plan B."

"We have a Plan B?" the other three asked simultaneously.

"Yes, I made a Plan B," she sighed, "but I didn't want to let any of you know, because, ideally, nothing would go wrong with Plan A. But—"

Harvard's face fell.

"You thought I was gonna fail!" he wailed.

"Well, to be fair," Princeton reasoned, "you *did* fail."

"I *didn't*," Columbia shot Princton a look, "think you were going to fail. I just thought a safety net would be useful."

"What is the safety net?" Yale asked. Something was wrong with them, too, but again, now was not the time to unravel everyone's anxieties. Now was the time to get the crab and get out. She produced a copy of the floor plan, the one Avi had lent them.

"The demo stage is here," she pointed, "which means in order to transport everything, they have to take everything from the storage room back here. There's not a back hallway that connects them, which means they have to move everything along the edge of the conference hall. There's five demos total, and we don't know when the demo with the crab is slated, but there should be enough of a crowd—"

Someone knocked on the door. There was a baby crying on the other side.

"Um...we're a family!" Princeton improvised. "And we're...taking a collective piss?"

"Princeton!" Columbia snapped.

"What was I supposed to say? It's the family restroom! Didn't you read the sign?"

"Keep going, Columbia," Yale said. The urgent edge in their voice was not lost on her. She nodded and turned back to the layout.

"This is certainly not as neat and tidy as the original plan, but we've always been scavengers, not thieves. If we can cause some kind of emergency while they transport everything—"

"I am great at causing emergencies!" Princeton beamed. Columbia knew Yale must be particularly worried because they didn't make a biting comment in return. In fact, they didn't even look like they'd heard.

"What kind of—" they started, but a noise from outside cut them off. Feedback from a microphone, and the muffled voice of someone speaking into it.

"What's that?" Harvard asked. Columbia pulled the conference agenda from her pocket.

"Um..." she scanned it, "I don't know. The demos aren't supposed to start for—"

Yale opened the door, pushing past a baffled father holding a crying infant.

"Who takes a baby to this kind of thing anyway?" Princeton grumbled.

"They started early!" Yale said, pointing to the stage where the demonstrations had already been set up. Tables were already lined up on the stage, bearing machines and computer monitors and vials and anything else that fell under the umbrella of progress.

"How...why..." Columbia glanced down at the schedule and back up to the stage incredulously.

"So, uh, Columbia," Princeton ventured, "You did come up with a Plan C, right?"

Columbia only shook her head mutely, watching as the corp representatives set up the stage.

"So this is it then?" Harvard asked. "We missed our chance? We've ruined it? We're just going to watch them as they kill that poor crab, then the desertwalkers will attack the city?"

"I...I don't know..." Columbia stammered.

Columbia watched, paralyzed, as a balding man in a lab coat took the microphone. He had the eager air of someone who spent far too much time researching behind closed doors and had finally been released to get a bit of sunlight and social interaction. He adjusted his glasses as he surveyed the crowd and began his speech.

"The Satsuki group is proud to present its latest advancement in chemistry."

The statement was met with polite applause. The man lifted a small canister.

"This vapor is harmful to desertwalkers. But it is *not* deadly. Why, you may ask, develop a compound to hurt the things when we already have a vapor to neutralize them? We can kill the monsters, yes, but killing is not the same as controlling. Imagine for a moment a world where we have no fear of the desert because we have made the monsters work for us. What you are about to see is the first step toward training these beasts. Humanity will once again rule the Earth."

A new kind of vapor, Columbia reflected, *one that doesn't kill. One that only...tortures.*

"Horrible," she said aloud.

The crowd, by contrast, whooped and hollered at the notion of taking the Earth back from the desertwalkers. The four Ivies, it seemed, were the only ones at the Conference not celebrating the notion that the crabs could be bent into submission.

"Thanks to the abilities of this new compound, as well as the assistance of the Delian Group," the presenter continued, giving a nod to some of the guards stationed around the conference center, "we were able to capture this rare specimen, alive, to demonstrate on for your today."

As the iridescent crab, scraping at its glass cage with stick-thin legs, was placed on the table, the crowd erupted into uproarious applause. A live desertwalker was rarely brought into the city safely, especially not one this large. The capture of the creature alone was a huge victory.

Yale's voice pulled Columbia away from the presentation.

"Harvard?" they asked.

Harvard wore a pained expression, one hand creeping into his hair. He stared absently at the stage, and the imprisoned crab.

"Harvard!" Yale asked again, but he didn't respond.

* * *

Harvard felt the creature the moment he saw it, lugged onto the stage in the glass case he'd seen in the storage room. It was the same kind of presence he'd felt when the Empress or Skrack was speaking, but it wasn't directed at him. It was a mind reaching out for someone, anyone, to hear it, a mind pleading for freedom. There were no words, no sentiments, conveyed in the message, only a call, screeching, pulling Harvard toward it with a kind of magnetism he felt in his chest.

"He's...speaking to me," Harvard said incredulously.

"The crab?" Princeton demanded.

"What's he saying?" Columbia asked.

Before Harvard could answer, the demonstrator flipped the switch and the show began. The desperate cries for help abruptly shifted to wails of anguish, as the creature writhed in its case. Harvard could barely hear their questions over the pleas that inundated his mind. He gripped his head, fingers curling into his hair, and let out an agonized cry. He reeled in pain, stumbling over his own feet. Yale was by his side immediately, one arm around him, bending over to make their faces level.

"What's wrong?" they asked.

"They're hurting him!" Harvard cried, squeezing his eyes shut. "We...we have to... make it stop—" he stammered, his face contorting.

The other Ivies were asking him questions, but he could no longer hear them. All he could hear was the wailing, and even with his eyes closed, all he could see were the crab's desperate attempts to free himself from his prison.

"MAKE IT STOP!" he screamed, this time drawing a few stares. He knew there were hands on him now—maybe Yale, maybe Columbia, and someone was whispering something in his ear but—oh, none of it mattered. Nothing human mattered. Nothing mattered but the crab. Harvard was not very good at thinking under pressure. So he didn't think. He simply leapt forward before anyone could grab hold of him.

For the first time in his life, Harvard felt perfectly steady. There was no trembling as he fought his way through the mass of spectators. He felt as though the pull of the creature was carrying him through the crowd— he hardly heard the shouts of dismay, or felt the bodies pushing up against him, or even the floor underneath his feet. The only things in the room were him and the cries of a creature in need, and the magnetism between them was a force greater than he could comprehend. All he could see was the creature needing his help, clawing at its glass case with delicate thin legs. All he could do was throw himself at it in hopes of stopping the agony.

* * *

Yale was on the stage behind Harvard before they knew what they were doing. Before any of the demonstrators could stop him, Harvard wrapped his arms around the glass case and yanked it free. One of the demonstrators made a move for him, but Yale was faster. With a quick swing of their arm they threw the woman off the stage. For the brief moment Yale was facing out into the crowd, they couldn't help but search for the bespectacled face of the Head Enforcer. Now the crowd went from concerned confusion to absolute chaos. There were shouts, screams, cries.

Then there was a gunshot.

* * *

Harvard heard the shot ring out, but he didn't feel anything. All he could feel was the glass case gripped against his chest. He'd heard the body goes into shock when it's fatally wounded. He was thankful for that. At the very least, the creature's cries had stopped. There was silence. For one blessed moment, everything was silent. What a peaceful way to die.

He swiveled to face the crowd behind him, time frozen in one quiet, crystalized moment.

Yale turned to face him, their face stony and impassive as ever—so placid that Harvard would hardly have known anything was wrong if it hadn't been for the crimson stain rapidly crawling up their new white shirt.

"You should go," they said to him. Then they crumpled to the ground.

The rest of the world snapped back into action. Delian Group guards converged on them. Columbia was there, somehow, dragging Yale away. Someone was closing their arms around him, lifting him off his feet. There was a horrible screeching sound coming from somewhere, coming from everywhere, and Harvard realized that it was *him,* screaming.

"No!" he was crying. "No!"

But Yale's crumpled form faded in the distance as someone carried Harvard away, through a doorway, and into the hall.

"I know this is bad, little dude," he heard Princeton say, "but right now we've got a crab to save. So we gotta *run.*"

CHAPTER THIRTY-TWO

The Surgeon

"Good shot," Devrin patted the guard on the back. He was still holding his glass of champagne. He loved a good show.

"Shall we go after them, sir?"

"Oh, focus your energy on the ones with the crab. The other one will be dead soon anyway."

"Yes sir," the guard nodded, and led his legion after the two thieves who'd disappeared into the back rooms of the convention center.

* * *

Columbia half-guided, half-dragged Yale through the back hallways. She hadn't memorized the floor plan Avi had given them like Harvard could have, but she remembered enough to know there should be an emergency exit.

Though they were growing weak, Yale was surprisingly compliant as she steered them toward an exit. Perhaps getting shot was not so bad.

It was only when they made it outside that Yale's knees buckled and they collapsed to the concrete.

"I'm sorry...I'm sorry," they panted. "I can't—"

They cringed, gripping their bleeding abdomen, and Columbia could see they were fighting back a scream.

She knelt beside them, holding them by the shoulders.

"Yale—*Chavi*—" she corrected. "I know it hurts. I know you're in pain. But we need to get out of here right now."

"I know, I know," they nodded. Columbia helped to pull them to their feet, but they only collapsed back into her arms, and both fell to the ground again.

"We need to go," Columbia repeated. "We need to go."

"I know, I just...I can't—" their words caught in their throat as they started taking quick, shallow breaths. They squeezed their eyes shut and groaned.

"*Chavi please!*" Columbia screamed, growing desperate.

She heard a car careening toward them, and she feared Conference security had already found them. The vehicle screeched to a stop and the door swung open.

"Get in. Now."

Columbia looked up to see the face of Avi Taheri staring back down at her.

* * *

"We have to go back! We have to save them!" Harvard cried, wriggling in Princeton's grip.

"Columbia's got it covered, I promise. The best thing for all of us is if we get that little fucker back where he came from, and we're done with all this crab bullshit forever. Got it?"

"They could be dead!"

"Then what help would we be, right?"

"But—"

"They told you to go, remember? Ya gotta listen to your captain."

The sound of thudding boots came behind them. They were being pursued—which really didn't come as a surprise, since Harvard still gripped the precious carcine cargo in the glass case. Princeton hazarded a glance over his shoulder before darting around a corner. He burst through an emergency exit and set Harvard down on the concrete.

"Here's the plan: We're gonna run down this street to the main gate," Princeton said, indicating the main road of Bastion.

"No," Harvard said absently.

"No? What do you mean no? We have to—"

"No," Harvard repeated. "I know a better way."

"How do you—"

Before he could finish, Harvard gripped his wrist and yanked him down a side street, guiding him through a weaving maze of alleys and passages, one that could only have been mapped by a boy who had needed to make some quick escapes.

* * *

Jasmine summoned all her strength and lugged Chavi into the van. They groaned in protest at being jostled around, landing heavily across the back seat. Jasmine climbed in after and slammed the door shut, kneeling in front of the seat where Chavi lay.

"Avi?" Chavi asked weakly, seeing her face in the rearview mirror.

"The one and only, buddy," Avi said as she slammed her foot on the gas and the car jerked into motion. Jasmine hurriedly placed a hand on Chavi's shoulder to prevent them from toppling off the seat.

"How did you know...why are you..." she stammered, looking up at the girl she hadn't seen in years.

"No offense," Avi said, focusing her eyes on the road, "but I didn't exactly expect you guys to heist a major corp without a hitch. I packed just about every first aid material I could grab. It's all in the bag. Find some fabric and apply pressure to the wound. Now."

Jasmine rummaged through the bag until she found a wad of gauze. She gingerly removed Chavi's blood-slick hands from their stomach and placed the fabric over the wound. A red stain spread through the fibers quicker than Jasmine had anticipated.

"They're bleeding a lot," she reported weakly. As if in response, Chavi groaned a half-scream, half-cry.

"I know," Avi said, "Gut wounds don't clot well. That's why we have to move fast. If we don't deal with this right now, they could be gone within the hour."

"But how—"

"Don't ask questions, Jasmine! Just make sure they don't lose consciousness and they keep breathing."

Jasmine wasn't sure how to do the latter, but the former seemed straightforward enough. She placed a hand on Chavi's cheek. They looked up at her with pained, frantic eyes.

"Avi's gonna take care of you," she said in the most serene voice she could muster. "You're gonna be fine."

"I...I don't think so—" Chavi wheezed, biting their lip to avoid crying out in agony.

Jasmine nodded. "Yes. Yes, you are. I promise."

Under normal circumstances, Chavi would have laughed at her face. They would have said, "You don't know that, Jasmine! How could you possibly know that?" But in their state of fear and pain, all they said was, "You promise?"

"Yeah. I do."

The car came to an abrupt stop, jolting Chavi forward into Jasmine's arms. They cried out, a proper scream this time. Avi was already at the door, helping Jasmine lift their body out of the vehicle.

"Where are we?" Jasmine asked.

"Bastion University of Sciences," Avi answered, hooking her arms under Chavi's and hoisting them out of the car. Jasmine grabbed their legs.

"Everyone's still in town for the conference. Place should be pretty much empty."

She fished around in her pocket, allowing one side of Chavi's body to sag toward the asphalt. Her hand emerged with a key card. The two awkwardly carried their friend up the stairs of the stone building, and Avi sidled up the keypad and tapped her card. The little panel beeped affirmatively, and the door slid open.

"Follow me," Avi commanded, as though Jasmine had a choice. Avi was leading the way and Jasmine was simply dragged along, struggling not to drop Chavi's legs on the tile floor.

Avi swerved to the left, pushing open a door with her back, and led them into an operating room. She led Jasmine toward an empty table, where they placed Chavi's body.

Jasmine watched helplessly as Avi donned her surgical apron and goggles, wheeling a tray of tools over to the operating table. Her face hard and determined, she immediately set to work with a pair of scissors, cutting away Chavi's clothing to reveal the bleeding flesh underneath. Once she had enough space to work with, she traded her scissors for a scalpel, prodding at the wound. By this point, Chavi's pained cries had become full-on wails. Jasmine wished impotently she could take the pain away from them. She couldn't imagine the agony they were in. This was the person she'd seen practically beaten to a pulp, and they'd shrugged it off—memories of the altercation with Carter Vik came all too quickly, the sight of Chavi smiling, *laughing*, as the blood ran down their face. How bad must this hurt to have them screaming in anguish? What kind of torture were they going through right now?

I wish it was me, Jasmine thought. *It could have been me.*

"Hold this," Avi said, gesturing for Jasmine to come over and hold some gauze against the bleeding. Avi rushed out and returned, wheeling an intravenous pole, a bag of clear liquid hanging from the hook. She went to the side of the table opposite Jasmine and jabbed Chavi's arm with a needle.

"What are you doing?" Jasmine asked.

"I can't explain everything!" Avi snapped. "We don't have time to sit around doing an anatomy lesson! Just do what I tell you, okay?"

Jasmine nodded. Avi ran around the operating table to Jasmine's side. She placed her hand over Jasmine, holding the gauze in place.

"I'm going to start working," she said. "Keep them awake, alright? Whatever you do, make sure they do not fall unconscious."

"Got it," Jasmine nodded again, releasing her hold on the gauze and gripping Chavi's hand.

"Hey," she said, moving up to where their head lay on the table. "Hey, Chavi. Look at me. Listen to me."

They turned to face her, and their cries of misery subsided a little when the two locked eyes.

"Jasmine," they managed to say, though Jasmine could tell speaking wasn't easy. She placed her other hand under theirs, and she found their skin slick with sweat. She held their head in place facing her.

"I've got you, okay?" she assured them, bending down. "Everything's fine. Avi's got this under control. You're gonna be fine."

"Jasmine, I don't—AUGH!" they cried as Avi set to work on the wound. Jasmine hazarded a glance toward where Avi was working and— oh Founders, that was so much blood. What was she doing? Was she making the hole bigger?

"Distract them, Jasmine!" Avi commanded without looking up from her gory task. Jasmine turned back to face Chavi.

"It's okay!" she said. "It hurts now, but it's all okay. Let's talk, let's talk about, um..."

Dusts. What the hell could they possibly talk about?

"Jasmine, listen to me," they hissed through gritted teeth. "I need you to tell my mother—"

"No," Jasmine shook her head, tears starting to burn her eyes as she squeezed Chavi's hand. "We're not doing this. You're going to be fine, okay?"

"Bullshit," Chavi breathed. "We both know I'm dying. So you need to tell my mom..." they groaned, taking a sharp breath. "Tell my mom I'm sorry. I broke my promise and I'm sorry."

Jasmine couldn't bear the thought of informing Rivka Chakrabarti that her only child had died. No, not just that. Her only child had returned from the desert alive, only to die just a few miles away from her. Jasmine pushed the thought away.

"And Harvard," Chavi continued after a few labored breaths. "Tell him...tell him it's not his fault."

But it is his fault, Jasmine thought. If he hadn't run off like that, then Chavi wouldn't have run after him and—no. She reminded herself of the same thing she'd been told countless times. By teachers, but her classmates, by Avi, and even by Chavi's mother: no one was responsible for Chavi's actions except Chavi. She couldn't blame herself, and she couldn't blame Harvard.

"Okay," she murmured. "But—"

"There's one...more thing," Chavi clenched their jaw, and Jasmine couldn't tell if they were crying, or if it was just the sweat dripping down their cheeks.

"I need you to...tell Harvard..."

"You can tell him yourself," Jasmine insisted, though she wasn't sure if she believed it anymore.

"No, Jasmine. Tell Harvard..." Chavi shuddered, then gave a pathetic groan, like a scared animal.

"I...I..." their eyelids fluttered. Jasmine felt a stab of panic.

"Chavi!" she screamed, shaking their head. "Chavi, listen to me! Stay with me!"

"I...I'm cold," they managed to say, barely moving their lips. Jasmine wasn't quite sure what this meant, but she doubted it was good.

"Avi?" she implored.

"I know! I'm working on it! I'm...I'm trying!" she cried, her arms now red to her elbows in blood. Jasmine turned back to Chavi, all their urgency having faded away, their words turned to incoherent mumbles. Jasmine didn't think she would ever hear anything more heartbreaking than their screams, but their silence was far, far worse.

"Chavi," she pleaded. "We need you to stay awake, okay? Just a few more minutes. And then we're gonna take you to see your mother, and—and—"

Chavi gave a weak smile and mumbled something unintelligible.

"Harvard! Think about him, Chavi! Don't you want to see him again? He'll be...he'll be so happy to see you!"

Her throat tightened as she thought of Harvard with his fiery curls and freckled face and stubborn optimism, and the way he'd blushed and turned away from Chavi at the conference only a few hours ago. *The two of you have a lot to talk about.* How could Jasmine tell him Chavi was gone? She thought of Rivka Chakrabarti with her long dark locks and cups of warm tea and gentle smiles. *Keep each other safe.* How could Jasmine tell her Chavi was gone? She even thought of herself. Didn't *she* matter too? She would follow Chavi anywhere. She would follow them to the ends of the Earth—in fact, she felt she'd already followed them there and back. She loved Chavi, not the same kind of love as Rivka or Harvard, but a different breed, the kind of love that only Jasmine Reyez could bear, and she was so full of it, and she didn't know what she'd do with it if her best friend was torn away from her. All she knew was she refused to let go.

She was pulled from her reverie when she noticed she was squeezing Chavi's hand, and their eyes were staring vacantly up at her, barely seeing her at all, their expression of fear having melted into one of sudden serenity.

"Shit!" Avi cried.

Jasmine looked up to see Avi no longer working. Instead, she buried her face in her palms, staining her headscarf with blood.

"What?" Jasmine asked tentatively.

"They've lost so much blood already...I'm doing what I can to staunch the bleeding, but stomach wounds are...I mean, if there's not enough blood in their body, their heart will seize up and...I thought the extra fluid would help but..."

Avi cut herself off, choked by a sob.

"We might be too late. I don't...I don't know what to do! They're already starting to get chills, which looks like it could even be the onset of sepsis..."

Jasmine grabbed Avi's shoulders.

"Avi," she said firmly. "It's okay. This is not your fault. You have done everything you can. You are *doing* everything you can."

"But it's not enough!" she cried, and Jasmine understood her anguish. Her entire life, everything Avi had ever done had always been enough. Avi Taheri had never once admitted defeat. And this moment, her first failing, would kill her best friend.

"Avi, you're probably the best doctor in Bastion. If what you say is true, then...then they were probably dead the moment they were shot."

Avi sniffled, nodding morosely.

"I just...I've missed them for so long. I can't...I can't let them go. Not now."

Jasmine glanced over at Chavi, who was in a state of semi-consciousness, breathing in uneven, shallow gasps and groaning weakly. She swallowed, tightening her grip on Avi's shoulders.

"What can we do?" she asked Avi, hating the sudden quiet of her own voice.

"We can make them comfortable until it's over," Avi said.

Jasmine felt that familiar fullness, the one she'd felt all the time at the Academy, when she'd thought of herself as a tea kettle without a spout. This time, she knew what she was full of: rage. And this time she was not going to let that feeling slip away from her like it had all those years ago, her head full of shame and the stench of vinegar.

"I have an idea," she said. It didn't make any sense—she wasn't even sure how or when she'd come up with it— but it was the last thread of hope she could cling onto.

Avi's brow furrowed. "But you don't...I mean, you haven't—"

"I know. It's a bad idea. And it probably won't work. But if it is the last chance we have, then we're going to do it. But you have to tell me: is there any way you can save them?"

Avi glanced back at the examination table, blood-soaked bandages littering the surface and falling onto the floor, her scalpel glimmering with crimson, discarded on its tray.

"No," she admitted in a whisper, tears again welling up in her eyes. "I can't save them."

Jasmine nodded. She knew this was stupid. But she would rather do something stupid than give up on Chavi so easily.

"Then help me get them back into the car and I'll take it from there."

CHAPTER THIRTY-THREE

Skrack's Mercy

"Where the hell are we going?" Princeton asked, allowing Harvard to drag him through side streets and alleys, a maze of secret passages in the city he had grown up in.

"The front gates! I mean, it's the only way out of the city, as far as I know. But they don't know that's where we're headed. So we might lose them!"

Harvard held the glass case to his chest with one arm, and he towed Princeton along with the other, gripping his hand.

"You've lost *me*, that's for sure. I have no idea where we are."

"South Side of Lower Bastion, right behind the mall that used to be an art gallery."

"How do you know that?" Princeton gaped.

"I've been here before. I've been everywhere in the city." He hazarded a surprised glance back at Princeton. "You haven't?"

"Um. No?"

Harvard jerked abruptly to the right, and Princeton followed willingly. Suddenly they were on the central street again, right in front of the main gates.

"Wow," Princeton marveled.

"C'mon!" Harvard continued to pull him forward, through the gates and into the dusts. Funny, Harvard thought, to have spent so much time trying to get back to the city, only to be leaving it in such a hurry. When Harvard felt they'd run far enough into the desert, he let go of Princeton's hand and attempted to pry the glass dome of the case.

"We're almost there, little guy," he assured the crab inside. "You're almost free!"

"Give me that," Princeton suggested. Harvard obliged, and Princeton easily ripped the dome free of its base, allowing the creature inside to leap off and skitter into the desert.

And suddenly they were alone. For the first time in what felt like centuries, there was quiet. Nothing but the sound of the wind whipping across the desert, and both of their heavy breathing.

"Did he at least, like, say thank you?" Princeton asked. Harvard was still staring after the creature, which had since disappeared in the yellow haze.

"No," he mused, "he didn't."

Princeton turned at the sound of a vehicle behind them. He nudged Harvard to turn too. Two Delian Group security trucks had pulled up behind them, and officers piled out, leveling their weapons at the two boys. One of the guards stepped forward, shouting to them, "You are under arrest as per the Bastion Code of Law for the theft of corporation property. If you cooperate with us now, we will not hurt you. However, we are legally permitted to use force if necessary."

Princeton dropped the glass case, putting his hands in the air to show he had no intention of fighting back.

"Harvard," Princeton hissed. "Do what they say, okay?"

Harvard, however, for possibly the first time in his life, was not in a mood to be doing what he was told.

* * *

"You have to help us!" Harvard pleaded, running up to the guard before Princeton could hold him back. "Our friend might be dying! We need to find them, we need to go to them, we need to—"

The guard in front swung his fist in an arc and caught Harvard squarely in the jaw, connected with so much force that he went down instantly.

"Hey!" Princeton shouted, putting his hands down. "You can't do that to him!"

"He was resisting arrest," the Delian guard justified.

"He was begging you for help!"

Another officer grabbed Harvard and dragged him to his feet, but Princeton shoved him away.

"Don't touch him!" he yelled. *So much for going quietly,* he thought.

By the time the two of them were haphazardly shoved into the back of one of the Delian vehicles, Princeton was badly battered, and Harvard had blood trickling from his temple.

"It's done," Princeton whispered in Harvard's ear as the officer in front started the van, hoping to comfort him. "We did it. It's over. We're free."

"What about Yale?" Harvard asked weakly. Princeton didn't respond to this. He didn't have an answer.

* * *

"Where are we going?" Avi asked without taking her eyes from the road stretching out in front of them.

"Just keep going straight," Jasmine commanded, her arms wrapped around a barely conscious Chavi, jostling them every so often to keep them from slipping away completely.

"We're about to reach the edge of the city," Avi warned.

"I know."

"You want me to leave the city?" Avi asked in disbelief.

"Just trust me, okay?" Jasmine asked. She took them beyond the city gates, the wheels of the car kicking up clouds of orange dust behind them.

"Here!" Jasmine cried, and Avi slammed her foot on the brakes.

"Help me!" Jasmine requested as she leapt out of the car and threw the back door open to lift Chavi out. Together, the two lowered Chavi to the sand.

"Skrack!" Jasmine screamed. "Skrack!"

Avi watched wordlessly, though her face was full of questions. Jasmine knew Avi probably thought her time in the dusts had eroded her mind. She kept calling anyway.

"Skrack!" Jasmine cried again to the barren desert plains. She fell to her knees.

"Skrack!" Her next plea sounded broken, almost defeated. Almost.

"Jas—" she began, moving to lay a hand on Jasmine's shoulder.

"He'll come. He has to," she insisted, then cried out again into the desert void, her voice choked with tears. "Skrack!"

"Jas, what—" Avi tried to ask, but Jasmine ignored her.

"Please!" she pleaded. "We did what you wanted. We did everything you asked. So please! Help us! Please!"

Still, no one came to answer her call.

"Skrack!" she cried again. Jasmine bowed her head in defeat, sobs wracking her body. Avi placed a gentle hand on her shoulder, when a rumbling sound made Jasmine's head snap up. Rising from the ground as a towering desertwalker, larger than any she had ever seen, emerging from a subterranean den. Avi's hand tensed on her shoulder.

"Jasmine," she murmured, "we need to leave. We need to run. There's a...a..."

Jasmine ignored her, instead running toward the creature.

Not long ago, the sight of a hulking crab barreling toward her would have filled Jasmine with panic, kicking her survival instincts into gear. Now she felt a wave of relief wash over her as she ran up to meet the beast. She doubted if he would actually help her, but Founders, she was going to try. His voice, projecting itself directly into her mind, stopped her in her tracks.

Your part in our affairs is over, the voice stated, *Why do you trouble us?*

Jasmine struggled to make sense of her maelstrom of thoughts. *We need his help. Oh Founders, a megacrab is speaking to me. Harvard was right. I should never have doubted him. We need his help. Chavi is dying. A megacrab is speaking to me? The Empress trusts us. We have gained the Empress' trust.*

"We need your help," Jasmine explained. "I don't...I don't fully understand, but I know you have some, some secret to life, and...and Chavi...Yale...is going to die! Because of the mission we did *for you.* You have to help us. Please." Jasmine hated the desperation in her voice, but she was ready to beg.

Our contract is complete, the sonorous voice declared. *The heir has been returned. The Empress is satisfied. You are no longer bound to us, and we are no longer bound to you. Your pleas mean nothing.*

"I know you don't like humans," Jasmine continued, choosing her words carefully, "and I'm not asking you to. But I know the Empress trusts us. Even if she doesn't want to."

At the mention of her name, the Empress appeared on the crest of Skrack's great shell, such a small creature dwarfed by the enormous beast.

I am grateful to you for your service, it is true, Jasmine heard the delicate sweet voice in her mind, *but Skrack is correct. Our two worlds are too distant to render further aid. I'm sorry. But our relationship ends here.*

Jasmine gestured wildly back to where Chavi lay in the sand, Avi now kneeling by their side.

"This is a person Harvard loves!" she shouted. "This is a person Harvard cares about so deeply. And if they were to die—*to die because of what they did for you*—it would break his heart. Don't do it for me. Do it for Harvard. You don't have to like humans. But I promise you, Harvard is the best of us. And I know you saw that first-hand. Please. Do it for him."

He did us a great service, the Empress conceded.

Skrack was not as easily convinced. *What's done under threat of violence is not evidence of kindness.*

"But that's not why he did it, and you know that," Jasmine said. "Even if you'd just asked him, he would have done it. Because he can't stand to see another creature in pain. And for all your talk about the cruelty of humans," she struggled to keep the acid out of her voice, "right now, that's more than I can say for you."

This last bit seemed to have moved Skrack, or at the very least touched on his carcine pride. He ambled forward, past Jasmine, examining Chavi.

I cannot guarantee the human's survival, he finally declared.

"All we ask is you try," Jasmine said, not allowing herself to hope.

Fine. I will see what my hatchlings and I can do. You will wait.

With that declaration, Skrack lifted Chavi's inert body in his claws and descended into a den, hatchlings following suit. Jasmine moved to follow him, but Skrack outstretched a thick leg to block her path.

Not you. You will wait.

"I need to be with them!" Jasmine said. "If something happens...if they don't make it...I need to be there!"

The ways of the desertwalkers are not for the human mind to comprehend. You may not bear witness. On this point, I am firm.

Jasmine looked up at the Empress for aid, but she looked on from her perch, silent. Avi lightly touched Jasmine's arm, and it occurred to her Avi wouldn't be able to hear the exchange. All she knew was that Chavi was losing precious time.

"Alright. Go," Jasmine stepped back, and Skrack retreated with Chavi into the den. For a long moment, Avi and Jasmine stood in silence, staring after Skrack. Jasmine wrung her hands. Avi eyed her.

"Why didn't you come back to see me?" she finally asked.

"We weren't supposed to," Jasmine said without turning to her.

"Chavi did."

"Well, that was a bad idea."

"Jasmine...Jasmine, look at me. What are you not telling me?"

Jasmine turned to face her friend, and the very sensation she had been fearing started to tighten her chest.

"I—" she started, and she felt her throat tighten. "I was afraid. I was afraid if I saw you, I would want to leave. To abandon the Ivies and go back to you. To the way my life used to be."

Avi laid a hand on Jasmine's shoulder.

"You can still do that, you know," she said. "You've still got the scores. You can come to school with me—or any university you want, for that matter! You could start a career. Live in the city. You don't have to go back to the dusts ever again."

Jasmine shook her head, sniffling. "No. I can't do that to Chavi."

Neither spoke it aloud, but they both shared the same unsettling understanding: *Chavi might be dead.*

"Jasmine...I know you care about them. I do too. But at the end of the day? They are not our responsibility. They are not *your* responsibility."

"But it's not just them," Jasmine protested. "It's the boys, too. What about Harvard and Princeton? I can't just leave them. Not after everything we've been through together."

"They're not your responsibility either!" Avi said. "Look, Jas. I know you. I've seen the way you give so much of yourself to people, and for years I thought that was just who you were. But I don't want to see you give yourself up anymore. I'm going to ask you what I should have asked you years ago: what do *you* want, Jasmine? What do *you* want?"

Jasmine broke into violent sobs, her shoulders shaking. Avi wrapped her arm around Jasmine, pulling her close.

"I just want things to go back to the way they were," Jasmine sobbed. "The three of us."

"Maybe they still can," Avi said, rubbing Jasmine's back.

"No. Not anymore," Jasmine pulled herself away, wiping her eyes with the heel of her hand. "I have a team now. They wouldn't leave me. So I won't leave them."

"But—"

"And I don't *want* to leave them."

"Okay," Avi nodded, a kind smile on her face as she ran a hand over Jasmine's hair. "If you're certain. The choice is yours. The choice has always been yours."

* * *

A voice cut through the haze that had descended on Chavi, a voice so heavy and all-encompassing they thought was the voice of the dusts itself, calling them into the deep, where they'd always known they belonged.

You will be changed. Do you still wish to live?

They could not speak. They no longer had a tongue. They no longer existed in the body that had once belonged to them. That body was flesh and bone, languishing somewhere dark and cold, but now, Chavi was elsewhere. They could not feel or smell or taste but could hear the voice addressing them and sense something pulsing and warm just beyond the edges of their perception, and with everything that was left of them they said, *yes.*

They knew it was not enough, because they had surrendered their body to the earth, and they could not will it to speak. But they still thought, *YES.*

And somehow, the voice answered.

Then I will do what I can.

The pulsing warmth faded, and Chavi felt themself dissolve.

* * *

Jasmine and Avi turned at the sight of the diminutive Empress scuttling toward them. Jasmine's heart hammered as she prepared to hear the creature's report.

Come with me, the Empress demanded. Both girls walked toward the crab, but she held up a claw.

No. Just one.

Jasmine and Avi exchanged a glance.

"You go," Avi said.

"But you're the doctor!" Jasmine exclaimed.

Avi gave a sad laugh and shook her head. "I'm not a doctor. And besides, whatever the crabs are going to do... is like no medicine I've ever studied. I want you to go. I'll go get your...your other teammates."

Jasmine's eyes widened. "You will?" She felt a stab of guilt for completely abandoning Princeton and Harvard in her frenzy. Avi nodded.

"Don't worry. They're safe with me."

Avi pulled Jasmine into her arms one more time, giving her a reassuring squeeze, then ran toward her van before Jasmine could protest. Taking in a shaky breath, Jasmine followed the crab down into the den.

Jasmine's blood pounded in her ears as she descended into the dim caverns. She followed a line of hatchlings, guiding her toward the center of the den like a line of ants marching toward their freshest bounty. She didn't like the thought of it. Ants prey on dead things, after all. She pushed away the nagging questions about what this could mean. Were the hatchlings guiding her, or were they...going to feed? She swallowed and pressed on, acutely aware of her shallow breaths echoing footsteps.

She was now so deep in the cavernous den she could hardly see, and she found herself reaching out to the clay walls for guidance. She saw a faint glow emanating from an arch ahead of her, some kind of greenish glimmer, and the shadows of hatchlings making their way toward it. She took a deep breath and followed.

Taking up most of the dome was Skrack, his legs folded under his shell. Laying in front of him was Chavi, motionless, looking paler than she'd ever seen them. Jasmine swallowed as knelt beside her friend, looking for signs of life. They breathed almost imperceptibly. Jasmine let out a sigh of relief and laid a hand on their arm. Still warm. Still alive.

"What did you do to them?" Jasmine asked, her question sounding more accusatory than she had intended.

The ways of our kind are not for your small human mind to understand, Skrack snapped. *You have no way of comprehending what I have done.*

"I...I'm sorry," Jasmine stammered, looking up at the crab. Perhaps it was the tears glimmering in her eyes that softened his tone.

I have...attempted to save your friend, he said more levelly. *But such a feat is not easily done. Desertwalkers and humans have no history of collaboration. My hatchlings and I have done our best, but our methods are...experimental.*

Jasmine examined the wound. It had some kind of herbal poultice on it, fastened with what looked like scrap fabric.

You've brought...human medical equipment, I presume?

"Yes," Jasmine said, opening the first aid pack that Avi had given her.

I suggest you apply it accordingly.

Jasmine nodded. Of course, these creatures had no bandages. They had no use for them. Jasmine was not a medical genius like Avi, but she knew how to clean and bandage a wound; right now, that was all that was required of her. Skrack watched her with a kind of quiet curiosity. She didn't dare speak during the task for fear of making some kind of mistake. For a long moment, the cavern was silent save for the trickle of peroxide, the rustle of the backpack, and the ripping of medical tape.

When she'd done all she could, Jasmine inspected her work. There was no more bleeding, which was good. But how much blood had they already lost? She could see the dark brown stains on the clay ground by the light of the shimmering fungus. Would this be enough? She took a shaky breath as she delicately mopped blood off Chavi's face with a wipe.

"Will they survive?" she finally asked.

I cannot say. All I can tell you is this: if they awaken, then they'll live. But if they have not awoken by the end of the night, I doubt they ever will.

Jasmine nodded, watching the rise and fall of Chavi's chest.

"Is there...is there anything I can do?"

You have already done it. Now there is nothing for you but to wait.

Jasmine bit the inside of her cheek and nodded again, willing herself not to cry again in front of the creature, despite the tightening in her throat. She could not speak, lest the deluge begin. Instead, she bent down, wrapping her arms around Chavi, and attempted to stand. For a brief moment she wondered at her own strength, hefting her friend with ease, until she realized Skrack was lifting Chavi's body as well.

I am sorry to make you wait. But I will not make you do this alone.

CHAPTER THIRTY-FOUR

Prison

Harvard had never seen the inside of Delian Group Detention Center. They weren't properly jails, just holding cells for perpetrators before the Group figured out what their fate should be. A few of the kids from the Shack had gotten locked in these before when they were caught, but mostly they were dismissed as harmless mongrels and let off with a little fine. Of course, to a kid living in the Shack, a little fine was a massive debt, so many of those kids were later taken in as recompense.

Harvard never thought he'd end up in one of these. He thought he was too quick and stealthy. He'd only been chased a few times while at the Shack, and he'd been able to lose his pursuers every time in the twisting labyrinth of backstreets. He'd almost managed to do that this time, but apparently releasing a crab into the desert was a bit of a giveaway.

"What do you think they're gonna do with us?" Princeton asked, reclining on the bench affixed to the wall, arms crossed. Harvard faced away, gripping the pale green bars of the holding cell and watching the Delian Group officer at the desk at the front of the building, in hopes the man might deign to give him some updates on the fates of his friends.

Harvard gripped the bars tighter.

"Talk to me, Harvard," Princeton begged. "Please."

"What is there to talk about?" Harvard asked, and he heard a bitterness in his voice that had never been there before.

"I don't know! Anything. I just...I don't know. If this is really it, I feel like I can't...I've gotta talk to you."

"Why?" Harvard pulled himself away from the bars to face Princeton. "You don't even like me."

"That's not true!" Princeton protested.

Harvard made no effort to hide his skepticism.

"Why don't you believe me? I don't not like you! I don't!" Princeton slammed a frustrated fist onto the metal bench. Harvard flinched. Princeton stared at him, wide-eyed as a too-late revelation crystallized in his mind.

"Are you scared of me, Harvard?"

Harvard stared at him blankly. Could he really have forgotten all the times he'd shouted at Harvard, the times he threatened him, the time he thrust him against the metal wall of O'Neill's pod in anger, when Harvard had been crying out apologies? Or did he just remember it differently?

"Uh, yeah," he said, marveling at Princeton's obliviousness.

"Why?" Princeton threw his arms up in the air. "Do you think I'm gonna hurt you or something?"

"No," Harvard said after a moment of consideration. "But I think you could. If you wanted to."

"Oh. Well. I'm not. So, like, don't be scared."

"Okay."

They held each other's gaze across the cell for a long moment.

"Are you still scared?" Princeton asked.

"Yeah," Harvard admitted.

"Why?"

Harvard sighed, searching for the words.

"Imagine you've been living with a...a big creature. I don't know. A big scuttler, let's say. And you knew that scuttler could kill you, and sometimes it gets so mad at you it feels like it wants to. Then one day the scuttler says 'are you scared of me?' and obviously you say yes because the scuttler has given you a lot of reasons to think it may kill you. And then when you say yes it says, 'well don't be scared.' Are you still scared?"

Princeton's shoulders slumped. "Am I the scuttler in this metaphor?"

Harvard rolled his eyes. "Yeah, of course you're the scuttler."

"Okay, point taken."

He crossed his arms and bent further down on the metal bench, staring at the cracked concrete floor.

"I think I'm scared of you too," he murmured.

Harvard couldn't help but laugh.

"You're scared of *me*? Why?"

"Look, I have been so shitty to you. And I keep thinking I should apologize but like if you forgave me? I'd feel like, 'damn I'll never be as good a person as this guy.' But the worst part is if you didn't forgive me...I mean you're like the sweetest guy ever. So if even you wouldn't forgive me...then I must be a real shit."

He leaned forward, burying his face in his hands.

"Listen buddy...I fucked up. Like, I fucked up really bad. And I know that."

"What do you mean?" Harvard ventured cautiously.

"I mean you're a really great guy. You're smart and you're nice and like...you're just so much better than me. In every way. And I kinda think I know that, and I get mad at you because...I mean, I just lose my patience so quick."

Harvard cocked his head to the side quizzically.

"Sorry, I'm...kind of lost? I mean, thank you, I think. But I'm confused. What are you saying?"

"I'm saying I'm sorry, Harvard!" Princeton stood up abruptly and grabbed him by the shoulders. "Can you just accept my quaking apology? I'm fucking sorry! I'm sorry!"

Harvard didn't know what to make of the shouted apologies. Flustered, he broke away from Princeton's grip.

"Sorry, that was, uh, that was kinda aggressive, huh? I'm not real good at this, I don't think. Shit."

Princeton rubbed his face in frustration.

"Do you mean it?" Harvard asked.

Princeton looked up. "Huh?"

"Do you really mean it?" Harvard repeated. "That you're sorry?"

"Yes!" Princeton said emphatically. "Of course I mean it!"

"Oh. Okay. Then I forgive you."

"You do?" Princeton gaped.

Harvard shrugged. "Sure."

"But that's...that's too easy!" Princeton protested.

"Lots of people have done bad things to me," Harvard explained. "Really bad, actually. And none of them ever apologized for it. You were always...I mean, yeah, you were mean to me. But that's all you ever were. Which is not that bad, all things considered. You were also really nice at times. And sometimes you even made me feel like we were friends. Plus, you apologized. So, I forgive you. I don't think it's too easy."

Princeton stared at him, dumbfounded.

"Harvard, you know you can tell me who hurt you," he finally said, "and I'll kick their ass."

Harvard laughed, blushing.

"I appreciate that," he said, "but I don't need you to do that."

Princeton put his palms up. "I'm just saying, the offer is open."

He eyed Harvard for a moment in disbelief.

"You actually forgive me? For real?"

"Sure."

"Great, now I feel like trash."

Princeton went over to lean against the wall, but a bit of the friction between them for years had evaporated, and Harvard felt he could breathe just a bit easier. A bit.

"You know what sucks?" Princeton mused, looking out at the Delian guard seated at the desk. "We might have just saved humanity, and no one will ever know. Even if we tried to tell someone no one would ever believe us."

"I don't know if *I* believe us," Harvard admitted, thinking back to the way he doubted his own sanity when Skrack had first spoken to him. Had it all really been in his head? Now they were trapped in this cell all because of him, the other two Ivies injured and unaccounted for respectively, it felt like some kind of bizarre nightmare that Harvard had somehow convinced the others was real. If it had been some kind of dusts-induced illusion...what then?

"What do you think the punishment is for stealing from the Satsuki Group?" Princeton asked. Harvard could hear that measure of casualness in his voice, unsuccessfully masking the fear that lay underneath.

"Don't know," Harvard said, as a feeling of detachment washed over him.

"Do you think they're gonna kill us?" This time Princeton's veneer had dropped completely, and Harvard could clearly hear the panic welling up inside him. By contrast, Harvard was starting to feel numb.

"I don't know."

He thought about Princeton's sudden moment of vulnerability, and wondered if maybe he should take a cue. If they were about to be executed, would he regret not saying anything? Even if he wasn't sure if it was true. He'd tried so long to convince himself it wasn't true. His life would be a little easier, a lot simpler, if it wasn't true. But he couldn't bear the idea of this little inkling of a notion dying with him, never being spoken aloud. He squeezed his eyes shut and forced the words out of his mouth.

"Princeton. If we're about to die then I think I need to tell you something."

He hoped Princeton might say something reassuring, like, "We're not about to die, idiot! Shut up!"—that was Princeton's version of reassuring—but Princeton, too, was caught in the throes of pessimism, so he only said, "Go ahead." And he was somber about it, which didn't bode well. Harvard took a deep breath, then blurted out, "I think I'm in love with Yale."

Princeton stared at him, wide-eyed. Harvard braced himself for some kind of mockery. Instead, Princeton said, "For real?"

Harvard nodded.

Princeton laughed, but not in the derisive way that Harvard had anticipated.

"Harvard, that's great!"

"I...it is?"

"Sure! I mean, love is, like, a beautiful thing and shit. And it needs to be protected at all costs."

Harvard gaped at Princeton, speechless.

"Listen, buddy. We're gonna get you outta here. And we're gonna fix Yale up, too. And you guys are gonna kiss or whatever. Okay?"

Harvard was too shocked to speak, so he just nodded rapidly.

Princeton ran his hand through his hair excitedly, holding up a finger as he said, "Hold on, I need to think back on things for a second."

For a silent moment he concentrated, then he said, "Yeah, okay a lot of things make more sense now."

Harvard cocked his head in confusion. "What makes more sense?"

"Oh, like the way Yale totally lost it when you were gone."

"What...are you talking about?" Harvard asked, his chest swelling at the idea of Yale "losing it" over him.

"Well first off, they were about ready to pummel O'Neill when they found out what he did to you. And when we got out of there, they would *not* let us go back until we found you. It was scary, honestly. Like, I just thought it was stupid. But it makes way more sense now that I know that you guys are, like, a *thing*."

"Um," Harvard wrung his hands, loathe to admit this was a question that had tortured him, "I don't really know if we *are* a thing, to be honest."

"Did you two..." Princeton made a lewd gesture. Harvard blushed. "Um. Yeah."

"How about—" he made another lewd gesture.

"Uh. A little."

"How about—" he made another lewd gesture.

"We tried it, but, uh, I didn't like it very much."

"How about—" he made another lewd gesture.

"I don't know what that means," Harvard admitted.

"I don't either! But one day, I'm gonna find out!"

Despite the severity of their situation, Harvard found Princeton's eagerness, the way his cynicism had just melted away, spread warmth in his chest. He laughed despite himself. Princeton clapped hands on both of Harvard's shoulders.

"Everything's gotta be okay! It's gotta!" Princeton declared.

"How do you know that?" Harvard asked.

"I don't! I'm just saying...it better be."

* * *

After what felt to Harvard like an eternity of waiting around in the cell trying not to imagine their fate—and worse, Yale's—someone burst into the office. She was a young girl, roughly his age, but she carried herself with the pride and confidence of someone much older. Harvard first noticed her headscarf. A spiritual symbol meant she must be someone important. Even the Bell family wasn't connected to a religion. Harvard pressed himself up against the bars, hoping to hear snippets of their conversation. She was arguing animatedly with the man behind the desk who had been charged with watching them.

"Ms. Taheri," the man was saying, "you must understand I have the utmost respect for you and your family. But the boys are charged with grand larceny, from the Satsuki Group no less. As much as we'd like to wave this away at your request, it won't be as simple as that."

She faltered ever so slightly, but recovered gracefully.

"So corp feud, then?" she threatened. "Bastion hasn't seen a conflict like that in some time, if I remember correctly, and you really want to start one over these two boys?"

"You keep using the word 'boys,' a lot," Princeton pointed out, gripping the bars, "but you know we're like, whole adults, right?"

The two ignored him.

"Look, Ms. Taheri, of course we don't want to take things that far—"

"Well then it'll be a damn shame when my parents publicly denounce the Delian Group."

"—but we simply don't have the power to override these charges. Even for someone of your stature. These kids—"

"Adults!"

"—will go through the same legal process as any other convicted criminals. Our branch of Delian Group only covers the catching and detaining of criminals. Everything else is up to the judicial branch."

"Well don't sell us short," said a voice from the back of the room, "we certainly do a bit more than *that*."

Harvard turned to see a suited man saunter into the room, his glasses glinting in the fluorescent light. Harvard remembered him from the conference—the same man who'd spoken to Yale: the Head Enforcer.

"Pardon me, sir! I didn't expect—" the guard stumbled over his words, reddening. "I thought you'd be at...I mean, if it's not too bold of me to ask, what are you doing here?"

Avi Taheri was not impressed.

"Who are you?" she demanded.

While the security officer looked stunned by the girl's lack of decorum, the man gave her an amused smile, as though he thought her brazenness was charming.

"No one you would know, Ms. Taheri," he grinned, pushing up his glasses. "I work with the Delian Group."

"Obviously," the girl's eyes flickered over to the stunned officer behind the desk. "And you're supposed to be important?" she ventured.

"Very, actually," he assured her before turning to the man at the desk. "I can smooth things over with the Satsukis, if things come to that," he explained, "so long as you don't mind me having a word with these fine gentlemen?"

"Of...of course, sir!" the guard said. "Go right ahead!"

"Greatly appreciated," he purred before turning to face Harvard and Princeton.

This was the first time Harvard felt the man's eyes on him, and the sensation was like an ice-cold hand being pressed against his spine. There was something about his smile, the way he moved, and the way his eyes sparkled—it was almost catlike. Predatory. Harvard remembered some kind of folklore from pre-Quake times about a dangerous smiling cat, but he couldn't quite remember the details.

The man delicately lifted a metal stool and placed it across from the two boys, only the bars and a few centimeters separating them.

"Lovely to see you both again, though I wish the circumstances weren't so unfortunate," he said. Something about his voice was warm and soft, and Harvard found himself stepping forward unwillingly. His eyes darted toward Harvard. Harvard's breath caught in his throat. "What can I call the two of you?"

"Well, the name I picked for today was Felipe," Princeton explained, "but honestly, I don't think it suits me."

Devrin gave an honest chuckle.

"You're funny," he said, pointing at Princeton. Then his eyes flicked back to Harvard again, and he felt that icy tingle on his back. "And you?"

"Don't call me anything," Harvard found himself saying.

Devrin nodded. "Very wise," he said. "Now, to business: I happen to hold a very important position in the Delian Group. The most important, as a matter of fact, if you can believe it."

"I've never heard of you," Princeton said. "I mean, no offense, but like, everyone's heard of the Rubiras and the Satsukis—"

"Yes, I like to keep it that way," Devrin cut him off. "Anonymity makes things significantly easier. I'm sure Ms. Taheri here can attest being rich *and* famous can sometimes be a little too much to bear."

He lifted a hand toward Avi, who crossed her arms pettishly.

"But trust me when I say I can have you released in an instant. I can't, of course, let you off the hook completely," he admitted. "It was, after all, the Satsuki Group you stole from, not my own. But I can let you out of here now—so long as you do one thing for me."

"Wh...what do you want?" Harvard stammered.

Devrin's eyes glinted mischievously. "Tell me why you wanted that crab."

Harvard and Princeton exchanged a look, and a silent panic passed between them. Harvard was the one who spoke, tentatively at first.

"I..." Harvard began, "I don't like to see creatures in pain. I wanted to free it because...it was hurt. And I couldn't bear to see that."

"Fascinating," the man murmured with a smile that said, *I know you're lying to me.* He gestured for the man at the desk to unlock the cell.

"You're free to go."

Harvard's brow creased. "Really?" he asked. There must be some kind of catch, right? They couldn't really be let off that easy. But Devrin was already standing, straightening his jacket.

"Oh, yes," he strode to the door. "I got what I came for."

"What did you—"

He was gone before Harvard could ask, and the cell door swung open.

* * *

"We're here," Ave announced as she pulled up to the curb on a side street in the west section of Midtown Bastion.

"What is this place?" Harvard asked as Avi led them toward a narrow building, other structures flush against it on both sides. It was a cramped townhouse, constructed in a gap between buildings that clearly was never meant to house anything. Of course, this was increasingly common in Bastion as housing demands skyrocketed. The townhouse looked oddly lopsided—its first floor was little more than a hallway, but its second floor extended on top of the building next to it, as though it were casually leaning an arm on its fellow houses for support.

Avi fished out a key and ushered the two boys inside. It was far from the affluence of Harvard's childhood, sure, but compared to the Shack or the Commission, a real life above-ground house was a virtual paradise.

"Townhouse my parents are remodeling," Avi explained as she ushered them inside. "They purchase old properties, squeeze a new building in, then rent them. It's like their side gig."

Princeton squinted at her. "So you're, like, rich?"

"Yeah, I'm 'like,' rich."

Princeton crossed his arms. "Well, that's some bullshit! You said you were Yale's friend, right? You could have helped them out! They wouldn't have even had to have become a scavenger, probably, if you just tossed them a little extra cash. This," Princeton waved his arms at the unfinished apartment, "is ridiculous!"

Avi sighed deeply, cast her gaze down.

"I wanted to," she admitted. "I don't control any of this money. Not yet. I want to do great things with it, I promise! One day. But right now, I'm just a student. My parents control everything. And my parents...were not fond of Chavi."

"Who?" Princeton asked.

Avi stared at him blankly for a moment.

"Right," she said, "you guys don't know, do you? You use brand names."

"So, Yale and Columbia—"

"Are Chavi and Jasmine."

Chavi and Jasmine, the names echoed in Harvard's head.

Chavi.

"Which brings me...to another crucial point," Avi added. "Since they are in the midst of redoing this place, they won't be keen on having guests—"

"We're not allowed to be here," Harvard surmised.

"Not as such, no," Avi said. "It was the only place I could think of. I mean, I can't very well take you to my dorm. And taking you to my parents' house would be totally out of the question. At least here...it's empty. It's secluded. And since they're still hiring contractors, no one is going to be around for a while. So it seems kinda like the perfect place considering the fact half the city is probably searching for you after that stupid stunt you pulled."

Princeton bristled. "Hey, you don't know the—" Avi held up a hand cutting him off.

"I trust you had your reasons. Believe it or not," she held his gaze for a long moment, "I trust you. Any friends of Chavi and Jasmine are friends of mine, and I know they wouldn't just go charging off into danger if there wasn't a *really* good reason for it. Well, Chavi, maybe, but definitely not Jasmine."

Harvard blinked, still struggling to grasp the new names. What was that supposed to mean? Yale was always very insistent about the very *opposite* thing—keeping the Ivies *out* of danger at all costs. Then again, when it came to their own safety, they were less than careful. Was the Yale Avi knew the same one that Harvard did? Surely, they were the same person, but...how much had they changed? Did Harvard really know them at all? Maybe they were still Avi's old friend more than they were his captain.

"You two stay here," Avi commanded, pressing a key into Princeton's hand before heading toward the door. "Whatever you do, do *not* leave. Do *not* show your faces. I'll bring you everything you need. Later. For now—"

"You're going to get Columbia and Yale?" Harvard asked.

Avi nodded gravely.

"Do you think...do you think they'll be okay?" He was terrified of the answer, but the question burned too much to go unasked. Avi sighed.

"I don't know," she said, then held up a warning finger. "Wait. Here."

She slammed the door behind her, and Harvard heard the lock click into place. He couldn't help feeling like he'd gone from being one person's prisoner to another. Princeton laid a hand on his shoulder.

"It's gonna be okay, buddy," he said, giving a gentle squeeze. "It's gonna be okay."

Harvard didn't believe that for a second.

CHAPTER THIRTY-FIVE

Return

Harvard watched from the upstairs window, waiting to see Avi's van pull up in front of the townhouse. Every car that passed, the sound of every motor, made his stomach flutter. What would he see when she finally arrived? Would he see Yale emerge from the vehicle, alive and well? Or would he see Avi and Columbia carrying a lifeless body, wrapped in sheets?

He felt a hand on his arm and turned to see Princeton standing above him.

"C'mon," he said, "let's do something. Let's...oh, I don't know. Play a game?"

"A game?" Harvard asked in disbelief.

Princeton shrugged. "Yeah. Sure. Whatever you want. Is there, like, a game you used to play when you were little?"

"Um...no? I didn't really...I didn't get to play a lot of games as a kid."

"What? No games?" Princeton gaped. "You're joking!"

Harvard shook his head somberly. Before he could turn back to the window, Princeton grabbed his arm and pulled him down to the floor, so they were both sitting across from each other.

"When me and my sisters were kids, we had to take our dad to the doctor a lot, right? So we were in the waiting room together, like, all the time. So we'd have to come up with games to pass the time."

"I—I didn't know you had sisters," Harvard admitted.

"Yeah! Three!" Princeton smiled, and without meaning to Harvard smiled back. Princeton grabbed his hands and held them out in front of him. "C'mon. I'll show you."

The games Princeton taught Harvard weren't particularly fun, interesting, or creative. In fact, they felt exactly like the kind of games that children would make up in the waiting room of a hospital. And yet, Harvard found himself laughing and playing along. Perhaps it was Princton's insistence, or just the fact Princeton had never *played* with Harvard. In fact, Harvard couldn't remember the last time anyone had played with him. So he found himself lost in the mundane rituals of the games, until Avi's car door slammed shut outside.

They both bolted up and bounded down the stairs. By the time they were there, Avi was already unlocking the door. Harvard leapt forward, but Princeton caught him around the waist and pulled him back.

"Give them space," he instructed gently. Harvard was thankful for Princeton's restraint, since if it weren't for his arm holding him in place, he would have pounced on Avi and Columbia when they came through the doorway, both carrying Yale's unconscious body.

"There's bedrooms upstairs," Avi told Columbia. "We can go up there."

So Yale was at least alive. That comforted Harvard. Princeton didn't let up his grip until Avi and Columbia were safely halfway up the staircase, and they could follow from a distance.

"Are they going to be okay?" Harvard asked from the doorway as Columbia and Avi laid Yale in one of the upstairs beds. The two girls exchanged a glance.

"We don't know," said Avi, "but we're gonna do everything we can."

Harvard couldn't resist the urge any longer. He rushed to the side of the bed, nearly knocking Avi out of the way.

"Do you want to...stay here, Harvard?" she offered.

"Yes please," he said, looking down at Yale's pale, expressionless face.

Avi wordlessly slipped out of the room and returned with a wooden chair. She placed it behind Harvard. Harvard glanced up at the other Ivies, and they shared an unspoken understanding. They shuffled out of the room, taking Avi with them, as Harvard lowered himself into the chair, still staring fixedly at the person in the bed in front of him.

Gingerly, he slipped his hand into theirs, interlacing his fingers with Yale's. Their skin was clammy and cold. Harvard gave their hand a squeeze. Then he slumped over and sobbed.

* * *

The sun hovered over the horizon, threatening to sink, and Yale had still not awoken.

"We should—" Columbia started. "We should probably start talking about what we do if—"

"No," Avi held up a hand. "Not yet."

Princeton was silent, leaning on the kitchen counter, his hands clasped together as is in prayer. His face, however, suggested nothing but concern. For the first time in a long time, he was completely silent.

Columbia had suggested they give Harvard space, so the three stood huddled together. Yale's requests to Columbia tumbled around in her mind—*tell him it's not his fault*. When should she do that? Would it comfort him if she went up there now to console him? Or would delivering the message solidify in his mind that Columbia had already come to terms with their captain's death? She hadn't, of course, but...she couldn't keep her mind from leaping to conclusions. Morbid conclusions.

Avi, despite her time apart from her closest friend, could still read her as clearly as she read those complex medical texts.

"It's not over yet," she said.

"It feels like it's over," Princeton whispered, his eyes cast down at his interwoven fingers. "It feels like everything is over."

* * *

When Harvard had been Ronan Bell, he had borrowed his mother's pen. Well, not *borrowed*, strictly speaking, since she hadn't actually given him permission, but he *had* intended to give it back. It was a beautiful fountain pen she kept in a stand on her desk, and it had probably cost her more than some of her more lavish jewelry. Young Ronan thought it would be perfect for his bird sketches. He needed a good pen to get the shapes just right, and surely that was the nicest pen in the house, and surely no one would see him slip into the study to lift it or slip back into the study to put it back. No one ever *did* notice him.

But he'd lost it. Before he'd even had a chance to draw any birds, he'd misplaced the little thing and couldn't find it anywhere. He tore apart his whole room, ripping the sheets from the bed and pulling shirts from the wardrobe, wondering where the pen could possibly be hiding. To a child, any crisis seems like it very well be the end of the world. He willed the pen to appear, silently begged the universe that the pen would just suddenly be there, sitting on his notebooks where he thought he'd left it. He desperately pleaded to turn around and he'd see it on the bed or on the floor or on the windowsill, and the world wouldn't end after all.

Harvard felt this same desperation as he sat watching Yale breathing, willing their eyes to open, begging the universe to see them awake and alive again. Every time he blinked, a part of him believed that when he opened his eyes again, Yale would be looking at him, smiling, and they'd say, "Did you miss me?"

But every time he opened his eyes, he saw their unmoving face, looking stonier than ever.

He never had found that pen. His mother had been furious.

Harvard was all grown up now. But the feeling that this truly was the end of the world had not gone away.

He still gripped their limp hand, massaging it with his thumb. *Please wake up*, he begged internally. Then, out loud, "Please wake up."

He knew they couldn't hear him but speaking out loud felt good. He couldn't change much in this world, but if the only thing he could do was speak, then he would do it. So he continued, his hand still caressing Yale's.

"Yale. I'm so sorry. This is all my fault and I...I just want you back. I don't know what I'm going to do without you. I know this sounds weird, but...I didn't know who I was for a long time. I mean everyone told me who I was. Stupid, useless—but I didn't think that was actually me. I didn't know what I wanted or who I wanted to be. And then I met you and—and, I did. I knew I wanted to be the kind of person that you would like. Founders, I sound like an idiot. I just mean...I always wanted to be better than I was. My whole life I just felt like I wasn't good enough. For anyone. But I was good enough for you and that— that made me feel like I could be good enough for me, too. And I don't think I could have grown up if I didn't feel that way. So you can't leave me. Because if you're not with me...I'll be alone again. So please stay with me. Please, Yale."

Now everything had fallen apart, now that they weren't in the dusts anymore and they were running from the Commission, it felt so wrong to still be calling them by their Ivy name. What was it Avi had called them?

"Please," Harvard whispered, "Chavi."

Chavi's eyes fluttered open, as though they'd only been napping. They let their head fall to the side to see who had said their name.

"Harvard?" they asked weakly. Harvard threw his arms around them, holding them tighter than he had ever dared.

"Yeah," he said tearfully, burying his face in their neck, "I'm right here."

"Wha—" Chavi started to form a question, but the words died on their lips. Harvard pulled away to look at them. They looked confused, like someone who hadn't fully woken up from a dream, too full of questions to pick one to speak aloud.

"It's okay," Harvard whispered. "Everything is okay."

This seemed to comfort Chavi.

"Good," they rasped, smiling, "good."

* * *

The next few days were a blur for Jasmine, with much of the time eaten up with caring for Chavi during their recovery. They were in and out of consciousness like someone with a persistent fever, often waking up confused about where they were and what was happening. Harvard's presence tended to calm them down, so Harvard would spend all day in the chair at their bedside, just in case they awoke and needed comfort.

Their befuddlement was nothing compared to the pain.

Jasmine, Princeton, and Avi would all rush to Chavi's room at the sound of their cries of agony to find them in a semi-lucid state, Harvard futilely attempting to wake them from what he thought was some kind of nightmare.

"They're not...I don't...I don't know what's happening!" he stammered the first time it happened, his eyes wide with worry.

"Chavi!" Avi attempted to shake them awake. "Chavi! What's wrong?"

But wouldn't answer. They only groaned until the pain subsided, then fell back to sleep.

The next morning, Chavi claimed not to remember it.

"I wish I understood what was happening," Avi shook her head. "It's just...this is exactly the kind of thing I'm supposed to know. But I don't fully understand what that crab did to them, so I don't understand what's going on with them. I—"

She cut off, burying her face in her hands in defeat.

* * *

It was a bit of a lie, admittedly. Chavi *did* remember it.

They didn't remember much from those few days as they slowly regained their footing in reality. It was a muddled mix of dreams, pain, and Harvard. Lots of Harvard, which they were thankful for. The pain, oddly enough, wasn't from the gunshot wound. It still ached, but it paled in comparison to the burning that woke them up at night, a feeling like molten stone pumping through their veins, like every one of their nerve endings was crying out all at once and there was nothing, *nothing* they could do to stop it. They didn't *mean* to scream. They would wake up and they were already screaming.

The problem was, Avi was already distraught about her inability to save them back at the university. Her impotence when it came to their bouts of pain worsened her slipping sense of capability. If there was something Avi Taheri always was, it was capable. Chavi couldn't bear to see her so flustered. So, they tried to hide it. It wasn't as though she could do much for them anyway, besides supplying them with painkillers that barely did anything to dull the burn. They didn't want to spoil this moment, the first period all the Ivies were healthy, happy and safe and back in Bastion proper, by worrying everyone about what sort of crab disease they had contracted. Either it would pass or it wouldn't. If it passed, no one would be the wiser. If it didn't...well, there wasn't much anyone could have done for them anyway, now was there? At least they got to see Harvard again, and when the right moment came they could let him know everything that passed between them before the Conference really meant something to them.

Harvard rarely left their side, and of course Chavi had no complaints about that. No matter the time of day, Harvard was always by their bedside when they awoke, sometimes sitting in the chair drawing pictures in a sketchbook Avi had no doubt sourced for him, sometimes even reclining on the bed beside them, dozing. On these lucky occasions, Chavi would wrap an arm around him and pull him closer.

* * *

"Harvard," Chavi said one day, Harvard seated in his usual chair by their bedside. Their voice was still quieter, weaker than it had once been, but Harvard hoped that would be temporary. "Do you...do you want me to call you a different name? By your, um..."

Real name, Harvard thought. What was a real name, anyway? Not the one he was born with. Not the one the Commission had given him. But the one he had chosen...well, no one had called him that name for years.

And it carried the weight of his mother, Kathy, Shila. He touched his hand to the back of his neck and idly twirled a strand of hair.

"You can keep calling me Harvard...you should keep calling me Harvard, actually. But...my real name is Ronan."

"Ronan," Chavi echoed, their voice barely above a whisper. "I like that."

Harvard grinned sheepishly, pushing a stray strand of ginger hair behind his ear.

"Thanks. I chose it."

It almost felt like a betrayal to leave behind the name he'd chosen for himself, but in truth, every time he heard it, he heard the acid in his mother's voice, see the scowl on his sister's face. He didn't want Chavi calling him by the same name he'd had in the Bell household. Who was to say he couldn't have different names for different people? He'd changed his name once, after all. He could change it again. He could have as many names as he liked.

"You're sure you don't want me to call you Ronan?" Chavi asked.

Harvard nodded. "I'm sure."

Chavi closed their eyes and laid back, and Harvard wondered if they were hiding another wave of the pain that kept them up at night. They exhaled slowly before opening their eyes again and sitting up.

"I'm sorry I must not be very good company," Chavi sighed, taking a sip of the water that Avi had left for them.

"That's not true," Harvard smiled. "You're always good company. I always like being with you."

"Really?" they asked.

Harvard nodded definitively. "I don't mind if you're too sick or tired to talk. I don't need to talk to you. I just like being with you. That's all that matters. As long as I'm with you, I'm happy."

Chavi smiled, and Harvard realized it was maybe the most genuine smile he had ever seen from them.

And I would spend every moment with you, he wanted to say. *I would spend every moment for the rest of my life with you because every moment with you is better than a moment without you.* But he didn't know how to say that, so he just smiled back. Chavi suddenly looked nervous, their eyes darting away as though the glass of water they held had just become incredibly interesting.

"Harvard," they rubbed the glass with their thumb, "do you, uh…do you wanna be my boyfriend?"

The question hit Harvard like a punch in the stomach, but in a good way somehow. Harvard felt his heart begin to pound as he started trembling.

"Oh. Um. Yes. Please. Yes. I was also…um, I was also wondering if I could be…if I could do that."

Chavi gave him a fond grin.

"I would be honored," they said, gently placing their hand on the back of Harvard's. He felt himself beginning to blush.

"You're shaking again," Chavi observed. "Are you nervous?"

"No!" Harvard said reflexively. "I mean, maybe. I'm not sure. I'm excited, I think. I've never…I've never had someone ask me to be their boyfriend before."

"Well, I've never asked that of anyone either, so I think we're on equal footing," Chavi sat up a little in bed, squeezing Harvard's hand.

"Why don't you come sit next to me?"

Harvard kicked off his shoes and slung his legs onto the bed, cuddling up against Chavi, who wrapped their arm around him and pulled him close. The trembling subsided a little when he felt Chavi's warmth. He nuzzled his head into them.

"Is this okay?" he asked.

"Yeah," Chavi said. "This is perfect."

Perfect. Chavi was the only person ever to call Harvard perfect. They bent over and planted a kiss in Harvard's mass of red hair. The two lay like that, enraptured in each other's presence, for a long, long time.

CHAPTER THIRTY-SIX

A Farewell

Harvard bolted upright, awoken by a stirring in the back of his mind.

Come now, or you'll miss your chance, said a familiar voice. Somehow, he didn't need an explanation. He knew where he was expected.

Not bothering to change out of his sleep clothes, he wore only a t-shirt and shorts. He slipped on a pair of shoes by the door, which he closed slowly behind him, careful not to wake anyone. He padded through the dimly lit streets of Lower Bastion, and though he'd been warned many times never to traverse Lower Bastion alone at night, he was not afraid. He knew that at least for tonight, there was someone looking out for him, someone who would come help him one last time if he was in danger. But he wasn't in danger, not really. He reached the city gates without incident.

Shrouded in moonlight stood Skrack, far enough into the dusts that no one in the city would worry, but close enough that Harvard could get to him. The beast extended a claw to Harvard, and on it he saw the Empress balanced daintily.

I could not bear to leave without thanking you, Harvard, she said. *We do not know what measures we would have been forced to take without your aid. Mryk is deeply grateful. This will not be forgotten.*

"Leave?" Harvard asked. "Where are you going?"

Someplace humans cannot follow, she answered, angling her shell down, like a human bowing their head somberly.

"Oh," Harvard said, not fully understanding, but also knowing he probably wasn't intended too. "Well, can you visit? We'd love to see you sometimes. We'd make sure no one in the city—"

Quiet, Skrack commanded. *The Empress would not deign to pay homage to a human city.*

It is a kind offer, the Empress added, *but I go to seek the Serenity. It is not a journey my kind return from.*

"I see," Harvard said, not really seeing. "Will...will you be alright?"

Both Skrack and the Empress made that scraping and clicking noise that Harvard had come to understand as laughter.

It is very kind of you to worry about me, the Empress said, *but your fear is unfounded. I have long awaited Serenity's warmth and I will embrace it with open claws. No, Harvard, it is you I worry for. That city of yours is more monstrous than any beast you will find in the desert.*

"Well, at least it's not trying to eat me," he said with a little laugh. Neither crab seemed to find it particularly funny.

I wouldn't be so sure, Skrack muttered. Harvard didn't know what this was supposed to mean.

Goodbye, Harvard, the Empress said. *I hope the world does not make you cruel.*

"Goodbye, Empress," Harvard pet her shell with two fingers, and surprisingly, Skrack did not protest. "Good luck with your serenity, whatever it is." The Empress laid her claw gently against his fingers, as though she were petting him back.

"And thank you Skrack," Harvard looked up to meet the creatures eyes, "for protecting me even though you obviously hated me."

Well. You Know. I do as my Empress commands. He shifted slightly in the sand, and Harvard was certain that if crabs could blush, he would be bright red.

"And...thank you for saving Chavi. I don't know what I would do without them."

The two creatures were oddly silent at this. For a fraction of a second, Harvard wondered if it was something that Skrack regretted.

Look after each other, he said. He withdrew his claw, and the Empress with it.

As Skrack began lumbering back into the wasteland of dust, Harvard gave them both a wave. He was almost certain that before they disappeared into clouds of sand, he saw the Empress waving back.

* * *

The time was close. The Empress could feel her Essence pulling at the chitin of her mortal shell, as though it were bursting to get out. *Soon, she thought, soon I will ascend. But not yet. There is work to do yet.*

Will you miss him? she asked.

No. Skrack answered too quickly for his answer to possibly be true.

Will you watch over him for me?

I will have your heir to protect. I have more pressing matters to deal with than the affairs of humans.

And you need all your many hatchlings to assist you in this task? You cannot spare the occasional pair of claws to aid the humans to whom we are so indebted?

Skrack brooded for a long moment before finally saying, *If you desire it, Empress, it will be so.*

The two traveled without speaking for a moment before Skrack asked. *What about you, Empress? Will you miss him?*

Once ascended, I don't expect I'll miss anything at all, she admitted. *But I suppose if I could, then I would. I would miss Harvard. I would miss Mryk. And I would certainly miss you, noble Guardian.*

Skrack laid her down in the sand, where she could travel under her own power. She would not need him anymore, not where she was going.

It has been an honor to serve you, he said.

I fear for the future of this land, she said, her diminutive black eyes scanning the dusts. *Protect it, will you?*

Before Skrack could answer, she let her Essence unravel, and as she joined with Serenity, she was finally free.

Epilogue

Delian Tower was the tallest building in Bastion. The reasons for this were manifold. One reason was the people of Bastion believed that in a dangerous, hostile world, safety and security was their prime value, and the tower should serve as a monument to those ideals. Another reason was the founder of the Delian Group ensured it was written in the Bastion Law Code that the building could exceed the maximum building height. It was all steel and glass that glimmered in the sunlight, tapered at the top—the jewel of Midtown Bastion.

The man called Pierce looked out on the city from the top office, hands clasped behind his back and a sense of dread churning in his stomach.

"Are you excited, Pierce?" his employer asked as he entered the office, easily balancing a teacup on a saucer in a practiced hand. He was in high spirits today. Then again, he was always in high spirits. At times, Devrin was a very tiring man to work for due to his incessant chipperness. At other times, he was a very tiring man to work for other reasons.

"Should I be?" Pierce asked, turning toward Devrin's desk.

"Yes! Yes, of course!" Devrin lowered himself into his plush chair, "Great things are afoot for the human race. Didn't you see all that science?"

"I got a little distracted."

Devrin nodded, sipping his tea. "I told you it was going to be interesting, didn't I?"

Pierce nodded. "Indeed you did, sir."

Devrin placed the teacup in its saucer with a pointed clink.

"The Galvin Conference gave me hope for the future. Do you know why?"

"Why?"

"Because it gave me faith that we are doing the right thing. There will be a new dawn for Bastion. And so soon! The plan is already in motion!"

Another of the many reasons Pierce found Devrin exhausting was that half the time, he had no idea what the man was talking about. He sometimes thought that Devrin was constantly forgetting what he'd explained and what he hadn't, but he mostly expected the man just enjoyed making those around him feel out of the loop.

"To be honest, sir, I'm not really sure I understand your plan," he admitted.

"Yes, that's by design. You see, if I were to verbalize it, that would give someone an opportunity to try and stop its momentum, and I can't afford to give anyone that opportunity. The rest of the Underground City is listening."

Pierce nodded. This, at least, Pierce understood.

"It doesn't matter, of course, because I've scrapped that plan completely."

Pierce couldn't help being a little taken aback.

"But you just said...what about the—"

"New plan!" Devrin announced abruptly, leaning back in his chair, brandishing a pen. "Forget the old plan. Stupid! Silly! Absurd! We have a new plan. Better plan! More interesting, more efficient, and more importantly, more fun. It's not worth it if you don't have any fun, right?" he grinned, raising his eyebrows at his assistant.

"Of course. We always have fun," Pierce agreed stoically.

"Fun fun fun," Devrin sang to himself, cheerfully rifling through the papers he had on his desk.

"And *this* is how the fun shall begin!"

Pierce glanced over at his desk to see his boss had already sourced pictures of the four scavengers who'd sneaked their way into the conference. Pierce always marveled at Devrin's ability to acquire information so rapidly, but it wasn't any wonder—any record that wasn't already available to him *would* be available to him if he set his mind to it.

"I believe," Devrin muttered to himself, clicking his pen, "there was a pre-Quake expression referring to 'those meddling kids,' but its meaning has been lost to time. In any case, I'm quite thankful for 'those meddling kids.' They've been such an inspiration to me."

"How so?" Pierce asked.

"Do you really think," he looked over the top of his glasses, "that four scavengers would risk arrest just to rescue a baby crab out of the goodness of their hearts?"

Pierce scratched his beard. "I admit, it seems...unlikely."

"You've been watching them for me, haven't you? And doesn't it also seem unlikely that the one we both saw receive a fatal gunshot wound seems to have a miraculous recovery?"

"I...suppose." Admittedly he'd been so relieved to see the scavenger had survived, he hadn't wondered how it had possibly happened.

"Evidently," Devrin spun his pen, "our friends the Ivies have a contract with our former friends out in the dusts. I'd like to get in on that contract."

With a flourish, he selected one of the four pictures and held it up to Pierce.

"This is how we start the new plan: bring this one to me."

END OF BOOK 1 OF THE BASTION CYCLE

ACKNOWLEDGEMENTS

If anyone ever told you that novels are written by one person, they are a liar. This novel has been shaped by the commentary of so many talented and thoughtful writers, and also probably indirectly shaped by everyone I have ever met in my entire life. But more specifically:

Thank you, William C. Tracy, for believing in my work, putting in the time and effort to help me get it where it wanted to be, and sharing it with the world. I am so ridiculously thankful that you took a chance on me.

Thank you to Rob Greene, my mentor from SFWA, who directed me to Reese Hogan's work, which in turn brought me to Space Wizard.

Thank you to the Silent Notetakers Writers' Collective, who have been workshopping this novel with me ever since it was just a concept. I fondly remember discussing the first three chapters in the Swarthmore rose garden during (has it really been this long?) fall of 2021. Thank you, Grace Griego, Shaoni C. White, and Yarrow Syskine, who were with me right at the beginning. Thank you, Elliott Yordy, who finished reading before anyone else because they were just so excited. Thank you to Alex Lakej, one of the first beta readers. Thank you, Delphi Foster, even if the first time around she "only read the parts with Harvard in it" because she is "Harvard's number one fan." Thank you to J.R. Steele for helping me with the beginning, and Emma Johanna Puranen, for helping me with the end. Thank you, Alexander Sheldon, with whom I bonded over a mutual love of Creatures. Thank you, H.R. Owen, who gave me confidence in these characters. You're all stars.

Thank you to my family, who supported me through the many years of rejection. Thank you to my dad for giving me artistic advice since I was a child, and thank you to my mom for being both my best English teacher and a shoulder to cry on. Thank you to Grandma for always reminding me to focus on what brings me joy. Thank you to Emily for doing silly goofs in my time of need. Thank you to Juliet, who read my short story collection and liked it so much she read it aloud to everyone she met.

Thank you to Vivian Lin, who sat with me at lunch every day in fourth grade so we could talk about books. I'm amazed and thankful that she supports me to this day.

And of course, thank you to Noa, who has supported me with everything I wrote, even though at the beginning, I didn't feel I deserved that support. Without his constant encouragement, I'm not sure if I'd be brave enough to write anything at all.

ABOUT THE AUTHOR

Alex Kingsley (they/them) is a writer, comedian, game designer, and amateur mycologist. They are a co-founder of the new media company Strong Branch Productions, where they write and direct the sci-fi comedy podcast *The Stench of Adventure* and other shows.

Their short fiction has appeared in *Translunar Travelers Lounge, Radon Journal, The Storage Papers*, and more. In 2023 they published their short story collection, *The Strange Garden and Other Weird Tales*. Alex's sci-fi play *The Bearer of Bad News* premiered in LA in 2022 produced by the Annenberg Foundation, and their sci-fi play *Unplanned Obsolescence* premiered in Philadelphia in 2023 as part of Cannonball Festival.

Alex's SFF-related non-fiction has appeared in *Interstellar Flight Magazine* and *Ancillary Review of Books*. Their games can be downloaded pay-what-you-will at alexyquest.itch.io. They live in Chicago, Illinois, with their partner Noa and their cat, Ford F150. You can find them at alexjkingsley.wordpress.com, on BlueSky at alexyquest.bsky.social, Instagram at hitchhikersguidetothealexy, Mastodon at alexyquest@podvibes.co, and on TikTok at alexyquest.

Please take a moment to review this book at your favorite retailer's website, Goodreads, or simply tell your friends!

www.ingramcontent.com/pod-product-compliance
Lightning Source LLC
Chambersburg PA
CBHW022301310726
48973CB00001B/161